A BRIGHT
AND
TERRIBLE
SWORD

A BRIGHT AND TERRIBLE SWORD

Book Three of the Soulvine Moor Chronicles

Anna Kendall

Indigo

Copyright © Anna Kendall 2012
All rights reserved

The right of Anna Kendall to be identified as the author
of this work has been asserted by her in accordance
with the Copyright, Designs and Patents Act 1988.

First published in Great Britain in 2012 by Indigo
An imprint of the Orion Publishing Group
Orion House, 5 Upper St Martin's Lane, London WC2H 9EA
An Hachette UK Company

A CIP catalogue record for this book is available
from the British Library.

ISBN 978 1 78062 072 5

1 3 5 7 9 10 8 6 4 2

Typeset by Input Data Services Ltd, Bridgwater, Somerset

Printed in Great Britain by Clays Ltd, St Ives plc

The Orion Publishing Group's policy is to use papers that are
natural, renewable and recyclable products and made from wood
grown in sustainable forests. The logging and manufacturing
processes are expected to conform to the environmental
regulations of the country of origin.

www.orionbooks.co.uk

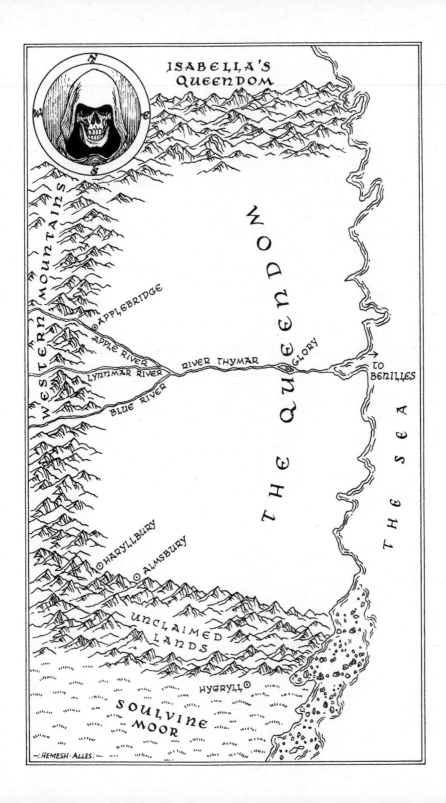

1

I watched the spider inch across its web towards the tiny mouse.

Neither should have existed, not this early in the spring, and not inside the cottage. Not even in such a mountain cottage as this one, snugly built but seldom swept and smelly with droppings from the pig that the children brought inside on cold nights. But the cottage, although filthy, was warm. Spiders had hatched, baby mice had been born, and overnight this small life-and-death struggle had begun in the dim chimney-corner where I lay, still weak from my illness, on a pallet of dirty straw.

I had lain here for over a month, dependent on the good will of the cottagers who took me in. Although perhaps 'good will' were not the right words. Without this family of John the Small (he had no other name), I would have died. And *with* this family—

'One Hand!' shouted Bets, the oldest girl, hurling herself down the ladder from the loft. They all shouted, all the time. She raced towards me.

'Hush your mouth!' cried Mrs John, coming from the bedroom, which was the only other room the cottage possessed. 'You'll wake him!'

'He's awake!' screamed Bets, jumping on top of me. It hurt, even though she weighed so little. Every move of my body still hurt.

'Get off!' yelled Mrs John, plucking her daughter up by her neck as if Bets were one of her scrawny chickens. 'Go get the wood!'

'That be Ned's labour!' Bets cried, suddenly all wounded injustice. She had not noticed the spider web.

'Do it!' Mrs John roared. She gave Bets a shove towards the door. To me she said nothing, as always.

Inches from my face, in the dim corner, the spider had reached its prey. The mouse was less than two inches long, although it had grown old enough to venture from its mother's nest in the wall and be caught by the sticky strong threads closest to the floor. The spider was huge, half the size of my thumb. As Mrs John lit a rushlight and stuck it into the holder on the wall, the spider's hairy body glittered a dark red.

'I be hungry!' yelled Ned, shooting down the ladder. The other three children followed. From the bedroom the baby wailed.

'Then fetch the water for gruel!' Mrs John bawled, 'or none of ye eat! John! Get up! Get up now!'

Robbie loomed over my pallet. 'Are ye still sick then, One Hand? Are ye dying?'

'Leave the lad be!' Mrs John shouted. 'Water! Now!'

'That be Bets's labour!'

Mrs John slapped both boys and shoved them to the door, all the while crying towards the bedroom, 'Get up! Get up, ye lazy no-good!' The baby screamed. The two smallest children had just made it laboriously down the ladder, although Jemima fell the last three rungs, lay in a crumpled heap on the floor, and screeched.

The red spider hung with four legs in its web and four on the struggling mouse. Its fangs closed on the mouse's skin.

John the Small slouched from the bedroom, scowling at his wife. 'Will ye not let a man rest, woman?' he bellowed, reached inside his half-tied trousers, and scratched his privates.

I had no idea why these people had saved my life. John the Small had found me collapsed in the snow on a track that led down the western mountains towards The Queendom. I had shivered and raved with illness. Unable to lift me – he was barely four feet tall – he had brought his wife and two oldest sons, of nine and ten, and the four of them had dragged me inside, dumped me on the hearthside pallet, and left me there for a month. It was an incomprehensible act of kindness towards a stranger, for although the season was wrong for plague, I might have carried any number of other diseases that could have killed them all. Incomprehensible, too, as since bringing me inside, husband and wife had almost completely ignored me. Neither ever addressed me. The children brought me food when they remembered. John and Mrs John treated me as if I were part of the pallet itself, and of far less interest than the pig. I had not washed in a month. I was not alone in that, and smelled no worse than the others.

The mouse gave a last desperate struggle to free itself. The spider hung on. The web trembled and its bottom strands tore.

'It be warm out!' Bets cried, coming back inside with an armload of wood. She dropped it onto the floor, where it clattered and rolled. 'Spring!'

'And the field not even turned!' Mrs John yelled, rounding on her husband. 'Ye'll never get the planting done in time!'

'Let me be, woman!'

'It be spring!' Ned bellowed, sloshing inside with the bucket of water. The bucket leaked. A trail of water spread across the floor as Mrs John lugged the bucket to the hearth and dumped the water into the kettle.

The mouse went still. Its struggles had further torn the web, and now only a single strand connected the spider

3

to the web above. It began spinning more threads to bind the mouse to the web.

'Well, bring the wood to the fire, girl!' Mrs John yelled at Bets. 'Be ye a half-wit? Jemima, stop that wailing or I'll give ye something to wail about!'

Jemima did not stop wailing. The baby bawled in the bedroom. The pig came in the open door and the three older children raced after it, yelling.

I sat up. It was the first time in a month, it took me a long time, and it made my head spin. But from this position, I could reach the web. Slowly I put out one finger on my one hand until it touched the centre of the web. The spider silk felt sticky, but strong. My touch did not break it, not even when I pushed on the interwoven strands.

The family sat or stood – there were not enough chairs – around the wooden table, slurping gruel and screaming at each other. However, my unaccustomed movement attracted attention. Mrs John looked right at me. Never before had she addressed me directly, so it felt almost shocking when she did.

'Ye call out in yer sleep, One Hand.'

I went still. My old fault, and the cause of so much grief in my life.

'Look – there be a web!' Robbie shouted.

Mrs John and I stared at each other.

'It hold a spider!' Bets screamed.

'Ye always call the same name,' Mrs John said.

'Get it!' Ned bawled. The two boys leaped from the table and scrambled over me to the wall.

'Look – it hold a *mouse*!'

'Kill it!'

Robbie's arm sliced through the web. It gave way. Ned, bouncing painfully across my legs, grabbed a stick of wood and smashed it down on spider and mouse alike.

4

I held my breath. The country folk, unlike those of the palace, are close enough to death to believe in the old ways. If in my sleep I had blurted out the words *hisaf* or Soulvine Moor ...

Mrs John said, 'Who be Katharine?'

'Got it!' Ned bawled, and the web hung in tatters.

'Katharine', not 'Maggie'. I had called not the name that filled my thoughts as I lay on the pallet week after week, but the name I tried nightly to forget. My mother's name, my sister's name. The name that used to invade and terrorize my dreams and did so no longer. Just as I no longer crossed over to the Country of the Dead. Whatever was happening there, my part was to stay away. Mother Chilton and her witch apprentice, Alysse, had made that very clear to me. I was to stay out of the war they waged with Soulvine Moor and, instead, go home to Maggie and my unborn child.

There was nothing I wanted more. Maggie, with her fair curls straggling over her forehead, her tart competence, her love for me that had been undeserved and unrequited for so long. I yearned to go back to Maggie, living in Tanwell with her sister as she awaited the birth of our son.

And I had lost so much time already! Mountain travel in winter had proved much harder than I had expected, especially with one hand. Time and again I had been forced to hole up at some remote farm or rough inn while snow storms raged outside. I would have died without Mother Chilton's money to buy such sanctuary. Then, nearly at the base of the jagged western mountains and nearly into spring, what did I do but fall ill and into the wild household of John the Small.

Maggie must, by now, be but a few months away from her confinement. It had been summer when I lay with her on that fragrant hillside, amid the scents of wild-flowers and the heavy drone of bees.

I did not answer Mrs John about the name 'Katharine', and a moment later her attention flew to Ned and Robbie, who were tossing the dead baby mouse back and forth across the table. 'Get that dung out of here – what ails ye?' she bawled. 'Yer daft, the pair of ye! Out! Out!'

The boys fled, shouting, outside. The morning chaos continued. Through the open door came sunshine and the intoxicating scent of sweet warm air. It was indeed spring. I must recover completely from my illness, must become strong enough for travelling, must return to Maggie. If, after all I had done, she would still have me.

Bets cried, 'Look! One Hand is standing up!'

'I—'

She barrelled across the room, jumped on me, and knocked me back down.

I persisted. Day after day I forced myself to stand, to walk, to strengthen my withered muscles. When I could, I went into the woods and gathered bird eggs, dug roots, found last autumn's nuts, brought back firewood – anything to help repay Mrs John's rough kindness. I had money left, sewn into a secret pocket of my cloak, but I didn't offer any, sure in the knowledge that this family would simply take it all. Mrs John took my contributions to her house-hold without comment. But the day Robbie tried to knock me over and I swatted him away with my one good hand, remaining on my feet, she smiled.

And it was so good to be out of that filthy cottage! Birds sang from every branch in the woods. Crocuses and hyacinths bloomed in the sun, lilies of the valley in the shade. One day I bathed in a forest pool, longing for Joan Campford's strong yellow soap. I washed my clothes as best as I could. With the little shaving knife in my boot I shaved off my tangled beard and cut my hair. Then I lay naked under the strong sun while my clothes dried and, weary from such unaccustomed exertion, fell asleep.

And dreamed.

Darkness—

Cold—

Dirt choking my mouth—

Worms in my eyes—

Earth imprisoning my fleshless arms and legs—

I was dreaming about crossing over. But the dream crossing brought me not to the Country of the Dead, which I had promised never to visit again, but rather to John the Small's disorderly cottage. Mrs John sat at the table, shelling nuts I had brought her, popping nut meat into little Jemima's mouth. The baby slept in its ramshackle cradle. For once, the cottage was quiet.

All at once, another presence entered the dream, although not the cottage. A shadowy presence ... No, not even that. A grey whisper, somewhere between a scent and a sound ... It was vague but unpleasant. Perhaps Mrs Johns felt it, too. For in the dream she stopped shelling nuts, her hand suspended in the air, holding a broken black walnut, and her eyes stared. At me, even though I was not in the cottage.

A long moment spun itself out.

Then I woke beside the forest pool and the sun had gone behind a cloud, leaving me shivering and cold.

I dressed in my still damp clothes. The dream had been so mild compared to those I once dreamed, so why did it leave me uneasy? That unpleasant whisper in my mind ... no, not even a whisper, merely a vague stirring of ... what? A faint animal scent, a nearly inaudible sound. Trivial things, nothing to make me afraid. Not I, Roger Kilbourne, who had caused a battle to be fought and a savage lord to die and a queen to burn. Who had killed the sister who once haunted his dreams.

Late afternoon shadows, long and deep, slanted over the cottage when I returned. Robbie, Ned and Bets screamed from atop the roof, where they played some game that threatened to topple them all into broken bones. Matt, too little to climb to the roof, had to remain below and bellowed at this foul injustice.

Inside was just as noisy. John the Small had not returned from wherever he'd gone, but Jemima cried and pulled at her mother's skirts and the baby wailed. In the middle of this din, Mrs John was a single point of stillness. Not a muscle of her face or body moved as she faced me across her dirty table. Her grey hair straggled around her face. Fear filmed her eyes.

'Ye maun go now.'

'What?' I said, inanely.

'Ye maun go.'

'I—'

'Ye did not say what ye be. Now you maun go.'

What ye be. She could have meant anything. A *hisaf.* A murderer. The former palace fool. Of all the things I could have said, I blurted, 'How did you know?'

'Go now.' And then, 'I have me bairns to think of.'

'I'm . . . I'm no threat to your children, mistress.'

'Go.'

She was implacable. She handed me a packet: my waterbag, Tom Jenkins' two knives, what smelled like food wrapped in leaves. And all the while her eyes held mine and I saw in them not only resolution but fear. It was the fear that decided me. These people, however crude and slovenly, had saved my life. I could not bring fear to them, not even when I believed there was nothing to fear. I took the packet and left.

But at the doorway I turned to try one last time. I must

know. I said, 'Was it . . . did you . . . did you happen to fall asleep this afternoon, mistress? To . . . to dream?'

'Go now.'

I went. From the roof top Bets, giggling, threw a pebble at me. This struck Robbie and Ned as a great idea and they scrambled to dig more stones from the thatch. There were none so they threw the thatch itself, and it was in a hail of straw that I left the cottage and set my feet upon the track down to the valley below.

2

In truth I was not sorry to go. It seemed to me that I was strong enough now for the journey or, if not, would soon become so. I had youth on my side; in another two months I would turn eighteen. And the weather had turned. When I tired, I could build a fire and stop for the night.

Exhaustion came earlier than I thought, before the thin track from the cottage had even joined a proper road. Sitting before my fire, eating the hard bread and harder roots that Mrs John had sent with me, I thought about her fear. The country people, not sophisticated enough to have abandoned the old ways, often believed in soul arts and *hisafs*. But that did not mean that they could recognize them. The only ones I knew of who could do that were women with talent in the soul arts themselves. Sometimes they didn't even know they possessed such untutored talent, like Princess Stephanie. Sometimes they knew they did not but longed for it, like Queen Caroline. Sometimes they made of their talent a weapon to fight the war against Soulvine Moor, like Mother Chilton. The web of these women stretched across The Queendom, the Unclaimed Lands, Soulvine Moor itself. And Mrs John must be one of them, in some minor and untaught way. She had recognized me as a *hisaf*.

But only after I had dreamed of crossing over. It was through dreams that my sister Katharine, now more than merely dead, had terrorized little Stephanie and me. Through dreams Katharine had even killed Stephanie's attendants. But my sister was gone. And I would never cross over again.

I banked my fire and put Mrs John from my mind. For me, the battle against Soulvine Moor was over. I was journeying to Maggie. Again and again I pictured my arrival in Tanwell. I would tell Maggie I loved her, that I had been a fool not to know it sooner. She would cry, perhaps, and I would hold her and kiss her fair curls and lay my hand on the bulge of her belly that was my son. Then, afterwards ...

I fell asleep smiling, happy to breathe in the sweet night air instead of the fetid cottage. I was journeying to Maggie.

However, the journeying was harder than I expected. I had not yet got back my full strength. The next day I had nothing to eat but some early strawberries. At the first farmhouse I came to, one cleaner and more prosperous than John the Small's, I was able to buy some food and rest in the barn. So I continued for a few more days, and I felt my body return to itself.

But then the weather changed. Cold rain woke me before dawn. With sleep no longer possible, I set out walking, grumpy and shivering. The sun had risen unseen behind grey clouds when I came, sodden and weary, to the first town of The Queendom that I had encountered since last autumn. The village lay at the base of a series of steep hills, with a small river on one side. Abruptly the road to the east had broadened from a rutted track to a hard-packed surface. Cottages appeared like those in prosperous market towns, with fenced kitchen gardens and well-tended sheep pens and scrubbed front doors. On the river was a mill. An inn, the Blue Horse, stood on the main road.

But the road was filled with screaming people.

I gaped, confused, as a young man rushed from one

11

cottage, an old woman from another. The man dashed through the pelting rain and pounded on the door of another dwelling, but the woman stopped in the middle of the road and just stood there, as if too bewildered to move. I went up to her and touched her shoulder. She screamed and leaped away from me. Two of the other people pouring into the street rushed up and a man seized me.

'Is it him? Is it *him*?' He shook me roughly, like a terrier with a rat.

'No, be ye daft, this one's got but one hand!' Someone said behind me.

The man let me go and ran to another cottage. As soon as he opened the door, screams poured out. The old woman still slumped motionless in the rain, her face a mask of dripping grief. I grasped her arm.

'Mistress, you should go inside.'

She looked at me but I knew she was not seeing me but rather some horror. All at once her knees buckled and I caught her. People continued to rush past, but none came to her aid, or mine. The woman sagged against me, a dead weight on my good arm. I could not leave her there in the mud of the road so, not knowing what else to do, I pulled her towards the shelter of the nearest cottage.

The door opened directly onto a kitchen with a stone floor, trestle table, herbs hanging from ancient beams. The room was jammed with cottagers, grouped around something I could not see on the hearth. A middle-aged woman spied us and elbowed her way through the moaning people. 'Mother! Thank you, lad, she was . . . it is . . . .' The woman began to cry. But she took her mother from me and eased her onto a settle before turning back to me. 'It is the shock . . . we . . . so many of them!'

So many of what?

I said as gently as I could, 'What has happened here, mistress? I just arrived on the western road, looking for an inn ...'

She nodded, distracted, and then abruptly focused her attention on me. 'The western road? Did ye pass anyone?'

'No.' Few travelled in the rain, and fewer still from the western mountains.

'You are certain? You didn't see a big man with a black beard and green eyes?'

Green eyes. My spine went cold. 'I passed no one. Was ... was someone like that here?'

'Yes. He – all the poor infants – oh!' She put her fist to her mouth and began to sob.

I elbowed my way through the crowd, which had begun to turn ugly.

'—find him and—'

'—can't have gone far—'

'—get Jack and Harry and Will and—'

The men began to pull away, organizing their hunt. A few glanced at me suspiciously but looked away as soon as they saw my one hand. The women continued to cry, their murmurs between sobs, almost incoherent. But I caught one word:

'—witchcraft—'

I pushed to the front of the crowd.

On the hearth sat a young woman, her face gone numb with grief, holding a baby in swaddling clothes. I thought at first that the baby was dead, so motionless was it, its blank eyes staring at nothing. But then I saw that the child breathed. All at once the mother shook it, crying, 'Wake up! Wake up, Neddie! Oh, wake up!' She shook the baby harder, until an older woman stepped forward and stopped her.

'There, Mary, leave off, it does no good, my dear—'

The girl crumpled, sobbing hysterically. The older woman took the infant from her. Another woman sat beside the girl, who in her wild grief shoved her comforter away.

'*So many of them*,' the woman on the road had said to me. I turned to the nearest person, a small fierce woman with red curls under her faded cap. 'There are ... there are more babies like this in the village?'

'Aye, five of 'em, all under a year old.' Her gaze sharpened. 'Do you know anything about this, lad?'

'No,' I said, trying to look stupid, 'unless ... could it be plague?'

Of course it was not plague: wrong season, wrong symptoms, wrong victims. The red-haired woman's interest in me vanished. It should not have.

I was the only person who understood what we all looked at it. No, that was wrong – I did not understand it, not at all. But I had seen it before: the blank stare, the inability to be roused, the breath without active life. I had seen it all my life, but not here, not in The Queendom nor in the Unclaimed Lands nor in the savage western mountains.

In the Country of the Dead.

Seven infants alive but not alive, five in the village and two more on outlying farms. By evening the local men, their hunt turning up nothing, had returned to take what comfort they could in the taproom of the Blue Horse. The rain had stopped but a dank chill outside made the innkeeper build up the hearth fire until it roared. Or perhaps it was a need greater than mere cold.

I had taken one of the small, clean, comfortable rooms upstairs, had paid for the luxury of my first hot bath in months, had slept off my weakness all afternoon, had

14

eaten a hearty dinner. Now I sat at one of the taproom's long trestle tables, a tankard of ale in front of me, as the villagers came one by one to the room.

'—cannot console her anyway, so thought I might as well hear what news to—'

'—no change in little Bess and—'

'—wanted me out of the way so she can—'

But their excuses for leaving their grief-drenched cottages did not last long. These men had spent all day searching sodden fields and woods for something they did not understand. They had found nothing. Faces tight, eyes hard, they turned to me.

'Ye say ye saw no one on the western road, lad?'

'No. No one.'

'What's yer name, then?'

'George Tarkington.'

'Where do ye come from?'

'From my uncle's farm in the high hills.'

'And what be yer business in Rivertown?' This from the roughest-looking of the men, who wore a *gun* strapped to his back. Had the blacksmiths of The Queendom learned in the last months to make *guns* and *bullets*, or had this one been taken from a savage soldier in some local skirmish before the invaders left The Queendom? I had been away since autumn; there was so much I did not know. The cottager eyed me suspiciously.

But I have had much practice both in lying and in looking innocent. 'I'm travelling to Fairford. My—'

'Where be this "Fairford"?'

'Near the capital. My uncle died and left me our farm. I sold it to Samuel Brown and now I travel to live with my other uncle, my mother's brother. He will apprentice me as an apothecary.'

'Yer old to be an apprentice.'

'I know,' I said humbly, 'but there is little else I can do.'

I raised the stump of my left arm. I could feel tension ease around the table.

'So the sale of yer uncle's farm is where ye got the money to travel?' another man asked. This one had a more kindly expression.

'Yes, sir.'

'Well, if ye go on spending it on hot water for baths ye won't have much left for yer apprentice fee.'

'Yes,' I agreed. 'It was only this once. I had such a chill from the rain.'

Easily chilled, one-handed, too stupid to hoard my farm-sale money. They lost interest in me. I sat quietly, sipped my ale, and listened, to learn what I could.

The seven infants had all disappeared from their cradles during the night. The cottage doors had been barred from the inside, and the bars not disturbed. No windows had been forced open. But in the poorest and meanest of the cottages, where the parents slept in the loft and four children huddled on straw pallets before the warmth of the fire, a small boy had stirred. He heard something, or glimpsed something, or felt some movement by the baby's cradle. Or maybe it had been merely a fancy, or a dream, or even a lie; the boy was but five years old and given to telling tales. Anyway, the men reasoned, gripping their tankards of ale and shooting furtive looks at each other, how could a stranger have broken into the cottages without using the windows and doors?

At first light, when the cottage women arose to start the fire and put on hot water for gruel, the thefts of the infants had been discovered. Wives screamed; children cried out in fright; men rushed in from the bedchamber or down from the loft or in from the well house. Then all seven babes were discovered lying in a circle on the village green, wrapped in their rain-soaked blankets. They had

16

not been there long; none had even caught a chill. But the babies—

'Dead and not dead,' one man said starkly. His hand shook as he lifted his ale to his lips.

'They might yet come from their trances and be well,' said a very young man.

'They can't eat, Will!' said a third. 'If a child can't eat ...'

The oldest man, surely a grandfather rather than a father, spoke to me. 'In yer travels, lad, have ye seen or heard of anything like this?'

Yes. 'No.'

'The only thing we can do,' said Will, 'is wait. The children may become themselves again. If not—'

'If not *what*?' shouted another man. In the hushed tap room, the noise was shocking. 'Ye all know what happened! That green-eyed stranger, the one we all sat with here last night – and clever we thought ourselves to let him buy us all ale – he witched them all! Jack, ye bragged about yer fine new son, ye know ye did! Ale loosened all our tongues, and so that bastard knew – he *knew*–' Abruptly he hurled his tankard across the room, where it clanked against the stone siding of the fireplace and rolled onto the floor. He put his head in his hands.

Will said unsteadily, 'I have no belief in witches.'

'Then yer a fool,' Jack said, 'but witches be female. Always. And they do not trance infants.'

'One just did!' shouted the man who had thrown his tankard. 'Can ye not believe what's in front of yer damn eyes?'

Jack rose, his fists clenched. The other stood to face him, so fast the heavy trestle table shook. The oldest man's voice cut across the sudden silence.

'Stop it, both of ye. That will not help us. Will is

17

right. We maun wait to see if the babes recover. Meanwhile there'll be no fighting amongst ourselves, and no murdering of the babes because they ain't right.' He stared hard at a man I had not noticed, a thin man with a face like a weasel, who sat nervously twisting an amulet between his fingers. The thin man dropped his gaze.

After that, little was said. The men drank in silence. In more silence, one by one, they left the inn. I groped my way upstairs – no candle was offered – to my tiny bedchamber, barred the door, and lay in darkness on the narrow bed.

Someone, or several someones, had entered the cottages without using doors or windows.

The stolen babes had been left in a circle on the village green.

They were 'tranced' – Jack's word – and so 'neither alive nor dead'.

I could not get warm. I pulled my cloak tight around me and pulled my knees to my chest, but still I shivered. I had the chill that the tranced babies had not, but it wasn't a return of my winter illness. I did not know why these children had been taken, but I knew how, and by whom. Memory shivered along my bones.

A snowy mountain meadow, wind whipping the snow in my face and slowing my attempts to flee. A figure materializes in the snow. Another. Then a third. The three men who had been with my mad sister. Hisafs, *holding knives. Tom Jenkins drops little Princess Stephanie and springs in front of me, and the* hisaf *vanishes. He has crossed back over. Back and forth they go, the rogue* hisafs, *crossing between the land of the living and the Country of the Dead, manoeuvring for position, until one of them appears right next to Tom and his knife finds its mark in Tom's side.*

And it was I who had made that possible. I, by

disturbing the Country of the Dead, who had so weak-ened the barrier between the living and the dead that now *hisafs* could cross over not only in trance, but bodily. Just as I could, had I not vowed never to do so again.

Hisafs in league with Soulvine Moor had stolen those infants and had ... what? It was the Dead who lapsed into quiescent trances, who sat in circles, who were being destroyed by Soulvine Moor. Not the living. I did not understand what had happened here in Rivertown. I only knew it terrified me.

What if my own son ...

But no. Mother Chilton had told me to go home to Maggie. She would not have permitted that if it endan-gered Maggie or our child. I carried no markers, which meant that neither the web women nor the *hisafs* – on either side of the war – knew where I was. In fact, they probably thought I had died in my battle with my sister. We had been alone and only she would have known differently. And Katharine could never tell anyone any-thing, not ever again.

In addition, Maggie would be well guarded by web women, although she would never know it. They would be there in Tanwell: the unobtrusive kitchen maid, the aged midwife, the white rabbit under the hedgerow, the hawk circling above the village. They would use their strange abilities to protect my son. '*He is our last hope*,' Mother Chilton had said.

But I pushed Mother Chilton's bleak statement from my mind and clung to the rest. My son was well guarded. No *hisafs* knew where I was. No woman here in Rivertown had recognized what I was, as had Mrs John the Small. But Mrs John was country folk, closer to the old ways, and the recognition had been merely bad luck. No *hisaf* would come for me here in the dark silence of the night, materializing in this cold bedchamber to slide a knife between my ribs. What had happened in this village was frightening and terrible, but it had – for once! – not been caused by me. Nor was it my task to set it right.

Idiot, my saner self whispered to me, *not the entire army of web women and faithful* hisafs *have succeeded in setting it right.*

But that brought another thought, one that made me jerk upright in bed. They would be here soon, the web women. Whatever was happening in Rivertown, it must be a part of the war with Soulvine. The web women would come, and perhaps even *hisafs*. Why had I not realized this before? They might – *would* – recognize me. My obscurity, on which I counted, would be lost.

Cursing, I got up from bed and unbarred the door. Carefully I eased myself down the dark stairs. The taproom had closed for the night. The door creaked when I unbarred it but no one came. I slipped outside. I had no way to rebar the door, but I hoped that come morning the innkeeper would merely think I had wanted to get the earliest possible start on my journey and so had left before dawn.

The rain had stopped. Wind had risen to send clouds racing across the patchy sky. By the intermittent light of a half moon, I made my way across the village green where the seven tranced babies had lain, neither alive nor dead. Was Will right, that the little bodies would wither and die since they were unable to eat? Or would the infants continue to breathe, as unchanging as the Dead in that other country on the far side of the grave? Unchanging for ever, rosy tranquil infants lying inert and unseeing in their cradles ...

A deep shudder ran along my whole body, which had nothing to do with the cold night. Under trees whose spring leaves still dripped with water, through air that smelled sweet and fresh as if horror had not happened here, I left Rivertown for the road east.

3

Long before dawn I could go no farther. Leaving the road, I plunged into a thick wood growing down the side of a steep hill. Parts of the underbrush were dense and tangled. I crawled into a clump of bushes, hoping to encounter nothing larger than I was, and fell asleep. When I woke, the morning was far advanced, another drizzly overcast sky. Good.

What was happening in Rivertown? Had the infants come out of their trances, had web women arrived, had . . . But it was useless to speculate. My task was to get to Maggie, and the journey was still a long one. I crawled out from under my bushes.

A dog sat waiting for me.

For a long moment, dizziness took me, a vertigo born of fear. This, I knew well, was not a dog, or not merely a dog, no matter how much it looked like one. And it did look normal, sitting on its great grey haunches, wagging its short tail, its green eyes alight with friend-liness. It even smelled like wet dog, a scent redolent of scampers through fields followed by cosy evenings by a hearth.

But I had seen dogs like this before. I had seen Shadow massacre four savage soldiers by tearing out their throats. I had seen Shep leap at men who threatened me and Tom Jenkins, and tear them to pieces. I had seen a pack of such dogs race into the firelight on Soulvine Moor and rescue me from the people of Hygryll moments before a knife descended into my heart. And I had seen such a dog materialize from nowhere, inside a tent, to take down Tarek son of Solek son of Taryn, before his soldiers shot it to death. Dogs like these had hunted food for me. They had been my guardians, my saviours, my salvation. And after a fortnight, each of them had vanished completely. They came from the Country of the Dead, and when the time allotted them in the land of the living had expired, they were gone.

Someone had sent this dog to me. Someone knew where I was.

The dog bounded over to me and licked my face. I pushed it away, got to my feet, and stood looking warily down at its hopefully upturned face.

'What are you, boy?'

Its tail wagged harder.

'Who sent you to me?'

It licked my hand.

Not the web women. I remembered Mother Chilton saying bleakly, '*Neither Fia nor the dogs are our doing.*' And my father, about the torture I had undergone in Almsbury: '*We could not get the dogs to you fast enough.*' This dog had come from a *hisaf*, although not from my father, damn him for his promise to me of a rescue that had never come. So what *hisaf*? And how? Things could only cross over from the Country of the Dead when they were carried by a *hisaf*, and the dogs had always arrived alone.

I did not understand. And I did not want this dog, marking my whereabouts as clearly as if I shouted my name to every traveller I passed: Here I am, Roger Kilbourne! Come and claim me!

'Go away,' I said to the dog.

To my surprise, it did. But then it dashed back and laid a stick at my feet to throw.

Memory pierced me: Tom Jenkins, the only friend I had

ever had except Maggie, teaching Shadow to shake paws.
Someone somewhere had taught this dog to fetch sticks.
Who? Why?

'Go away! Bad dog! Go!'

The dog's ears drooped. It looked at me reproachfully.
It did not budge.

There is no way to make a big dog leave you if it does
not want to, short of rock or knife. I didn't dare; I had
seen what these dogs could do when angry. Besides,
I have never hurt an animal in my life. The only weapon
left was shunning. I picked up my pack, walked back
towards the muddy road, and pretended the dog did not
exist. If I ignored it for long enough, perhaps it would
give up and go away.

It did not. We walked for the rest of the day, the dog
and I, with many pauses to rest and occasional ones to
hide whenever a farmer's cart or a lone horseman passed
us on the road. There were not many. No one from
Rivertown came after me. The dog had far more energy
than I. It trotted tirelessly along the road. Whenever
I stopped to rest, it brought me sticks, which I studiously
did not notice. It chased three squirrels, catching none of
them. It lapped water from roadside ditches. It scratched
its fleas, looking up at me and wagging its tail hopefully.
I ignored it.

When I stopped at dusk and made camp, exhausted but
pleased with my returning strength, the dog disappeared
briefly and then brought me a rabbit. This it laid at my
feet, tail swishing madly, green eyes liquid with dumb
hope.

'Thank you,' I said, before I thought.

At the sound of my voice, it practically turned itself
inside out with happiness.

I was stuck with this dog. Even if I had succeeded in
sending it away, whoever had sent it already knew where

I was. And clearly the dog itself meant me no harm. I skinned and roasted the rabbit and shared it with the creature.

'You need a name, dog.'

It regarded me thoughtfully. Another memory sliced through me: Maggie suggesting names, all of which I rejected, for the first dog. Was she considering names even now, for our child?

I said, 'I'll call you Hunter.' An innocuous, common name, and if it meant more than it seemed, only I would know that. The dog finished its share of the rabbit.

Hunter curled up beside me as I slept, and both his warmth and his presence were comforting.

I dreamed. It was, and was not, the same dream I had had in the disorderly cottage of John the Small. Once again I dreamed of crossing over, with–

Darkness—

Cold—

Dirt choking my mouth—

Worms in my eyes—

Earth imprisoning my fleshless arms and legs—

The dream crossing brought me not to the Country of the Dead but to the road I had just left, running between crop fields and thick woods and small scattered villages. I stood alone in the middle of the deserted road until I became aware of an unseen presence, a shadow whisper, vague but not as vague as before. A scent I could almost but not quite identify, a sound I almost heard . . .

Then I was awake, Hunter stretched out beside me, the dog's front legs twitching as, in some doggy dream of his own, he ran after bright images in his own unfathomable brain.

Hunter and I travelled together many more days. The weather cleared and turned warm. Here in The

25

Queendom, so much lower than the mountains I had left behind, it was already early summer. Cattle moved slowly over meadows thick with sweet clover. In the golden light of late afternoon they stood beside farm ponds, their reflections undisturbed in the still waters. Barley and hops and cabbages grew in neat fields bordered by buttercups and daisies. Hunter and I clattered over wooden bridges built across lazy streams clogged with lily pads, and blue and green dragonflies darted over the waters below. And always the air was filled with sound: birdsong, croaks of frogs, the lowing of cattle, the deep *whoooo* of an owl at dusk.

Settlements grew closer together, travellers more frequent. Once I allowed myself the luxury of a night at an inn. And so late one afternoon we came to Stonegreen during its spring faire.

I did not recognize the village until we were in it, and then my bile rose. I had been here before, three and a half years ago, with Hartah. Here my brutal uncle had forced me to work for him as he preyed on the grief of women who had lost a loved one. Here I had met Cat Starling, the beautiful half-wit girl later burned as a witch. Here Hartah had made, or strengthened, his plans for the shipwreck that had altered my life for ever.

Unchanged was the huge, moss-covered boulder that gave the village its name. Unchanged, too, the painted caravans with the itinerant faire folk: jugglers and fire-eaters and sellers of pewter plates, coloured-glass jewellery, hand mirrors with carved gilded frames – things that village folk could not obtain save twice a year. This was the spring faire, to celebrate the end of planting; there would also be a harvest faire. The booths had been set up in a field at the far end of town. Caravans and worn tents and sale goods remained the same, but nothing else did.

Silence, thick and heavy as wool, hung over the field. Only a few villagers had come to the faire. Except for a boisterous group under the ale tent, who did not seem to be local, people stood in small serious clumps between tents, talking in low tones. Even the few children seemed subdued, gawking at the booths but not clamouring to be taken inside.

A figure approached Hunter and me. My stomach clenched. I remembered him: Kah the Fire Eater, a small wiry man in bizarre turquoise breeches, soft slippers like a lady's, and swirls of colour on his face and naked chest. He had been travelling faires when Hartah had had his booth. 'Sir, be ye from this place?'

'No,' I said, with relief. He did not recognize me. Bearded, one-handed, years older, there was little to connect me with Roger Kilbourne, Hartah's timorous and resentful nephew.

'Ye be a stranger here?'

'Yes.'

'Then ye don't know what has happened.'

'No – what?'

'That's what I be asking *ye*,' Kah said. His face furrowed in frustration, creasing the bright paint. 'The folk be not coming to the faire! How are we to eat if they don't come and buy?'

'Has there . . . has there been plague here?'

'Plague? No! Nothing like that, nothing a man can *understand*. I think the villagers all be daft. They talk on and on of their babes, as if the small ones all died, but from what I hear, they ain't!' He glared at me as if I were responsible for these babies, dead or alive.

'Then what—' I had trouble getting the words out '—what did happen to their children?'

'I don't know,' Kah said, disgusted. 'Not dead, not sickly, not stolen. Just gone quiet. What be ill about a

27

quiet child? A blessing, if you ask me – children make too much by damn noise anyway.'

Gone quiet. Like the infant in the cottage at Rivertown? Like all the infants under a year old at Rivertown? I managed to say, 'How many babies—'

'I don't know, and it makes no cheese ale to me.' All at once he looked hopeful. 'Would ye like to see a display of fire-eating, sir? Fresh from performing afore the Princess herself and all her titled court and—' He scanned my tattered clothing, and hope wilted. 'No, I suppose ye would not.'

'Are the infants—'

But he had turned and strode off.

So it had happened here, too. But ... *what* had happened? Infants put into the quiescent trance of the Dead, but here in the land of the living. How long ago?

All at once I had to know. Did the babes relapse into mindlessness, then wither from lack of food, and die? If so, this could be no more than a new, terrible disease to which the infant brain was particularly susceptible. But if the children did not wither, if they remained as whole and plump as the Dead did on the other side, then this was no mortal illness.

I ran after Kah so fast that Hunter gave a startled bark and then a great bound to catch up. 'Kah! How long ago did the babes here—'

He turned and stared at me. 'How do ye know my name?'

'I ... you told it to me!'

'I did not. Do I know ye?' He squinted at my face, and my heart began a long slow thud in my chest. 'Ye do look familiar, lad ...'

'I don't think so. But I ... I heard your name at the inn. From some boys in the stableyard, who wish to come to your performance.'

'Oh.' He scanned the forlorn faire. 'Then where be these boys?'

'I don't know. But can you tell me if the babes—'

'Pox on the babes!' Again he strode off.

I let him go. I could not stay here at Stonegreen. If Kah had almost recognized me, then others might do so. I walked towards the river, Hunter at my heels. Once away from the faire, I struck out across the fields back towards the main road.

Someone followed me.

At first, I wasn't sure. The figure stayed far enough behind me that I could not tell anything about it – a man? Woman? The figure seemed to be carrying something. Some poor farmer lugging home on foot goods bought at the faire? Perhaps a girl, blanket in hand, stealing away from her parents to meet a youth in the woods. Or had someone in Stonegreen recognized me? There were many in The Queendom with good reason to wish me ill. Loyalists to Queen Caroline. Kin to soldiers I had caused to be killed in battle. Those who would burn anyone suspected of witchcraft.

As the miles increased and the figure neither disappeared nor gained on me, I became certain. I was being followed. 'Hunter, go see,' I said to the dog. He wagged his tail, licked my hand, and stuck his nose in a rabbit hole under a hedgerow.

Nonetheless, Hunter made me feel safer. I had seen what dogs like him could do. Even though I knew that, having had Hunter more than a week, I would not have him much longer. And then – would I be sent another dog? Sent by whom?

The figure was no longer behind me.

Startled, I put up my hand to shade my eyes against the lowering sun, setting at the western end of the road. Had the person turned off into the woods to follow some track to cottage or wood cutter's hut, or to make camp in the woods?

Uneasy, I left the road to make my own camp. A half mile through the trees, walking as carefully as I knew how to leave no trail. The evening was far advanced but enough light lingered for me to discover a spring of sweet fresh water gushing from a hillside. I would not risk a fire lest it call attention to me; the night was warm enough and I had bread and dried cherries in my pack. I ate with my back against an old oak, Hunter curled beside me. The moon rose, full and round and yellow as one of Maggie's sweet cheeses.

Maggie ... what was she doing right now? Asleep in her sister's house at Tanwell? Sitting beside the hearth, sewing garments for our child? Or maybe gazing at this same moon in sorrow at the wreck I had made of her life: a fatherless babe, a husbandless mother. Did she hate me for abandoning her? *Maggie, I will make it up to you, all of it—*

'Hello, Roger Kilbourne,' a voice said behind me, and my world shattered.

4

I leapt up to face the intruder. He was small, a few years older than I, much shorter and even scrawnier. He wore rough brown clothing, old boots, and a large pack strapped to his back. With the moonlight falling full on his face, his scar stood out vividly, a long half-healed gash from hairline to chin running over the left side of his mouth, so that both upper and lower lip swelled and twisted. He pointed a *gun* directly at my heart.

And Hunter merely gazed up at him curiously.

I fought to control my fear. 'Who are you? What do you want?'

'What I don't want is to hurt you. This savage weapon is merely because I don't want you to hurt *me*. I am not much of a fighter.'

This last was said with bitterness. But I could see that he would indeed be bad in a fight. His shoulders were no wider than a girl's, and the hands that held the gun were small-boned and dainty. Even I, one-handed, could probably take him in a struggle. But there was nothing dainty nor timid about the dark eyes above the barrel of his *gun*. They burned with feeling.

Hunter scratched absently at a flea.

Irritation at the dog kept me silent. Wasn't Hunter here to protect me? He was doing a piss-poor job so far. But I have learned that if one says nothing, often the other person will begin to talk. Few can bear an unbroken and tense silence.

This youth was not one of them. His voice, high with strain, tumbled out words as a grinder tumbles out sausage meat. 'I said I mean you no harm and it's true, Roger Kilbourne. You must believe that. I will put down the *gun* as soon as you assure me that you won't harm me. Nor will your dog.'

My dog found another interesting flea on his backside.

I said, 'How do you know my name?'

'That is part of what I will tell you as soon as you tell me that you won't harm me.' The *gun* had started to wobble slightly, from either heaviness or fear.

'What is your name?'

'Leo Tollers. You see how frank I am with you.'

'It could be a made-up name.'

'It is not.'

'Then Leo—'

'Answer me! Have I your assurance or not?'

'After one more question. If I give you my assurance that I will not harm you, why would you believe it?'

'Because I know a great deal about you, Roger Kilbourne. And I have information you would like to hear.'

'But if I—'

His tone became sharper. 'You are trying to wear me out! No, don't get to your feet, don't try to rush me, I tell you I will shoot!'

If it hadn't been for those eyes, I might have tested him. A single leap would gain me the *gun*, which now wobbled even more in his unsteady grip. But his eyes stopped me. They held utter desperation. The desperate, I have learned, often stop at nothing.

Slowly I eased back to the ground until I sat cross-legged. Hunter, finally aware that something was happening, raised his face to me questioningly. I did not know what 'information' Leo Tollers had for me, but

I did not trust him. And I did not want anyone in The Queendom tracking me. I was going home to Maggie, and I must not lead anyone to her and my unborn son. Of all the things Mother Chilton had told me, that was the one I believed most.

There was only one way to escape Leo Tollers. And although Mother Chilton had told me not to do it, my father – curse his faithless bones – had told me it could do no harm. There was no longer any danger to me in the Country of the Dead. My mad sister was gone. I would rather do anything at all than either endanger Maggie or give up going to her.

With Leo's *gun* pointed at me, I bit my tongue hard, willed my mind, and I crossed over.

Darkness—

Cold—

Dirt choking my mouth—

Worms in my eyes—

Earth imprisoning my fleshless arms and legs—

And then I stood on the far side of the grave. I had not been here in months, not since the onset of last winter, but the Country of the Dead had not changed. Here was the sunless grey sky, the motionless trees, the hillside I had just left. Here, too, was one of the circles of the Dead.

They sat motionless, fourteen of them, facing the centre of the circle, dressed in whatever clothing they had died in. Around each of their heads was a thick, dark grey fog, completely hiding their faces. If I touched that fog I knew I would feel it vibrating like a hive of bees. In the centre of the circle was another patch of the grey fog, humming and spinning. As yet this patch spun slowly, the humming barely audible. But I knew what that patch of fog really was, and what it would eventually do. These were watchers from Soulvine Moor, preparing to destroying these

Dead for ever and to take unto themselves the power that the Dead slowly accumulated in their long wait for eternity. That was how war was being fought between Soulvine Moor and those struggling to preserve the barrier between life and death. It was only because of that war – and my past actions – that the barrier had eroded as much as it had.

But this was no longer my war. My need was simpler. As part of that erosion, I stood here now in body as well as soul. Only a *hisaf* could do so. I planned to walk towards Tanwell on this side of the grave, for perhaps half a day, then cross back over. There would be no way for Leo Tollers to track me. Even now he must be standing, bewildered and terrified, staring at the spot where a moment before I had sat cross-legged on the ground. Would he fire his *gun* at the place I had been? I hoped he would not hit Hunter.

I started to climb the little hillside, hoping for a break in the trees through which I could take my bearings. Land stretches or shrinks in the Country of the Dead according to need. Where many have died, a mile in the land of the living can become ten on the other side. A pond may become a vast lake, a stand of trees a huge forest. Conversely, if few have died on a mountain or desert or wild ravine, ten miles may become one. I put my boot firmly on the hillside.

Something made me turn, some shimmer of the still air or motion at the edge of my vision, and so I saw Leo Tollers, still holding his *gun*, materialize beside me.

He was a *hisaf*.

I must have gaped at him because a smile flickered on that scarred face, curving up the one side of his lips that could still move. 'Close your mouth, Roger.'

'You are—'

'Even as you are, yes. You cannot escape me by crossing

34

over. And I am still waiting for that assurance that you will not harm me.'

It suddenly seemed ludicrous. Here we stood, two living men in the Country of the Dead. Both with talent far beyond what ordinary people could command, both knowing that the Dead go on, although in a form neither of us relished – one no longer even assured since the war began – and we argued over bodily harm from a weapon foreign to both of us. If Leo Tollers had planned to shoot me, he would already have done so. I could not escape him, so I must put up with him. Although why he should believe my assurances, I didn't know.

I said, 'I promise I will not harm you.'

'Good.' He lowered the barrel of his *gun*, but did not replace it on his back. I suddenly saw what was slung there, which he must have been carrying when I first glimpsed him: a lute. He looked around and said, 'I don't like it here. I never have. Let us go back.'

'Yes.'

Darkness—

Cold—

Dirt choking my mouth—

Worms in my eyes—

Earth imprisoning my fleshless arms and legs—

I was the first to appear in the land of the living. Hunter had curled up on my cloak and gone to sleep. Some protection he was! For a moment I wondered if Leo would actually follow me back but a moment later he appeared, pale and looking ill.

'I *hate* that.'

I said nothing. Of course he hated it; I could not imagine any *hisaf* enjoying the passage through the grave. But Leo seemed far more affected by it than I had ever been. Sweating, his free hand on his concave belly even as the other clutched his *gun*, he seemed to be fighting nausea.

35

I watched, taking his measure: a naturally squeamish and timid man who had steeled himself to this task involving me. Whatever it was.

Eventually he regained command of himself, and I risked a question. 'What do you want of me?'

'To give you a message. First – have you water?'

I handed him my goatskin bag, filled at the spring that gushed a mere few feet behind him. He was clearly not accustomed to travel; no one sets out on foot without a waterbag. He drank deeply, water dribbling from the scarred side of his mouth, and swiped his hand across his lips. 'Thank you.'

'You are welcome. Now – who sent you?'

'I belong to the Brotherhood of *hisafs*, those fighting Soulvine Moor. As I suspect you already know.'

He did not look to me to be a likely fighter. 'How did you know where I am?'

'They knew.'

'*How?*'

'I don't know.'

'Did they tell you why you should follow me?'

'To give you a message from your father.'

It was like a blow. Watching me, Leo again gave that faint, twisted-lip smile from half his ruined face.

I said, 'My father? In . . .'

'Yes. He is still imprisoned in Galtryf. As was I, but I escaped. Rawley could not.'

Rawley. It was the first time I had ever heard my father's name. Rawley and Katharine. Who birthed Roger and the second Katharine, the half-sister I had killed. Rawley, who had abandoned my mother and who had abandoned me. Twice.

'Roger?' Leo said.

More harshly than I intended, I said, 'I want no message from my father.'

'That's too bad, because he sent you this.' Leo drew from a small bundle from his pocket, wrapped in the same rough cloth as his tunic, and held it out to me.

I did not take it. 'If you escaped from Galtryf, why can my father not do so? *Hisafs* can cross bodily now—' as we had both just done '— so how can stone walls hold him? How can they hold any of your Brotherhood?'

'Stone walls cannot. When the bodily crossings became possible – and I think you know how much you had to do with that change, Roger Kilbourne – many of us escaped, including me. But Rawley was held by the threat of harm to your mother if he left Galtryf.'

'Harm to my mother! My mother is dead!' I wanted to strike him for even mentioning her. My mother, whom I had last seen in the Country of the Dead, in the centre of one of those cursed circles.

'And you of all people know what can be done to the Dead, don't you? You have done it to many. The rogue *hisafs* threaten to carry your mother back to the land of the living, where she would have a fortnight before she crumbled into nothing, losing all chance at eternity. Just like the Blue army you brought back, like Lady Cecilia—'

'Stop!'

He did, raising the *gun* again at my angry tone. Hunter woke and looked at me in puzzlement. The dog had not objected to Leo, which lent belief to his tale that he meant me no harm. But just as my dislike for him hardened, Leo's face changed. The burning dark eyes softened into compassion.

'I'm sorry, Roger,' he said with more gentleness than I would have suspected him capable of. 'I lost my mother, too, and not very long ago. Just before this was done to me.' He touched the hideous scar on his face.

He was giving me a chance to shift the conversation

away from what pained me. 'What was done to you?'

'Badger baiting. Only instead of a dog, they used me.'

Badger baiting had been staged at the rougher of the country faires Hartah had once dragged me to. A badger was put into a small enclosed space and a dog dropped in to fight it. Wagers were laid. A full-grown badger, thirty-five pounds of terrified wrath with sharp teeth and powerful claws, would often win, killing the dog. Leo was larger than a dog but far less equipped to fight, even if he had been given a knife. I looked at Leo's face. My imagination is too good; I could picture the scene in all its cruel horror. That, and the compassion he had shown me, wakened mine towards him.

I said awkwardly, 'I am sorry you had to endure that.'

He shrugged. 'In Galtryf, Rawley was kind to me. So I said I would carry this to you.' Again he held out the small bundle and this time I took it, untied the string, and unwrapped the cloth.

A miniature portrait of my mother, just as I remembered her. She wore a lavender gown, with lavender ribbons in her hair. The same brown hair and eyes my half-sister had had, although my sister's eyes had been darker. My sister—

'Roger?' Leo said softly.

'I don't want it. Here, take it back, I remember her well enough without this. Why did my father send it? We have no more to do with each other!'

'Why do you hate him so?'

'He promised me a rescue that never came!'

Leo's face furrowed. 'But he had been captured and so could not rescue you. Surely you make allowances for that?'

Yes. No. Of course a man who was in prison could hardly rescue one who was not ... but I had relied upon my father's promise, had held it to me during the long weeks of being carted over the mountains towards the savage kingdom, forced to teach the Young Chieftain what could not be taught. All the fear and helplessness of those weeks I laid at the door of my father, who had insisted that I, a lad of seventeen, undertake this hopeless mission. And that mission had ended with Tom Jenkins, my only friend, killed in battle. I did not trust my father, who had deserted my mother and me, and I no longer believed his statement that he had done so only for our own safety. He was an adventurer, and we the victims of that lust for adventure. I could not forgive him, and I did not trust him. In memory I could still feel the blow he had given me in the palace dungeon.

I said, 'The miniature is a marker, isn't it? So that your "Brotherhood" will always know where I am.'

Leo looked surprised. 'I don't know.'

'I thought you were a member of the Brotherhood.'

'I am. That does not mean that I am told everything.'

I could believe that. Skinny, timid, huddled in his cloak against chill even though the summer night was not cold, Leo Tollers looked completely ineffectual, someone whom nobody would tell anything much. Probably he didn't know if the portrait was a marker, and probably it was. I took one long last look at my mother, wrapped up the miniature, and handed it back to Leo.

'What am *I* supposed to do with it?' he said, and now compassion had been replaced by querulousness.

'I don't know.'

Hunter looked from one of us to the other and back again, puzzled by the sharpness in our voices. Then Leo's demeanour changed once again. 'May I sleep here tonight? Near you and your dog?'

'I suppose so.' We could just as easily part in the morning.

'I'm afraid to be alone.'

'All right.' I felt uncomfortable with his timidity and abasement. My last camping companions had been Tom Jenkins, brash and confident, and Jee, who had the survival skills of a boulder.

'Where are you going, Roger?'

'East.' That much was already evident.

'But where?'

'Go to sleep, Leo.'

'Can I go with you?'

'No.'

He looked at me bleakly, his ruined face grotesque in the moonlight. 'I have nowhere else to go.'

'I'm sorry to hear that, but you cannot come with me.'

'Are you going to find work on some farm someplace?'

I didn't answer, merely lay on the ground and pulled my cloak loosely over me. Nonetheless, tension shot through me like lightning. Leo's questions implied that the Brotherhood of *hisafs* did not know about Maggie and my son. Was that true?

The web women knew: '*He is our last hope.*' My sister, too, had known: '*The child is the one! Your son!*' But my sister was gone for ever, and the web women and *hisafs* were at odds with each other over strategies to fight Soulvine Moor, none of which I understood. I believed that this Brotherhood was ignorant of my destination and my unborn child, but I waited in the darkness for Leo to say something that might contradict my belief. And if he did? What would I do then?

He said humbly, 'Maybe you have other kin to take you in? An uncle or brother?'

'I do not.'

'Nor have I. Perhaps two maimed youths could better find work together than separately. We could offer two workers for one pay.'

He waited, then, for me to agree. I did not. The minutes

stretched out uncomfortably. I thought that he must give up and go to sleep, but instead he surprised me.

'Would you like to hear a song on my lute?'

I could not say no, not after my much greater refusal to take him with me. Ungraciously I said, 'All right', and there was much sighing as he drew the lute from its oiled bag, plucked a few strings, tuned it. He began to play, and I sat up once more, in surprise, and stared.

His voice was astonishing: pure and clear, a man's voice but with the sweetness of a girl's. The plaintive tune of love's loss was commonplace, but Leo's singing of it was not. At court I had heard many musicians. He bested them all.

> Although you to the hills do flee,
> My love you can't escape.
> Your heart, my sweet, belongs to me
> Though you may change its shape.
>
> Never, never will I cease
> To follow where you go,
> And ever, ever will I be
> The hound upon your doe.
>
> Do what you will and what you can,
> Employ the arts you know —
> Ever, ever will I be
> The hound upon your doe.

Leo raised his gaze and in the moonlight filtering through branches of the oak, his eyes met mine. *Never, never will I cease to follow where you go* ... Still that steady gaze held mine, and I saw in them the same burning look as when he first trained his *gun* on me. *Ever, ever will I be the hound upon your doe* ...

Then Leo laughed. 'It's merely a song, yes, Roger?' He put away his lute, lay down, and went to sleep.

But I lay awake for a long time.

5

We travelled together one day more. I set a punishing pace, one that tested my returned strength to the limit. I wanted to tire Leo as much as possible so that he would sleep deeply. Before my illness I had been toughened by months of mountain walking; it was clear that Leo was unused to moving much at all. He was meant to be a musician or a scholar. Why had the Brotherhood chosen him to follow me? There must be a reason. I needed to know what it was.

'That's a village ... ahead,' Leo said, panting. 'Could we stop ... for ale?'

'I have no money,' I lied.

'I have money.'

'Then you may stop. I will go on.'

He scowled, his dark eyes flashing with the strong feeling that always seemed to lie just below the surface. I quickened my stride. He kept up, with difficulty, and so we passed through the tiny settlement, which did not seem to be having any trouble with tranced children.

The village was followed by fields, which gave way to sheep pastures thick with clover, and then to rolling hills dotted with great tracts of wood. Here the road, obviously less used, dwindled to a track. The long afternoon was warm and fragrant, and it was The Queendom at its loveliest. Wild cherries and plums blossomed pink and white. The nightingales had returned from their winter home. Finally, just as the sun set in tender pinks and golds, I left the road to camp by a noisy stream bordered by bulrushes. Weeping willows grew along the bank, dipping their branches into the water and filtering the light to a green glow. I dropped my pack under a huge willow tree. Leo, groaning, sank to the ground.

'Hunter, go find!' I said. He bounded off. 'Leo, gather some twigs for a fire.'

'I can't. I can't move any more.'

I snorted and left the willow. When I returned with twigs Leo had unwrapped his lute and was strumming it softly. His whole body drooped with weariness.

'Do you think,' I said sarcastically, 'that you can bestir yourself enough to skin a rabbit if Hunter brings one?'

'You skin it, Roger, and I'll make the fire.'

'Don't tire yourself too much.'

He raised those burning eyes to me. 'I cannot help it if I am not strong.'

'No, you cannot. But since you are not, why did you agree to bring me that miniature?'

'I told you, your father was kind to me in Galtryf.'

I made the fire while Leo rested. Finally I said, 'So you knew my father in Galtryf.'

'I already told you so.' He had laid his lute aside and sprawled full-length on the ground.

'And what is "Galtryf"?'

'It is an old castle used by the Brotherhood as their command post.'

'How did you come to be there?'

'I was captured in the war we wage with Soulvine Moor.'

We had come to the information I wanted. Hunter returned with a rabbit and I took it from him, drawing out my knife and making a great show of skinning the rabbit so that Leo did not have to. I wanted him to feel in my debt.

I said, 'What was your part in the war?'

Leo took a long time to answer me. 'I was a decoy.'

'A decoy?'

'You don't know how the war is waged, do you, Roger?'

'Tell me.'

'I cannot tell you much because I don't know much. Until I was approached by the Brotherhood, I lived at the manor house of Lord Jasper Vincent, at the northwestern edge of The Queendom, in the mountains near the border with the country of Queen Isabelle. I was musician there. And a kitchen boy and jack-of-all-work; whatever was deemed within the feeble powers of a weakling like me.' His voice held bitterness.

I could picture the remote, rough-country manor house. The pages and young lords, as wild as the landscape, would not have used a boy like Leo gently.

'Was that where the badger fighting took place?'

'Yes. There was a wedding, my lady Judith with a rich lout from Her Grace Isabelle's queendom. The feasting and drinking went on for three days. The night of the third day the merry sweet lads ... they ...' His fingers, as if of their own volition, touched the scar on his face.

'Leo, did the older nobles not recognize your talent? Not treasure it?'

'That lot could not recognize any talents but fighting and whoring. Except Lady Judith. She was married against her will to that ... that oaf ... she with her sweet heart and beautiful ...'

Hs voice had dropped in pitch, full of emotion. I knew what I was hearing; I had once felt it myself. Leo Tollers, kicked and ridiculed, the butt of vicious pranks, had loved a high-born girl he could never have.

I said, 'Why did you not cross over to escape the badger?'

'I did. But this was before the breach between the lands of the living and the Dead had crumbled enough to permit *hisafs* to cross bodily. My body remained behind, and so I was maimed. And crossing over ... I hate it. I always have. How can you do it so blithely? The passage through the grave .... ' He shuddered.

'Doesn't that make you an odd recruit to your Brotherhood of *hisafs*?'

'They saved my life,' he said sharply. 'One of them chanced to be at Lord Jasper's manor; he stopped the lordling's sport and saved my life. A week later more arrived with a spare horse and took me away.'

'Then how did you end up in Galtryf?'

'I don't want to talk about it.' He bent over his lute, strumming and tuning the strings. I reached out and put my hand across the fret.

'I know you don't want to talk about it, Leo. But I must know. I don't understand this war, and now that the Brotherhood has found me, I must. Why were you sent to me? I do not wish to take part in the conflict, and the web women have told me I should not.'

Leo spat a curse, so filthy it startled me. 'The "web women"! Those old hags! They would lose us this war with their prattle about the web of life and death and their cowardly reluctance to kill anything!'

It seemed an odd statement, given that Leo did not seem very brave, but perhaps he did not see himself as a coward. Men seldom did. I ignored his anger about the web women and returned to my question.

'What is the Brotherhood trying to do? And why are you with me?' Certainly it was not as protection.

In the dimming light under the willow tree he gazed at me a long time. Finally he said, 'The Brotherhood is trying to kill all the *hisafs* who are making the obscenities performed on Soulvine Moor possible. You know about those, I think. You have been there.'

I had. Twice. The second time I had barely escaped

46

with my life. 'How many *hisafs* have sided with Soulvine Moor?'

'I don't know.'

'How many have the Brotherhood succeeded in killing?'

'I don't know.'

'What do they want with me?'

'They only want to know where you are.'

'Why?'

'I don't know.'

'You brought me this marker so that I may be located at any moment, and yet you don't know why?'

His temper flared. 'I told you, I am here only because your father was kind to me! I don't care about this war any more than you do, not really! But I must live and eat the same as any other beast!' He picked up his lute and began to strum, harsh angry chords. I could see that he would tell me no more tonight. I left the willow to gather more wood.

As I hunted for dead branches, I considered Leo's story. Some parts of it did not seem consistent. If he were really an intimate of my father at Galtryf, wouldn't he know more than he professed to? And if the Brotherhood had rescued him once, from Lord Jasper's manor, wouldn't they continue to see that he could 'live and eat like any other beast' without setting him the task of bringing a marker to me – a task for which he seemed very ill suited? Dissatisfied with what he had told me, and insufficiently moved by pity for his helplessness, I was more determined than ever to shed him. Now. Tonight.

There was no moon, but the stars shone brightly: the Weeping Woman, the Cat, the Wagon Wheel, the Southern Star. Leo, exhausted by the day's hurried pace, slept deeply. His concave chest rose and fell; a soft whistling noise came from his thin nose above the mangled lips. Hunter, too, slept, curled up tightly as a coil of rope. But I knew that the second I stepped on a twig, or perhaps even rose, the dog would wake. So I left the only way I could. I jabbed my small shaving knife into my thigh, willed my passage, and crossed over.

Darkness—

Cold—

Dirt choking my mouth—

Worms in my eyes—

Earth imprisoning my fleshless arms and legs—

And then I stood in the Country of the Dead. The landscape seemed exactly like the one I had left, except for the light fog, and even that seemed to diminish as I moved towards the road – or where it would be if this place had any roads. My plan was to walk for several hours across country. If Leo woke, he would not know in which direction I had gone in either landscape, even if he could steel himself enough to cross over after me. And by the time I returned to the land of the living, I would be too far away for Hunter to sniff me out.

As soon as I emerged from the woods onto a broad field, I came across the Dead. Widely scattered in ones and twos, they sat in the places where they had died. They gazed at nothing, their faces tranquil and calm. None of them were old women, who were usually the only ones I could rouse, and anyway they would not be able to tell me anything I wished to know. I trudged on.

The Country of the Dead is perpetually silent. Ordinarily I don't mind it; ordinarily I don't even think about it. But now the quiet felt leaden, as oppressive as the low grey sky and the dim, even light. I began to hum, and then to sing, and the words were the troubling ones of Leo's song:

Never, never will I cease
To follow where you go,
And ever, ever will I be
The hound upon your doe.

Well, I had shaken my hounds – both of them – and in another week I would be with Maggie. I would hold her in my arms, feel her fair curls against my cheek, endure the deserved tongue-whipping she would give me for abandoning her – probably many tongue-whippings – and then we would make our life together with our son. Maggie, who had always loved me better than I deserved and—

Something flickered at the edge of my vision.

I stopped and peered through the pale fog. An object appeared on the ground in the middle distance, disappeared, appeared again. A small object, no larger than a pie. My heart began a low, hard thumping in my chest.

Should I cross back over? But I might not have walked far enough to be beyond Hunter's ability to find me.

Cautiously I approached the object. Again it flickered out of existence. When I reached the place it had been, there was nothing there.

But there had been. Here, where nothing ever appeared except—

'*Waaaaahhhhh!*'

My heart nearly jumped from my body as the thing reappeared, and this time there was no doubt what it was. A child, red-faced and screaming. Its blue eyes glared at me, the smell of its full diaper hit my nostrils, its indignant yells pierced my ears, and then it was gone again. And I understood.

This was an infant *hisaf*, unable as yet to control its coming and goings across the barrier of the grave. When I had been such a babe, such crossings had probably happened mostly in my dreams. Back then *hisafs* had not been able to cross over bodily. There must have been times when my infant self lay asleep, restless and feverish from some childish illness, pain in my head or belly or throat. That's what is required – pain, plus a kind of letting go that, paradoxically, is also an act of will. Babes cannot control their will, and I did not remember crossing over until I was six years old.

But this child was not six, nor anywhere near it, and it was awake. Awake and in infant pain from hunger or its bowels or fear. And the abilities of *hisafs* had grown with the growing breach between the land of the living and the country of the Dead.

What was this babe's mother seeing, as she cared for it? Did she know what her child was? Could she accept it? I could imagine the terrible pull between love of one's child and fear of witchcraft. But, no – this baby's father must have been a *hisaf*, too. The mother, like mine, must have known what her son would be.

I reached out my good hand towards the child, who screamed louder and then vanished. It did not reappear. His mother must have risen from her sleep, stumbled to the cradle I could not see, and tended to her son. On this side there were few Dead in sight; the parents of the little *hisaf* lived isolated from other people, perhaps the better to protect their child. So must my mother have once protected me.

Longing to see her again – alive as I remembered her at six years old, not as she was now – hit me so hard that my eyes watered. Then the longing for my mother, unseemly in one my age, became renewed longing for Maggie. *Soon.*

Another mile or two and the Dead became more numerous. There must be a village here, on the other side. Then, beside a swift downhill stream, I came to something I had seen before and hoped never to see again.

A large circle of the Dead, thirty or thirty-five, all facing inward towards the centre of the ring. The Dead wore clothing from many different eras and seasons: coloured wool, linen shifts, heavy crude furs, old-fashioned far-thingales, bronze armour, tattered night shirts. Old men, little girls, young women, half-grown boys, soldiers – each of their heads was densely shrouded in dark fog, obscuring their faces. In the middle of the circle spun a vortex of even darker fog. Faster and faster it spun, now starting to hum, now the hum rising to such a loud pitch that I clapped my hands over my ears even as I started to run forward.

'No! Don't!' I screamed the words, but of course there was no one to hear. And the words were stupid anyway – as if I could stop the horror about to happen! The vortex spun faster, there was a huge clap of sound, like lightning striking the ground, and all the Dead disappeared, along with the vortex.

Gone. Just gone.

I sagged to the ground. The light, pervasive fog over the landscape had also disappeared. I could see for miles, along the mountains and valleys of the Country of the Dead. But there was nothing to see where these Dead had sat awaiting eternity. The grass was not even charred. It was as if nothing, and no one, had been here at all. The men and women of Soulvine Moor, present in the vortex in ways I did not understand, had sucked the power of the Dead unto themselves. They had annihilated bodies and souls both, so that these Dead existed no longer anywhere, their chance for eternity lost for ever.

Just as I had hurled my mad half-sister into such a vortex, depriving her of her own eternity. But that had been different. My sister had been used by Soulvine Moor to kill innocent people, and would have been so used again. She had been stalking my unborn son. The people who had just vanished into the vortex had, in contrast, been blameless, tranquil and mindless Dead who threatened no one.

I don't know how long I sat on the ground, gazing as sightlessly as the Dead themselves, but eventually I pulled myself together and stood. Behind me someone moaned.

I spun around so fast that I nearly lost balance. 'Who's there?'

Another moan, from close by. I followed it to a man lying behind a bush. I could not tell if he was asleep or very ill, but one thing was certain: he was not dead. I drew my big knife. If he was here and alive, he must be a *hisaf* – but for which side? A deep groan and he opened his eyes. They were bright green.

'*A big man with black beard and green eyes ... He witched our babes in Stonegreen ...*'

The bearded man stared at me and groped for his weapon, but he could barely move his arm. I knelt beside him, swiftly found and confiscated two knives, and put my own blade at his throat. 'Who are you?'

Glaring at me with hatred, he tried to speak but managed only a hoarse, unintelligible whisper.

Unbidden, words of Mother Chilton's floated into my mind: '*Everything has a cost, Roger Kilbourne – when will you learn that?*' She had meant the web women who became birds to rescue me and nearly died from their transforming effort. But *hisafs* could not become animals. Of what action was this man paying the cost? No *hisaf* was necessary for the spinning vortex to rob the Dead; I knew that much.

I said, 'What have you done here? Tell me or I will kill you.'

He *smiled*. A feeble smile, barely a bending of his lips

between the black beard and bristly black moustache, but a smile nonetheless. His green eyes shone with contempt. And I understood. He did not think I was capable of murder.

He was right.

I had killed Hartah, but that was in the heightened passion of fear and unexpected grief after he had just slain my Aunt Jo. I had killed my sister, but she had caused the deaths of two people I cared about, menaced me and threatened my son. To drive my knife into the throat of a stranger – I could not do it. I was either not hard enough or not courageous enough, and I could not even tell which.

So instead I said fiercely, inanely, 'What did you do here that depleted you so?'

Again that contemptuous smile.

'What did you do to those infants in Stonegreen?'

This time he turned his head away from me. It took all his strength, and his eyes closed in exhaustion.

I tied him hand and foot with what was left of Tom Jenkins' rope; the odious children of John the Small had stolen most of it for their games. Too bad those children had not been tranced into quiescence!

The *hisaf* did not rouse as I bound him. I was just wondering what to do with him now when another sound took me. Something crashed through the under-brush across the stream – something moving fast where nothing should move at all. Once before I had heard such a sound, right after I hurled my sister into the vortex. I did not know what it had been then, although I assumed it was more *hisafs* coming to rescue her, and I did not wait to see what it was now. With both hands I seized the inert body of the bound *hisaf*, bit down on my tongue so hard that blood filled my mouth, and crossed over.

We emerged inside a structure. Dim light, even dimmer

than in the Country of the Dead, filtered through two very dirty windows. As my eyes adjusted, I saw that I stood inside a mill, undoubtedly built beside the swift stream I had noted on the other side. The great millstone did not turn; the mill was empty; the door wide enough for wagonloads of grain was closed. But outside, loud enough to be heard above the mill race, people shouted and screamed.

'The babes!'

'—witched—'

'Help me! Help my child – someone, anyone! Oh please help!'

So it had happened here, too. The black-bearded *hisaf* had stolen children, as he had done in Stonegreen, and left them neither dead nor alive. At that moment, I could almost have killed him – except that these villagers would do it for me, as was their right. But if I were caught with him, they would kill me, too.

I spat out a mouthful of blood and turned to the two dirty windows overlooking the stream. I unlocked one, shoved open the casement, and climbed through onto a narrow shelf of land between the building and the mill race. The red of a summer dawn streaked the sky. There was no way to move away from the mill without being seen except to descend into the water, crouch between its banks, and waddle along until I reached the cover of a wooded bank about a quarter mile upstream.

The water, icy from the mountains, came to my waist. Gasping with cold, I held my pack above the stream, cursing each time it was splashed by water breaking on a rock. By hugging the closer bank, I made it to the woods. The whole way, the wails and shouts of the villagers followed me, grief become heart-piercing sound.

I hoped they found the bound *hisaf* before he revived enough to cross over.

I shivered in my wet clothes. It would be at least an hour before the sun shone warmly enough to dry me, and I dared not risk a fire. The best I could do was shed my sodden tunic, breeches, and small clothes, pour the water out of my boots, and wrap myself, naked, in my dry cloak from my pack. I wasn't as far from either the village or from Leo Tollers as I wanted to be, but cold kept me from going any farther.

It turned out not to matter. Something thrashed through the underbrush to the east. Moments later Hunter ran up to me. He licked my hand, leaping and frisking like a demented thing, and shortly after Leo followed him.

'Roger, you moron – you cannot rest here! Don't you hear them? The villagers? If they find us—'

I looked up at him from where I sat huddled in my cloak. Slowly I said, 'How did you know something had happened in that village?'

'I came that way! Hurry, get up!'

'You did not come that way.'

'Yes, I did – I circled back to avoid the town. Get up!'

His fear seemed real. Perhaps he *had* circled the village to reach me when Hunter finally sniffed out my trail. And perhaps his fear was what it seemed: terror of having to cross over to escape a band of furious men hunting whoever had tranced their children. But even though singing seemed the last thing on Leo's mind at the moment, I nonetheless seemed to hear the words of his song in my mind:

> *Never, never will I cease*
> *To follow where you go,*
> *And ever, ever will I be—*

Hound. I looked more closely at Hunter, studying him

even as Leo dug frantically in his pack for something I could wear. The dog looked like all the others sent to save me over the last months: grey coat, big snout, short tail, green eyes brimming with doggy devotion. But no two living things can ever be completely identical. I had memorized the small white patch on Hunter's left hind leg, the scratch on his haunch where he had tangled with a thorn bush, the way one toe grew slightly over another on one paw. This was not Hunter.

And ever, ever will I be
The hound upon your doe.

6

We walked away from the village as fast as I could travel. Exhaustion kept me from talking, even from thinking. There was only the road, dusty and too bright on my tired eyes. When we halted at mid-morning, I fell asleep so swiftly that I didn't even remember lying down.

I dreamed. Not of crossing over, but of . . . I wasn't even sure what. Vague shapes, vague animal smells, a greyness that was not fog but wasn't anything else, either. The dream felt disturbing enough to wake me.

'Good morrow, sleeping lad,' Leo said mockingly. 'You left me to do all the work, you know.'

I sat up, my heart still thudding from the dream. It was twilight, still warm, and Leo had made a fire. The good smell of roasting meat banished the scents of my dream. Hunter, who was not Hunter, had caught a brace of rabbits. Leo had even gathered wild strawberries, which astonished me until I realized I was lying on a bed of them. All he had to do was reach out his hand. The fire burned in a little clearing ringed by birch and oak.

'Thank you, Leo,' I said. 'Are you sure you're not tired from such extensive labour?'

He laughed, and for the first time I almost liked him.

'Don't burn your fingers. Here, Hunter, have some rabbit. You earned it.'

Did he really not know this wasn't Hunter? I ate greedily but my mind was not on the food. When we finished and were sucking our fingers while the dog crunched rabbit bones, I began.

'You said you circled back through that village and so knew what was happening there.'

'Yes.' He unwrapped his lute.

'No music, Leo. I want to talk.'

He ignored me, strumming softly. 'You can ask, Roger, but I told you: I know very little.'

'Not as little as you profess, I think.'

'You're wrong. I know exactly that little.' He began a lilting air I had heard at court. Queen Caroline and her ladies had danced to it.

'You know at least what you heard in the village. What happened there?'

'The same thing as in Stonegreen. You were there, Roger. Babies vanished from their cradles and were found at dawn, as tranquil and mindless as the Dead.'

'Where were they found? What exact spot?'

'I don't know. Maybe somewhere near the stream you waded along.'

'Listen to me, Leo. When I crossed back over from the Country of the Dead, I found myself inside the village mill, beside that same stream. On this side was the circle of tranced babies, on the other side I saw a circle of the Dead. And those Dead just vanished. They were sucked into a sort of spinning grey vortex. Do you—'

'They were what?' Leo looked up, startled and then afraid. 'The Dead were sucked into something? That's impossible!'

'No. I saw it.' More than once.

'I don't believe it. The Dead never go anywhere! They're dead!'

I believed him. His whole body had gone rigid with shock and fear. Leo hated to cross over; probably he had never seen the vortex, or even the fog that formed it. He knew nothing. And in talking to him, I knew no more than before.

'All right,' I said. 'Let us forget that I ever spoke of it.'

'Gladly. I think you must have dreamed all that, Roger. You were dreaming today, just before you woke. You called out a girl's name.'

Alarm shot through me. 'What name?'

'Maggie. Who is she?'

I managed to grimace and shrug. 'A girl I once bedded. The only girl, in fact. She was a kitchen maid.'

He nodded, not very interested. 'I have never had a girl.'

'Oh.' I didn't know what to say. This was the reverse of Tom Jenkins, who had boasted to me of his many conquests.

'What girl would have me?' Leo said bitterly. 'Look at me. Puny and weak and scarred. Even my Lady Judith was only kind to me from pity.' He struck a harsh chord on his lute and reached for its wrappings.

'Leo—'

'Shut your mouth, Roger. I'm going to sleep now. You clean up.' He rolled in his cloak beside the fire, face turned away from me.

In the gathering darkness I buried what was left of the rabbit – not much, after the dog was finished with it – to keep predators from camp. Under the oaks I gathered more deadwood for the fire. Water was harder; I could find neither spring nor stream, which was probably why Leo had not filled the waterbag here. And he had not filled it as we walked earlier because water was heavy to carry. 'Puny and weak' he had described himself – he'd left out 'lazy'. Which made it all the more puzzling that he was here, sticking to me like pine tar.

But no longer. What had failed last night, I would try again tonight. I was leaving Leo Tollers and the dog that was not Hunter, as soon as the animal was asleep and so could not bark and wake Leo.

At the moment, however, the dog sat wide awake, gazing at me with its green eyes as I sat by the fire. Occasionally it licked my hand. The stars emerged in a deep blue sky but tonight their beauty captured me less than did my own troubled mind.

What had the stolen, tranced infants to do with the circles of the Dead? What was the connection? And why hadn't the sucking of the Dead into vortexes disturbed the Country of the Dead? Three years ago I had begun to disturb that calm landscape. I had carried back first a half-wit sailor, then Lady Cecilia, and then over a hundred soldiers. My meddling had caused storms, earthquakes and withering in that landscape on the other side of the grave. Eventually it had summoned that bright and terrible thing, which I had merely glimpsed, to rend the sky. Later one of the web women, Alysse, had called that monstrous shining 'the sword', and she had turned pale with fear when she spoke of it. So why now didn't the loss of so many Dead also disturb the landscape?

I had thought to leave all this confusion behind me for ever. I had thought to find Maggie and make a new life with her and my son. I didn't want these questions, didn't want any more—

Grrrrrrffffff!

All at once the dog growled, leapt to its feet, and raced towards the oaks, barking frantically. Leo jerked awake and sat upright. In the starlight the scar across his face shone dully. 'What? What is it?'

'I don't know! The dog just went mad!' I drew my knife.

'Stay here!' Leo said, and somehow he didn't sound like himself. I did not stay there. Leo ran into the trees but I, faster, got there before him. At first I could not see in the dimness under the canopy of leaves. Then I could, and I cried out.

The dog had caught a rabbit. His jaws with their vicious teeth closed on the rabbit's neck. It gave a high, inhuman scream and then, even as I watched, the rabbit became human. A woman, and the dog's jaws were closed on her neck. Blood spurted in a powerful jet high into the air. The dog shook her body as if were a rag, then dropped her.

'Stay away!' Leo cried.

I knelt beside the woman and turned her face upward. She was dead, and the dog had mangled her face. But I knew her. Alysse, the web woman who was Mother Chilton's apprentice. She had come to me and to Tom Jenkins as we were being taken by savages over the western mountains. She had told me Soulvine Moor was destroying the web of being that weaves life and death together. She had reprimanded me for tearing that web, and when she was done scolding me and warning me, a white rabbit had hopped away from me into the moon-light.

Another life lost because of me, and another frustrating mystery: What had Alysse wanted to tell me that now I would never know?

I straightened and faced Leo. Bile rose in my throat. 'You knew.'

'Knew what? What are you talking about, Roger?' He stared at the bloody pulp of Alysse's face, then abruptly dashed behind a tree. I heard the sound of retching.

I was wrong – *wasn't* I? How could Leo have known what Alysse was, or that the dog would attack her? But he had yelled, 'Stay away!' with something very like authority. And it was unlike his passivity to dash after the dog; it would have been more typical of him to huddle beside the fire, *gun* ready and face fearful. On the other hand, here he was vomiting at the very sight of blood – not the reaction of a man who anticipates a murder. I had no real reason to believe that Leo 'knew' anything about this attack.

But the dog knew. It had made an unerring leap at the rabbit that was Alysse, and not with its usual joyful hunting of food for us to eat. This had been a snarling attack with bared teeth. Just as when other dogs had protected me: in a cottage in Almsbury, on a rock beside Hygryll on Soulvine Moor. But Alysse had been no danger to me. So why had the dog killed her?

It sat with blood on its muzzle, looking at me. Stifling my fear, I squatted beside it and looked into those green eyes. I saw nothing but dog. Pleased by the attention, it tried to lick my hand, and I snatched it away as if from a fire. 'No!'

The dog looked puzzled and scratched at a flea.

Gently I covered Alysse's face with the spare cloth from my pack. She had died trying to reach me to tell me something, of that I was sure. The web women knew where I was. But the web women were no danger to the Brotherhood of *hisafs* fighting Soulvine Moor. The two groups had different ideas about how to fight and so did not work together; both my father and Mother Chilton had told me that. But they did not kill each other.

'*We could not get the dogs to you fast enough*,' my father had once told me. The Brotherhood controlled the dogs. I did not know how, or why they had been able to find dogs in the Country of the Dead, where no animals lived. But only a *hisaf* could bring anything back from there, so the *hisafs* must control the dogs – although no *hisaf* ever accompanied them in their crossing. How was that possible?

None of it made sense. Only one thing was clear: this dog was no friend to web women, and so not to me either. No matter how it acted. If the Brotherhood could send dogs from the other side, then maybe the faithless *hisafs*, those working with Soulvine Moor, could do the same. And if this dog had not killed me, it was because the rogue *hisafs* wanted me alive.

They knew where I was.

That meant I could not, must not, lead them to Maggie and my unborn child.

Anguish flooded me, so strong that for a moment I could not even see. All I wanted was to go to Maggie, and now I could not.

Leo came from behind his tree, wiping his mouth on his sleeve. He shrank from looking at Alysse, even with her head covered. He said, 'Why did Hunter do that?'

'I don't know.'

'Do you know this woman?'

'I did once,' I said.

'She was a rabbit ... then a woman ... she must be a witch!'

'She was ...' I looked up at him. 'In Galtryf you never discussed the web women?'

'The what?'

'The Brotherhood never told you about them?'

'I don't know what you're talking about.'

I straightened. On my feet, I stood nearly a head taller than he. Leo shrank back a step. I said, 'You were imprisoned in Galtryf – imprisoned there with my father – and the two of you never talked about the women of the soul arts? You were recruited by the Brotherhood and they never explained to you who fights on which side of this war? I no longer believe you, Leo.'

'I can't help what you do or do not believe.'

We faced each other across the clearing. Both of us drew our knives. I said, 'Alysse came here to warn me about *you*, didn't she?'

'Hryffl grut!' Leo cried, and the dog sprang at me. But I was no longer there. I crossed over.

Darkness—
Cold—
Dirt choking my mouth—
Worms in my eyes—
Earth imprisoning my fleshless arms and legs—

I stood in on the edge of a field in the Country of the Dead, not in the woods I had left behind, although a thick stand of trees grew to my right. Beside me sat Alysse.

She had already lapsed into the mindless quiescence of the Dead, her face not bloody and mangled but serene, the pale flesh smooth and unbroken. Some part of my mind was glad that my last sight of her would be like this, and not the horror on the other side. For I could not stay here. In a moment Leo would appear beside me – or would he? Overmatched in strength here as well as there, and with his hatred of traversing the grave, it was possible he would not follow me at all. If so, I had a chance to escape.

'Thank you,' I whispered to the unmoving figure in the unmoving landscape. Then I ran into the trees for better cover, thrashing and stumbling over roots and branches. The grove wasn't large and on the other side was a long, gently sloping hill dotted with boulders, wild-flowers, and the Dead. I ran down it to the shallow river at the bottom, waded across, and entered the forest of pines and birches bordering the far bank.

This was a more open wood than the one on the top of the hill, with wide spaces beneath the high branches of pine and a soft carpet of pine needles underfoot. Walking was easier here. I moved rapidly for nearly a mile, then sat down to rest.

Leo had not followed me. Nor had the dog. That dog – it had appeared right after I left the bearded *hisaf* tied up in the mill. So even then Leo's allies had known where I was. Then – but not now. I was safe now, so I could –

I could do what? Could I still go to Maggie? I didn't see why not. Once again, no one knew where I was. I could travel still farther here, cross back over, and make my way to Tanwell, to Maggie and the child.

Tears of relief came to my eyes. But not only of relief, not while I remembered Alysse. She had died trying to warn me about Leo. Although Leo made no sense, either – if he was indeed one of the rogue *hisafs* rather than one of my father's, then why had they sent someone so weak and cowardly to follow me? But Leo did not stay in my mind. Alysse did, dying for me.

As had so many more. I could not believe I was worth it.

The baying came an hour or so later.

It was not the sound of someone, or even many some-ones, crashing through the forest. That would have been preferable. This was a noise I had heard only once before, when I had been briefly in the Country of the Dead with my father. It sounded like the royal hunt, and now that I knew the grey dogs could belong to the rogue *hisafs* as well as to those protecting me, I didn't hesitate. Even as the baying rose in both volume and pitch I crossed back over—

—to find myself in a circle of men with *guns* pointed at my chest.

Not savages. Men of The Queendom. 'Hello, Roger Kilbourne,' one of them said, and another was on me before I could so much as blink. Something hard and cold clasped my one good arm. Biting down again on my still bleeding tongue, I crossed back over.

Darkness—

Cold—

Dirt choking my mouth—

Worms in my eyes—

Earth imprisoning my fleshless arms and legs—

In the Country of the Dead the baying had ceased, but the man who had spoken had crossed over with me.

He said nothing. The cold on my arm was an iron cuff, chained closely to one on his. He yanked it hard, did something with his left hand that I did not see, and once again we were in the barrier between life and death, fighting our way through the grave. He was a *hisaf*.

In the land of the living, the men had lowered their *guns*. The man who had said my name laughed. 'You, Roger, of all people – you should know that what is fastened onto you, crosses over with you. Wherever you go, Kelif goes with you. And contrary-wise. We have you at last.'

'Who . . . how . . .'

'How did we find you? Oh, that was easy.' His free hand reached across his body and fingered the hem of my wool tunic. He stretched out his palm before my face. On the calloused flesh lay a small burr, so tiny I had never noticed it to pull it off. He said, 'Did you not know that markers could be so small? Consider it part of your education, lad. Yes, you're right . . . I can see it from your face. Our Leo put it there.'

Our Leo.

'But you're hungry, am I right? All this running and escaping and hiding – surely it tires a man out. Come and eat. I am Straik, by the way. Your servant, sir.' He made a little mocking bow and laughed again.

My captor dragged me under a tall pine, where the other three men were opening packs and building a fire. They were large men, but Kelif towered over them all, a giant with hands like sides of pork and a broad, blank face. Straik, in contrast, had the thin sharp face of an intelligent stoat. His eyes seemed never to be still, darting constantly about, missing nothing. All wore tunics and

66

breeches of rough brown wool, knee-high boots, and thick short beards. Only Straik seemed to be clean. As soon as I heard the others speak, their accents told me they came from the Unclaimed Lands or even Soulvine Moor. But Straik spoke like a man of The Queendom. All four, excepting only the silent Kelif, laughed and joked among themselves as if I were not there. I stayed mute with terror.

What did they know? They clearly came from Soulvine Moor. Did they know about Maggie and our son? I could think of no other reason that they might want me – unless it was something to do with my father, supposedly their prisoner in Galtryf. Unless Leo had lied about that, too.

Oh, let my capture be due to my father and not Maggie!

One of the men under the trees turned full face towards me, and I recognized him. He was the *hisaf* who had stolen the children in Stonegreen, the stranger with black beard and green eyes. I had last found him in the Country of the Dead, moaning and barely able to move, beside the circle of the Dead that disappeared into a vortex. He was the man I could not bring myself to kill and so had left bound hand and foot. Obviously he had wriggled free, or had been rescued.

He smiled at me, a smile so full of nasty promise that I had to look away. I should have killed him when I had the chance. My compassion, or squeamishness, would cost me now.

Mother Chilton's words echoed in my head: *'Everything has a cost, Roger Kilbourne – when will you learn that?'*

Another man, younger than the rest, brought Kelif and me bread, cheese, and a goatskin bag of sour ale. I could not eat; my stomach churned too much. But I drank some ale, lifting the tankard with the hand chained to Kelif.

67

'Sleep now,' Straik said, even as Kelif stretched out wordlessly on the pine needles. The iron chain pulled on my wrist. 'We all need sleep, probably especially you, Roger. No, I will not answer any questions now, so do not bother to ask any.'

I thought that fear would keep me awake. I was wrong. The ale, my exhaustion, the warm summer sun filtering through pine branches all sent me to sleep before I even knew it was on the way. And I dreamed.

I stood in Queen Caroline's privy chamber in the palace, where I had not been for years. A bright fire burned in the hearth, and goblets of wine stood on an ornately carved table. Mother Chilton sat on a small stool, her simple grey gown puddling on the stone floor, her back bent with age. She threw something powdery onto the fire. Beside her stood little Princess Stephanie – no, Queen Stephanie now – her six-year-old eyes wide and solemn. 'Breathe,' Mother Chilton said, and the child breathed deeply. Then she turned and her grey eyes seemed to look directly into mine. 'Say it,' Mother Chilton urged.

Stephanie said, 'Roger! Run!'

The dream woke me. It seemed so real – because it *was* real. Once before, my mad half-sister had used Stephanie's inherited gift for the soul arts in order to kill. Now Mother Chilton used them to warn me. But Stephanie's warnings, like Alysse's, came too late. I could not run.

Kelif slept on. I sat up, which stretched the iron chain between us to its limit. The setting sun shone redly between the trees. Meat roasted on the fire, where one of the men slept and the others talked and laughed softly. It looked like any hunting camp where jovial moods rose from a successful hunt. The youngest man, scarcely more than a boy, whittled on a willow whistle. He brought it to his lips and blew softly and a high, sweet note sounded on the warm air.

From somewhere came an answering note.

The camp changed instantly. Kelif and the other sleeper woke. The three men by the fire jumped to their feet, but not in alarm. If anything, they looked happier than before. I heard the rumble of a wagon in the distance, then shouts.

'By damn – they're early!' Straik said. 'That can only be good!'

Kelif pulled me to my feet and dragged me forward through the trees, followed by the others. The pine woods thinned and ended very close to the camp, giving way to gentle hills covered with clover and buttercups and scrub bushes. Lurching over the trackless ground were two wagons, each drawn by a broad-backed, hard-working horse and driven by a man in rough brown clothing. More such walked beside the horses. Each wagon carried supplies and riders. In one were a woman and a girl of about ten or eleven, both bound. In the other rode Leo.

When the wagons reached the edge of the wood, Leo jumped down and came over to me. I stared, my fear momentarily drowned in astonishment. For he was utterly, completely changed.

7

'Good morrow, Roger,' Leo said mockingly and made me a comic bow. He seemed to have grown two inches and five years. No, of course he wasn't taller – but surely he was broader? He stood with such confident swagger that his chest no longer seemed concave. His dark eyes sparkled. In a single fluid motion he reached up and pulled at his face, and the scar from his badger fight came away with a ripping noise and a smear of adhesive and grease paint.

'You're ... you're an *actor.*'

'At your service.' He grinned, enjoying my outrage. All the pity I had expended on him, all the protectiveness for his craven timidity ...

'I recognized you at Stonegreen,' he said. 'A good piece of luck, since we had of course been looking for you. We were in the ale tent, touring the provinces. Stupid audiences in those villages, but one must eat.'

I remembered the one noisy group at the spring faire, laughing and talking when everyone else wandered in dazed anger at seven tranced infants neither dead nor alive. I blurted, 'But when—'

'—did I see you first? At court, of course, when you were Queen Caroline's fool. We played before you one winter night. We did "The Hero of Carday". I gave you my Prince Channing, and it played very well indeed. Your whorish queen could not take her eyes off me.'

I vaguely remembered a troupe of actors presenting a play to which I had paid little attention. I'd had eyes only for Lady Cecilia. But that had been over three years ago, and—

'I never forget a face,' Leo said. 'Not even when I last saw it dyed yellow in fool's paint. Here, Kelif, has our Roger been giving trouble?'

Beside me, Kelif scowled and spoke for the first time. His voice was slow and slightly garbled, as if words must be forced up his throat. 'Straik wants ye.'

'What for?' Leo still grinned, preening over his triumph over me.

'Maybe to dig a piss hole,' Kelif said, and Leo's grin vanished. He stalked off.

'Kelif,' I said, 'are all these men *hisafs*?' But the question was asked from desperation; I did not really expect an answer. Nor did I get one. Kelif sat down again under the tree, and I of necessity sat with him. There was nothing to do but watch, learn all I could, and hope to discover something that would let me escape.

Escape how? I was securely chained to a *hisaf* who possessed all my 'talents', half again my bulk, and twice as many hands.

Six men besides Leo had arrived with the wagon. Two of them lifted down the bound woman and girl. The woman said something in a low voice and the girl nodded. I saw that she, unlike the woman, had been gagged with a strip of cloth tied tightly across her mouth. One of the men ungagged her. He cut both their bonds with a short knife with carved handle. The woman rubbed her wrists with her fingers.

She was in her mid-thirties, the age of Queen Caroline when I had first seen her, and like the queen this woman was beautiful. Her hair was dark red, plaited around her head; her eyes bright blue with long dark lashes. She wore a simple gown of blue wool, now mussed and soiled with travel, and shadows and lines ringed her eyes. They roved desperately around the camp until they came to me. She gasped, turned pale, and started towards me. The man with her grabbed her arm and held her, looking questioningly at another man.

The girl had followed every gesture, only she was too quick for the man who clutched at her and he got only air. Darting through the camp, she stopped dead in front of me and demanded, 'Are you Roger?'

I stared at her. Gawky and thin, she also had red hair and blue eyes, but they were utterly different. The rich copper tresses of the mother – the woman had to be her mother – had become carroty and lank on the girl, worn in two tight and unbecoming braids. The woman's bright blue eyes here were a washed-out, watery blue. The girl had spots on her skin. Her teeth were crooked.

'I asked you a question!' she said, and only her voice was lovely: musical and deep for a girl. 'Are you Roger Kilbourne?'

There seemed little point in denying it. 'Yes.'

She spat at me, the thick gob of spittle landing in my beard just as the mother, followed by her guard captor, reached us.

'Rawnie! Stop that! Roger, I'm sorry, she ... I ...' A slow blush mounted from her neck to forehead. Almost she seemed about to cry, which seemed too much reaction to a daughter's crude manners. Abruptly she seized the child and dragged her off, the guard following both silently. Ten feet away the mother turned back to me. 'I *am* sorry. We can talk later, perhaps.' The girl glared at me, hatred animating her pale blue eyes.

Dazed, I turned to Kelif. 'Who are they?'

He didn't answer.

The wagons were drawn close to the fire and supplies unloaded. A second fire was built so that the two wagons and two fires made a square. Only then was I brought to the centre, where Kelif and I were given a blanket to sit on and another to, presumably, cover us at nightfall. The others stayed by the fires. I guessed that they would continue to surround me, taking shifts at night, so that I could not be approached by web women in disguise as animals, nor rescued by anything less than an army.

Why? Was I to be tortured in order to find out about my son? If so, why had these men not done so this afternoon, before help could arrive? And I didn't understand at all why the woman was here or the girl, Rawnie, who so obviously hated me for reasons I could not fathom.

She began to shout in her oddly deep, musical voice. 'Don't put that thing on me again or I'll kill you! I will!'

'Rawnie,' her mother said despairingly, 'if you're quiet they will not gag you. So be quiet!'

She might as well not have spoken. Rawnie screamed, kicked, bit. It took two men to hold her down while a third approached with the gag. The mother pounded him ineffectually on the back and then, far less ineffectually, hit him over the head with a stick of firewood. He crumpled to the ground. Two more men rushed to restrain her. Everyone shouted and cursed. Into this melee, from out of the forest, strode Straik, easily identifiable as the leader here. He took the fighting girl from his men, got her into a headlock, and vanished.

Another *hisaf*.

The mother held her hands in supplication. 'Please, oh please, she's just a little girl . . . .'

'She be a she-cat,' said the man who had tried to gag her, and whom the mother had hit with firewood. 'And so be you. If you try that again, you slut, I'll—'

'Jol,' another man said warningly, 'Straik said she is to be used gently.'

'I'd like to use her,' Jol muttered, but he glanced

73

fearfully at the spot where Straik and the girl had vanished.

The other man said, 'Trip through the grave will do that young one good. Frighten her into next sen'night.'

It did not. Straik and Rawnie reappeared and she looked as furious as ever, and not at all frightened. Her mother rushed to hold her and Rawnie shoved her away. But she had stopped shouting.

'We have a bargain,' Straik said to the mother. 'She will not shout and I will not leave her alone in the Country of the Dead without water or food.'

Rawnie said loudly – but not quite a shout – 'You said I could have what I want.'

'So I did,' Straik said, clearly amused.

The mother said fearfully, 'What did she want?'

Rawnie said, 'To kick Roger!' She dashed over and did so, right in my belly, leaving me gasping for air. Rawnie walked placidly back to Straik. 'Thank you. I hate you, too, but I will keep my half of the bargain. But *not* because I'm afraid of being left in the Country of the Dead!'

'Why, then?' Straik was enjoying this.

'I have to stay here to look after my mother.'

'So you do,' Straik said. 'And Leo shall look after you. Leo, she's your charge. Lose her at your peril.' Straik went to the other fire and called his men to him.

Leo came forward, looked distastefully at Rawnie, and said, 'If you try to run, I shall beat you.'

'You couldn't beat a puppy. Look at you.' Rawnie stalked towards the second fire and flopped beside it. 'When will that rabbit be ready? I'm hungry.'

Kelif smiled contemptuously at Leo, who flushed. I saw my chance.

'Who is she, Leo?' I made my tone as humble as possible.

I have never known any professional actors, but at

court the lords and ladies were forever amusing themselves with masques. A few courtiers always clamoured for the best roles, sulked if they did not get them, and strutted like peacocks about the stage, displaying their dramatic feathers. Leo, now that I saw him as he really was, struck me as one of these. Such actors had resisted no chance to feel important.

Nor did Leo resist. 'Who is she? You're so ignorant, Roger!'

'I know I am,' I said, more humbly still.

With his free hand Kelif made a gesture that might have meant *Be quiet*. Leo ignored him.

'I would think, Roger, that you wouldn't be so ignorant about your own family. Don't you recognize—' long pause, for effect '— your *other* half-sister? Nor your father's second wife? No, I guess you don't, you poor doomed idiot.'

Satisfied with his triumph, he followed the girl to the fire.

Rawley. Rawnie. Rawley. Rawnie. All night the names clanged in my head, like rusty and misshapen bells. *Your father's second wife.* He had married again, then, after my mother had died giving birth to Katharine and I had been abandoned to Aunt Jo. *Your other half-sister.* This one born here in the land of the living, unlike Katharine, whom I had killed. *Rawley. Rawnie. Rawley. Rawnie.*

I could not sleep. Hatred for my father boiled through me. For his irresponsibility, his deceit, his failure to protect either of his families. I hoped they kept him in Galtryf for ever. I hoped he died there.

Rawnie's mother had recognized me. I had seen my father only once, but I knew that except for his green eyes and my brown, I looked like him. Perhaps Rawnie had recognized me, too. But why did she hate me so?

75

And what did the Brotherhood of *hisafs* want with either of them? For it was clear that Leo had told me the truth about that, or at least half the truth. The Brotherhood existed. But they were fighting on the side of Soulvine Moor, not against them. The only thing I was sure of was what Soulvine Moor wanted. They wanted to live for ever, and to channel the power of the Dead to do so. *'The Dead grow in power over years, over centuries – how could it be otherwise?'* Mother Chilton had once told me. *'Even stupid youths like you know how much power death has.'*

I knew. I knew better than most. I did not want to die, but I would do so if it meant keeping these monstrous men from my son.

As I lay beside the snoring Kelif and listened to the night guards moving around the edge of camp, I could not make my mind rest. Rawnie and her mother slept alone in one of the wagons. The guards talked softly, one of the horses whinnied in its sleep, an owl hooted in a pine tree. My heart began to beat faster. But it was just an owl.

Rawley. Rawnie. Rawley. Rawnie.

Maggie.

The thought of her should have been comforting. Her competence, her acerbic resourcefulness, her unwavering love for me. Instead it was a torment. If the Brotherhood knew where she was, if they came after her to obtain my son . . .

The mind can travel endlessly in the same worn rut, but the body must sleep. Towards dawn I came finally to the end of the rut, but what followed was somehow worse. I dreamed.

I crossed over to the Country of the Dead, emerging in a vast stone chamber with crumbling and uneven walls. Something lay in one corner. I walked closer. It was one of the grey dogs, like Shadow and Shep and Hunter and the nameless others. The

76

dog lay unmoving but not dead. The dog opened its green eyes and tried to snarl. But it had not even strength enough to draw its lips back over its teeth. Only its eyes glittered with feeling, and a vague animal scent came not so much to my nose as to my mind—

I woke. The camp began to stir for the day. Kelif woke. Someone brought me cold meat and bread for my breakfast. To eat, Kelif and I must raise our hands, his left and my right, at the same time. It was awkward when his ale spilled, he cursed at me in his slow, thick voice.

Straik appeared and studied me in the growing light. 'Look at you. Did you sleep at all last night, boy?'

Kelif said, 'He sleep all yestreen.'

'So I heard. I'm sorry you can't have a break from him, Kelif. Take him into the woods to piss and then into the wagon. He can ride and sleep, and you can ride, too.'

Kelif scowled. 'I want to walk.'

'I know. But it can't be helped. Your aid is crucial here, my friend.'

Kelif, clearly unhappy, tried one more time, gesturing wordlessly at Rawnie and her mother.

'They can tell him nothing he doesn't already know, thanks to Leo's dramatics,' Straik said. 'And it doesn't matter anyway. Our only task is to get him there.'

'Aye,' Kelif agreed, still unhappy. He dragged me to the woods to piss and then back to the wagon, where he sat beside me in resigned silence. The wagon bed was cushioned with three or four rumpled blankets, a waterbag, and a half-opened pack. I glimpsed red cloth and a wooden comb painted with flowers.

When Rawnie and her mother returned to the wagon, I heard the girl before I saw her. 'No, you don't have to, you stinking ugly *hisaf*! You don't have to chain me! I promise not to get out of the wagon if you leave me unchained!'

'And if I believe that,' said Leo's voice somewhere beyond the high sides of the wagon, 'next you'll tell me how you can turn the river into honey. Into the wagon with you.'

'I won't.'

'Rawnie,' her mother said helplessly.

'Just don't *chain* me,' Rawnie said.

Leo yanked down the backboard of the wagon. He was pretending amusement but his acting skills appeared to be eroded by irritation. The amusement was distinctly sour. He said, 'I think you've overlooked one good reason to get into the wagon, Rawnie.'

'Oh? What reason?'

'Can't you guess?'

He could have bodily thrown her into the wagon. I guessed that Leo – all of them – were under orders not to touch either of the women.

Rawnie said, 'No, I can't guess!'

'In the wagon you can abuse Roger instead of me.'

Rawnie's head popped above the wagon side, saw me, and she hissed. She ran to the back of the wagon, where Leo stood in with an air of elaborate nonchalance, and kicked him hard in the shins. Then she leapt onto the wagon bed and kicked me in the side.

'Rawnie, stop that this moment, or you know what I will do!' her mother said, looking fearfully at Kelif. Kelif said and did nothing. The mother's voice did not carry much authority, but Rawnie looked fearfully over her shoulder and then, mercifully, settled into one corner of the wagon. The mother said, 'I'm sorry, Roger.' She climbed into the wagon.

The kick had hurt. I concentrated on trying to breathe while Leo snapped an iron cuff, the twin of mine but with a longer chain, onto Rawnie's ankle. Her skinny wrist would have slid right through it. He fastened the other end of the chain to the same ring as mine. He left Rawnie's mother unbound and then climbed from the wagon with evident relief. But he could not resist one last mockery.

'Enjoy each other's company, Rawnie and Roger.'

'Eat dung,' Rawnie said.

Her mother and I stared at each other.

This was the woman my father had chosen to set in my mother's place. She did not look formidable. Her face, pale and pinched this morning, nonetheless looked kind. She had been left unchained because there was no chance she would try to escape without her daughter. But she was not an escaper, anyway, nor a fighter. I was forced to admit to myself that I hated that she looked gentle and soft. She reminded me too much of what I could remember about my own mother. Evidently my father had fixed tastes in women.

'Roger,' she finally began, 'I know how much of a shock this must be to—'

'You know nothing about it,' I snapped.

Rawnie said, 'Don't be rude to my mother!'

I ignored her. She started to get up, probably to kick me again, but her mother repeated, 'You know what I will do!' and the child sank back, glaring, into her corner.

I said to Rawnie, 'If you'd really wanted Leo to let you stay unchained, you shouldn't have called him a "stinking evil *hisaf*". That's hardly the way to get people to help you.'

'I hate you,' she said, but something shifted behind her pale eyes. I hadn't really meant to instruct her, only to return her insults, but it actually looked as if she was thinking about what I'd said. I didn't care if she considered it or not. My attention returned to her mother.

I said, 'Rawnie is how old? Twelve?'

'Eleven.' Her voice held reluctance; she already knew my line of thought. Not stupid, then.

'Eleven. So she was born the year after my mother died and I was sent to my Aunt Jo. Rawley did not waste much time mourning, did he?'

Her lovely face hardened, but into pleading rather than disdain. 'You don't understand, Roger. He thought you were dead, too. He was so distraught at being unable to protect Katharine, out of his mind with grief, even though he had left for her own safety—'

'Don't bother. I've heard this all before "Mrs Kilbourne". He left my mother to be taken by some other man, my sister to be born and go mad on the other side, and me to a life of beatings and starvation from that brute my Aunt Jo married.'

'He didn't know!' she cried.

'I have met him, you know. Once. He did not look like such an ignorant man to me. He did look like a faithless and cheating liar. Although of course he had you to console him for his losses. Tell me, was my mother even in the Country of the Dead before he took you?'

Her gaze radiated despair. Rawnie, wide-eyed, watched us both; evidently some of this information was new to her. Even Kelif, normally stolid as a boulder, had opened his sleepy eyelids and sat listening.

She said, 'I had not expected to find you so bitter, Roger.'

'I have cause to be.'

'Yes. But not at your father. He did the best he could in difficult circumstances.'

'Oh, I'm sure he did. His best was an abandoned wife and child, another child raised beyond the grave, a gullible mistress and a bastard second daughter.'

Rawnie leapt up and rushed at me. 'Don't talk about my father like that!'

Her chain would have been long enough to reach me, and her mother's cry ineffectual to halt her, except that

Kelif reached out with his free right hand and stopped her as easily as if she had been made of paper. He pushed her away and said simply, 'No.' Rawnie fell heavily back into her corner. Tears came to her eyes, gone in an instant.

The wagon lurched forward. I had not even noticed the driver climb aboard, nor the camp being struck. In truth, I was appalled by my own outburst. I had not intended to spew so much venom upon this woman. My anger was with my father, not her.

But she had the last word. With quiet dignity, she said, 'My daughter is not a bastard. I *am* Mrs Kilbourne. My first name is Charlotte.'

I said nothing. And the wagons, guarded by the Brotherhood of rogue *hisafs*, started south in the sweet summer sunshine.

8

I was not only ashamed of my outburst to Charlotte, but also shaken by the unsuspected depth of my own bitterness towards my father. In addition, I had lost my chance to obtain information. Charlotte might know where we were headed, and why. Shortly after the wagons started to move, she fell asleep. I guessed that she had slept as little the previous night as I had. Rawnie and I glared silently at each other for a while, and then she, too, nodded off, her hand protectively on her small pack. Kelif may or may not have been sleeping; it was always hard to tell.

I gazed at Charlotte as she lay at the very rear of the wagon, against the backboard. One of her plaits had come unfastened from around her head and it lay on the blanket, thick and shining coppery red. In sleep the pinched look left her face. I should not have spoken to her as I had. Her daughter may or may not have been a bastard; my son certainly would be unless I could reach Maggie and marry her. Charlotte clearly loved my father and had probably tried to comfort him for his loss, which was just what Maggie, in her acerbic way, had done for me after Cecilia's death. How could I revile Charlotte for her actions and yet treasure Maggie for hers? No, it was my father who deserved reviling, not this woman.

When Kelif began to snore, perhaps lulled by sunshine or the motion of the wagon or sheer boredom, I touched Charlotte's outflung hand. She woke instantly, gasping, and looked around for Rawnie. The wretched child still slept.

I choked out, 'I am sorry for what I said.'

Her face lit up, with no trace of grudge-bearing. 'That's all right, Roger. I know Rawnie and I must be a shock to you. And I hope you will believe that Rawley—'

'I don't want to talk about him.'

'All right.' Some of the light went from her face, but she continued to smile at me. When she sat up, the loose braid swung across her face. She groped among the blankets in the wagon bed, looking for the wooden hairpin to put her braid back in place.

I said, 'May I ask you some questions?'

'Of course.'

'Do you know where they are taking us?'

'No. Do you?'

'I know almost nothing. Why were you and Rawnie captured? Is either of you ...' I glanced at Kelif, but he still snored. I kept my voice low. 'Do you or Rawnie have talent for the soul arts?'

'No. Not at all. I don't know why these *hisafs* took us.'

I could think of only one reason: their connection to my father. I still did not know how you keep a *hisaf* imprisoned in Galtryf, or anywhere else, when he could escape bodily to the Country of the Dead, unless my father were chained night and day to a half dozen of the Brotherhood as I was to Kelif.

Charlotte gave up the hunt for her hairpin. She took down the other braid, unwound them both, and began to comb out her hair with the painted comb from her pack. I had to look away. Just so had Cecilia combed out her shining hair by a campfire, and Maggie in the taproom of our inn. In such a moment a woman looks intensely feminine, vulnerable, and desirable.

'Roger,' she said very low, 'do you know where they're taking us, and why?'

All morning the wagons had been climbing increasingly steep hills. We were leaving, or had left, The Queendom for the higher terrain of the Unclaimed Lands. Presently, I knew, the landscape would become even wilder, dotted with ravines and cliffs, until it once more levelled off into high, peat-laden moor.

'Roger?'

'I think,' I said, forcing the words past my suddenly tight throat, 'that we are going to Soulvine Moor.'

The wagons halted at noon for a midday meal. I could not eat, nor could Charlotte. Both of us knew what happened on Soulvine Moor; I had experienced it twice before. First Cecilia had died there. Then I had almost died, stretched out and bound on a flat rock while the drum sounded its deadly rhythm and the knife was held to my throat by the old man with green eyes. Only the dogs had saved me, the dogs and Tom Jenkins. Yet although I feared death as much as the next man, it wasn't the thought of death that churned my stomach and tightened my throat. It was the sure knowledge of what the Soulviners would then do to my body. How they would use it in their obscene ritual, symbolically 'drawing strength' from their victims' flesh in the land of the living, exactly as they did from their souls in the Country of the Dead. And would some *hisaf* of the Brotherhood then cross over to sit me in a circle, to watch as I was consumed by a spinning vortex of grey fog? And my chance at eternity lost for ever . . .

Charlotte's gaze met mine only once during that uneaten meal. Immediately she looked away. I knew that she could not bear to see mirrored in my eyes the knowledge I saw in hers. Instead she watched Rawnie, and for a moment I almost transcended my own fear in the greater one she must feel for her child.

For my child was still safe. We were not headed towards Maggie at Tanwell, but in the opposite direction. The Brotherhood did not know about her, or my son. And when I was dead, they never would. Charlotte had no such consolation.

And Rawnie no such fears. She was less obnoxious than usual, but not from fright. At first her behaviour made no sense to me, and then it did.

As soon as we were unchained from the wagon for the noon halt, Leo reappeared. Evidently he was still in charge of Charlotte and her daughter, and evidently he still did not relish the task. Probably he expected more kicks, more insults, more noisy resistance. He under-estimated Rawnie. So did I.

She must have remembered what I said to her at break-fast: *'If you'd really wanted Leo to let you stay unchained, you shouldn't have called him a "stinking evil hisaf". That's hardly the way to get people to help you.'* As soon as he freed her ankle from its long chain, she smiled at him.

'Thank you, Leo.'

He started in surprise.

The four of us, stiff from sitting in the jolting wagon, climbed down and were led to the woods to relieve our bladders. Since there were no women to attend Charlotte, Leo must do it. The scowl stayed on his face; probably he didn't like turning his back on Rawnie, but Straik had ordered that she and Charlotte be treated with all possible respect. However, before they entered a thick grove of trees, Rawnie laid a hand on Leo's arm. They were close enough that I heard what she said.

'I'm sorry I was so difficult last night and today, Leo. It's just that I was scared. I've never been away from home before, not like you, and I don't know how to be brave.' A pathetic smile. 'You've been all over, I know, so it's different with you, because you're an actor. When Mama told me, I couldn't hardly believe it. An actor! You must have done such wonderful things!'

Charlotte stared at her daughter with disbelief, Leo with suspicion. Rawnie disappeared modestly behind the trees.

She returned before her mother did, walked up to Leo, and clasped her hands before her beseechingly. 'Can I make a bargain with you? If I am really, really good all the rest of the day, would you do some acting for me when we stop tonight? Not a lot – I know somebody like me can't expect somebody like you to give a free play – but just a tiny bit of one scene?'

'No,' Leo said.

She lowered her head and whispered, 'I understand. Great actors don't do acting for free.' Her whole small body reflected penance and disappointment.

'No, they don't,' Leo said. But he stood a little taller and a smile lurked at the corners of his mouth.

Suddenly Rawnie brightened. 'But I can pay you! I have two pennies all my own!'

He smiled. 'Two whole pennies? Really? Such a fortune!'

'I know you probably get hundreds of silvers for acting, even gold pieces!'

'Well ... yes.' He was, not unexpectedly, a convincing liar. 'But do you really promise to cause no trouble at all? None?'

'None!' She was transfigured; light shone from her face; she rose on her toes with excitement; she almost levitated. 'Oh, Leo, *would you*?'

'I make no promises,' Leo said loftily. Charlotte returned and we were once more loaded into the wagon.

Rawnie held out her foot for the chain. She looked at Leo as if he were a prince, a hero, a god.

Once he had gone and the wagons and men had resumed their march south, Rawnie glared at me. 'What are you staring at, Roger?'

'Nothing,' I said. In truth, I was comparing her to my other half-sister, Katharine, whom I had murdered. Katharine had been mad, and she had been used by the Brotherhood for their own ends. She had killed people. Rawnie had been loved and sheltered all her life, and she was clearly not mad. She was in complete control of her devious self. But she seemed just as unpredictable. I didn't like her, I felt no kinship with her, but neither could I stand the thought of what awaited her on Soulvine Moor.

Late in the afternoon we halted on a rise above a poor, hardscrabble farm in the Unclaimed Lands. Usually in such wild terrain the farms were far apart, but this one had several ramshackle dwellings and a larger-than-usual goat shed. Peering over the high side of the wagon, a movement which strained the short chain between Kelif's wrist and mine, I saw figures far below. A woman raised her face to us, then scurried into one of the huts. Two more women carried a bucket of water from a mountain stream. Children dashed around, chasing each other.

Straik and two of his men went down the hill, returning later with their arms full of bundles and leading two goats. Food, I guessed, bought from whatever meagre supply the farm had, in return for coins rarely seen here. Straik strode to the wagon, followed by Leo. Straik said to Kelif, 'Watch him well.'

Kelif's sleepy eyes opened wide. 'Be ye—'

'Yes.'

'*Here?*'

'The men are all gone on a long hunt. And this circle is ready. Leo—'

Leo said, 'I want to go with you.'

'No. Your job is the wife and daughter.'

'It is my right. I would be in command here but for your—'

'No,' Straik said. He started down the hill towards the farm, followed by every man except Leo and Kelif. Leo scowled fiercely. Rawnie made a movement towards him, studied his face, and subsided into her corner. No flattery would work just now. My stomach tightened until it felt a hard stone.

'*This circle is ready.*' I knew of only one kind of circle Straik could have been referring to, and it did not exist in the land of the living.

The Brotherhood reached the farm. I rose to my knees to watch over the wagon side. Kelif rose with me, which somehow frightened me even more.

One of the men grabbed the first woman he reached. She screamed, which brought Rawnie upright. I said sharply to Charlotte, 'Don't let her watch!' Charlotte grabbed for her daughter, but it was Leo who shoved her back into the corner and kept her there.

The *hisaf* bound the woman's hands behind her and carried her to the closest hut. The other men did the same, catching and carrying women and children into the same hut. I heard one woman shout 'Run!' and two older children vanished into the woods. The men did not chase them. Screaming continued to come from the hut, so at least the men were not slaughtering their captives. Instead they methodically carried something from that hut, from all the huts. At first I thought they were stealing more supplies, but the bundles were not food.

They were infants.

'What are they doing?' Rawnie cried. 'Let me up!'

'If you move,' Leo said, 'I will hit you.'

'I don't care!' Rawnie said.

Scuffling behind me, but then Charlotte's voice shrilled high-pitched with fear. 'If you don't stay still, you know what I shall do!'

No more scuffling. The men below had imprisoned everyone in the hut. In the area between huts, worn to bare earth by many feet over much time, they carried six infants. The babes' wails sounded thin and high on the errant breeze. Straik and two others vanished.

I knew where they had gone. No matter the punishment from Kelif, I bit my tongue and crossed over.

Darkness—

Cold—

Dirt choking my mouth—

Worms in my eyes—

Earth imprisoning my fleshless arms and legs—

Kelif and I stood in the Country of the Dead. Huts, goat shed, screaming women had all been left behind. In the dell, under the unvarying dim light of this side, sat a circle of the Dead. Beyond them the fog was thick as soup, although the air surrounding the circle was clear. Each of the unliving heads was obscured by more thick, vibrating grey fog, and in the centre of the circle spun a humming vortex. Faster, faster . . .

Three *hisafs* appeared, each with an infant on either arm. I could barely glimpse them through the fog. Then a clap of noise like thunder, light brighter than the sun, and the Dead vanished, sucked into the vortex.

That was all I had time to see. Kelif gave a great bellow, seized me, and we were again back in that terrible place between countries, that eternal grave. This time it seemed to go on for ever, although probably that was only my own horror. Then we were back in the wagon, peering over the side. A moment later the *hisafs* reappeared, infants still in their arms. The babes' cries had ceased. The *hisafs* laid them, inert and tranquil, in a circle on the ground.

Kelif cuffed me on the side of the head and I staggered against the side of the wagon, unable to fall because of the chain between us. The blow hurt, but not as much as what I had just seen.

So it was true, what Mother Chilton had told me so long ago. *'Don't you understand? Life and death are both part of the web of being, and both have power. When power is made to flow unnaturally from death back to life, as Soulvine Moor is doing, there must also be a flow in the opposite direction. Or else the whole web will become more and more disturbed, until it is destroyed. There are terrible times coming, more terrible than you can imagine.'*

That time was here. I had just seen it. Soulvine Moor had sucked the power of the eternal Dead into themselves, to use in their quest to live for ever. They had thereby robbed eternity from the Dead in that circle. To balance their theft, they had taken life from the infants, putting the babes into the unchanging, quiescent trance of the Dead. That was why the Country of the Dead had not been disturbed into storms and quakes, as it had when I had brought back the Blue army. Soulvine was preserving the balance in the web of being, so they could go on plundering it for their own gain. *'Everything has a cost,'* Mother Chilton had said, but she had not said the most monstrous part. Sometimes the cost is paid by the innocent.

Which did not include me. If I had not meddled with death, if I had not brought back Bat and Cecilia and the Blue army, if I had not carried Tom and Jee and the princess across the grave – then would any of this even be possible? Mother Chilton had told me that the war with Soulvine Moor began even before I was born – but how much had I advanced it?

All those infants, neither dead nor alive ... all those grieving parents ...

Behind me Charlotte said tremulously, 'Roger?'

Kelif growled, 'Get back down, ye.'

Leo said anxiously, as well as with rage that she was a cause for anxiety, 'Rawnie, I would not really hit you.' Which meant, *Don't tell Straik I threatened to do so!*

Rawnie said in her new, warm, lying tone towards Leo, 'That's all right. I'm sorry.'

I was back in the world of captives, of complicated politics, of solid wagon and hard-edged trees, of clear unfogged summer air. But I had seen what Soulvine Moor was doing. My father's *hisafs* and the web women – whatever they were doing to stop Soulvine Moor was not, apparently, succeeding. I did not see how it could. Life and death, both, were under siege.

I sank down against the side of the wagon, turned my face to the rough wood, and spoke to no one for the rest of the day.

9

It was twilight before we halted for the night. Probably Straik wanted to put as much distance as possible between the Brotherhood and the farm plundered of its babies' life force. The first stars had already appeared. A half moon rose, buttery yellow. The horses had been labouring all day as they climbed uphill and now they stood, panting and covered with foam, as men rubbed them down and watered them. Leafy trees had given way almost entirely to tall pines and then to more scrubby ones, and I knew we were nearing the end of the Unclaimed Lands and the beginning of Soulvine Moor.

Straik and his men, including Leo, were in a jubilant mood. They built cooking fires. They bathed naked in a frigid mountain stream, shouting and laughing, men who acted as if victory were close at hand. In contrast, Charlotte and I barely spoke nor moved, avoiding each other's eyes. Charlotte sat by the fire with her head down and her hands clasped tightly together. She seemed frozen with fear.

Not so Rawnie. She concentrated on Leo, watching him so intently that my gaze, too, was drawn to him, and I saw things I had not noticed before. His swagger and self-importance I had set down to an actor's confidence, but now I saw that some of the other men – not all, but some – deferred to him as well. They listened as he talked and laughed. The talk was light: of women, of inns in The Queendom, of ale and wine. But Leo was listened to, and when he interrupted another's speech, the other man instantly fell quiet.

I remembered what Leo had said to Straik: '*I would be in command here but for your–*' Your what?

Straik said, 'Leo, give us a song.'

'Perhaps later.'

'Now,' Straik said, and it was an unmistakable order.

The two men locked gazes, and it was Leo who looked away first. Sulkily, all laughter gone, he unwrapped his instrument. His head bent over it as he sang, so that I could not see his face.

> Although you to the hills do flee,
> My love you can't escape.
> Your heart, my sweet, belongs to me
> Though you may change its shape.
>
> Never, never will I cease
> To follow where you go,
> And ever, ever will I be
> The hound upon your doe.
>
> Do what you will and what you can,
> Employ the arts you know —
> Ever, ever will I be
> The hound upon your doe.

His voice was as clear and strong as when he'd sung the song to me, and the words as chilling. But when Leo raised his head, it was not me he stared at but Straik, and the look was a challenge.

Straik laughed. 'A pleasant enough tune. If we fail in this war, you can always earn your living singing for pennies in alehouses.'

Leo flushed. 'I'm no alehouse singer. I was an actor.'

'Oh, I'm sure you were very fine,' Straik said jeeringly.

'For now, you'd best escort Mistress Rawnie to the woods again. She is squirming.'

Anger blazed in Leo's eyes. One of the older men frowned, clearly uneasy with Straik's bullying, although he said nothing. I had the sense that the Brotherhood had a rigid order of succession of leadership but that not everyone was happy about it. Could I somehow use that to my advantage? I did not see how.

Rawnie looked uncharacteristically frightened, although only for a moment. She had indeed been squirming in her place around the fire, but not for the reason Straik suggested. Rawnie had been trying to get something out of the pack on the ground beside her, or possibly put something back in, without being noticed. Now all eyes turned to her.

Charlotte put out her hand, as if to give her daughter a gentle shove, and let it fall atop whatever the thing was. 'Go with Leo, dearest. You will be more comfortable.'

They left, Leo flushed with anger, Rawnie unembarrassed but looking thoughtful. No one watched Charlotte, except me. A pink twitching tail suddenly poked from between her fingers. I glimpsed the mouse as she swept it back into Rawnie's pack and drew the drawstring tight.

Charlotte had seen my gaze. She sat cross-legged on the ground, and now she bent her head forward as if to tighten the laces on her boot. With her face thus hidden she said so softly that Kelif could not hear, 'Don't tell. Her pet of two months now. The only way I can compel her obedience.'

So that was what Charlotte had meant when she'd told Rawnie to obey 'or you know what I will do!' And Rawnie believed that her mother would deprive her of her pet. That suggested a steeliness in Charlotte that I had not yet seen, as well as a certain desperation about controlling her daughter. Two months – how long did mice live? If the rodent died, how would Charlotte discipline Rawnie?

Rawnie and Leo returned to the fire. Straik was holding forth with some tale of casting dice at a country inn. Rawnie stepped in front of him and said loudly, 'Leo is going to act for us!'

'I think not,' Straik said, his feigned amusement not quite masking his real annoyance.

'Oh, yes, he is!' Rawnie cried, all childish excitement. 'And he's going to give "The Hero of Carday" because both John and Tarf love it so! Don't you?'

Two men looked up. I hadn't even known their names, although I had noticed their open-mouthed pleasure in Leo's lute song. Both faces now brightened into uncertain eagerness. They glanced at Straik, at Leo, at Rawnie. I guessed that they harboured a hunger for stories, that polished entertainment had rarely come their way, and that were they not born *hisafs*, they would still be doing simple work somewhere, ill used by the sharper wits around them.

'Don't you love that tale?' Rawnie insisted to the two men. 'Isn't it wonderful to hear about heroes?'

'Heroes,' John said, with a pleading look at Straik. 'You said *we* be heroes.'

Tarf begged, 'Leo be an actor. He played at court!'

Straik chose lordly indulgence. He waved his hand negligently. 'If you must. Begin then, Leo.'

So his hold upon his men was not as firm as he wished. If it had been, he would not have given way. This bit of information, too, I turned over and over in my mind like a bright stone.

Leo strode into the firelight. The others shifted to face him, taking places on the ground behind Rawnie, Charlotte, Kelif and me, so that we all became an audience. Only Straik stayed on the other side of the fire, so that

Leo's back was to him and Straik would see nothing of the performance.

I had seen Leo change from a timid and scarred waif to a confident swaggerer. That should have prepared me for how thoroughly he could transform himself. It did not. As he stood beside the fire, one side of his face illuminated by its flames and one side in shadow, he seemed to grow taller and broader. His stance took on gravity. Nothing moved but his eyes, and they burned with the fire of idealism and sacrifice.

'The Hero of Carday' is one of The Queendom's most beloved epics. The poorest band of troubadours knows the play, and they give it often. But this was no alehouse recitation, chosen so that the richness of the words might disguise the poverty of the performance. Leo *became* Prince Channing, Lord of Fire. He stood not in a wooded mountain clearing but on the ramparts of a castle, as he prepared to trade his life for that of his people. Leo's voice quivered with feeling, the controlled emotion of a man choosing death for a greater good.

> But let me be remembered.
> This is all I ask – to be remembered
> As I was. Remembered in the morning
> At the rising of another day,
> Remembered in the evening
> In the ache of weary bones
> Glad of weary duty. Remembered—

The faces around the fire were rapt. Even I was swept up in the speech – I, who faced death soon, and not with Prince Channing's noble courage. Even though I knew full well that there was nothing noble about sitting for centuries, mindless, in the Country of the Dead. The play was a lie, but in Leo's rendition it was a lie of

96

overwhelming power and beauty. Such words could never—

Aaaiiieeee —

A scream, deep and agonized, abruptly cut off. And a snarling and tearing of flesh such as I had heard too often before. Men leapt to their feet, shouting. A moment later the crack of a *gun*, and the terrible sounds ceased.

'Jol got him!'

'Who—'

'How—'

A string of curses. Confusion, shouting, men thrashing off into the dark woods. Kelif leaped to his feet and ran around the fire, dragging me with him.

Straik lay in the firelight, his throat torn out, blood everywhere. Atop him lay a grey dog, shot through the head. Both were dead.

John dropped to his knees and began to cry.

This seemed to turn the rest of the Brotherhood either stony or angry. Tarf tried to pull John to his feet. 'Stop that!' John, his simple face contorted by grief, shoved Tarf away. Everyone began to talk.

'They know where we are!'

'Find the *hisaf*!'

'You know we'll never find him.'

'Double our speed to—'

'Safe in Galtryf—'

'I said we needed dogs! I told Straik from the beginning!'

'And we shall have them,' Leo said.

Another shift in everyone. They glanced at each other, down at Straik, and then gave their full attention to Leo. My guess had been right. The Brotherhood – or this little piece of it, anyway – had one absolute leader at a time. It had been Straik. Now it was Leo. I didn't know why; he was younger than most of the others. But now his leadership was unmistakable. He donned it as easily as he had taken the part of Prince Channing and if this, too, was acting, it was of the same high order.

Kelif, surprisingly, spoke first. 'Who?'

'Not you,' Leo said. 'You are needed to guard Roger.'

Kelif's great shoulders stiffened but he did not argue.

Leo's gaze travelled across each man's face. Eventually he said, 'Dick and Macon.'

One by one, the others nodded. Charlotte, whom I had not realized stood beside me with Rawnie, drew in a sharp breath. I whispered to her, 'What are they going to do?'

She raised a shocked face to mine. Firelight played over her wide eyes. 'Don't you *know*?'

'Know what?'

'The dogs ... why, that was the only reason Rawley could marry me!'

Marry her? What did that have to do with the grey dogs that had followed me since Shadow, all those months ago? I knew that the dogs came from the Country of the Dead, because each of them vanished after a fortnight, crumbled into nothingness and were gone for ever. Like Cecilia ...

I would not think now of Cecilia. Something important was happening here, and I needed to know what it was. Unexpectedly, Leo aided me. He had noticed that Charlotte and I were whispering, and he said, 'Roger will see this.'

The youngest *hisaf* scowled. 'Why?'

Leo said, 'Because I suspect he does not already know. And he should witness what awaits him.'

Someone else laughed, with such cruel relish that my spine froze. 'He doesn't *know*?'

'I don't think so. You don't know about the dogs, do you, Roger?'

I said nothing. Beside me, Charlotte trembled.

The scowling *hisaf* said, 'It's dangerous, Leo. They know where we are. They could be waiting. Why risk losing him on the other side?'

'We won't risk it. Roger waits here until Macon and Dick are ready. It shouldn't be long – there's a kennel right over the border.'

'They might have *guns* by now.'

Macon said angrily, 'Oh, stop whining, Gregory. Dick and I can take care of ourselves. Nobody's asking you to risk anything.'

The scowler flushed a mottled maroon. Macon and Dick glanced at each other, took their *guns* from their backs and drew their knives. I did not see what Macon did, but Dick drove the tip of his knife into his thigh, and both vanished. They had crossed over.

Leo said, 'John and Tarf, bury Straik. Gregory and Stuart, you have perimeter guard. Kelif, keep Roger and the women in the wagon. Ned, come with me.'

Everyone obeyed, except Rawnie. She ran after Leo, calling, 'Wait! Your acting was *wonderful*!'

But for once he had no time for adoration. Kelif dragged me to Rawnie, caught her in the powerful hand not chained to me, and dragged her into the wagon. Charlotte climbed in after her daughter.

All at once an eerie silence fell on the camp. Leo and his lieutenant conferred out of earshot. The guards had disappeared into the woods. The only sounds were cracklings from the fire, the hoot of an owl, and then the scrape of shovels on earth as John and Tarf dug Straik's grave.

I said, very low, to Charlotte, 'Tell me. What are those dogs?'

She glanced at Rawnie, who said irritably, 'Oh, Mama, I already know all about it!' She rose on her knees to peer over the wagon side, watching the men dig the grave.

Charlotte sighed, but did not dispute this. Probably it was true. If it were not, Rawnie was about to learn, because I was determined to acquire all the knowledge Charlotte had. I should have done so earlier. Straik might have wanted me ignorant but Leo was in charge now, and Leo could not resist drama. '*Let him see what awaits him . . .*' Kelif, accepting the change in leadership, did not interfere as Charlotte and I talked.

I repeated, 'What are those dogs?'

Charlotte seemed to search for a place to begin. 'They come from the Country of the Dead.'

'I knew that much.'

'Rawley . . . your father made them.'

'"*Made* them"? How can—'

'Not made them. Those are the wrong words.' Then all at once her speech flowed freely. 'They are born, of course, there on the other side. It first happened when a *hisaf* had a pregnant hound. The *hisaf* crossed over with his dog and so the puppies were born in the Country of the Dead. Like . . . like your sister.'

So that was how living dogs had appeared in that place where there was no living thing, save *hisafs* and Katharine. Now I understood the baying I had heard on the other side.

Charlotte continued, 'This was long ago, before I met Rawley. The breeder thought the dogs might be useful to track the Brotherhood, and Katharine, too. Which, of course, they were. Rawley has a talent for handling animals and he spent a lot of time training the puppies. After your mother died, and he thought that you died too, it was a distraction for him. Although, of course, the Brotherhood were quick to learn about the dogs and did the same thing.' She glanced at Kelif. He listened, his eyelids half closed, his face expressionless in the starlight.

I said, 'Go on.'

Charlotte twisted her hands together. Rawnie still watched the grave-digging. 'Then Rawley had another idea. Do you ... Roger, have you ever seen ... Rawley wasn't sure how much you know about the ... the women who practise the soul arts.'

More than I wanted to know. Mother Chilton, endlessly scolding me, prematurely aged to avoid capture when she was with me. Alysse, dead because she tried to warn me against Leo. Even little Princess Stephanie, whose dream, undoubtedly directed by Mother Chilton, had tried to warn me. I told Charlotte none of this, but merely nodded.

'They can change into animals, you know, into their soul sharer. Each one of them has one. Into other animals, too, although the cost of doing so is very high. It saps their life force, even unto threatening death, until they recover.'

Yes. I know.

'Rawley thought the soul arts must be related to what Soulvine Moor is doing on the other side. The Soulviners can't cross over, of course. But they can ... have you seen what looks like a cloud of fog, over ... over there? Rawley says it spins. It is—'

'I know what it is,' I said, more harshly than I intended. 'A vortex.' I had seen it suck in an entire circle of the Dead. I had seen it devour my sister when I threw her into it. 'The Soulviners remain in the land of the living, but something of them is present in the Country of the Dead.'

'Yes. It is the essential part, the ... the life force itself. They learned to do it with the aid of potions from soul-art women and acts of will from rogue *hisafs*. Rawley took this knowledge and he made trial after trial, until he ...'

101

She stopped. My heart began a long slow thump. 'Until he what? What did my father learn to do, Charlotte?'

'Did you know that Rawley's mother was a woman of the soul arts?'

'No. How does that matter?'

'Many *hisafs* marry such women. They understand each other. Or at least they did, until they conceived such different ideas about ... about this war.' She glanced fearfully at Kelif, who appeared to be asleep but probably was not. 'It's unusual for a *hisaf* to marry a woman from the The Queendom, one without talent in the soul arts, as Rawley did.'

Twice, I thought, but did not say aloud. My father evidently preferred women who could not rival him. I said, 'Charlotte, tell me what my father learned to do!'

'I think it would be more interesting to show you,' a voice said outside the wagon. Rawnie, still hanging over the opposite side, immediately leaped across the blanket-strewn wagon bed. 'Leo!'

'Kelif, bring him,' Leo said. 'They're back already. It seems the handlers were training dogs nearby. This is such a lucky expedition. We are blessed.'

Rawnie gaped at his mockery. John and Tarf continued to dig Straik's grave. Kelif rose, bringing me with him, and pulled me from the wagon. When Rawnie tried to follow, Charlotte grabbed her. 'Stay here!'

'No!' Rawnie shouted. She slipped from her mother's grasp.

'Yes! Or you know what I will do!'

I glimpsed Rawnie's glance at her pack, where the pet mouse lay hidden, just before Kelif took me into the woods.

We stumbled a short way under the trees to a small clearing. Moonlight streamed through the break in the trees. Here Stuart and Gregory waited, along with Macon and Dick. The latter two seemed pale. As I watched, Macon and Dick vanished.

A second later, so did Kelif and I. He had crossed over, taking me with him.

Darkness—

Cold—

Dirt choking my mouth—

Worms in my eyes—

Earth imprisoning my fleshless arms and legs—

We stood in a featureless meadow in the Country of the Dead. This, then, was one of those places where the landscape differed from that in the land of the living. And differed in another way, as well. Two dogs barked at our arrival, straining at the leashes held by men armed with *guns*.

The dogs looked like every other dog that had come from here: big, grey, with short tails and green eyes. At least a dozen years since the first pregnant bitch had been brought over. Something about breeding live animals in a dead place must make the strain run true. My flesh crawled. These dog were not, had never been, truly alive or dead. They were unnatural things, and what had my father been doing with them that was more unnatural still?

One of the unnatural things wagged its tail and licked my hand.

Charlotte had spoken of the web women, of 'trial after trial', of Soulvine vortexes. I couldn't see how the pieces fit together. None of this made sense.

Leo appeared beside us; apparently his reluctance to cross over had been as pretend as everything else he'd once told me. The older of the two men said, 'Where's Straik?'

'Dead,' Leo said briefly. 'Killed by a dog from the others.'

Kelif said to the men holding the leashes, 'Ye won't leave them?'

'One of us will stay guard,' the older man said.

Leo frowned. 'Both of you stay.'

'We can't. Leo, you know that. There is too much to do, and not enough of us to do it. You should know *that*.'

Kelif said, 'Then why this open place? They maun see ye for miles!'

'Then we maun see them,' the second man said, less deferentially than the first. 'This be easier to defend. Tell him, Leo – even though ye be an actor and not a soldier.'

Leo's eyes blazed. The challenge to his authority set him to issuing orders. 'Nonetheless, I want Macon and Dick under cover of trees.'

'As ye wish,' the second man said, with contempt. Tension among the five *hisafs* prickled like heat. Silently we hiked across the silent meadow and into a stand of silent trees.

'I'm ready,' Macon said. Was that a slight tremor in his voice?

'Aye,' Dick said.

Leo turned to Macon and Dick and clasped each of their hands, his face theatrically solemn. 'Good luck, my brothers.'

They yanked their hands from his and knelt beside the two dogs, who quivered with pleasure. Macon and Dick placed their hands on the dogs' heads. The men's faces contorted with intense concentration. All at once both dogs yelped, and the two men toppled to the ground.

At last I understood.

Images whirled in my mind. The web women who became a rabbit, a white deer, a black swan, two diving raptors . . . the *hisaf* I had found beside a vortex just before it sucked in a circle of the Dead, whom I had not been able to bring myself to murder. He had taken the babes from the village beside the mill and then lay moaning on the even grass of the Country of the Dead, so weak he could barely open his eyes. At the time I had assumed that his weakness was due to something connected with the vortex. But I had never seen such a half-dead *hisaf* beside any other vortex. So I'd thought his depletion must be connected with the theft of the babes – except that Straik and the others had shown no such weakness after stealing the babes at the farm in the Unclaimed Lands.

It was the dogs. Always, from Shadow on, I had known that there was something strange and terrible about the grey dogs . . .

Macon and Dick gave a great cry and collapsed to the ground. At the same moment, the two dogs threw back their heads and howled in pain. Kelif dropped to his knees, dragging me with him, and bent over the men. Macon's eyes rolled back in his head. Dick gasped as if he would never catch his breath. It took several moments for them to stop convulsing, and then both moaned.

Leo stood above us, his voice filled with satisfaction. 'A good inhabiting.'

Kelif looked at him, and for once there was a complex expression on that sleepy broad face: concern for his brother *hisafs* mingled with contempt for Leo's lack of it. Leo did not notice. He had raised his gaze to the dogs, led a little way off by the other men, who now slipped the leashes from their great heads.

The dogs looked no different. One sniffed at a *hisaf's* boots; the other scratched its flank. Were Macon and Dick really 'inhabiting' – that was the word Leo had used – these animals?

Yes.

Such a dog had killed Straik. Such a dog had attacked Tarek, the savage chieftain. Such dogs had saved my life.

They were dogs, but they were somehow directed – or partially directed – by the *hisafs*, who were simultaneously in their depleted bodies and in the animals. Just as I had been able to be, until recently, both in my tranced body in the land of the living and simultaneously walking in the Country of the Dead. Just as the men and women of Hygryll had been both in the round stone hut and also present as watchers in the grey vortex on the other side.

And my *father* had created this living weapon, which had now spread to the Brotherhood. Just as the savages' *guns* had spread to The Queendom and the Unclaimed Lands. Was it always thus, so that the world would always grow more dangerous with each new discovery?

Leo pulled me to my feet, which led Kelif to rise, too. His eyes burned, just as when I had met him, with some hatred or fervour I did not understand. He put his face very close to mine and said softly, 'I wanted you to see what awaits you.'

I managed to say, 'I cannot become a dog. I will not.'

Leo gave a great shout of laughter, perhaps the most cruelty I have ever heard in a single sound. 'You don't understand yet, do you, Roger? But you will. Kelif, bring him back.'

Leo vanished without another look at his barely conscious men. It was Kelif who said sadly to the strangers, 'Ye maun guard them well. Please.'

'Aye,' one said, while the men lay weak on the ground and the dogs sat on their haunches, regarding us with their green eyes under the bleak and unchanging sky.

'How does it work?' I said softly to Charlotte. Rawnie lay asleep beside her, Kelif beside me. Sometime during the night the wind had risen, clouds had raced in, and drizzle had begun to fall. The four of us had been moved to sleep underneath the wagon, close to the fire, which had since sputtered and gone out. Rain pattered softly on the wagon bed above us, which smelled of wet wood. The ground felt hard beneath my back. Charlotte could not sleep, no more than I. 'The dogs – how does it work?'

'What do you mean?' she said.

'How much of a dog's brain becomes *hisaf's*? How much is still dog?' Clearly the men could exert some control, including attacking at will.

She whispered, 'I only know what Rawley told me.'

'Tell me.' One of the two dogs padded into view, patrolling the camp. The Brotherhood would not be taken by surprise again, as they had with Straik's death. Charlotte waited until the animal had passed, a grey shape in the grey drizzle.

She said, 'The dog is still a dog. The man's soul rides quiescent most of the time, as if dreaming. Rawley says it's not exactly boring, it's more like dozing. But when the soul becomes alert, it can direct the dog's actions, although the exertion is exhausting.'

Mother Chilton admonishing me: '*Everything has a cost, Roger Kilbourne – when will you learn that?*'

I said, 'And afterwards? The dogs are from the Country of the Dead, they cannot stay here past a fortnight. They ... disintegrate and melt away.' Like Cecilia.

'The full life force returns to the *hisaf*, and that is the most dangerous time. It's like an attack on the body. Sometimes the *hisaf* does not survive the end of the inhabiting.'

'And my father has done this? More than once?'

'Yes. Rawley is very strong. It takes not just a strong body, you know, but also a strong will.' Her soft voice held pride.

'But how ... what does he do to ...'

'He tried to explain it to me, but I didn't understand.

107

Maybe you will. He said that when he crossed over, instead of falling down a well, he made his mind climb up, out of the well. Does that make sense?'

'No.' Crossing over had never felt to me like falling down a well, but rather travelling through a grave. Was it different, then, for every *hisaf*? I didn't know; I had never met another *hisaf* until this past year. I said, 'How many *hisafs* are there? On either side of this war?'

'I don't know. Rawley never told me.'

My mind raced. Ten men left here now, although I didn't know if all of them were *hisafs*. But a pack of the grey dogs had rescued me once, on Soulvine Moor. A small pack but each animal carried the soul of a *hisaf* who was risking his life for me. Had my father commanded that? Why did the *hisafs* consider me worth so much trouble?

I could not ask Charlotte that. But the question suggested another idea to me.

'Charlotte – I don't think Leo is going to turn us over to the men of Soulvine Moor to use in their ... their ceremony.' I could not bear to name it, nor to think of it.

She stirred slightly. 'You don't?'

'No. We're certainly heading towards Soulvine, but I think we're going beyond some border village. I think they're taking us to Galtryf.'

'To Rawley?' she breathed. And then, 'But why?'

'I don't know.' Leo's words howled in my brain: *'I wanted you to see what awaits you'*. But I didn't know what he meant. If I was to be torn apart by a dog, as Straik had been, the Brotherhood could have done that already. If I was to 'inhabit' a dog, I did not see how I could be forced to do so, or why the *hisafs* would want me to. So why did they want me – and Charlotte and Rawnie – at Galtryf?

Charlotte laid a grateful hand on my arm. I felt her

relief; I had given her hope that she and her daughter would not die in the monstrous 'ceremony' practised by Soulvine Moor. Even without knowing what awaited us at Galtryf, my speculation felt like a reprieve to her. She would not have to watch Rawnie stretched out on a flat rock, stabbed through the heart, and then her young flesh . . .

As always, my mind rebelled from the image. It was too close to what I had nearly endured, to what had been done to Cecilia. Instead, I dwelt on my own relief. If we were going to Galtryf, the Brotherhood was not using me to reach Maggie. They did not know about Maggie. She and my son were safe.

And so, in pathetic gratitude for the lesser horror rather than the greater, Charlotte and I were both finally able to sleep.

10

The next day we crossed the border onto Soulvine Moor. The change was apparent immediately. Woods and wild, ravine-cracked mountains gave way to a vast, high, treeless plain. The undulating ground was covered with peat or coarse grasses between clumps of low purple flowers. Occasionally huge outcroppings of rock thrust up from the springy peat. These granite outcroppings somehow looked older than any stone in The Queendom. The occasional curlew wheeled overhead, crying shrilly.

The wagons made slow progress over the uneven ground. Rawnie hung over the side, watching the monotonous landscape when she could not watch Leo. She missed nothing. 'Mama, did you see that?'

'No. What was it?'

'A nest of birds – under those purple bushes. Oh look – a rabbit! Why are their ears so long?'

I rose to my knees to peer over the side of the wagon, straining the chain between Kelif and me. He grunted in mild protest but did not pull me back down. 'Those rabbits are a different breed from the ones in The Queendom. Cousins.' Jee had told me so.

'Nobody asked *you*, Roger,' Rawnie snapped. 'Oh, there's a— What are those?'

'I don't know,' Charlotte said wearily.

In the far distance, barely visible, moved a herd of wild ponies. Rawnie's eyesight must be almost as good as mine. I said, 'Those are ponies. They breed wild on the moor.'

'Ponies!' Rawnie breathed. 'I wish I could catch one!' Her voice turned wistful. 'I have a horse of my own, at home. Papa taught me to ride. He said I have a very good seat.'

Immediately she regretted the confidence. A kick was aimed my way, but her chain would not stretch that far. She settled for making a dreadful face and turned her attention back to the moor. Her hand tightened on the little pack with her pet mouse.

All at once I understood her dislike of me. Rawnie was jealous. Spoiled, petted, indulged, she had been her adored father's only child until she learned about me, in the same moment she and her mother were ripped from their cottage, her horse, her life. In her child's mind, I stood for loss and fear. It softened me towards her.

Or perhaps I simply felt guilt for bringing yet another child into danger. Jee, Stephanie, Rawnie. And of course Katharine, whom I could barely stand to think about.

I said, 'Look over there, Rawnie – another rabbit!'

'Eat dung, Roger.'

I gave it up. Anyway, I wanted to think in peace. Climbing up a well instead of falling down into it ... Had Charlotte remembered my father's words correctly? If so, what did they mean?

Throughout the day the wagons rumbled along, staying as much as possible on higher ground. Once a wheel sagged into a particularly spongy patch of peat and we were all ordered out while Straik's men, cursing, lifted the wheel. Later one of the dogs startled a nest of grouse and they rose nearly straight up into the air, scolding and flapping. Rawnie turned to me almost defiantly.

'What are those birds?'

'Grouse.'

'Do you know much about the moor?'

Too much. 'I know some.'

111

'How?' she demanded.

'Friends taught me.' Jee. Fia. Tom Jenkins, the best tracker in three lands. Pain smote me. I would never see Tom again.

'Why do you look like that? Are your friends dead?'

She missed nothing. I said, 'Some of them are.'

'Oh.' Then, a moment later, 'What are those flowers called?'

The rest of the afternoon she asked me questions. When I didn't know the answers, I made them up. During a brief respite, while Rawnie dozed with her head on her mother's lap, I studied the dogs. They looked like Shadow, like Shep, like Hunter, like every other of their kind that I had seen. Were they really carrying the life force – the souls – of Macon and Dick, as quiescent in them as were the Dead on the other side? And like the Dead when I roused them – the ones I could rouse anyway, which were mostly old women – Macon and Dick could be roused to direct the dogs to attack, to kill.

Climbing up a well instead of falling down into it . . .

I picked one of the dogs, concentrated on it, and then changed my mind. No. Too dangerous. If I succeeded— but, no, I would not succeed, Charlotte said my father had needed much practice to cross over into the mind of a dog. That was a web woman's art, not a *hisaf*'s. But if I should succeed, then Macon or Dick would be there already, and then what?

No.

Rawnie was back, standing beside me in the swaying wagon. Either her resentment of me had lessened or she was hiding it for reasons of her own. I was beginning to think her fully as good an actor as Leo.

'Roger, there's a light!'

Dusk had fallen. At the bottom of a long sloping hill an eerie light shifted over the ground, pale and flickering and somehow cold. The country folk thought it was the souls of the dead who could not cross over. I knew better. All Dead crossed over.

'It's marsh gas. There's a bog in that low-lying place. Bogs are very dangerous. One can swallow a grown man.'

'It can!' She was thrilled. 'And what's *that*?'

I didn't see anything.

'There, Roger! Are you blind? It's moving slow and careful ...'

With difficulty I made out the skulking animal, all but hidden by bushes and dusk. Although I had never seen one before, Jee had told me about them. 'It's a moor cur.'

'A dog?'

'No. A beast somewhere between a jackal and a wolf.'

Rawnie strained to see. 'Is it dangerous?'

'They can hunt. But they prefer to eat dead things. Carrion.'

She turned her head to look at me, her thin face alight. 'How dead?'

I shrugged. 'Dead is dead, Rawnie.' Although not if Soulvine Moor succeeded in their quest.

Rawnie snorted. 'Don't be so stupid, Roger! I mean, how many days does something have to be dead before it's too rotten for moor curs to eat?'

'I don't know.'

She rolled her eyes and went back to peering at the moor cur. 'It's coming closer. Do you think it's hungry?'

The beast had crept towards us. Larger than I had thought, it had silver-black fur and big, pointed ears. Its hindquarters were so large and powerful that it looked misshapen. The wind shifted and I caught its scent, pungent and raw.

'Probably it's hungry, yes.'

'There are two! See that other one way back there –

I'll wager that's his wife. Do you think they would eat me if I was dead?'

'Yes.'

'What if I were still alive?'

'Yes, if it cornered you and it was hungry enough. They have powerful jaws.'

'Can it run faster than me?'

'Much faster.'

'I would fight it,' Rawnie said seriously. 'I would outwit it.'

'I doubt it,' I said.

'Yes, I would. I would kill it dead, dead, dead and then I would skin it and make myself a cloak of its fur. But before that I would bash in its head and gouge out its eyes and—'

'Rawnie,' Charlotte said, without hope.

'—and cut out its heart and . . . oh! We're stopping. That's good, I'm hungry.'

The wagons halted for the night. The moor curs disappeared. Leo shouted directions at his men, who were already doing what was necessary. We had stopped at the base of a great hill topped by a tor, a rounded outcropping of bedrock. Coarse grasses blanketed the area, dotted with patches of low green moss and waist-high clumps of heather. A golden plover, startled by our arrival, took wing from a stand of grass and one of the dogs streaked after it, barking furiously. From the side of the hill a spring burbled, forming a small pool before the water was sopped up by the damp peat. We made camp far enough from the spring to avoid the worst of the dampness, and men filled our waterbags.

It is wearying to ride all day in a jolting wagon, chained to a taciturn giant and a chattering child. As soon as we had eaten, I wanted to return alone to the wagon, or under it, or perhaps just lie on the open ground and sleep. But Kelif sat by the fire, and so I did, too, staring blearily into the night. Stars blazed overhead.

Rawnie, also tired, said little. She didn't even try to convince Leo of her adoration, or ask him for another display of acting. She sat with her head bent over the pack on her lap, one hand thrust inside it. For just a moment I glimpsed her mouse, its pink nose and quivering whiskers, before she pushed it back inside, glancing fearfully to see who had noticed. In that moment she seemed less an obnoxious and conniving nuisance and more a pathetic child.

She caught me looking at her and stuck out her tongue.

I gazed into the night. The larger moor cur had crept towards the pool under the spring. So far the dogs, both asleep by the fire, had not scented it. I could barely make out its silver fur as it moved, and then drank.

Climbing up a well instead of falling down into it ...

Staring at the moor cur, I concentrated my will, just as I did when crossing over. Charlotte had not said that pain was necessary for this, but in case it was, I bit down on my tongue. *A well, a well ...* I pictured myself wedged inside a stone well such as Maggie and I had had at Applebridge, about a metre from the top, my back braced against the curved side of the well and my good hand extended to hold myself in place. I could almost feel the stone at my spine, smell the water below, see the gleam of sky above me. Climb, climb by inching my body upward—

Nothing happened. I did not cross over to the Country of the Dead, and I did not inhabit the moor cur. I stayed beside the fire, and nothing had changed. I was still headed to Galtryf and whatever terrible fate Leo had planned for me there.

*

Several nights later, lying under the wagon on that barren and wild moor, I dreamed for the first time of my son.

But it was Princess Stephanie that I actually saw. The little princess, who would be seven years old in a few weeks, appeared in a wavering landscape I could not identify. It might have been a garden, or a wood, or even a courtyard. Although the surroundings flickered and flowed, Stephanie seemed almost shockingly solid, as if I could reach out and touch her. The lessons she was receiving from Mother Chilton must be refining her talent. Her forehead crinkled.

'Roger, your baby got born.' More creasing of the forehead. 'And another, too. I don't understand ... oh, be careful, that one is such a bad thing!'

'Your Grace,' I tried to say, and the effort woke me. I lay under the wagon. Rain pattered lightly on the wood above. One of the dogs passed by on silent patrol. Kelif and Rawnie both snored. And the sweat of pure panic soaked my already chilled clothes.

Another? Another was born? Did that mean that Maggie had had twins? Or that another child had been born somewhere else? But Stephanie had called it a 'bad thing', and I didn't think she would refer to a baby as a 'thing'. Most little girls loved babies. So what had Stephanie meant?

Then, all at once and as quickly as they had come, my fears left me, lost in awe. *My son had been born.* I was a father. And Maggie ... was Maggie all right? Why hadn't Stephanie said? Women died all the time in childbirth; my own mother had. Why hadn't Stephanie reassured me about Maggie? But a dream was not a letter, carefully composed and full of news – it was a vision. I knew that. Visions cannot be controlled. But why hadn't—

I had a son.

Was Maggie all right?

What 'bad thing' was also born?

When we reached Galtryf and Leo subjected me to 'what awaits you', my child would lose his father. Just as I had. I would never see my son.

Was he a *hisaf*? I remembered the *hisaf* baby I had seen flickering in and out of the Country of the Dead, unable to control his infant talent. Was my son already doing that? He was the child of a *hisaf*, after all. What would Maggie, who knew nothing of what I had wrought in the Country of the Dead, make of her babe's appearing and disappearing? And Maggie lived with her nasty sister. Would the sister take the baby for a witch? What then?

Maggie—

My son—

'Stop twitching,' Rawnie said crossly. 'You woke me up with all that shifting and moaning! What's wrong with you, Roger?'

Everything.

And the next morning, even more.

The attack began at dawn. A light rain fell from clouds that had blown in from the west. The clouds paled without colour or sun, and the moor was grey and misty. I had not slept since my dream, and the view from under the wagon looked eerily like the fog in the Country of the Dead. Its chill tranquillity broke when the dogs began to bark frantically.

'What the by damn!' Leo shouted. Someone else began to curse. The dogs raced off through the mist until all I saw was two dark blurs. Then another blur leaped to join them.

Two blurs, three.

'Rawnie! Into the wagon!' Charlotte screamed.

'What – oh!' the girl cried. 'The dogs are fighting!'

A single shot sounded, frighteningly close. It was

followed by a volley of firing from the camp. I couldn't see anything except the dogs, all at once clear as the fight broke off, the animals circled each other closer to the wagon, and then leaped at each other's throats again.

'Shoot!' Leo screamed. But no one could get a clear shot. Three dogs attacked the Brotherhood's two, snarling and rolling over each other. Blood spouted in foaming jets onto the moss and bracken. And all five grey dogs looked alike – which ones carried Macon and Dick? There was no way to tell. A snarl from forty-two bared teeth, a howl of anguished pain, a tearing of flesh . . .

One dog fell and did not rise. Impossible to tell which.

'Shoot them all!' Leo cried. 'Damn it, fire!'

No one did, at least not at the dogs. Shots rang from the mist, some from above us. Charlotte, having shoved Rawnie into the wagon, pulled her out again and pushed her back underneath; the shots seemed a greater threat than the surviving dogs. I grabbed at Rawnie with my one good hand and tried to crawl on top of her to protect her. The short chain between my wrist and Kelif's prevented me. More *guns* fired.

I cried to Kelif, 'Help!' He did not move. I shoved at him, and my hand came away covered with blood.

Gathering both Rawnie and Charlotte into my good arm, I crossed over.

Darkness—

Cold—

Dirt choking my mouth—

Worms in my eyes—

Earth imprisoning my fleshless arms and legs—

Only this time the women came with me, as well as the dead weight that was Kelif, and the crossing seemed longer, harder. I could not breathe, could not move . . . Then we were over.

'Don't shoot!' someone cried. 'It's Roger!'

We stood at the base of the hill, here without obscuring mist. The next moment two of Leo's men appeared nearby, and a second later, Leo. They, too, had crossed over to escape the *guns* coming from the mist, the *guns* so hard to see through the morning mist on the moor. The escape did not work.

Crack! Crack! Shots sounded, deafening, an obscenity in that calm landscape. They came from the tor atop the hill. Two of the *hisafs* fell. It was an ambush.

Leo vanished. Another *hisaf* appeared, looked wildly around, and swung his gun towards me. I crossed back over, dragging the other three with me, and we were back under the wagon in the land of the living.

Men appeared, disappeared, fired the *guns* stolen from savages. *Crack!* Charlotte cowered beside me, both of us covering Rawnie. Kelif's blood soaked into our clothing and the ground. I couldn't tell who was winning. The dogs continued to fight, but now I couldn't see them and I didn't know how many were left alive. Was there less snarling, fewer howls of pain? Were men rushing down from the tor on this side, having made the laborious climb up the other slope during the night?

Everything depended on how many *hisafs* fought on each side. Charlotte said there were not many in total. And now, from the bodies I could glimpse on the ground, there were fewer. *Hisafs* could die, both here and in the Country of the Dead. If this was truly a rescue and it succeeded—

Under the wagon, in the blood and dirt and noise, my heart began a wild thumping of hope.

Crack!

And then abruptly it was over. Quiet, except for Rawnie's sobbing. A pair of boots appeared beside the wagon. The man bent, in a moment I would see his face and then I would know which side—

Shouting from the opposite direction, another crack of a gun, and the man toppled forward, falling face up, his eyes gone wide with shock. He was not one of Leo's, and now he was dead.

The gunfire resumed, filling the air: from behind the other wagon, from the tor, from the moor. People ran towards us, so many pairs of feet that I groaned. Abruptly, for the second time, the *guns* ceased.

Charlotte cried, 'What is it? Who won?'

I said, everything in me gone numb and cold, 'Leo did. With help.'

Warriors from Soulvine Moor had arrived, running flat out across the moor. The *hisafs* trying to rescue us had crossed over from the Country of the Dead to the equivalent positions on the tor, but they had been outnumbered. The Soulviner warriors had *guns*, too. Not all of them, and some had been shot before the *hisafs* on the tor had given up and crossed over to escape death, retreating to the Country of the Dead where the Soulviners could not follow and our rescuing *hisafs* had the advantage of numbers. Whatever numbers were left alive.

Had the Soulvine warriors not arrived, their rescue would have succeeded. Had this been my father, coming for me half a year later than promised? And if so, did his body now lie among those broken and bleeding in the morning mist?

Sick at heart, I crawled off Rawnie. I couldn't crawl out from beneath the wagon while still chained to Kelif, and Charlotte seemed too paralysed with fright to move. But Rawnie cried, 'Let me up! My mouse!' and slithered out from between us. She straightened up beside the wagon and gasped.

I knew what she was seeing. I had seen it before.

Leo still shouted orders. 'Get him out of there and

chained to somebody else – they're still over there!'

Still over there. The rescuers still held the Country of the Dead. I could grab Charlotte and Rawnie again, drag Kelif with me, cross over to safety with the *hisafs* who had come for us. I seized Charlotte. Rawnie, however, had climbed onto the wagon – I could hear her above me – and Charlotte must have guessed what I intended.

'No, Roger! Not without Rawnie!' She struggled free of me.

Should I leave them here? I could escape by myself, think of a way to come back for them later once I had the other *hisafs* as allies—

Then all choice was taken away from me. Leo crouched by the wagon and hit me on the head with the butt of his *gun*. Blinding light tore through my head, and then all went black.

11

When I woke, the wagon was moving. Never had my head hurt so much. The pain became even more agonizing when I opened my eyes to the sun. I groaned and closed them again. It didn't help. Spears shot through my head, and when the wagon lurched suddenly, I nearly cried out.

'I thought you were dead,' Rawnie said conversationally.

I didn't answer. But slowly, by tiny and wrenching movements, I opened my eyes. Something was wrong with my vision; there were two of her, wavering in and out of existence as if she were a *hisaf*.

'Your head is turning purple,' Rawnie said, leaning closer to inspect me. 'Leo hit you really hard.'

Of course he had. Knocking me out was the only way to keep me from crossing over. The wagon lurched again, and this time I cried out.

'Poor Roger,' Rawnie said, although more with interest than compassion. 'Does it hurt?'

'Yes.' Speech was the only thing that didn't hurt. 'Where's your mother?'

'Walking behind the wagon. She got tired of riding so she's talking to Leo. Do you know you're chained to John now? Kelif got killed.'

I turned my head slightly; it was torture. A very blurry John sat next to me, staring at nothing, his face slack and mouth open. I had the same impression I'd had when he dug Straik's grave: that John was, if not feeble-witted, then at best very stupid. But he was big and he was armed. I would not be able to escape him by crossing over, even if I had been able to summon the necessary will. The pain I already had.

Rawnie put her face close to mine and whispered, 'We almost won the battle. But only almost.'

I said, 'Where are we now?'

She shrugged. 'I don't know. Somewhere on this moor. It all looks alike.'

She was wrong. I made myself sit up, biting my lip to keep from crying out at the pain. As before, my chain was just long enough to permit me to rise to my knees and peer over the side of the wagon. John did not try to stop me.

Everything looked blurry, but I was able to discern Charlotte trudging alongside Leo. She looked weary but not grieving. So my father had not been among the defeated rescuers. Once again he had not even tried to come through for me.

The monotonous peat moor was giving way to a landscape of greater variety. We were surrounded by tors, higher and more numerous than before, with swift streams running down them. More boulders and great outcroppings of rock. But I also saw clumps of trees, although they looked neither tall nor healthy. A roe deer broke from one grove and streaked across the heather. Still, I knew what Rawnie meant. There were no villages, nor even isolated farmhouses, probably because the soil here was as poor as on the peat moor. In that, the moor was unvarying.

A band of Soulvine warriors walked beside the wagon. Looking at them, I felt a deep shudder shake my entire body. These were the people who had taken Cecilia and—

I couldn't think of that, I would go mad.

The warriors included both men and women, all young, all fit. A few carried *guns*; all had spears and knives. At Hygryll I had seen them dressed in ceremonial white robes, but now they wore rough leggings and tunics of animal hide. They all had green eyes. My stomach churned at the sight of them.

'Rawnie, did any of the dogs—'

'They all got killed, ours and theirs. I don't care – they weren't nice dogs. Other pets are better.' Shielded from John's sight by my body, she opened her hand and finally showed me her mouse. The small rodent, brown with a long pink tail, looked resigned, or perhaps only hungry. If Charlotte had been in the wagon Rawnie would not have dared take the creature from her pack.

'How many of Leo's men survived?'

'Just John and Tarf. But now we have all these other stupid people guarding us.'

'Did Leo, or anybody else, say where we're going?'

'No.'

'Or when we will arrive?'

'No.'

'Or—'

'Nobody told me anything, Roger! Nobody ever does! They think I can't— She's coming back!'

Rawnie stuffed the wretched mouse back into her pack just as Charlotte climbed into the wagon. Charlotte sagged with exhaustion but nonetheless tried hard to smile at her daughter, now innocently sitting with her hands folded in her lap.

'Roger, you're awake – does your head pain you?'

'Yes.'

'Let me bathe it with a little cool water. I wish I had some semintha leaves, those are good for pain.' She dabbed at my head with a cloth moistened with water from the waterbag. It made no difference at all. But as she leaned close to my face she breathed, 'We arrive at Galtryf tomorrow morning.'

'And then—'

But she only shook her head, and tears filled her eyes before she blinked them away. 'I tried to talk Leo into freeing Rawnie. She is but a child, no threat to anyone. He said no.'

'They want you – both of you – as hostages to compel Rawley.'

'Perhaps,' she said. But neither of us knew what they wished to compel my father to do. And I – I didn't believe that was my purpose in being carried to Galtryf. I was not a woman nor a child, I was a man grown. Leo and the Brotherhood had something else in mind for me: '*Let him see what awaits him.*'

What could it be?

Tomorrow I would find out.

All day my vision blurred and my head throbbed, like hammers hitting directly on my brain. I drifted in and out of sleep, all of it uneasy and none of it restorative. At one point late in the afternoon, I woke to find only John and I in the moving wagon. Charlotte and Rawnie must be walking again. The back of the wagon had been left down, and I watched boulders and stunted trees blur past.

A moor cur followed the wagon, just at the edge of my vision. At least I think it was a moor cur; it might have been a wolf (if there were wolves here), or a dog, or even a delusion. But from the way it kept behind rocks and bushes, I guessed it was a cur, attracted by the smell of the food in the supply wagon. Or perhaps by the blood on my head.

My head hurt so! How long could this headache last? I wanted to escape the relentless, pounding pain, escape myself, escape everything, go somewhere else. But if my body crossed over, John would come, too. And there was nowhere else to go.

Climbing up a well instead of falling down into it . . .

Carefully, as if an effort of will might jar my body, I pictured that well and myself wedged into it, a metre from the top, my back braced against the curved side of the well and my good hand extended to hold myself in place. Above me loomed the dirty-silver fur of the moor cur. Climb, climb by inching my body upward— Now do it more—

A scent in my nostrils, a black-and-grey landscape alive with smells, food food food danger danger food—

I gasped and pulled back, and instantly my headache was thrice as bad, so bad that I nearly fainted with pain. So this was the agony felt by the *hisaf* I had found in the Country of the Dead, unable to breathe from the effort of returning from inhabiting one of the grey dogs. This, too, the agony of the web women who had become diving raptors, afterwards left gasping and barely alive from the effort. And I had scarcely touched the mind of the moor cur.

But I *had* touched it. I couldn't do so when I'd tried before – what was different now? Was it that I was in so much pain? Charlotte had mentioned nothing about pain being needed to cross into the dogs, only the agony and risk of returning. So what else was different?

I lay the rest of the afternoon, pondering this, pretending to sleep. No answers came to me. Gradually my headache returned to what it had been at first, which was terrible enough but now, in contrast, seemed bearable. So does greater pain reconcile us to lesser.

As evening fell the wagons halted. John hauled me down to sit with the rest around the fire, but I could not get warm. My head did not stop blazing with pain.

I couldn't eat, although Charlotte urged me to do so. I could not even listen to Leo, who boasted about 'his' victory over the *hisafs* who had tried to rescue us.

Finally one of the Soulviners, a young man whose green eyes had grown sharp enough to cut glass, said in the accent of the uplands, 'T'wasn't your victory, but ours.'

'I am in command,' Leo said, 'by order of—'

'Hush,' a young woman said. 'We don't speak his name.'

Leo smiled, a look tolerant of less civilized beings with their primitive superstitions. He didn't even realize what a mistake he was making. The Soulviners gazed at him steadily, and it was not with contempt but with something more dangerous: doubt.

The young man with the cutting emerald eyes said, 'Had it not been for us, ye would have lost all. As it be, ye lost the dogs.'

'And they lost theirs!' Leo retorted.

Rawnie said, 'Leo, give us another play!'

Did she do it deliberately, to defuse tension? She looked all childish enthusiasm at the moment, but I did not believe that. Although why would Rawnie wish to lessen tension? She thrived on it. No, she was still trying to work her way into Leo's approval, for reasons of her own.

'Well,' Leo said, 'if I must—'

The Soulviners did not speak, any of them, but they could not keep flashes of interest from their faces. Possibly none of them had ever seen a play. But they knew Leo was an actor, and they were curious.

I suppose that if you hope to live for ever, you expect to have time to be curious about everything, including plays.

But I did not want to be again enthralled, half against my will, by a performance from Leo. With an aching head, and sick at heart, I wanted only to sleep. I said to John, 'I would sleep.'

'Aye.' He stood, pulling me up with him. Laboriously, my head throbbing at every movement, I got to my feet. We climbed into the wagon. Instantly John fell asleep, his mouth open, his slack features gone even duller than when awake. I heard Leo say imperiously, 'Not a play tonight, I am not thus moved. A song, I think.'

I lay as far away from John as my chain would allow and thought of Maggie and my son. I would never see either again. I would never hold my child. Did he look like me, with my nondescript brown hair and eyes, or did he have Maggie's fair hair and grey eyes? Was he, in infant *hisaf* dreams, flickering back and forth between the land of the living and the Country of the Dead? How was Maggie keeping that from her sister? Was she—

Rawnie's pack stirred. Her mouse crept out.

I reached for it with my one hand, stirring the chain between John's wrist and mine, but before either he could awake or I could grab the mouse, it was no longer there. Instead a woman lay full length beside me on the wagon bed.

'*What—*'

She clamped a hand over my mouth and scowled, as my dazed mind tried to capture this new truth. Rawnie's mouse was a web woman. As Mother Chilton had become a black swan, as Alysse had become a white rabbit.

I whispered, inanely, 'But you were with her so *long*—' Two months, Charlotte said, Rawnie had had her mouse – two months before this journey even began! Why wasn't the web woman weak and nearly dying, as Alysse and that other girl had been when they became raptors and—

All at once I understood. A bird had not been Alysse's

chosen 'soul sharer'; a rabbit was. This woman was naturally a mouse. The word turned me giddy – 'natural' to become an animal! To become a—

'Hush,' the woman repeated, still scowling. 'I must go. I cannot enter Galtryf with you. That would be possible only if I had assumed my soul-sharer shape while on the castle grounds, which I did not. But before I leave, I would tell you some things.'

John stirred in his sleep. By the fire Leo plucked a few notes on his lute, tuning it. I held my breath, half expecting the web woman to vanish. But then John only snored more deeply. And so we lay side by side in the wagon bed, stretched out under the stars above Soulvine Moor, the woman a slender half-glimpsed shadow against the rough side of the wagon. Only her hair, unbound and flowing towards me, seemed solid and real. Her words, too, showed me shadowy realities, glimpsed before but never understood, and beyond her words and woven into them was Leo's music.

'You have made grievous errors, Roger Kilbourne. You were told last winter not to cross back over, and yet you did so. You destroyed your sister. Katharine was—'

'She was going to kill my son!'

'—was the conduit,' the woman continued, as if I had not spoken. 'It was through her that the accumulated power of the Dead first could flow into the Soulvine watchers in their vortexes. Those living and those dead are connected, of course – how could it be otherwise, when the Dead were once alive and the alive must someday join the Dead? When Soulvine, with the help of the rogue *hisafs*, began to pervert that connection, it was through Katharine that the balance was maintained, because the life power of newborn babes could flow in the opposite direction, from the land of the living to the Country of the Dead. When you—'

'That is not true!' I whispered hotly. 'My sister was not this "conduit"! She couldn't have been because now she is gone, but the robbing babes of their souls still continues! I have seen it!'

'You don't know what you have seen, and you must stay quiet now and let me finish. I have not much time.'

'But—'

'Hush!' she said, at the same moment that Leo began to sing.

> Although you to the hills do flee,
> My love you can't escape.

'When you threw Katharine into the vortex, first we feared the entire web of being would break. When it did not, we thought as you do. *It is over*, we thought, and rejoiced. But Soulvine Moor has learned much, and the circles of Dead continued to disappear, and infants to be robbed of their life force. The web is further strained, almost to the breaking point.

'And the *hisafs*, on both sides, have made it worse with these dogs. Soul arts grow and change, Roger Kilbourne, like all the rest of life. Thus your father was able to combine the gifts of a *hisaf* and the training of a woman of the soul arts, and so inhabit the dogs. But not all growth is necessarily good. It may instead be stunted, misshapen, a tumour upon the intentions of life. As is Soulvine's quest to life for ever, and as are those dogs. A *hisaf* has no calling to cross into animals. The *hisafs* should keep to their gift, and we of the soul arts to ours.'

> Your heart, my sweet, belongs to me
> Though you may change its shape.

130

I said, 'Are you sure you are not just jealous, now that *hisafs* are using your art?'

'They are not "using" it, they are perverting it. Animals have their own web of being, and it must be respected. Try to understand, you obstinate boy! The—'

'I am not a boy!'

'—centre of the web is Galtryf. That has always been so. We women of the soul arts originated there, long ago when Galtryf was a force for good in the world. As did the *hisafs*. The city is very, very old. Now it lies in ruins, city and castle both, but it was the original source of all the transcendent arts, great and small. Galtryf is the shadow of The Queendom, that dark part that the oblivious farmers and blacksmiths and wheelwrights and courtiers have chosen not to acknowledge. Nonetheless, the shadow is there, in all of us. And in Galtryf, now, the perverted use of the soul arts is the shadow of the shadow.'

> Never, never will I cease
> To follow where you go,
> And ever, ever will I be
> The hound upon your doe.

I said, 'But ... but why can the circles persist and the babes be robbed when my sister is gone? I murdered her, I—'

'I told you, Soulvine moor has learned to do many things, things no mortal should do. We do not know. But all may change again when your son is born. Your father had unusual powers from his mother, your grandmother. She was a very great practitioner of the soul arts. *You* have proved to be nothing unusual, but your son may be. We have reason to believe so. He is our last hope, because Galtryf is winning this war.'

Do what you will and what you can,
Employ the arts you know —
Ever, ever will I be
The hound upon your doe.

My grandmother was a web woman. I had not known that – how could I? My son was a 'last hope'. My mind reeled. I started to say, 'My son *has* been born,' because clearly the woman did not know this. She had, after all, been a mouse for the last two months. But before I could speak, someone outside the wagon thumped it hard, crying, 'John should hear this, he loves music – John!'

John awoke. And there was no one else beside me, just a small brown mouse, disappearing over the edge of the wagon with a flick of its long pink tail.

12

Rawnie was inconsolable at the loss of her mouse. Her grief took the form of rage. She pounded on the wagon bed and screamed until John casually reached out his huge hand that was not chained to mine and cuffed the side of her head. Rawnie stopped in mid-yell, stared at him with wide shocked eyes, and began to cry.

Charlotte leapt at John like an enraged she-bear. 'Don't you touch her!' She pounded ineffectually with her soft fists on John, who looked at her with the astonishment of a man whose hat has been blown off by a slight breeze.

The din attracted Leo. 'What goes on here? Charlotte, stop that. No, John!'

John had reached out to cuff Charlotte as he had Rawnie. At Leo's command he halted, looking confused. He lowered his hand, raised it again, held it halfway to Charlotte's head and gazed piteously at Leo. All at once I knew why John had never been selected to cross over into one of the dogs. The dog was smarter.

Charlotte cried, 'He hit Rawnie!'

Rawnie, as if cued, sobbed harder. 'He lost my mouse!'

'Mouse? What mouse?' Leo said. 'John, you know that striking any of them is forbidden.'

Forbidden by whom? Why? Did that include me?

Rawnie said, 'My pet mouse! Tickles! He was in my pack and John let him go!'

'I never did,' John said.

'Yes, you did! You *did*, or Tickles would still be here!'

Leo said, somewhere between amusement and disgust, 'Well, stop crying. We'll get you another pet. How would you like a ... a baby curlew?'

'It would fly away!'

'Then ... a kitten?'

Rawnie stopped crying. Her face brightened so quickly that suspicion took me: had the tears been an act? No, she had genuinely wanted her mouse. But now that it was gone, little schemer that she was, she seized the opportunity to endear herself to Leo. And under her adoring and hopeful gaze he visibly expanded, like bread dough rising on warm air. He was the hero of the moment, even if the next moment he might execute us all.

'A kitten!' Rawnie breathed. 'Oh, could I? Where would you get a kitten?'

'I'll get it,' Leo said. 'But no more screaming, there's a good child. And Charlotte and John, no more fisticuffs.' He swaggered off, having restored order to the Fiefdom of the Wagon Bed. His back turned, Rawnie stopped beaming and gazed after him thoughtfully.

I wanted to be alone, to think about what the web woman had told me. Since I could not be alone, I did the next best thing and feigned sleep. But Charlotte and Rawnie's whispered conversation kept me from my thoughts.

'Do you think he'll really get me a kitten?'

'I don't know, Rawnie.' Charlotte sounded close to tears.

'There might be cats at Galtryf.'

'How did you know we're going to Galtryf?'

'I listen,' Rawnie said scornfully. 'I learn things. Galtryf is a big, old, scary place. The bad *hisafs* there will torture Roger. Papa is there and they think they can make him help them, but I know that he would never do anything

134

bad, so they're wrong about that. And everybody here is afraid of somebody's sword.'

No response. Then Charlotte said in a strangled voice, 'Never mention that again.'

'Which part?'

'Any of it, but I mean the . . . the last thing.'

'The sword? Whose sword is it?'

'You will heed me,' Charlotte said in an entirely different voice, so firm and menacing that it silenced even Rawnie. For a moment.

'Piss-pots!' she finally said. 'I'm not afraid of anybody's sword. All it can do is kill me dead, and then Papa would come and get me from the other side.'

A low despairing groan from Charlotte, who nonetheless did not correct her daughter. Charlotte, if not Rawnie, evidently knew that you could not cheat death for long.

Although that cheat was exactly what Soulvine Moor was trying to do.

No one else spoke that night. Perhaps they slept, perhaps not. I did not.

'*The bad hisafs there will torture Roger.*'

What was the sword?

'*Your son is our last hope, because Galtryf is winning this war.*'

Would my father join Soulvine Moor if the Brotherhood threatened to torture Charlotte and Rawnie? I did not know him, did not understand his mind. And Rawnie, for all her precocious plotting and listening, was blind where he was concerned. She thought him a hero, out of one of Leo's plays.

'*Galtryf is the shadow of The Queendom.*'

Shadows and swords. Alysse had spoken to me of the sword. And three years ago, when I had brought the Blue army back from the Country of the Dead, something bright and terrible had roared out of the sky. It lasted only a small piece of a second, but my telling of it had made Alysse gasp. Alysse, who never showed any emotion towards me except impatience! She had called it 'the sword' but I had seen no weapon, merely glimpsed blinding light and heard wordless sound. The Dead awaited the sword, Alysse said. She had not said why. But none of this seemed of use to me now.

'Soul arts grow and change, Roger Kilbourne, like all the rest of life. All may yet change when your son is born.'

But he was already born, or so the little princess in faraway Glory had told me, and nothing had changed. I was still captive, headed for pain and death. Infants were still sent into trance, neither living nor dead, their life force sucked away. Circles of the Dead were still being sucked into vortexes of watchers from Soulvine Moor. The breach in the wall between the living and dead – in the image of the *hisafs* – grew wider and wider. Or – in the image of the web women – the web of being grew more pulled, torn, misshapen. Nothing had changed.

'The bad hisafs there will torture Roger.'

I lay awake for hours, but when I finally slept, I had a plan. It was not much of a plan but, facing agonizing death, anything is better than nothing.

Perhaps.

Or so I hoped.

I made myself wake before dawn. There had been no dreams. Over a large hill to the southeast the sky had begun to pale, a chill grey like an icy sea, although the day promised to be warm and fair. Today we would arrive at Galtryf. I had not much time.

Pulling myself to the limit of my chain, I peered over the side of the wagon. The moor curs were there, just beyond shooting reach of the Soulviners' *guns*, or what

I thought was their reach. Did the animals know that, or was it coincidence? I had no idea how intelligent moor curs might be. Yesterday I might not have been able to see them all, but at least this morning my vision was again clear. The headache was not as bad, either.

Two – no, three moor curs. Did they travel in packs, then? How aggressive were they? Not that it mattered; I had little choice. These were waiting until the wagons moved on, to scavenge the bones and intestines of last night's roasted rabbits, plus whatever else we had left. I picked a cur, stared at it, and made pictures out of mind and will.

A well. It extended deep below me, but only a metre of curving brick wall above. I was wedged against the stone, my back braced on one side, my feet and hand holding my body in place. From below came the scent of water, above was grey dawn sky and the sudden song of a bird. All was pictured in as much clarity and detail as I could manage. I climbed, inching my body upward. One tiny bit closer to the top, then another, and always with the act of will that I had used in crossing over . . .

Darkness, cold, dirt choking my mouth—

No! Not the grave! Climb upward, upward, out of the well, cross over into the moor cur—

The grave disappeared. So did the well. Instead the world suddenly became black-and-white-and-grey, and infinitely strange. The air was layered in scents, richer than the dull sights, except when something moved – there, the flash of a curlew taking wing, and something in the distance was falling—

The falling thing was me. My body hit the wagon bed with a thud that woke John. He glared at me, rose to his knees to survey the camp, found nothing amiss. Instantly he went back to sleep.

I lay on the rough wood, Charlotte and Rawnie snoring

softly at the other end of the wagon, and I squeezed my eyes shut in gratitude. I had done it. For just a moment, I had entered the mind of the moor cur and left my body behind. If I could do it with a moor cur, then perhaps I could do it with a rat, a bird. I could not escape death in Galtryf, but now at least I could escape the pain of torture. The Brotherhood would kill my body. But now they could not force me to talk, as men have always been forced under great and continuous pain to tell their secrets. When the pain became too great, I would cross over into any creature available, and so would not babble of Maggie and my son. I would not betray them. Nor would I tell Soulvine anything that would aid them in their war.

But I must be able to sustain the crossing longer than a moment. I must practise.

Again I rose to my knees, this time wedging myself in the corner of the wagon in such a way that my body would not fall. The moor curs were still there. I didn't know why I could do this – it should not have been possible. My father's dogs had all been animals born in, and sent from, the Country of the Dead.

'*Soul arts grow and change, Roger.*' The web woman had thought me 'nothing unusual' – but I had known web women to be mistaken before. The well, the climb upward, the act of will, and again I crossed into the moor cur. Of all the strange sensations I had known on both sides of the grave, this was the strangest. I was the moor cur, and I was Roger Kilbourne. All I could see, hear, smell – and how keen were both hearing and smell! – came to me as the moor cur received them. And yet I knew I was a man, too. A man inhabiting an animal, but not bodily. My body stayed tranced in the wagon, as I used to leave it tranced when I crossed through the grave.

I made the moor cur turn its head. It did, without resistance or protest. Was its own will thus gone? No, for I sensed its fright at my presence, but it was fright muffled and ineffective, as if a fly buzzed beneath a pile of blankets.

A second moor cur approached me – us? it? – and sniffed. Had it sensed that I was somehow different? Apparently not, for the female stood beside me, her body relaxed. Was this my mate? I tried to reach the moor cur's own mind – to reach beneath the blankets – and immediately found myself back in the wagon.

Pain throughout my whole body. Weakness, gut-twisting hurt ... I reached for the side of the wagon, to hang on to it, and my arms were too feeble to hold it. I did not have even enough strength to cry out.

This, then, was the cost. This was what had weakened the *hisaf* I had found in the Country of the Dead, nearly dead himself. This was what Macon and Dick had risked to cross into the dogs guarding Leo's wagons. This was the cost to the *hisafs* inhabiting Shadow and Shep and the other grey dogs that had rescued me time and again. I had not known. And I had crossed into the cur only briefly. Would practice make the return any easier?

There was only one way to know.

When the weakness and dizziness had passed, I tried again. This time I was not thrust out of the beast but instead chose the time to return, which was when I saw the first man stirring near the embers of last night's fire. The eastern sky blazed pink and gold. I crossed back into myself.

'Roger's sick!'

Rawnie, the first awake in the wagon. Her cry roused Charlotte and John. I slumped in my corner and believed I was dying. It would be better than this. A blaze of pain, like standing in a fire. I could not move my arms or legs. I could not force words past my throat.

'Roger?' A cool hand on my forehead: Charlotte. 'Why, you are burning with fever! Did you eat something bad last night?'

I could not answer. Nothing on my body worked. My bladder let go.

'Faauughhh – he wet himself!' Rawnie said. 'Roger, you stink.'

I was glad to faint.

Nonetheless, I did it again. And again.

All that day, I practised. Whenever I felt strong enough to pull myself up on the side of the wagon, I leaned over it and pretended to retch. Each time there was some creature to cross into: a rabbit, a vole. Each time I crossed, my body collapsed into insensibility. Each time I returned, I was weak as an infant, not able to so much as lift my head.

'He needs a healer,' Charlotte said.

'There are healers at Galtryf.' Leo's voice, full of rage. 'He had best not die before we arrive there!'

If I could have, I would have smiled. Leo wanted me alive so he could kill me.

Someone pried open one of my eyelids. Rawnie. 'Roger, are you still breathing?'

'Leave him be, Rawnie!'

'I just want to know if he still breathes!'

I breathed. I felt strength ebb and flow in my body. I felt pain and relief from pain. I saw the sun climb high in a blue sky and sink again, until shadows were long and the moon appeared, once again waxing towards full. And I practised.

I saw the world as a rabbit sees it, alive at ground level with a thousand rustlings and scents. I crossed into a deer, seen fleetingly as it leaped a small swift brook and dashed away. I crossed into a swallow soaring above the wagon and became so dizzy with the strangeness of flight that I had to return to my body before I fell out of the sky.

In the evening I was too weak to leave the wagon and sit beside the fire. Charlotte tended me, putting crumbs of food into my mouth, holding the waterbag so I could drink. She stripped and washed my body, and I was too depleted to be shamed by her ministrations. That night I fell into sleep like a man tumbling off a high cliff and striking solid rock below.

Into such insensibility it seemed that no dreams could penetrate. But one did, although it came as *grey and blurry as if my vision were still affected by the blow from Leo's gun. A figure, small, flickering – was it waving its arms? Yes. Somehow I sensed it was a girl, a child – oh, no, no . . .*

Katharine, the little sister I had murdered?

But it was not. Colour flickered in and then out of the dream, reducing it to the grey tones of my sight as a moor cur. But the colour had been purple, and the girl waving her arms was little Princess Stephanie. She was crying.

'Roger—' Her voice came as from a great distance, which was true in life but never before in my dreams. Barely could I hear her. 'She . . . is . . . almost . . . ready.'

'Who?' I shouted back across that unbridgeable distance. But I was not a web woman; I could not at will bridge the gulf between dreams. Stephanie did not answer me. More arm waving and then another voice, one I knew well, without body but as clear as if she stood at my elbow. Mother Chilton.

'Where do they go?' Mother Chilton asked, in the tone she had always taken with me: acerbic, slightly impatient, constantly reminding me of my shortcomings and failures.

'Where do who go?' I shouted back, but both of them had

gone, the crying princess and the disembodied voice. I woke.

The sun had already risen. The camp bustled around the wagon. I could sit up without pain, although I still felt weak. And in mid-morning, we came at last to Galtryf.

13

If I had imagined what Galtryf would look like – which I had not, having too many more pressing things to think of, such as torture, death and Maggie – I would have pictured a place like a slightly larger Hygryll. That settlement on Soulvine Moor had consisted of low, windowless rooms dug into the sides of low hills, each faced inside with stone and covered outside with the coarse grasses of the Moor. Peat fires had burned, and the simple furniture had been of stone or of scarce wood hauled many miles. Galtryf was nothing like that.

'Is *that* where we're going?' Rawnie breathed, hanging over the side of the wagon.

I pulled myself upright to look. Even John, roused to lethargic curiosity, raised his head and squinted ahead. Only Charlotte, nearly paralysed by the conflicting claims of desire to see her husband again and fear for when she did, took but one quick glance and sank again to the bed of the wagon.

'I'm going to ask Leo about that place,' Rawnie said, hopping out of the back of the wagon. 'By damn, it's big!'

'You climb right back in here,' Charlotte said. 'And do not use such rough language, young woman.'

Rawnie scowled, but she obeyed. She was no longer chained since there was no longer anyplace to go. Standing upright in the swaying wagon, she repeated, 'It's so big!'

Big, and formidable, and ruined.

Built atop a wide, flat tor, Galtryf rose in jagged, broken

chambers and towers and grey stone battlements. Once it must have been even larger than the palace at Glory. Once it must have been impregnable, a fortress of the ancient kind I had seen in paintings at court. Once it might have been magnificent in an austere, belligerent way. Now whole sections had caved in on themselves, creating piles of rubble. Roofless walls loomed jaggedly over rooms choked with weeds. Lonely towers poked at an indifferent sky.

A man, silhouetted against the sun, strode out to meet us. 'You have them?'

'Of course,' Leo said.

'Well done,' he said, but it did not sound like a genuine compliment. Tinged with amusement, the comment was a tolerant dismissal of a boy who has correctly fingered his lute. 'They are well?'

'Well enough.'

'And what does that mean?'

'Roger has been ill. It's not my fault!'

'Nothing ever is,' the man said. 'Very well, go to the kitchen and get something to eat. I will take this over.'

Leo scowled but, at another dismissive look, he stalked off. The other man came to the back of the wagon and stared at us. Even Rawnie fell silent.

He was neither tall nor broad, and had nothing like John's imposing size. But every line of his face conveyed command. Dark-eyed, beak-nosed, he had cheekbones like chisels and close-cropped grey hair. He looked preternaturally hard, as if he were only half flesh and the other half were carved from the granite that lay all around us. I knew instantly, as I had never known of anyone else, that he was a *hisaf*.

He glanced briefly at Charlotte and Rawnie, then turned his full gaze upon me. 'So you are Roger Kilbourne.'

I said nothing.

'You have made great difficulties for us, Roger. But not for much longer. She is almost ready.'

The same words Stephanie had said in my dream. I found my voice, although it came out almost as a croak. 'Who?'

He only smiled, and I hope never to see such a smile again. To the wagon driver, waiting respectfully, he said, 'Bring them in. The south gate.'

'Aye, Lord Jago.'

Lord? Nothing in the man's rough dress set him apart from the travel-soiled driver, and nothing about him spoke of the manners and breeding I had learned to recognize at court. The 'lord' strode away, and the wagon lurched forward.

Rawnie said, 'What a by damn piss-pot.'

'Rawnie!' Charlotte said, without hope.

We drove for a long time, circling the ruined fortress, over stony and uneven ground without so much as a wagon track. The horse laboured and sweated. The wagon passed great open pits which might once have been rooms or perhaps outbuildings, most surrounded by the traces of crumbling walls. Finally we rounded a section of wall more intact than most, and below us lay the sea.

I had not smelled it; the breeze blew from the land. Nor had I realized that this far out on Soulvine Moor, the coast curved abruptly inward. The eastern edge of Galtryf stood on a high cliff, with a dizzying fall to rock-strewn water below. To the south the high moors gave way to a gentler landscape: undulating hills, some wooded and some grassy, that descended gradually to the distant horizon. In morning sunshine this unknown country looked fertile, inviting, and empty of people. But no sunshine could make the vast decayed pile of Galtryf seem inviting.

145

We passed more of the open, low-walled pits, and then under a huge gate from which all wood and ironwork were gone. Only the stone arch remained. The keep beyond the gate was a dirt courtyard ringed by closed wooden doors on three sides and a partially caved-in wall on the fourth. Here the wagon stopped. Dogs rushed to meet us and fear sliced through me, but these were merely ordinary hounds such as noblemen keep to hunt, although skinnier and mangier.

Lord Jago said, 'Put them in the prepared chambers.'

Two young Soulviners pulled down the wagon back and reached for Charlotte and Rawnie. Rawnie said, 'Don't touch me, you piss-pot!'

The younger man smiled. 'I will not, young Lady Rawley.'

Rawnie looked as astonished at the title as I was at the Soulviners' dress. Unlike Lord Jago, these wore silks and velvets so worn that bare patches showed in the cloth and the hems trailed frayed threads. The brocade of the younger man's old-fashioned doublet bared one entire shoulder. The once-red hat of the other drooped over his brow like a flat pancake. With their green eyes glowing bright – too bright, as if drunk on much wine – and their decrepit finery, they looked like players in some comic masque.

Charlotte said, 'Rawnie, get out of the wagon.' Charlotte climbed down and held firmly to her daughter's arm. 'You will not separate us.'

'Of course not,' the Soulviner said. 'And Alice will attend you.'

A young girl, only a few years older than Rawnie, came nervously around the wagon. She, too, wore faded finery eaten with moth-holes. Eyes downcast, she dropped Charlotte an awkward curtsey.

Fia, curtseying to Tom and me in the middle of a forest:

146

'Perhaps I was a lady's maid'. The memory pierced me, sharp as a dagger. Fia, Mother Chilton had said, came from Galtryf. She was an apprentice there before she escaped to bring the web women the terrible tidings of what went on there. *'Galtryf poisoned her. It keeps all of its young on a steady low dose of poison until it is sure it has snared their minds. Without the antidote in the food that Fia ate every day, the sickness took her.'*

I looked again at the maid's eyes. Too bright, too green, like the two young men. Galtryf was adept in the use of potions and drugs.

Charlotte regarded the serving maid with bewilderment, Rawnie gazed at her with suspicion. John pulled me from the wagon and led me, stumbling in weakness, behind yet another Soulviner. The youth unlocked one of the doors giving on to the courtyard and John and I entered. Behind me Rawnie yelled, 'I'll come visit you later, Roger! After I see my father!'

I did not dare turn around, lest she see on my face the knowledge that I might never see her again.

The chamber behind the door was stone-walled and windowless, but the door was set with a barred grille that admitted some light. A narrow straw pallet with thin blanket, a bare table with one of its four legs a rough stave, an equally battered chair. Silently John unlocked the chain around my wrist and left. The Soulviner locked the door.

For a long moment astonishment held me motionless. I was free of my captor *hisaf*. Why?

Before the door could open again, I bit my tongue hard and crossed over.

Darkness—

Cold—

Dirt choking my mouth—

Worms in my eyes—

Earth imprisoning my fleshless arms and legs—

But I could not reach the other side. I struggled in the grave – for such a long time I struggled in the grave! And then, all at once, I was back in the locked stone room at Galtryf, sitting on the floor and trying to determine what had just happened.

It had felt like a solid wall between me and the Country of the Dead. Everywhere, or just here? Perhaps my gift was gone for ever, taken from me by soul arts I did not understand. But I did not think so. I had crossed into the grave easily enough – I just could not cross out of it. Something in the Country of the Dead prevented me from doing so. I could not imagine what it was. Such a thing had never happened before.

But one thing was clear. I had been unchained because here I could not escape. This was how my father had been held at Galtryf and not, as Leo had claimed, by threatened harm to my dead mother. I, too, was as bodily confined as if I were not a *hisaf*. Did that mean that I couldn't inhabit an animal either, nor escape the agony of the torture to come? If that were so . . .

In panic I pressed my face against the window bars set into the door. The horse stood still hitched to Leo's wagon. I pictured the well, concentrated my will—

Flies and hunger and smells something behind snort startle tense to kick no it's not—

I stayed only a moment in the horse's mind, but that moment was enough to collapse me to the floor, panting and gasping, pain lancing my head. No matter. I would recover. And my escape – pitiful though it might be – was still intact.

Thus do we learn to be grateful for what should never have been necessary at all.

*

For the rest of the day people came and went in the courtyard. I spent the time peering through the bars, learning what I could in case it might prove somehow useful. The mangy, underfed dogs slunk about. After a time the same people appeared and reappeared; either not that many lived at Galtryf, or else they did not pass through this courtyard. I saw 'Lord Jago', some of Leo's men, John fetching water from the well, a dozen Soulviners dressed in the same fantastic rags as the first two, Alice the serving maid. 'Alice' was not a Soulviner name; it belonged to The Queendom. This place was a mockery of the royal court at Glory, which Soulvine perhaps hoped to take over when they had won this secret war and could live for ever. Galtryf was also a centre of command, lightly staffed but used as a place to dispatch *hisafs* and Soulviners on their missions of war. A mock court, a military command post – and what else?

Why could I not cross over?

The long summer twilight began. Now fewer people crossed the courtyard, and the aroma of cooking drifted on the warm air. My stomach growled with hunger. I was just about to rattle my bars and shout for food when two figures, one large and one small, unlocked my door. It was hard to see in the gloom, but the small figure carried a tray with a lighted candle.

'I have brought your dinner,' said a woman's voice, unknown to me and yet somehow familiar.

The man said, 'Stand away from the door.'

I backed up against the far wall, the stone chill at my back. Tempting odours wafted from the tray. The woman set it upon the rickety table and straightened. In the candlelight her face looked middle-aged, and almost familiar. She curtseyed to me, a graceful drooping that somehow conveyed resigned despair, the kind that has been going on a long time. She glanced timorously at the man, much older than she but still powerfully built.

The woman said, 'May I ... may I stay and talk with Roger? About *her*?'

He scowled. A look between them that I could not read, but his seemed both defiant and ashamed. He growled something under his breath; it might have been an oath. Then he said, 'He be dangerous.'

'Do you care?' she said, but without spirit. 'Lord Jago does not.'

'Ten minutes, then.' He left, locking the door behind him.

The woman came closer. She raised her face to mine, and the candlelight fell straight upon it. Green eyes, like all of them, but a peculiar shade, neither emerald nor moss nor grass but only their own colour. Skin as white as her still-thick hair, small and delicate features in the lined face, a tilt to the nose ...

A black swooping dizziness took me, gone in a minute. I said, 'You are ... you ...'

'Yes, Roger Kilbourne. I am Cecilia's mother.'

14

Did she know what had happened to Cecilia? That was all I could think of as I stared at her, unable to move or speak.

'I know that Cecilia died at ... at Hygryll. Hemfree brought her there. I know that because you followed her, and tried to rescue her, you were nearly sacrificed to the soul eating, too. I want to thank you for your attempt to save her.'

She smiled, surely the saddest smile I have ever seen, and shame washed through me. She did not know. Not that I had brought her daughter back over, or that after a fortnight Cecilia, like all those carried back from the Country of the Dead in the arms of *hisafs*, had lost her chance at eternity. She now existed in no realm. I had watched her beautiful flesh melt and rot and disintegrate in the most terrible instant of my life. Cecilia's mother did not know that, and so she stood there and *thanked* me—

I could not stand it. I looked away and stabbed around in my mind for something, anything, to turn the talk away from Cecilia. I blurted, 'I will die here at Galtryf, won't I?'

She could face truth better than ever Cecilia could; her life had forced her to. 'Yes.'

'When?'

'When she is ready.'

'Who is "she"?'

Her eyes widened. 'You don't know?'

151

'Know what?'

'Lord Jago didn't tell you? Or Leo?'

All Leo had said was 'Let him see what awaits him', when Macon and Dick had crossed into the dogs . . .

In one stride I crossed the small room and grabbed her small shoulder with my one hand. 'Who is "she"? Tell me – not knowing is worse!'

So softly that I almost didn't hear her, she said, 'Perhaps not.'

'Please,' I said. '*Please.*'

She seemed to visibly gather herself together, pulling from the air sufficient courage, or will, or perhaps even cruelty. 'You killed your half-sister, Rawley's second child, that was born and raised in the Country of the Dead.'

'Yes.'

'You threw her into a soul crossing.'

'A spinning vortex, yes.'

'And you thought her power – the power of a conduit between the living and the dead – you thought her power had vanished, too.'

'No,' I said. 'I thought it had been dispersed, distributed among the watchers in that vortex. I knew it made them stronger, but it obliterated Katharine.'

'No,' Cecilia's mother said, 'that is not what happened. It's what should have happened. It's what might have happened if there had not been another nearby.'

'Another *hisaf*? One of the Brotherhood? I saw no one!'

'No. Not a man, nor woman either. Did you not hear it? I have heard that it was very close.'

A crashing through the underbrush just as I threw my mad sister into the vortex. I had fled that crashing, crossing back to the land of the living to escape what I assumed was a *hisaf* racing, too late, to rescue Katharine. But it was not a *hisaf*. It was . . . it was . . .

152

Cecilia's mother saw the truth on my face. 'Yes. It was one of the dogs. And Katharine had some inborn power as a woman of the soul arts, or she could not have become what she did. She was untutored and unpractised, but her mad brain had seen Lord Jago and the others with the dogs. Perhaps she had even tried it before. One of the dogs had been sent to rescue her – so much faster than mere men! – after you and yours killed her *hisaf* guard in the mountains. She crossed to inhabit the dog.'

My knees gave way and I sank to the edge of the narrow bed.

Cecilia's mother sat beside me and took my one hand in both of hers. Even through my horror I somehow noted how small her hands were, how delicate the bones. Like Cecilia's.

'Your sister did not know how to do the inhabiting correctly, or perhaps it was the death of her body that made it so hard. At any rate, the crossing nearly killed them both, her and the dog. It did kill the *hisaf*. For a long time the beast, too, seemed certain to die. But it did not, and now she grows stronger and stronger.'

I remembered the dreams I had had of a vague greyness, an animal scent, something unformed but uneasy. My sister, slowly gaining strength in the habitation of a dog in the Country of the Dead. I got out, 'And soon it – *she* – will be ready.'

Cecilia's mother didn't answer me. She didn't need to. Leo had told me about a badger baiting that had scarred him. That had been a lie, but this baiting would not be. Katharine wanted revenge. I would be put in a pit with this dog that was my mad sister. One-handed, unarmed, unable to cross over. The dog would leap upon me, and it would be as it had been with Straik, with the savage singer in the cottage at Almsbury, with all the maiming and killing I had seen such dogs do. Go for the throat, the eyes—

'Roger!' Cecilia's mother said. 'Drink this!'

Wine. I gulped it down. It did not steady me, but her gesture of kindness did. And I remembered my own practice with the rabbit, the deer, the swallow . . . If I could find any creature near the dog baiting, I could at least escape the pain.

I demanded, 'Is the place where I will die outdoors?'

She must have thought it an odd question, for her lined face wrinkled even more. 'Yes. Why?'

A rat, a bird in the sky above, anything at all. I said, 'I would prefer to die under the open sky.'

She answered nothing, because what could one say to that? For a long moment neither of us spoke. Then all at once words tumbled out of her, as if they had been kept inside a long time.

'When Queen Caroline sent word that she wanted a child from Galtryf to raise, a child with talent in the soul arts, I persuaded Lord Jago's father to send Cecilia. She was five years old. I have no talent, but my mother did. I lied and said I had seen the glimmerings of talent in Cecilia, and so she was taken to court. I wanted to get her away from here. The Brotherhood had just been formed, and had joined Soulvine Moor in its quest to live for ever. I thought my Cecilia would be safe at court in The Queendom.'

'Why did you not go yourself?'

'No one left Galtryf without permission, not even then when there were so many apprentices here, both web women and *hisafs*. Later there was the poison.'

Poison. 'Fia said—'

Her green eyes sharpened. 'You knew Fia?'

'Yes.'

'She, too, escaped Galtryf, but I don't know how. One

day she was just gone. How did she live without the antidote in her food every day?'

'She didn't,' I said flatly. The memory of Fia was almost as painful as that of Cecilia. 'She died of the poison.'

'Ah.' A soft, desolate syllable. 'Cecilia would have lived had she not been betrayed by Hemfree.'

'Why did Hemfree bring Cecilia back to Soulvine Moor?' For years I had puzzled over this. 'Mother Chilton trusted her to him!'

'Yes. But he had been turned by the Brotherhood. Mother Chilton did not know that. Hemfree, too, wanted to live for ever, and so he joined Galtryf and gave Cecilia to the Soulviners.'

'I would kill him if I could!'

She gazed at me, and I saw myself through her eyes: ineffectual, one-handed, doomed to be killed. I sounded inane, even to myself. But then another thought struck me.

'The poison – is it in the food here?'

'Yes, and the antidote. After a fortnight a person cannot leave here without dying.'

Her look said: *But you do not have that long.* She did not say it aloud. I said, 'Charlotte, Rawnie—'

She nodded sadly. 'Soon they will never be able to leave.'

'And my father?'

'He is here. But *hisafs* do not seem susceptible to the poison. It— Oh!'

The door unlocked and my jailer came in. He jerked his head at Cecilia's mother, who stood and walked towards the door. She risked only one sentence more, said back over her shoulder as if it mattered much to her. 'My name is Joan.'

'Get ye out,' the man growled. He looked at me then,

with the strangest combination of defiance, anger, and shame.

'And mine be Hemfree,' he said, and was gone.

That night was long. I could not sleep. Repeatedly I tried to cross over, but always I could not get past the grave. The mouse-woman had said she could not enter Galtryf unless she had changed to her soul-sharer while still within its walls; something blocked the soul arts in this place. Galtryf was a huge dark blockage that nothing external could pass.

But I was wrong. Dreams could pass. Towards morning I fell into fitful sleep, and somehow I knew even in sleep that this was one of the sent dreams, but sent neither by Stephanie nor by the dog which Katharine struggled to inhabit. In this dream all was blurry. No defined land-scape, but instead a meaningless swirl of colours. No figures, but instead a wavering form that might have been a person or a piece of furniture or a colourful tapestry. From this shifting blur came a sensation of need, of seeking something.

'What?' I said in my dream. 'What are you seeking?'

The answer came not in any clear voice, but in a sort of sing-song repetition, such as a parrot bird will use to speak words it does not understand. 'Where ... do ... they ... go?'

'Who? *Who*?'

More swirls of colours, somehow conveying distress. The swirls began to fade.

Where do they go? The same words Mother Chilton had spoken to me in Stephanie's dream. Then they had been clear and crisp, but no less puzzling. Where did who go? And why should I, imprisoned and soon to die horribly, have any knowledge about the matter?

'I don't care where anyone goes!' I shouted at the

156

retreating colours. They vanished, I woke, and Rawnie stood clutching the bars of my window and peering through them.

'Who are you shouting at, Roger?'

'What ... why ...'

'Wake up, lazy head, it's almost midday. Who were you shouting at?'

'I ... I dreamed.'

'Oh,' she said, without interest. 'Well, wake up. Your meal is coming. Joan is getting it now in the kitchen.'

'Rawnie,' I said, now fully awake, 'You must not eat the food here! It's poisoned!'

She considered this, her thin freckled face pushed as far between the bars as it would go. 'I ate food last night and I don't feel sick.'

'No, it takes a long time. You and Charlotte must not eat!'

'We have to eat or we'll die,' she said reasonably. 'Besides, we ate the exact same food as everybody else and they're not dead.'

'But—'

'There isn't anything else to eat,' she said impatiently. Clearly she didn't believe me about the food, preferring to trust her own observations. 'But listen, Roger, I don't have much time. I came to tell you things. First, Papa is here. I haven't found him yet but I'll make Leo tell me just where he is. Second, I'm going to rescue you.'

I stared at her.

'Don't look so doubting! I can come and go as I please here and—'

'You can? Can Charlotte?'

'No. Just me. I follow Leo around and pretend he's wonderful, so I'm not caged. Mama is and she doesn't like me gone from her, but Leo lets me out just to annoy her. Also—'

'Rawnie, Leo is dangerous. You can't—'

'Be quiet and listen! I don't have much time! I'm going to get a knife and bring it to you and – here he is!'

Leo appeared beside Rawnie. Instantly she turned her face towards his, and it was like a flower – or at least a small weed – turning to the sun. Leo smiled at her, condescending to accept her adoration, before unlocking the door.

'Good morrow, Roger. Did you sleep pleasantly?'

I stared at him in hatred.

'Perhaps not – you seem a bit out of sorts. Maybe breakfast will help.'

Joan entered, eyes downcast, and placed a tray on the table.

'That's all, Joan,' Leo said. 'You may go.'

She curtseyed to him and left without looking at me. Behind Leo's back, Rawnie rolled her eyes and made vomiting gestures.

'Eat well,' Leo said. 'A few days from now I will have a surprise for you.'

I glanced at Rawnie, who shrugged.

'Come, child. You can watch me groom my horse.'

'Oh,' she breathed, 'can I help? Please, Leo? I can learn so much from helping you! You know how to do everything!'

'If you're very good, you may help.'

She clapped her hands like a girl much younger than eleven. Wouldn't Leo, an actor himself, recognize her performance for what it was? Apparently not. His vanity outweighed his judgement, and he swaggered away with Rawnie at his heels.

Could she really find our father? Or bring me a knife? I would not put much past her. But I didn't see how a knife could help me. It would not hold off a dozen men, or even one, not when I had but a single hand to wield

158

it with. And I doubted I would be allowed to bring a knife into the pit against ... her. The dog. Katharine.

Don't let those pictures form in your mind.

My stomach growled. I gazed at the food, but on this Rawnie was right: there was nothing else to eat. So I ate the coarse, dense bread, the cheese made of sheep's milk, the summer berries. If there was poison in any or all of it, I didn't taste it. Afterwards I wanted to lie down on the straw and give myself to despair, but instead I made myself stand at my barred window and observe what I could. Watching the life of Galtryf from the shadows of my prison became both distraction and tutelage.

A girl, a green-eyed Soulviner dressed in tattered brocade and torn lace, drew water from the well.

Two men crossed the courtyard, deep in conversation.

Two more men mounted horses and clattered through the gate, accompanied by the pack of hunting dogs.

A rat scuttled from a hole in the keep wall to a different hole in a different wall.

Leo also scuttled across the courtyard. That's how it looked, his confident swagger replaced by a resentful hurrying. Lord Jago's voice pursued him, issuing mocking orders.

A cart pulled in, laden with casks and bundles. Women unloaded it and carried everything through a far door.

In late afternoon something changed. At least three dozen people, taut with excitement, assembled in the courtyard. The *hisafs* wore their usual wool tunics and breeches but the Soulviners were even more fantastically garbed than before in ragged gowns with court trains, moth-eaten hats with fresh feathers, soiled velvet doublets slashed over even more soiled cloth-of-gold. Glimpsed between the bars of my window, the strange parade seemed both solid and unreal, like faire puppets that disappear and reappear at the will of someone unseen. Leo, Jago, Tarf – none of them so much as glanced towards my cell.

A wagon pulled into the courtyard. Someone – the crowd blocked my view – was helped down from the wagon box. Everyone collapsed into curtseys and bows, and a murmur ran through the courtyard. Awe, respect – who was this? He or she vanished into a doorway and the entire gaudy, tawdry group dispersed.

The sun lowered in the sky and the shadow of the western wall, dark and cold, fell across the courtyard. Rawnie slipped through that shadow, furtive as a small animal.

'Here, Roger, take this, I have to go!' Something pushed through the bars, and she was gone.

A knife. Small, intended for bread, not sharp enough to even cut meat. The tiny shaving knife in my boot was more deadly. I wished I had back Tom's two knives, taken from me when I was captured. Since I didn't, I put Rawnie's knife into my other boot, trying to keep myself from either laughter or tears. She had tried.

I went back to my straw pallet, lay down, and gave myself to despair.

The next three days were much the same as the first. I watched from my cell, saw nothing of note, and was never taken out of my comfortable prison. Rawnie came and went, but she had no new information for me except that the new arrival was 'really really old'. She had not found our father. People passed through the courtyard, and it seemed to me that each day they looked more tense, more excited. Apprentice girls, not Joan, brought me my poisoned meals. They all curtseyed to me, and the curtseys were a mockery of what was already a mock court. I did not see Hemfree, nor Jago, nor Charlotte.

At sunset on the fourth day my door unlocked and Leo

stood there with a candle, which he ostentatiously lit. 'Now, Roger, you can see the surprise I promised you.' Another figure stood behind him, too tall to be Rawnie. The candle flared.

All at once the air went from my lungs and the strength from my limbs. My mouth fell open. Standing behind Leo was Maggie.

15

'Roger!' She rushed forward, threw her arms around me, sobbed once, then pulled back and hit me on the shoulder. 'You left me again!'

That had been a year ago. Before I could react, she had again collapsed against me, and her whisper in my ear was both urgent and frightened. 'Say nothing of the baby! Nothing!'

Over Maggie's shoulder my eyes met Leo's; his grin was nasty as always, but it did not seem to promise further cruelty. Maggie trembled against me, her belly flat. If the dream from Stephanie had been accurate, Maggie had given birth not very long ago. *Where was my son?*

Leo said, 'She's here to watch you die, Roger. You didn't think we knew that you had run off from court with a kitchen maid all those years ago, did you? A mistaken notion on your part. The Brotherhood knows everything.'

Against my shoulder, Maggie gave a tiny shake of her head.

Leo put his hands on his hips and surveyed us with a vicious smile. 'Such a touching reunion. I think I will leave you two alone for a while. That will make it all the more painful for her to witness what will be done to you.' Ostentatiously he banged the cell door closed and locked it, taking the candle with him.

I pulled Maggie to my straw pallet and lay with my

arm tight around her. My mouth moved against her ear. 'Are you all right?'

'Yes.'

'Is he … is he …'

She stirred against me, her mind quick as always, her voice low. 'How did you know it was a boy?'

'Too complicated to explain. Where is he?'

'Three strange women came for him, the night before these men took me … oh, Roger, they were witches!'

Web women. Relief washed over me like sunlight, and just as warming. If Mother Chilton had my son, he was as safe as was possible in what the world had become.

'It's all right, Maggie. The women come from Mother Chilton and—'

'Her!'

'You must trust me on this. They are the only ones who might be able to protect him.'

'How do you know?'

How to explain it all to her? There was so much, and she knew so little of it: the soul arts, my long history with Mother Chilton, all that Fia and Alysse and the mouse-woman had told me, the Brotherhood, the war that my father's *hisafs* were losing against Soulvine Moor. She knew nothing of Tarek, of Princess Stephanie's talent, of my dreams, of my mother. Most of all, she knew nothing of Katharine, the mad sister I had murdered who had crossed over into one of the misbegotten dogs born in the Country of the Dead. She knew nothing, and I did not want to take hours to tell her. I wanted to clasp her tight and hear about my son.

I repeated, 'You must trust me on this.'

But had she done so, she would not have been Maggie. 'Tell me! This is my child we are discussing!'

'And mine. Oh, Maggie, I have longed for you so! I love you, my sweetheart, and I have been The Queendom's biggest fool not to realize it before all this happened. If I could, I would ask you now to be my wife.'

That stopped her. She rose on one elbow and stared at me. In the gloom I could not see her face but I knew from hours of imagining how her wide eyes and the fair curls straggling over her forehead would look. She would be dirty from travel, eager with hope, sceptical with her own acerbic Maggie-scepticism. Never had I loved her more, now when it was almost too late.

She breathed, 'Lady Cecilia . . .'

'A boyish dream. Even if she were not dead, it's you I would want.'

Tears fell onto my face before I even knew they had filled her eyes. They tasted salty on my lips. But Maggie was Maggie still. She said, 'And you could not have realized all of this three years ago, when it might have done us some good?'

I pulled her towards me and kissed her. She gave a low, strangled gurgle that might have been sobbing, or laughter, or protest. If it were the latter, it did not last long. The last light faded from the cell. And finally, in the darkness of my last prison, I made love to Maggie as I should have long ago, with my whole heart, a fool no longer.

Only afterwards, as we lay close together in the darkness, did I remember her condition. I whispered frantically, 'Maggie! Should we have . . . you gave birth not so long ago!'

'I wanted to,' she said simply.

'But did I hurt you? Did anything . . . anything . . . .' I knew little of women's insides.

'I'm all right. I'm strong, Roger, and it was a very easy birth. The midwife would scarcely believe it was my first.'

All at once I was hungry for information about the

164

child I would never see. 'Tell me about him. Please. Everything.'

'He is beautiful. Strong, healthy. With your brown eyes but fair hair, although not much of that. He nurses well . . . oh, Roger, the women who took him promised a wet nurse but he needs his mother!'

There was nothing to say to that. 'What is his name?'

She hesitated. 'I know it's odd, but there was a friend of yours whom I treated badly even though he was only trying to help me . . . He brought me to you, or tried to, but I was so upset at the time that I never appreciated his kindness and so . . . well, I named the baby "Tom".'

All at once I saw Tom Jenkins, brash and kind and feckless, with his great height and his fresh blue eyes and his bright yellow hair. The only friend I had ever had, and I the cause of his death. He died helping me, as he had tried to help Maggie. My throat closed, but I managed to get out, 'How did the web women take the baby?'

This time she paused for a long time before answering. Painful memories. But Maggie could always face truth. 'It was at night. My sister had given us, Tom and me, a stall in the stable to sleep in. She counted me a disgrace to her, unmarried with a child. But the stable was warm and the Widow Lampthol, in the next cottage, had given me a blanket and bits of old furniture, so we were comfortable enough. Long before, Tom had brought me some baby clothes – I don't know from where – and I still had them. That night I heard my brother-in-law's horse neigh and stamp; it woke me. Moonlight came in the window and I saw three mice creep towards my pallet. Then all at once they turned into three women.'

Maggie shuddered at the memory – Maggie, who feared almost nothing! But she went on.

'One of the women was quite old, the other two mere girls. The old woman said that on the morrow some evil

165

men who could cross over into the Country of the Dead were coming to take away my babe. That little Tom had special talent, beyond even what his father had shown. How did they know who his father is, Roger?'

'I don't know,' I said, although I did. Mother Chilton would have told them.

'How did they become ... I know I saw them first as mice ... how do they ...'

'That I truly do not know.'

'I think,' she said, with a flash of her old tartness, 'that you know considerably more than you are telling me.'

'Later,' I said. 'Go on about the mice women.'

'They said that the men sought to kill my infant because he is yours, and that my only chance was to let them take him. I refused and picked up Tom and started screaming for help. And then – I don't know how it happened – everything went black. When I came to, I was alone in the stall and Tom was gone. But this was in my hand.'

She groped at her gown, still rucked up as high as her knees, and put something in my hand. In the darkness I couldn't see what it was. But I felt it: a willow whistle, with rough letters carved onto one side. I laid the whistle on Maggie's breast so that I could trace the carving with a finger on my one hand: JEE.

Maggie said with desperate hope, 'They might have stolen it from him – but who would bother to steal a whistle from a child? It wasn't stolen, was it? Jee sent it, so I would know it was good people who took Tom?'

'Yes, Maggie, yes. Jee is with Mother Chilton, and she sent the web women that took Tom.'

'That's hardly reassuring to me! I don't want our baby caught in those women's schemes!'

'Better their schemes than our prison here.'

That quieted her for a moment. Finally she said, 'Where

is Jee? He left The Queendom with you and Tom Jenkins
... where is Tom?'

'Tom is dead. Jee is at court with Princess Stephanie.'

Maggie caught her breath. 'With the princess? *Jee?* How
did that happen?'

'It's a very long tale,' I said.

'Tell me. All of it. Leave nothing out. Start with those
"web women" – how do they change into mice like that?'

'Maggie,' I said, with the same resistance I had always
felt to her probing. But now my resistance was untinged
with resentment. She was Maggie. She would always
question everything, and I would always resist, and that
was part of the preciousness of our bond. 'I cannot explain
the soul arts. I cannot explain my own talent. I cannot
explain even what I do know because we have no time.
But you must tell me this about our son. Did he ever
flicker in and out?'

'Did he ever *what*?'

'Flicker in and out of existence. One moment be in
your arms, the next moment vanish, the moment after
that return. Did he?'

'No.' Her tone said I had taken leave of my senses.
Unlike me, she had not seen the infant *hisaf* flickering in
and out of the Country of the Dead.

'Did he ever do anything unusual?'

'No! He is – was – *is* a normal baby, and so good,
he hardly ever cried ...' She was crying now, with the
desolation of bereavement.

And I was helpless. I could do nothing to restore our
son to her, or to rescue her from Galtryf, or to prevent
my own terrible death on the morrow. The web women
who might have saved us could not penetrate the blockage and corruption that was Galtryf. My father was as
imprisoned as I. His *hisafs* were losing the war with
Soulvine.

'Tell me all you do know,' Maggie said through her tears. 'Everything, from the time you left me.'

I began. But despite what she had told me, Maggie must have still been weak from childbirth, from her abduction to Galtryf, or from both. For the next moment she was asleep, despite her best inquisitive intentions. I pulled the blanket up over her and nestled her against me. If this was the last night of my life, it was also the sweetest, with her warm body in my arms and her living breath against my cheek, all the night long.

The next day they took me to the pit.

16

'Get up, Roger Kilbourne,' Leo said, unlocking my cell door. 'You too, slut.'

Maggie, who either woke quickly or was already awake, got wordlessly to her feet. The silence was so unlike her that instantly wariness penetrated my dread. What was she going to do?

'I said get up!'

Staggering to my feet, I glanced at Maggie. She held both hands at her sides, concealed in folds of her gown. I transferred my weight to the balls of my feet, shifting my feet in my boots. My knives were gone.

It burst out of me before I even thought: 'Maggie! No!'

Too late. She darted forward and thrust both pathetic knives, my tiny shaving knife and Rawnie's small trinket, at Leo's chest. Rawnie's 'weapon' missed. The shaving knife penetrated Leo's thick leather doublet about half an inch. He looked down at it, surprised, and gave a roar of laughter. His arm came up and, spindly though it was, knocked Maggie across the face hard enough to send her staggering sideways.

I was on him in a moment. My one hand slammed into his belly and doubled him over. But John came through the door and plucked me off Leo before I had gotten in more than the one blow. John, grinning, pinned me easily against his massive chest. 'Ye be peppery this morning, Roger?'

'Take ... him ... !' Leo gasped, his face purple with pain or rage or both.

Maggie hit John from behind with the wooden chair.

He turned ponderously, like a great millstone on its axle. If Maggie had been taller and able to reach his head, she might have felled him. As it was, the chair had crashed across his broad, muscle-padded shoulders and not even dazed him. One arm still pinned me; with the other he grabbed Maggie around the throat and squeezed.

'No! She ... must ... watch ... .' Leo wheezed. The words seemed to take a long time to reach John, as if they – or he – moved not in air but in some thicker substance, molasses or tar. Maggie's eyes bulged in their sockets and her feet kicked frantically, uselessly, against the floor. When John finally opened his fingers, she crumpled like a doll.

'Maggie!' I cried. 'Leo, let me ... please for sweet pity's sake ...'

'Take ... him ...' Leo said. The fury in his dark eyes did not even seem human. But as John dragged me from my cell, I saw that at least Maggie still breathed.

The courtyard was deserted. No maids at the well, no boys attending to horses, no Joan, head bent and figure hunched, hurrying on some errand in her enforced slavery. After my dim cell the light seemed blinding, even though the sky was grey with clouds. The wind smelled of rain. A gull wheeled overhead, crying. All my senses sharpened almost to pain, to blot out the pain of knowing I would soon die.

'Come,' John grunted when I sank to the ground. If I were an inert weight, maybe that would slow us down, postpone the inevitable, give me a few more precious moments to smell the wind and hear the gull ... *anything for a few more moments ...*

John picked me up as if I were a child, slung me over his massive shoulder, and trudged on.

We went out the gate and rounded the corner of the

castle, towards the rubble that was the rest of the ancient city. John picked his way over the rough ground. Clasped tight against his shoulder, I could see nothing, but I heard the sounds of many people. Shouts, murmurs, laughter. Someone called, 'Breathe your last, boy!' More laughter.

And so we came to the pit where I would die.

It had once been a large underground room, a guard-room or storage cellar, under the keep's vanished for-tifications. Now it stood open to the sky, its stone walls grown with moss and weeds. The bottom of the pit had been cleared of rubble, exposing the original stone floor. Above the walls a few broken pillars jutted into the sky like accusing fingers. John dumped me into the pit. I fell heavily, amid cheers from the people, Soulviners and Brotherhood alike, ranged around the two sides closest to the keep. They had dressed again in their 'finest': soiled silks and velvets and brocades whose tatters stirred in the breeze.

I rose to my feet and stared up at them, their jeering mouths and green eyes. Each person seemed etched against the grey sky, preternaturally clear. A young girl, lovely as Cecilia had once been lovely, her pink mouth twisted with hatred. Leo, recovered from my blow, watching with arms folded and bloodlust in his dark eyes. Hemfree, who had sold Cecilia in return for induction into the Brotherhood. Charlotte, tied to one of the stone pillars, weeping. Was Rawnie there, too? Would they make her watch this? I didn't see her, nor Joan either, and Leo was somehow fond of Rawnie so maybe he would excuse her from—

I saw my father.

He was tied to another pillar, far from Charlotte. I rec-ognized him instantly: the man I had met only once, in the palace dungeons last autumn. His was the older version of the face I saw whenever I had a mirror. He gazed at me with so much anguish that, for that moment at least, I could not hate him for his many abandonments of me. He made an odd motion of his mouth, and I knew what he was doing. He was biting his tongue, trying desperately to cross over. But none of us *hisafs* could cross over while in Galtryf, not even my father. Although with one last desperate effort, standing there in the bottom of the pit, I tried.

Darkness—

Cold—

Dirt choking my mouth—

Worms in my eyes—

Earth imprisoning my fleshless arms and legs—

The grave, stretching on and on, while the darkness that was Galtryf, heavier than the world, would not let me cross further, pressing on me until I went back.

'No path out that way, boy!' someone called to me, amid laughter and jeers.

Slowly the jeers quieted, giving way to murmurs. Heads turned. Someone else approached. I did not see him until he reached the edge of the pit, but I saw the crowd part for him. Women curtseyed, men bowed. Then he stood above me, an old man with a white beard, dressed in a long white robe, his face familiar if only I had had time to study it.

I had no time. My eyes darted around the pit, searching for some creature I could use. A rat, there must be a rat, people were now sitting on the edge of the pit and passing cheese and bread back and forth, picnicking on my coming death. Where there was food there would surely be rats. If I could find a rat, a rabbit in the brush above – anything! But even the birds seemed to have left the sky.

The people above shouted and pointed. Words drifted down to me.

'Here she comes!'

'—tear apart—'

'—finally ready—'

'—his blood—'

The crowd parted again. Jago appeared on the rim of the pit, holding the leash of a huge grey dog. Its green eyes met mine and it leaped forward, restrained only by the leash. Grey lips drew back over white fangs, sharp as swords. From deep in the dog's throat rose a sound that made the crowd draw back, and me turn cold and dumb.

Katharine. She was finally ready.

'We maun wait!'

'Hold her, my lord!'

'Blood—'

Jago could barely hold the dog. Two of his men leaped to help, pulling the animal back from the edge of the pit. Again I searched frantically for a rat, a bird, anything living in order to escape the pain, even if I could not escape death. An image flashed in my mind: myself, sitting quiescent and mindless in the Country of the Dead, until one of the Brotherhood dragged me into one of the circles consumed by a vortex from Soulvine Moor.

My father called something to me, of which I caught the despair but no words. He called again, but I didn't listen. Turning away from the terrible sight of Katharine-as-she-was-now, I spotted the moor cur.

It skulked in the brush on the other side of the pit from the ruined keep, attracted by the scent of food. No one looked in that direction; they all gazed at me or at the dog. I could see the moor cur only from the corner of my eye and only because I stood below it. It crouched in the shadow of rubble, waiting for scraps of offal or carrion.

Relief struck me so hard that my vision blurred. I did not have to endure being torn apart by the dog, did not have to hear my bones break nor feel my throat spurt blood. There was a way out – not from death, which none of us can escape for ever, but from the pain of this particular terrible death.

But I could not take it yet. If my body collapsed too soon, Jago and Leo might simply wait until I returned to it. I had no idea how long I could inhabit the moor cur – I could only hope that it might be long enough.

And still the killing did not start. The dog strained at its leash, my father strained at his bonds, Charlotte wept, the crowd grew restive. What were they waiting for?

A few moments later I had my answer. A Soulviner dragged Maggie to the edge of the pit and held her there.

For a long terrible moment I thought they would throw her in with me. But no, the man merely held her so that she, too, would be forced to witness my death. Her mouth moved but I could not hear the words; perhaps they could not issue from a throat still damaged by John's strangling her. I could not hear her words, nor make them out on her lips, but nonetheless I felt them. *I love you, Roger.*

Jago bent to release the dog from its leash.

It sprang forward, and for a long suspended moment as the dog hung in the air in its leap into the pit, it seemed to me that I saw Katharine in its eyes. Then I was gone, crossed into the moor cur.

Confused jerks of a foreign body, sharp scents on the air, fear fear fear run run run—

I was in the moor cur, and I was the moor cur. Growls from behind me: there was a *pack* out there. I was Roger, I was the moor cur ... why could I not gain complete control? I was Roger, Roger was in my pack, I was the moor cur and a dog attacked me—

Throwing back my head, I howled the signal, and we dashed towards the pit.

Roger's body lay limp on the stone, a grey dog circling and snapping at it. I smelled the dog's confusion, and into that confusion we attacked.

174

Shouts, screams, snarls ... some of the pack fled. But my jaws had closed on the dog's throat and my mate's on her belly. We bit and tore and the taste of blood was good was sickening was good I was Roger I was the moor cur ...

The crack of a *gun*. My mate fell to the stone. I leaped from the pit and raced away, flesh still in my jaws. More *guns*. They could not catch me ... but now the Galtryf hunting hounds raced after me, baying. They leapt over the remains of ancient walls, over piles of rubble, closer, *closer* ... The hounds were built for greater speed than I. Then the moor cur's mind was gone and I was Roger, myself, in the body of the moor cur, and death that I had just defeated was gaining on me once more.

No.

I had come this far, done this unimaginable thing. *No.*

The swiftest of the hounds now raced only a few yards behind me. Then his jaws snapped on my hindquarters. Pain flooded me. I had but one choice left. Using the pain, I willed my moor cur's body and my human mind, and I crossed over.

Darkness—

Cold—

Dirt choking my mouth—

Worms in my eyes—

Earth imprisoning my fleshless arms and legs—

And then I lay, panting, with my tail between my legs, on an empty plain in the Country of the Dead.

Hours passed before I could rise.

My cowering on the ground was not due to the moor cur's body, which had not been damaged badly by the dog's bite. It was Roger's mind – *my* mind – that kept me whimpering. There is only so much strangeness that can be tolerated at once. In the last few years my life had

175

been passing strange, but nothing such as this. Never anything such as this.

I inhabited a moor cur.

I had killed – for the second time – my half-sister.

I could not return to my body. It must still live – or I would not, in *any* form – but my body lay limp in Galtryf, where there was no crossing over in either direction.

Maggie was imprisoned in Galtryf, without our son.

I inhabited a moor cur . . .

Would Jago and Leo and the others realize what had happened? I thought not. They didn't know – no one knew – that the arts of the web women and those of the *hisafs* were not so far apart as either group, in their arrogance, imagined. I didn't think Jago would realize that I had crossed into the moor cur. More likely, they would assume that I had found some unfathomable way to penetrate the barrier that was Galtryf Keep and had crossed over as Roger, as myself. Not in body but in essence, as *hisafs* used to do. Perhaps they would try the same thing. Perhaps they would keep my body alive in the hopes that it might yield some clue about what I had done, and how. I could hope.

But if a *hisaf* walking in the Country of the Dead caught even a glimpse of a silver-backed moor cur, the Brotherhood might deduce the truth. I could not stay here, not this close to Galtryf. In fact, I could not stay at all in the Country of the Dead. The grey dogs were here, and they might scent me. I had to cross back over to the land of the living. Besides, my belly rumbled with hunger.

But first, there was something I must do.

Raising my head, standing erect on my four legs, I sniffed the wind. No scent of man. How did I know that? I don't know, but I knew it. The senses of the moor cur body were freely available to me, as were its limbs and jaws and ears that caught every sound. But of its mind, there was no trace. I could not feel it. For that, I was grateful. If I were to survive this most extreme strangeness, I needed all my wits, without distraction.

The body moved easily under my command. Every sense alert, I trotted back towards Galtryf, the centre of all strangeness.

On this side of the grave, it was not a castle at all. Instead of a ruined pile of stone, there loomed a ... a *darkness*. Denser than fog, the darkness seemed solid, and yet it shifted subtly as I watched from a safe distance – or what I hoped was a safe distance. Flecks of silver seemed to appear and then disappear in the blackness. My hackles rose. The thing reminded me powerfully of Queen Caroline's eyes: black with submerged flecks of silver, like the shifting of stones under dark water.

No longer did it seem so bizarre to me that a *hisaf* could not cross over from Galtryf Keep into this structure of darkness. The thing looked impenetrable. Solid yet shifting, neither alive nor dead, neither grave nor landscape ... I did not know what it was. Nor did I want to know. I wanted only to be away from it.

My moor cur's body ran so easily! I covered a few miles in a random direction, until the empty plain gave way to a copse of stunted trees. I lay, panting, in the shade. My hunger had worsened. But in the Country of the Dead there was nothing to eat, for neither man nor beast.

I crossed back over.

The same woods, although not the same tree. Now I lay under a stunted pine, bent by the wind from the sea, which seemed closer here. The coastline must be altered. My moor cur's ears pricked at the sound of distant waves. Salt wind blew in sharp gusts. A storm was blowing in from the sea.

A rabbit hopped across the moor beyond, stopped to nibble at some green shoots.

Nothing in me felt moved to follow it. But for the first time, I realized what eating would mean to me now. I, Roger, had none of the moor cur's desires, or its tastes. Yet unless I wanted to starve, I must chase game, must kill it with my mouth, must devour it raw ...

I could not do it. I was not a moor cur, I was a man! I could not hunt like an animal, feel a helpless living creature's blood fill my mouth, tear it apart.

Yet I had done so with my sister Katharine.

Something did not fit. I could remember killing her, but it was as if the deed had been done by someone else. And so it had. At that moment in the pit I had not been Roger Kilbourne but rather the moor cur. Just as in the moment I saw the female cur shot, I had been Roger, and so felt no mourning for the moor cur's mate. Evidently I could shift back and forth.

Again my belly ached with hunger.

Cautiously I ventured from under the pine tree. The rabbit still nibbled on its shoots. It had not scented me; the wind blew in the other direction. I felt for the moor cur's mind beside mine, but could not find it. Instead I willed my own to recede, using the same well image that had brought me here. But I must not crouch all the way back inside the well or I would be back in my limp, tranced body in Galtryf. Picture Roger glancing back towards the well, thinking of climbing back in, of abandoning this brain to the beast that it had originally—

I found myself in the Country of the Dead.

It took several more tries to get it right, while the wind blew harder and dark clouds raced in from the sea. Eventually I could control the crossings between the land of the living, the Country of the Dead, and the mind of the moor cur. By that time the rabbit had long gone, but I glimpsed a grouse seeking the cover of its nest in the bracken. I shifted my mind – for such it felt – to the back of the moor cur's brain.

The moor cur shot forward in pursuit of the bird, and caught it. With greed and satisfaction it tore the grouse apart and ate. I was there, too, but at a great distance, as if I were witnessing any bestial killing that had nothing to do with me. And when the moor cur had finished eating, I once again took command of it.

Strangeness indeed. The bloody feathers blowing across the moor now sickened me. But there was no time for squeamishness; the storm began. Rain pelted me hard, mixed with hail. I ran back towards the little wood, until another sound froze me to taut stillness.

Someone cried out.

The growl deep in my throat was involuntary; perhaps I was not as in command of the moor cur as I thought! But I, Roger, realized this was not the cry of a hunter, nor even of a man. My ears swivelled to find the woman over the keening of the wind and the smashing waves below the cliffs.

It was scent that eventually found her, not sound. And it was not a woman. She lay crumpled on the moor, soaked through, curled into a mewling ball that looked even more frightened when I appeared above her. It was Rawnie.

17

Terrified though she was, she would not have been Rawnie if she had not tried to attack. As I loomed above her, she pulled a carving knife, considerably more substantial than the one she had brought to my cell, and thrust it at me. A moor cur is much quicker than a child. I danced away.

'I'll kill you, I will!' she screamed over the wind. 'Go away!'

I smelled bread, cheese, terror. How does a moor cur tell a child that he is not a moor cur? Rawnie had no soul arts to guide her to the truth – she had, after all, carried around a web woman guised as mouse for months and had never known it. Now she backed away from me, waving the knife feebly, sodden and screaming curses. Hail pelted her. When she tried to stand, she toppled over in a faint.

Carefully I took the neckline of her gown in my teeth and tugged. The cloth was tightly woven and substantial; Rawnie's pack had included but two dresses and Charlotte had sewn them to endure. I dragged Rawnie across the short stretch of moor to the relative shelter of the stunted trees. Then I went back for her little bundle. The faint had turned seamlessly into deep sleep. I lay atop her to keep her warm with my animal heat. There was no more I could do. If her bundle contained the means to build a fire, I could not use them.

After a short time she woke, screamed, and shoved at me. I had had time to plan. I leaped off her, picked up her pack, and laid it at her feet. Still screaming, Rawnie groped frantically for her knife, taking a full minute to realize that a moor cur does not ordinarily bring belongings to a shrieking child.

Rawnie stopped shrieking. The wild burst of rain had also stopped. In the sudden silence under the dripping pines, we looked at each other. I touched my front paw to the ground once, stopped. Twice, stopped. Three times, stopped.

Her eyes grew enormous. She shivered, with either fear or cold. But neither could stay her tongue for long. She whispered, 'Are you a *witch*?'

I moved my head from side to side: *No*. The motion felt stiff and odd in this moor cur's body.

'Are you a dog *hisaf*?'

No.

'Then what the by damn piss-pots *are* you?'

There was no way to tell her, or at least no way I could think of. And her fertile mind had darted on. 'Where is my *knife*?'

I trotted out of the copse and onto the moor, found the knife, and mouthed it gently by the handle. When I dropped it at her feet, she seized my neck and looked deeply into my eyes.

'You're a person, aren't you? I heard Mama talking once with Papa, they thought I was upstairs asleep, they said that some witches can change to . . . I didn't believe them. Daddy likes to tease, to tell me things that aren't true to see if I can figure them out, but . . . *are* you a witch?'

No.

'You're not lying to me?'

No.

'I better not discover you're lying to me!'

No. My neck was getting tired of shaking side to side.

'But there is a person in there, yes? You're really a person?'

Yes!

'Are you Papa?'

No.

'Leo?' She scowled. 'Because if you're Leo, I'm going to slice you into little pieces!'

No.

'Lord Jago?'

No.

'Well, I know you're not Joan 'cause she can't leave Galtryf or she'll die. She told me. She was here way too long, years and years, and if you stay that long you can't leave. She set me free, though, so that she "does not lose yet another child to evil". That's what she said, but I don't know what it means. So you're not Joan?'

No. If there is anything odder than playing Trumpet-The-Name with a shivering child while trapped in the body of a moor cur, I hope I never encounter it in this life or the next.

Rawnie frowned. 'I must make a fire, I'm so *cold*, damn there's no dry wood anywhere ... go fetch, boy! Find some dry wood!'

I was not a dog. Rage filled me that she, my little half-sister whom I had just rescued from freezing, should try to use me as one. That she considered a fire more important than my identity. That this damp and helpless child should be my only ally in impossible circumstances. My lips pulled back over my teeth, a low snarl escaped the back of my throat, and remorse for both of these made me lie down and whimper.

Rawnie said, '*Roger?*'

There is apparently more than one way to trumpet one's name.

*

By evening we had made camp. I had led Rawnie across the moor to the shelter of a shallow crevice in the side of a tor, beside a stream. With dry gorse twigs she laboriously built a fire. Never once did she stop talking.

'I'm so cold, how much farther, Roger, it's so weird to call you "Roger" when you're a moor cur, I wish you could tell me how you got that way, do you think Mama misses me? I thought Papa would rescue us at Galtryf but I never even saw him so I guess he wasn't there although Leo said he was but Leo lied a lot, I'm so cold! Oh, dry twigs, well it's not all dry, is that the best you can manage? It's a little wet where you slobbered on it, I suppose it's hard carrying things only with your mouth, Roger how *did* you get to be a moor cur? The bad *hisafs* can only become dogs and then only on the other side. I'm not supposed to know that. I used to tease Papa to take me to the other side but he never would, I wasn't even supposed to know about it but of course I do, and anyway Straik took me that one time, they treat me like a small child, I'm almost twelve already, by damn I'm cold! Oh, there goes the kindling, it's caught now, you may have to bring more wood, only don't slobber on it this time, all right? The fire feels so good, are you afraid of fire now that you're a moor cur? No, I guess not, there you are lying beside it, Roger are you going to stay a moor cur for ever? Are you?'

I lay close to the fire and willed her to shut up. It did not work.

'When my clothes are dry I'll fill the waterbag from the stream, Joan gave it to me along with the knife and those other things, she was crying when she helped me escape from Galtryf. I said I wouldn't go without Mama but Joan said that Mama would want me to escape and I guess that's true. Joan said three times that she would not lose another child to evil, I wish I knew what she meant, but once she called me "Cecilia". Roger, do you know who Cecilia was?'

For the first time, I was glad I could not speak.

'I guess not, after all none of us ever met Joan before and you were in your cell, they brought your wife to you, didn't they, or is she just your lover? She's not as pretty as Mama. I saw her ride in on a wagon, even though by then Leo had me locked upstairs in this smelly stone room, that's where Joan let me out of while everyone was somewhere else in the keep, I think something was happening but Leo said I should not see it. I wish you could tell me what I missed! Joan said my best chance was to walk south across the moor and hide if I heard anyone, until I reached the Unclaimed Lands and could find someone to help me rescue Mama. But something wasn't right, Roger. I know you can't just stroll into a stranger's house and organize a rescue. Joan said that only so I would be willing to leave Mama and save my own life, because Jago did not intend to let any of us live long. He had the death-look on him – not his death, but the kind of man who loves death for other people. So I left, and I left Mama, and ... oh Roger, should I not have? Did I desert her? Am I coward?'

She burst into tears.

It had not occurred to me that this spoiled, loquacious child could have her own doubts besetting her. Like most of the world, I had underestimated Rawnie. All I could do now was lay my head in her lap. She clutched my dirty fur and sobbed until she was cried out, then turned brisk and practical. All at once she reminded me of Maggie.

'Well, crying doesn't help, does it? We need to go on. The bread Joan gave me is all wet and ruined, but the cheese is still good. Do you want some? Do moor curs eat cheese?'

No. I left her gnawing on a large chunk of yellow cheese and made my way back to the moor. There I shifted into the cur, caught and killed a fawn, and ate until my belly felt like a hard taut drum. No scent of man came to me on the wind. When I returned, Rawnie was asleep by the fire. I lay beside her, sleepy myself from exertion and food, but also filled with anxiety for Maggie. What would Jago do with her now that I had gone?

Eventually I slept, and the dream that had deserted me in Galtryf came again. The same blurry swirl of colours, *although not so blurry as before. Stephanie, too, seemed clearer, her thin little face pinched and drawn, although her gown was merely a shifting swatch of purple. 'Roger,' the princess said, 'where do they go?'*

'Where do who go?' I tried to say, but no words came.

Stephanie looked puzzled. 'Roger?'

Then someone else was there, someone more solid, a source of comfort and food – how could that be? Mother Chilton had never fed me, not even once. How could she, I was only a moor cur – it was not Mother Chilton but rather someone else and—

Then I was awake, lying close to Rawnie in order to warm her, and the stars had come out to shine through a small break in the trees. It was not yet dawn. I did not know what the dream meant. Where did who go? But the dream had nonetheless served a purpose. It decided me where *I* must go, which was to Mother Chilton, in the palace at Glory. She was the only other person who might recognize me for what I was. She knew my whole history. She knew where my son was. She was my only possible help in rescuing Maggie.

Rawnie slept on. I sat beside her, scratched my haunch with my hind leg, sniffed the wind.

'Everything has a cost, Roger Kilbourne – when will you learn that?' But no cost was too great to get Maggie out of Galtryf. My last sight of her had been of her held above

the pit, forced to watch me die, her sweet body bruised with her effort to save me. Maggie, my love and my life. I would do anything, risk anything. Galtryf was a fortress, but a ruined one; the Brotherhood was an army, but a scattered one. And within Galtryf no *hisaf* could exercise his gift. Inside the keep, the Brotherhood were merely men. Therefore, Galtryf could be taken by a relatively small army of soldiers.

Where was I going to get even a relatively small army?

There was only one possible place: Glory. Mother Chilton was in the capital, teaching Princess Stephanie, and with her was that whole shadowy web of women who practised the soul arts. She had always helped me. She would help me now.

She must.

'No,' Rawnie said.

She had woken cold and cross. As she ate Joan's provisions, offering me none, she appeared on the edge of tears. I gazed at her helplessly. Even as a man, I would not have known how to handle Rawnie. She was a child, with a child's need for bed, dinner, warmth, safety. And I was a moor cur.

'I won't go anyplace with you until you tell me where it is! I have to rescue Mama. I can't just leave her there with Leo and Lord Jago!'

I barked at her.

'Oh, stop that stupid noise! I can't understand you, Roger. Where do you want to go? Here, draw it in the dirt – you can at least do that, can't you?'

With a half-consumed stick from the remains of the fire she scraped the forest floor clear of leaves. I put out a tentative paw, tilted so that only one of my claws touched the dirt, and drew ... what? A wobbly tower with a triangle-shaped flag on top of it.

'A boat? You want us to find a *boat*? With you like that?'

I scratched a lopsided ring around the tower: the wall around the island of Glory.

'A boat in a little pond? What good will that do?'

A snarl of frustration burst from my furry throat.

'Well, don't growl at me, it's not my fault you're a stupid moor cur! Try again. And clearer!'

I scratched a crude crown, and Rawnie caught her breath.

'A crown! You want to go to court!' And then, 'But why?'

It was far beyond my powers to draw an army.

'No, wait, I can guess! You were at court once, weren't you? Mama told me, although she wouldn't tell me what you did there, only that you lost your hand in a fight. I was so jealous, Roger, I never got to go anywhere! So you must have been a soldier at court, yes? And you have soldier friends who will help us get Mama! All right, that makes sense. Except for one thing ... I really have no finery to wear at court. This dress will not do.'

I stared incredulously as she fingered her plain, soiled gown. Nothing to wear? But she was a child, and a girl, and the only girl children I had known were Stephanie, always garbed as a princess by hands other than her own, and Katharine, who had been mad. If I could have been said to 'know' Katharine at all. Nothing to *wear*?

'Well, it matters not,' Rawnie finally pronounced, getting to her feet. 'I daresay some of your soldier friends have wives who can clothe me properly. Only we must hurry, you know. Court is probably a fair walk from here.'

It was at least two weeks' walk, perhaps three, for a

child. My heart shrivelled. My plan – if it even deserved that name – was stupid. By the time we reached Glory, my body back in Galtryf would have died from lack of food and water, and so I would die, too. Never had I left myself in trance to cross over for more than a few days. Perhaps I, running as a moor cur, could make it to Glory in that time. But Rawnie could not.

But once more I had underestimated her. 'Come on, Roger,' she said, hoisting her little pack. 'We need to reach some farmhouse or village where I can steal a horse.'

She found one by early afternoon, following the smoke that drifted high above the moor from a chimney. We had travelled northwest, away from Galtryf and towards the Unclaimed Lands, and had seen no one. No one was looking for us. The Brotherhood would be searching for me in the Country of the Dead. If Leo knew yet that Rawnie was missing and not merely hiding somewhere within the keep, he would probably assume her dead on the moor, prey to the same mad pack of rabid moor curs that had killed Katharine.

'You stay here,' Rawnie told me, from the cover of a low tor. 'If that horse scents you, it will probably neigh or bolt or skies-know-what. I can do this.'

I shook my head, the gesture still feeling as unnatural as it had yesterday.

'Yes, I can,' she said irritably. 'Nobody ever thinks I can do anything! But Papa taught me all about horses.'

Nobody had taught her about tracking. She was no Jee, who was her age but who had grown up in the Unclaimed Lands and could move through woods and fields so stealthily that he was barely glimpsed. Rawnie crouched, but anyone glancing from the window of the small hut would have seen her barrelling across the open space to the barn. No one glanced. In fact, I could scent no trace of man, despite that smoke, and all at once my ears flattened and my hackles rose. The hut was surrounded by no fields, no sheep pens, no byres. It was not a farmstead but a way station, maintained for travellers who needed a bed, a meal, and a change of fast horse. The only such people I could imagine on this desolate moor were those engaged in the hidden war of Soulvine and the Brotherhood against my father's *hisafs*.

I almost sprinted after Rawnie. Someone was in that hut or there would not be smoke drifting above it. What if they had dogs? But Rawnie was right: any closer and I would scare the horse whose scent twitched in my nostrils. Taut with indecision, I watched her unlatch the barn door and slip inside.

A minute passed. Two. Five. Did the smoke burn thicker, as if someone inside and awake had thrown more peat on the fire? No, it was only my fear misjudging the smoke. *Come, Rawnie, come back—*

She did, bursting from the barn on a huge brown charger, looking small in the saddle. The horse's hoofs thudded on the ground. 'Go!' Rawnie screamed at me, even as the charger shied away from me and the hut door burst open. Rawnie kept her seat as the horse thundered past me. I heard the crack of a *gun*, accompanied by shouts I couldn't distinguish. Then we were racing across the moor.

When she finally pulled up her mount, Rawnie's face shone with triumph. She laughed aloud, while the horse pawed the ground and rolled its eyes at me. 'We did it!' Rawnie cried. Her teeth flashed in laughter; her straggling braids danced. She easily held the horse in check; evidently our father had taught her well.

He had never taught me anything at all.

When she was done laughing and gloating, Rawnie

leaned down to me from the saddle. 'Which way, Roger? Which way to court?'

Sullenly I trotted off, leading the way northwest, towards The Queendom. Away from Maggie, trapped at Galtryf Keep.

18

By evening we reached the border between Soulvine Moor and the Unclaimed Lands. After this, progress would be slower as we left the open moor and took the rough tracks down through the mountains. Rawnie slid from her saddle. Her mood had changed, from elation to weariness and fear. How much did she know about making camp? I could not even ask her.

At least she could make a fire. 'I have only a little cheese left, Roger,' she told me petulantly, 'so you can't have any. And what am I supposed to eat when that's gone?'

I thought of Jee, her age, but able to snare game and find edible plants. I thought of Tom Jenkins, the best woodland tracker I had ever seen. I thought of Fia and Maggie, both competent women able to care for themselves and everyone else. But Rawnie was not a woman; she was a spoiled child about to cry, or rage, or both. How was I going to feed her?

'My legs hurt,' she said. 'I'm not used to riding any more!'

Nor I to being a moor cur.

'And *you're* no help,' she said spitefully. 'If I didn't need you to bring back an army for Mama, I'd just get on my horse and leave you, Roger Kilbourne!'

At that moment, I wanted her to.

'Where are you going? Don't leave me, you piss-pot!'

I trotted back and lay beside her, resentful and miserable. Rawnie knotted her hand in my neck fur. Within three minutes she was asleep by the dying fire.

I trotted past the horse, tied to a tree and hungrily cropping whatever grass it could find. During the long day's ride it had grown more accustomed to me. A half mile away, I shifted from Roger to the moor cur, hunted and ate, and returned to Rawnie. When I slept, I again dreamed of Princess Stephanie, this dream marginally less murky than the last: *'Where do they go?'*

I didn't know. Not where, not who, not anything.

The second day we crossed the entire Unclaimed Lands, Rawnie on that superb, tireless horse. She raced past the few travellers we encountered before they could question her. I kept pace, hidden in the woods. With daylight both Rawnie's hunger and her natural toughness had returned. She ate some wild berries and a few nuts, but by evening she was ravenous. And at evening we crossed into The Queendom and came to our first farming village.

'You stay here,' she said to me. 'You'll be no good to me in this place, Roger. Watch my horse.'

What?

She tied the horse to a tree within a grove by the small river that ran through town. I danced around her, frustrated beyond belief by my inability to tell her anything. Or, short of biting her, to keep her from doing anything. With a last contemptuous glance, Rawnie left me and walked towards the village. She knocked on the first door she came to, a prosperous looking cottage with thatched roof, dormer windows, roses and hollyhocks growing by the well tended path. A woman opened the door, stout and middle-aged. I could not hear what was being said. But after a few moments the woman grabbed Rawnie, pulled her inside, and closed the door.

What had Rawnie told her? I could guess. A lost or abandoned child, hungry and dirty, looking piteous ...

perhaps the little liar said she'd run away from a wicked uncle, or been abducted by bandits, or whatever else that fertile brain could concoct. She would have widened her eyes and squeezed out a few tears. Probably right now Rawnie sat in a warm kitchen cosy with firelight, gorging on ham and preserves and fresh bread. Why had I assumed that Jee's and Maggie's way of caring for oneself was the only way?

Maggie. Our son. Both were a constant pounding in my mind, like the drumbeat during battle. And all I could do was skulk here in the shadows, as mired in being a moor cur as once I had been mired in being a fool.

Sometime before morning, a sharp scent brought me from my fitful sleep.

A man appeared on the road, not twenty feet from my hiding place. One moment he was not there, and the next he was. A *hisaf* crossing back over.

And then another. And another. And one more. Their smell filled my nostrils.

Had they come for Rawnie? But the four, not talking, walked briskly away from the outlying cottage and towards the cluster of those around the village green. Each chose a different dwelling, stood by the barred kitchen door, and vanished. All at once I understood.

They had crossed back to the Country of the Dead, where each would take a few steps and then cross back over to appear within the kitchens of those cottages containing infants. I stood, trembling. But there was nothing I could do. Soon the men had all reappeared outside, each carrying a sleeping child. One man carried two, twins born to some woman whose grief would shatter the dawn. The men took the children a short way down the road and then all four *hisafs* vanished. Gone to that other, larger circle on the other side, where the hapless

193

Dead would be sitting around a spinning vortex.

There was nothing I could do.

The *hisafs* reappeared. They laid the babes in a circle in the road. After the men had once more disappeared, I crept towards the infants. All five lay as if among the Dead: quiescent, mindless, neither animated nor decaying. One lay wrapped in a yellow blanket woven with cheerful daisies, hours and days and weeks of loving work by some woman who cherished this child.

'Don't you understand, Roger?' Mother Chilton had said to me. *'Don't you understand what Soulvine Moor is doing? When power flows along the threads of the web of being, when it is made to flow unnaturally from death back to life, there must also be a flow in the opposite direction. Or else the whole web will become more and more disturbed, until it is destroyed. There are terrible times coming, more terrible than you can imagine.'*

I was looking now at those times. When, on the other side, that circle of Dead had vanished into the vortex of watchers from Soulvine Moor, the life force of these babies had been drawn into the Country of the Dead to balance what had been taken by Soulvine Moor.

A light came on in the closest cottage. A woman screamed. She had found an empty cradle.

I sprinted for the shadowy trees, reaching them just as the first door was flung open and the first cottager tore out. In a few moments came the entire terrible scene I had witnessed twice before: distraught parents discovering their babies, cottagers running from door to door, wailing and shouting, the parents almost as mindless in their grief as the infants they cradled in their arms.

To my intense relief, Rawnie, too, came running from the outlying cottage. 'What is it? What happened?'

No one had time to answer her. She stood, barefoot and dressed in a white nightshirt too big for her, staring at the closest of the babies. I didn't know how much she understood, how much Charlotte had told her or she had overheard in her incessant eavesdropping. Expressions came and went on her freckled face: horror, curiosity, horror again. Did she realize that soon someone would cry out 'Witchcraft!' That all strangers would become suspect?

I could not go to her. Not even when she turned and ran back inside the cottage. She didn't understand, didn't guess, had been too sheltered all her life by Charlotte and our father, who had never sheltered me—

She ran out of the cottage, still in the nightdress but carrying her little pack, just as the first man cried, 'Someone did this! A witch!'

Rawnie ducked behind a stand of hollyhocks and rose bushes.

Men shouted now, torn between grieving and organizing. The outrage built, the human need to find someone to blame, to avenge themselves on. Rawnie was just a little girl, would these men dare—

Cat Starling had been but a girl, and a half-wit, when she had been burned as a witch.

Rawnie was no half-wit. I watched as she moved stealthily away from the cottage, darting from the shadow of rose bushes to the deeper shadow of a willow, crouching behind the well house. The men still stood shouting at each other in the middle of the road. Another few minutes and one dashed towards that farthest cottage, but Rawnie had already gained the grove, appearing beside me in her white nightshirt, looking as insubstantial as marsh light on the Moor.

'Come, Roger, why are you waiting stupidly like that? We must leave!'

We ran through the woods, and the crashing attracted the men's attention. 'This way! Someone is there!'

In the clearing there was no time for Rawnie to fasten

the saddle on the startled horse. She slipped the reins from the tree where she had tethered him, climbed on with the aid of a low-hanging limb that nearly broke under her weight, and clattered away bareback. The woods were thin, and even as the men reached the clearing, she had guided the horse through the trees and onto a field of barley, where she whipped it into a gallop.

I raced behind her. Another minute to reach the road at a point well beyond the village. The horse was fresh; they would never catch us. When Rawnie finally pulled the animal up to let it rest, just as the sun broke over the horizon, I saw her face. She was crying so hard she could barely see.

'Stupid Roger! Why couldn't you have warned me? Didn't you guess they would blame that on me? That . . . that . . . whatever somebody did to those babies! Mama always said I must never do anything that anybody could think of as witchcraft, even stupid people – you're the stupid people, Roger! You're supposed to protect me! Oh, those poor babies . . . what happened to them? What? But you don't know, you're a stupid moor cur!'

She went on like that for several minutes, taking out on me her fear and horror. I understood. And even if I had not, what could I have done about it?

Finally she calmed enough to look around her. We were on a desolate section of road, here barely more than a cart track between distant villages, heading northwest. Rawnie didn't know where we were, but I did. Two more days' hard travel would carry us through The Queendom to the capital, Glory, on the broad and placid River Thymar.

Would my body back in Galtryf last another two days? What if it died before I reached Mother Chilton?

'This was a stupid idea,' Rawnie said. 'Nobody is going to give me an army to rescue Mama!'

I swung my head from side to side: *No.*

'You even agree with me!' Rawnie cried, and I swung my head again, harder: *No, I don't!* But my supposed disagreement had fired her up again. She needed to feel angry. It strengthened her.

'Stupid Roger! They *will* give me an army – I'll make them give it to me! Why are you always so disagreeable? I hate you!' And she was gone, spurring the horse with her bare heels, her braids flying angrily behind her. All I could do was try to keep pace. And to keep hope.

Travel all day, with a brief early stop to eat, the food stolen from the cottage of the night before and hidden in Rawnie's pack. She changed from the nightshirt into her filthy dress and stout little boots. The horse looked strained, and she soothed it and rubbed it down and found sweet grass and water for it, but none of that helped much. Villages became closer together. We developed a rhythm: trot between villages, race through them before anyone could stop or question us. The summer weather was warm and sweet, and Rawnie looked with longing at children playing on village greens, girls drawing fresh water from cool wells, a farmer carrying an immense wheel of yellow cheese along the road to some neighbour or market. But she did not stop. That, too, I understood: if she stopped, despair might take her.

By evening, however, the horse could go no further. I thought that Rawnie could not, either, despite her desperate bravery. She slid from the saddle and crumpled to the ground. 'By damn!' she said, somewhere between a sob and a snarl. 'My stupid legs!'

You're unaccustomed to a full day of riding, I wanted to say, and could not. When I lay down beside her, she pushed me away. 'Go! Who wants a stupid moor cur for company!'

She did, despite what she said, but not just now. I stalked along the edge of the stream she had chosen to camp beside, and stared at the water. It reflected the rising moon, a long swath of silver on the dark water. An owl hooted in branches above. On the opposite bank a brown rabbit appeared, twitching its nose, and I prepared to shift my mind and hunt.

The rabbit became a woman dressed in a gown of rough brown wool.

I blinked and peered, but I was not mistaken. A girl stood there, beckoning to me. One of the web women. So all this time we had been carrying a marker – what? It could have been anything, put into Rawnie's pack by the mouse-woman. I should have thought of this earlier. If I had not been a moor cur, I would have cried from relief. Rawnie and I were not alone. Mother Chilton knew where we were, and what I was now.

The reflection of the moon dissolved as I splashed across the shallow stream. The girl knelt to bring her face level with mine. No more than eighteen and very pretty, she gazed at me with neither a smile on her pink lips nor warmth in her dark eyes. 'Roger, I am here from Mother Chilton.'

My son? What of my son?

'She – all of us – are astonished at what you have done.' Her voice, however, held not astonishment but disapproval. 'It was not thought possible that a *hisaf* could cross into a living being here, in the land of the living. You are untutored in the soul arts and should not have been able to do this.'

What of my son?

'I am sent to tell you that no other *hisaf* must see you like this. If the Brotherhood knew that what you have done is even possible ... .' She shuddered in the moonlight, and I wanted to bite her. More reproaches from yet another web woman, and all I wanted to know about was little Tom.

'You understand that, don't you?' she went on. 'If the Brotherhood begins crossing into animals here, we will surely lose this war. We are already losing it. Do you think you are some variety of hero, creating what could be yet another weapon for Soulvine Moor? And the number of children taken by the Brotherhood grows and grows, and we don't understand how that can be without destroying the Country of the Dead, as you yourself once nearly destroyed it. Oh, why is everything so monstrous?' she cried, and I realized she must be younger than eighteen. The cry was the wail of a terrified child. Had Mother Chilton's forces become so depleted that she must enlist children?

It was a stupid thought. This war had always enlisted children. Stephanie. Jee. Katharine. Rawnie. My son.

What of my son?

The web girl jerked her head sideways to peer back over her shoulder. I strained my senses but could detect nothing. She said hurriedly, 'I must go. But listen well, Roger Kilbourne. Let no *hisaf* see you like this, no matter which side you believe him to be on. Mother Chilton will meet you at the junction of the Rivers Thymar and Albustrine at dusk tomorrow night. If you hurry, you can be there by then. I must go!'

I bit the hem of her gown and held on, growling deep in my throat. She looked startled, then angry. 'Let that free! Oh, yes, your son is safe with us. Now stop you – I must go!'

A brown rabbit stood before me, and the next moment had raced into the brush.

I still could not see what had prompted her to leave. No scent came to me, no sound. Unless it was the owl hooting in a distant pine, but I did not think so. The web women, as always, shared as little knowledge as possible with *hisafs*, even me. Perhaps especially with me.

When I returned to camp, Rawnie was nearly asleep. She raised her eyelids to half-mast and said scornfully, 'You were gone long enough. And why are you all wet? Don't lie next to me!'

I growled at her, lay down, and tried to remember where the River Thymar met the Albustrine. *'Do you think you are some variety of hero, creating what could be yet another weapon for Soulvine Moor?'* the web girl had said. I did not feel like a hero. Or, if this be heroism, I would rather it had fallen to someone else. Anyone else.

And the next day, I wished it even more.

19

With hard travel that strained my every muscle, left the horse covered in foam, and made Rawnie cry out every time she slid from her mount to crumple to the ground, we reached the place of two rivers by dusk the next day. No one was there.

'Roger, why did you push me so hard?' Rawnie said. 'I can barely feel my legs. And I'm so hungry! Why, Roger? This place looks no different from anywhere else!'

Petulance and weariness blinded Rawnie; this place *was* different. We had travelled by fields and woods, leaving the main road until we'd reached the Albustrine, a swift small river frothing with silvery rapids. Then we had followed the river. The Albustrine was too shallow for boats, and so the countryside had been peopled only with far-flung farms and the occasional mill village, all easily avoided. As it neared the Thymar, the Albustrine flowed wider and slower and then, with a last tumble of small waterfall, joined the great river.

I stood on its south bank. Broad and slow, the Thymar was the main navigation route for The Queendom, and tonight the moon was full and the air warm. In the blue twilight lighted barges glided downriver as silently as stars. The barges would be empty, having left their rich cargoes of vegetables, meat, wine, cloth, artisan works at the island capital of Glory.

Above me a great willow dipped its branches into the water. Across the river a few barges made for shore to tie up for the night, but none would choose this place.

Beyond this bank the land made a shallow shelf, thick with reeds and cattails and sedge. Only a small, light boat could reach my hidden place under the drooping willow.

Small craft were out there among the barges, everything from boys in leaky wherries, hooting at every passing vessel, to the sumptuous pleasure barges of the quality. On such a boat, thick with cushions and graced with musicians, had Cecilia and her friends passed summer evenings on the river.

Cecilia. Was her mother being punished for having helped Rawnie to escape Galtryf? That ruined, grey pile of rock seemed another country from the River Thymar. Yet it was Galtryf that so lethally threatened the prosperity and peace spread out before me on the river.

My nose twitched. A small skiff, without lights, glided through the reed-choked water towards me. Someone guided it with a pole, someone I could see only in silhouette, someone seemingly too small for the task. Behind me Rawnie still complained; above me a mourning dove gave its low single note. Frogs jumped from hummocks into the river, away from the skiff. It neared the bank and through the blue dusk I saw that the poleman was Jee.

He had grown since I saw him last, but not by much. Across ten feet of water we stared at each other, boy and beast. Jee wore rough riverman's garb with high boots, but not as if accustomed to it. For more than half a year now he had been at the palace, page to the young queen.

'Roger,' he said to the moor cur on the bank, and it was not a question. I could smell his acceptance of me, in whatever guise I appeared, just as he always had. Bred in the Unclaimed Lands, Jee had the countryman's knowledge of how bizarre the world can become, but the gaze he turned on me was more than that. Loyalty was hardened into Jee's bones, liquid in his blood, woven into the sinews of his strong little heart. He would die for me, for Maggie, for the little Queen Stephanie, and never count the cost.

On the skiff stood a small crude tent. Jee poled the craft to shore as the tent opened and Mother Chilton crawled out. She did not try to stand on the bobbing skiff but stayed in a spiky crouch. 'Well, Roger Kilbourne, we encounter each other again, and even more strangely.'

Was she going to reproach me, as the web girl had done? I didn't care. She was here, which meant I was no longer alone. Although, looking at Mother Chilton, she did not seem much of an ally: so old that her spine curved like a weighted sapling. Her face creased into wrinkles deep as valleys among dry hills. But her eyes still pierced me, those grey, almost colourless eyes that seemed to gather all light into themselves.

Jee tied the skiff to the willow and helped Mother Chilton ashore, she leaning on his shoulder, both of them splashing through the reeds and hummocks. Rawnie limped through the farther branches of the willow.

'Roger! I heard voices! Are you—' She stopped, peering through the gloom at the two strangers.

'Come here, child, so I can see you,' Mother Chilton said. 'No, not there – stand in the moonlight by the water. Do so now.'

Scowling, Rawnie obeyed, although I suspect she did so more to see the two strangers than to be seen. 'Who are you?'

'I am Mother Chilton.'

'I don't know you. Who are *you*?' she said, swinging her gaze to Jee, who said nothing.

'That is Jee,' Mother Chilton said.

'Can't he talk?'

'He talks when he has something to say, which would

be good advice for you, too, daughter of Rawley and Charlotte.'

'How do you know that? Roger, who are these people?' Rawnie demanded, obviously expecting no answer. Her scowl deepened; her freckled little face shone taut and pale in the moonlight.

Mother Chilton said, 'I know a great deal about you, child. Since Roger has inhabited a creature he should never have meddled with, I will need to talk to you, too, about Galtryf. But Roger first. Roger, you can at least indicate yea or nay, can you not?'

I nodded, the gesture feeling as stiff as ever.

'Good. What happened at Galtryf? We know that Katharine was there, that you did not succeed in destroying her in the Country of the Dead. We could feel her growing, a centre of power in the web of being, but we did not know in what form. Stephanie tried to reach you in dreams. Did she succeed?'

I nodded.

Rawnie said, 'Who's Stephanie?'

Mother Chilton ignored her. To me she continued, 'Then, abruptly, that centre of power disappeared. What form had Katharine taken, Roger? She was the granddaughter of one of us and obviously had talent, but we did not know how tutored it was. What did she become?'

Mother Chilton's eyes, sunken in her fantastic mass of wrinkles but still clear in the moonlight, pierced me. But without speech, how could I possibly answer her? Frustration swamped me.

Rawnie said defiantly, 'There was a *hisaf* dog that Roger was supposed to fight.'

'A dog?' Mother Chilton said. 'That could not have been Katharine.'

'Who's Katharine?'

'Be quiet, child, you know nothing.'

'I know everything, you old witch!' Rawnie shouted. 'Roger, tell her! You were supposed to fight a bad dog and I think you killed it!'

Three faces looking at me. I nodded.

It was the only time I have ever seen Mother Chilton wordless. And I felt a mean, stupid satisfaction: For a moment she was as mute as I. But how had Rawnie known that? By eavesdropping of course. Skulking into corners, creeping behind furniture or rocks, straining at keyholes.

She repeated, 'Who's Katharine? Who's Stephanie?'

Jee spoke for the first time. 'Queen Stephanie to ye.'

'Oh!' Rawnie said. '*That* Stephanie! And she sends you dreams, Roger? How come you never told me? I tell you things! Is she a web woman?'

Mother Chilton ignored all this. To me she said, 'We had hoped the growing source of power was connected to the children . . . where do they go, Roger?'

I stared at her with incomprehension, shook my head. The children went nowhere. Their tranced, undecaying bodies stayed with their grieving kin, and their souls were devoured by Soulvine Moor in its lust to live for ever. Mother Chilton already knew that. I didn't even understand her question. Hadn't the web women witnessed the Brotherhood stealing children? They seemed to know so much. They must have at least witnessed the half of that monstrous procedure that took place in the land of the living.

But if they had not, I could not tell them about it.

Mother Chilton saw my frustration and turned to simple questions, to which I could nod or shake my head.

'Are Rawley and Charlotte in Galtryf?'

Yes.

'And Maggie?'

Yes.

'When you left, all three lived?'

Yes.

'And you do not know, learned no clue, about where the children go?'

Again I did not understand the question. Mother Chilton sighed. 'I had hoped for more information from you, Roger Kilbourne. Child, tell me everything you witnessed, from the moment you and your mother were taken. Leave nothing out. Begin now.'

Rawnie, torn between fury at these imperious commands and the desire to accomplish what we'd come for, glared at Mother Chilton, kicked at a root by her feet, and began to talk. She recounted everything in great detail, warming to the attention as she was allowed to speak without interruption. But what she recited that was new to me, mostly details of her abduction and captivity, was not important, and what was important, I already knew. She finished with, 'So that's why we need an army, Roger and me. With an army we can rescue Mama and Papa and Roger's friend Maggie. If you know Princess Stephanie – I mean, Queen Stephanie – you ought to be able to get an army for us. If the queen is sending dreams to Roger, especially!'

Rawnie took a step backward, an actress thrilled with her own performance, a seeker confident of being rewarded with what she sought.

Mother Chilton said, 'That is not possible, child.'

'What?'

'I said that is not possible. There will be no rescue.'

'But you have to! You must!' Rawnie clenched her fists and advanced on Mother Chilton. Instantly Jee was between them. Mother Chilton spoke over his shoulder; in her stooped age, she was little taller than he.

'Listen, Rawnie, and you, too, Roger. I know what you hope. Inside Galtryf, the Brotherhood have no more

206

power than we do, that much is true. *Hisafs* may not cross over, and women of the soul arts may employ neither dream arts nor soul-sharing ones. That is the result of the terrible battles that brought Galtryf Keep to ruin, battles fought long before Roger was even born. So you believe that within Galtryf, both *hisafs* and Soulviners are just men and may be attacked like men. The fortress is ruined, the men and women within are few in number, and a small force of trained soldiers could capture the whole easily. In that, you are right.

'But consider further. Even if I were to convince Lord Robert Hopewell that The Queendom is in danger from Soulvine Moor – and I could perhaps do so – his army must first travel to Galtryf. They must cross a third of The Queendom, climb through the Unclaimed Lands, ride or march across Soulvine Moor itself. The Brotherhood and Soulvine have so few people at Galtryf because they are spread thinly across the countryside. The Brotherhood steals children. The Soulviners gather as watchers, to form what you call "vortexes". Both groups have spies everywhere. Lord Robert's army would be seen before it had so much as crossed the River Thymar. Long before it could reach Galtryf, Rawley and Charlotte and Maggie would have been murdered. And you, Roger – how long can your body stay alive in Galtryf while you parade across three lands in that animal guise you have so unwisely adopted? You, too, would be dead before Lord Robert's army reached Galtryf.

'I am sorry, children. It cannot be done.'

Silence, heavy and terrible as the grave pressing on me when I crossed over. I was being made to cross now, into truth. Mother Chilton spoke truth. The thing could not be done.

Rawnie burst into wailing tears and flailed her arms, her fists harmlessly glancing off Jee, who still shielded

Mother Chilton. He pushed her away and she fell to the ground, sobbing. Jee knelt beside her, making soft ineffectual noises of consolation. Mother Chilton watched me.

'Roger Kilbourne, you have fought well, if mistakenly, for what you love. I am sorry it must end this way. I must return now to Stephanie, who may say her good-bye to you in a dream. Or not – she has enough control now to use the conduit, even though he himself still has none.'

None of this made sense to me, and I didn't care. I cared only about Maggie. I could not rescue her, and I myself must die soon. *Maggie, Maggie, once more I failed you . . .* But such thoughts were intolerable. Better to think of something else, anything else! So I looked at Mother Chilton, and something in my stance must have conveyed information to her, because she said, 'You do not know?'

Know what?

'No, you do not,' Mother Chilton said. 'I thought that Stephanie might have . . . I am losing control over what she dreams to you. As I said, she is growing stronger in her arts. But only when she uses, as we all do, the conduit that replaced Katharine. Do you not remember, Roger, that I told you once she was the conduit for Soulvine Moor? Her unnatural living presence among the Dead made it possible for Soulvine Moor to begin their unnatural quest. Now they are strong enough to do so without her. But we, too, have our centre of power, one such as is born once in a thousand years. He can affect nothing himself, no more than can the centre of a spider web move into action. But all strands of the web flow through him. He is the conduit for others' power. He is our last hope.

'Do you really not remember this, Roger, even in your

current form? I have told you before, and so did Alysse. The conduit is unclear still because he is so young. He is your son, Roger. He is the one. As I have told you before.'

The skiff had left, Jee poling silently through the marsh and then rowing upriver in the growing darkness. Numbly I watched the little craft, its tent hiding Mother Chilton, grow smaller and smaller on the black waters, until I could see it no longer. Rawnie still lay on the ground, sobbing. Mother Chilton had tried to persuade her to go with them to Glory – 'What will happen to you if you stay here, child?' – but she had refused, kicking so hard that even Jee had given up. He had left her a bundle taken from the tent. He had also bent to give me a look of compassion so painful I had run off into the trees rather than endure it. But now I was back, having no place else to go, and not caring much if I had.

My son, the centre of Mother Chilton's web. Maggie, whom I could not help and would never see again. Myself, soon to die when my body expired in Galtryf. And then I would sit mindless in the Country of the Dead, until I was devoured by Soulvine Moor.

My son, the centre of Mother Chilton's web. Maggie, whom I could not help and would never see again ...

An owl hooted in the willow above. The river lapped gently at the shore. Frogs splashed into the water. A hundred night sounds came to me, a hundred night scents. And soon I would experience none of them, and neither would Maggie. Unless she was already dead.

Rawnie had stopped crying; perhaps she had sobbed herself to sleep. The night was warm enough that I did not try to cover her. This might be my last night alive. I fought to stay awake so as to miss none of it. And yet I could not really see it, really hear it, really smell it while my thoughts tumbled in their bleak pain.

My son, the centre of Mother Chilton's web. Maggie, whom I could not help and would never see again ...

No creature can hold off sleep for ever. I had travelled hard all day. Despite myself, my despair slid into sleep. The moonlit grotto formed by the willow faded around me, the coarse river grass beneath me, the rustling leaves above me. Into the void of their passing came Stephanie's dream.

And all changed yet again.

20

Swirling colours, vague shapes. But I was half awake under the willow, or perhaps I dreamed that I was half awake, or perhaps both were true at once. At any rate, a part of my mind understood that the shifting colours and half-distinguished shapes were in the infant mind of my son, through which the dream came. The conduit.

A figure emerges from the bright swirl, a small figure with something bright on her head. A crown. Stephanie's voice comes shockingly clear and unchildlike – shockingly because, for the first time ever, she sounds as commanding as her dead mother. I had not thought that possible. 'Roger,' Stephanie says, 'wait there. Do not leave. I so order.'

I try to answer, but no words come from my moor cur throat, and so—

'Roger!' Rawnie screamed in my ear. 'I dreamed!'

The scream sent me leaping to my feet, teeth bared. Rawnie ignored my teeth, my raised hackles, my attack crouch. She threw her arms around me and went on screaming. 'The queen said to wait here! I think they're coming!'

One should not throw arms around a confused moor cur. Only with the greatest difficulty did I jerk my head to the side so that my teeth closed on air rather than on her arm. This, too, Rawnie ignored.

'Did you hear me, Roger? That little queen sent me a dream and told us to wait right here! They must be going to send an army after all!'

Even with my wits once more assembled, this did not

211

seem likely to me. Stephanie might have meant ... oh, anything. That she would send more food, that she would send soldiers to claim Rawnie. This last seemed most probable. I was going to die, and without help Rawnie might, too. Or so Stephanie, delicate and usually timid, might think. (But, some part of my brain whispered, she did not sound timid in *your* dream.)

It was not yet dawn. The moon had set and a thousand stars danced on the dark river. On the opposite north shore, a distant light bobbed as some boatman or fisherman made an early start on the water. I could barely see Rawnie in silhouette, but I could smell her joy.

'I'm so hungry! Oh, look, that boy must have left this bundle last night – do you think there's food in it?'

Of course there was food in it. Not only could I smell it, during the night I had growled sleepily at one badger and two squirrels who had approached the pack. Rawnie tore it open.

'Bread and cheese and oh, look! Meat tarts, you shall have one too, silly Roger. Probably we will set out today for Galtryf and you will need your strength. Here, you may have the biggest one – aren't I thoughtful of you? Here's something! Trousers and a tunic! Mama would never let me dress as a boy no matter how much I begged her but I see that old woman knew better, or maybe it was the boy. What a strange boy! He hardly spoke at all. Oh, there's ants on the bread, they get into everything, no matter, I can brush them off ... How long do you think it will be before the army arrives?'

For once, I was glad I could not answer. Not that Rawnie would have listened to my nay-saying anyway. She believed what she wished to believe.

Throughout breakfast she went on prattling. The east brightened and then the sun rose. It would be a hot, clear day. Rawnie changed into her boy's clothing, first making me turn my back. She made a neat pack of the remaining food, her warm cloak, and the rest of her meagre belongings. Then she sat on the riverbank, boots off and toes dangling in the shallow water, to wait for the army that would not come. I lay beside her, dreading her inevitable disappointed rage.

As the morning wore on, boats crowded the river. Barges were pulled upriver by horses or mules on the opposite bank. Skiffs and wherries were rowed by stout men. Pleasure craft drifted downriver or were poled closer to shore, although not so close as the wide, marshy shelf of land before Rawnie and me. When a craft came close enough, she hallooed and waved, while I shrunk back into the brush. Nearly always the people aboard hallooed or waved back.

So much peace and prosperity, and The Queendom at its loveliest summer best. Was all this to be destroyed by Soulvine Moor, in their unnatural quest to live for ever? I did not know what the Moor and the Brotherhood would do next. Perhaps destroying enough of The Queendom's children would gain them their aim, perhaps not. How many children would be required? And had they some further means of harvesting more of them, once their power had grown sufficiently? My killing Katharine – twice – had apparently not even slowed this monstrous war.

No country can survive without its children.

By noon, Rawnie was restless. She waded in the marshy river, caught a frog, let it go. She washed the horse, tethered a short distance away, with river water, a task to which the horse objected. She made a daisy chain and tore the petals into tiny bits. She hunted, vainly, for a four-leaf clover among the coarse river grasses, which held no clover. Finally she burst out, 'Where the by damn *are* they?'

I said nothing.

'How far away is that stupid palace? You know how far, Roger, you've been there! Mama said so! Tap your paw for how many miles it is!'

I had no idea how many miles.

'Stupid Roger. And Mama told me you had such wit! Of course,' she added, in a generous attempt to be fair, 'she didn't know you were going to become a moor cur.'

The mention of her mother seemed to sober Rawnie. She sat on the bank, staring sullenly at the water. A skiff went by, hallooing and pointing at us, and she didn't even respond.

The hallooing and pointing grew louder. And it was not at us, but a little way upriver.

Then I caught the scent. Men and horses.

By the time they reached us, riding over fields on our south bank of the river, I knew that they had not come merely to escort Rawnie to the palace. Fifty men fully armed, and at their head, two figures. One was Lord Robert Hopewell himself, mounted on his magnificent black charger. Beside him, looking small on a large roan and holding on for dear life, sat Jee.

Rawnie capered and yelled. I sat on my haunches in the shadow of a gorse bush, stunned. Had Jee not heard what Mother Chilton said last night? No army could approach Galtryf without causing Jago to kill Maggie, Charlotte, and my father and then flee. What had happened at the palace to bring an army here?

'Look, Roger!' Rawnie shouted. 'Don't they look fine!'

Lord Robert halted his men in the meadow behind the willow tree and beside the Albustrine, where Rawnie's horse had been the sole contender for the field grass. He dismounted, lifted Jee from the boy's uneasy saddle, and strode towards us. When I glimpsed Lord Robert's face, I almost could feel pity. When I had known him, he had neither believed in nor trusted what he called 'witchcraft'. First I had challenged that stance and now, I guessed, Stephanie had. His handsome face had aged much in the past year.

Rawnie rushed forward. 'You came! You, boy . . . what's your name again?'

'Jee.' He gazed at Rawnie, in her boy's clothing, with open distaste. Stephanie, dainty and small, always wore modest gowns and spoke in a soft, feminine voice.

'Jee, thank you for bringing the army! Who are *you*?'

'Lord Robert Hopewell, Regent for Her Grace Queen Stephanie and High Commander of Her Grace's army,' he said, somewhere between irritation and amusement. Rawnie's mouth made a round pink O. Then, with some remembrance of the manners Charlotte must have desperately tried to fasten onto her, she made The Queendom's most awkward curtsey, nearly tumbling over onto the grass.

But Lord Robert's attention had already left her. His gaze found me, and now his expression was too complicated to read, although I would not have liked to encounter it over duelling pistols. He spoke to Jee. 'This is really Roger Kilbourne, the erstwhile Queen's Fool?'

'It be Roger, my lord.' Jee's soft voice, still in the accent of the Unclaimed Lands that had bred him, held tension. And I could smell it on both of them. The lord regent, the most powerful man in The Queendom, and the upcountry page insisted on by the little queen, had clashed on this matter, perhaps on many matters. Life at court must still be as complex and faction-ridden as I remembered from Queen Caroline's reign.

Lord Robert gazed down at me. 'The same Roger Kilbourne that rescued Her Grace from Tarek's army, the same that . . .' Abruptly he swung to face Jee. 'You are *sure*, page?'

'I am, my lord.'

Rawnie said loudly, 'Of course that's Roger! That old woman knew it last night, why don't you?'

'Be quiet, child,' Lord Robert said. 'How dare you speak to me like that?'

Rawnie's face went white, then red. She kicked Lord Robert in the shin. Outraged, he grabbed her, held her at arm's length so she could not repeat the offence, and swatted her behind. She began to shout curses, so he swatted her again. Jee ignored all of this, dropping to one knee beside me and speaking urgently into my ear.

'He did not wish to come to ye, Roger, but Stephanie made him. She be the queen, and she maun do what be best for The Queendom. I told her of Maggie in the fortress, and of ye witched into what ye be now, and of the babes being tranced like the Dead. Can ye believe it, Lord Robert had not told her! I learned of it in the city, and if it be not for me, my lady would never know aught. Lord Robert treats her like a child.'

Stephanie was seven years old, Jee eleven.

'I told her, too, of what ye had done to save the palace from the Blues, those years ago. To save her mother. And she did not know that, either. And then I told her what she maun do now.'

Jee had told *her*, the queen. Jee, whom Stephanie had clung to on our journey months ago through the Country of the Dead. Jee, whom Stephanie apparently trusted with that blind loyalty of which her ruthless mother had been incapable. Jee, who had convinced Stephanie to order Lord Robert here in order to do – what?

Jee gazed at me, his eyes dark and shifting as ash, and all at once I knew what he intended. For a moment I could not catch my breath. We stared at each other, and he nodded quietly.

Rawnie, not quiet, had been turned over to one of Lord

Robert's lieutenants, who had dismounted and walked through the drooping branches of the great willow. He held Rawnie firmly and I heard him say, 'Touch Lord Robert again and I will bind you, see if I do not. And stop that screaming or you stay here when we march.'

He meant it. Rawnie stopped yelling and flailing, although her expression was murderous. But I knew she would not have been left behind, not even if she grabbed Lord Robert's sword and thrust it through his belly. Lord Robert was no longer directing this campaign. Nor, except for whatever assistance she might have given the little queen, were the elderly Mother Chilton and her web women. Nor were my father and his *hisafs*, sworn enemies of The Brotherhood and of Soulvine Moor.

This part of the war would be directed by children. Jee, Stephanie, Rawnie, my infant son. Four children and a moor cur, poised to save two realms, the living and the dead, through a plan that made even my animal blood run cold in its foreign veins.

21

We could not bring the horses. That much was clear even to Lord Robert, who nonetheless hated the idea. But, then, he hated everything Jee had planned, everything Jee had asked Queen Stephanie to order done. As Lord Robert gave commands to his men, his face looked like a man eating pickles.

'Dismount. Grooms, assume control of mounts. Captains, tight three-column formation.'

Much shuffling of men, hooves, armour. The wild-flowers in the little meadow became trampled. On passing boats, people craned their necks to see and shouted indistinguishable words. The soldiers made three columns of sixteen men, a captain heading each and Lord Robert with his man-at-arms in front.

Rawnie knelt beside me. 'What are they doing?' When I did not even glance at her, she turned reluctantly to Jee. 'Boy, what are they doing?'

He did not answer either.

She rolled her eyes and said, with an elaborate show of mock courtesy, '*Jee*, what are they doing?'

'They be invading Galtryf.'

Rawnie frowned, and then her eyes widened as she worked it out in her mind. Springing forward, she grabbed her little bundle, raced back to me, and twined her grubby hand firmly in the fur of my neck. I shook her free. She grabbed my tail.

Lord Robert choked out, 'Each man grab hold of the one ahead of him. Hold on tightly.'

The men looked at each other, scowling or puzzled or already angry. On a few faces, older men, I saw the first dawning of comprehension. They remembered the battle three years ago at the palace. Heads swung around, looking wildly for the queen's fool. The three captains looked grim but unsurprised. They had known what was coming.

'This will provoke you,' Lord Robert said, and I wondered how long it had taken him to choose that particular word. 'It will not be pleasant. But when we arrive at Galtryf, remember that you are fighting the enemy there in the name of The Queendom and of Queen Stephanie. Long live the queen!'

'Long live the queen!' the men returned. This, at least, they understood. Their fear stank in my nostrils, and it would only increase.

No *hisaf* could cross into or out of Galtryf from the Country of the Dead. But I was not coming from the Country of the Dead. No web woman, the mouse-woman had told me, could enter the gates of Galtryf as a mouse, a swan, a deer, a hawk: 'That would be possible only if I had guised to my soul-sharer while inside the castle's reach, and I did not.' But I was not a web woman, nor was I entering the gates of Galtryf in a soul-sharing state. My body was already there.

Anyway, this plan was all we had.

Jee stepped forward and wrapped one arm around Lord Robert's waist. The three captains and the man-at-arms locked arms around each other's shoulders, and Lord Robert did the same to the captain at the left. I moved forward from the hidden shelter of the bushes, rose on my hind legs like a faire dog trained to amuse the crowd, and planted my front paws on the back of Jee's shoulders. The soldiers broke discipline to murmur – one even cried out – but at a sharp word from Lord Robert they fell silent, taut as lute strings. Rawnie gripped my tail so hard I nearly shook her off again, but her grip was the only thing preventing me from sticking the tail between my legs.

And so I crossed back into my body.

It was just as three years ago, and it was not. Then I had crossed the grave, bringing the Blue army with me. It was not the grave I crossed now, but the weight of the men dragged at me just the same. I struggled to surmount the well, and the struggle went on and on and on so that there was time for a thousand thoughts, all black with despair:

What if this bastard art, half *hisaf* and half web woman, did not permit me to cross back with others attached to me?

What if the chamber in Galtryf that held my body was too small for so many? Would soldiers end up inside solid rock?

What if this unnatural effort killed me – what then of these others?

What if—

What—

On and on and *on*—

In the distance someone was crying. How could that be, in the grave? How could I hear it? All at once, a woman's scream, and then I lay on a pallet of straw, unable to move from weakness, labouring hard just to breathe. A woman bent over me, whirling around and crying out as soldiers abruptly filled the room.

Maggie.

Maggie *lived*.

A long bare room, rubble at one end. Lord Robert shouted commands and his soldiers rushed the door. It was not locked. In a moment all were gone except for two, guarding the door. Rawnie would have rushed after them, crying 'Mama!' but Jee tackled her to the hard floor.

'Ye maun stay here till the place be secured.'

'Let me go!' Rawnie screamed.

Maggie gaped at us. *'Jee?'*

Rawnie tore free and ran for the door, only to be stopped and thrown back by one of the guard. Jee got to his feet. Maggie threw her arms around him and burst into tears. 'But how . . . how . . .'

She looked back at the pallet and my gaze met hers.

Her face went dazed and still, as if hit on the back of the head by a rock. When she finally managed to speak, her voice did not sound like Maggie. 'Roger . . .'

Jee said simply, 'He be back. And he brought the rescue.'

She looked wildly from me to the straw, back again, and put her hands over her face. A long shudder shook her entire body. But Maggie was still Maggie. The next moment she had thrown off her fear and she bent over me, raising a waterbag to my lips. 'Roger . . . drink . . .'

I could not. Everything went dark, came back, wavered again. I was dying.

And yet I was aware of all I could not see, almost preternaturally aware. From the corridor beyond came screams and the clash of swords. Rawnie argued with the guard. Jee went to Maggie and put his arms around her, and she hung on to him like a drowning woman to a raft. But Jee pushed her gently away, drew a pouch from his belt, and forced something from a vial into my mouth.

'This be from Mother Chilton. It might not be enough but it be the best she could do.'

The liquid from the vial tasted bitter on my tongue. I was too weak to speak. My eyes sought Maggie, who clutched my hand hard and started to cry. The last things

I saw were her tears and then Rawnie's face, thrust angrily over the pallet.

'What the by damn is wrong with *you*? Roger, don't you dare die before we find Mama and Papa! Don't you dare!'

Darkness.

I was in the Country of the Dead, and then I was back in the land of the living. No, that was not possible; it only felt real. Others flickered in and out with me.

I saw Stephanie, and the little queen was crying.

I saw Maggie, also crying, who laid a cool hand on my forehead and said something I could not hear.

I saw Alysse, who said to me, 'I told you already, Roger, that those living and those dead are connected in a vast web. How can it be otherwise, when the Dead were once alive and the alive must someday join the Dead?'

I saw Jee carrying a sword too large for him. The sword flashed in sunlight, vanished in a clap of sound.

I saw Tom Jenkins, playing at dice with Fia, while a moor cur capered around them like a court fool.

I saw my mad half-sister, a dim figure in the fog, mourning, 'Why did you do it, Roger? Why did you kill me?'

I saw Lord Robert, scowling as he said, 'We have won.'

And I saw Mother Chilton say back to him, 'You understand nothing.' But I could not have seen Mother Chilton, she was too old to travel to Galtryf. I could not have seen any of them, because weren't Alysse and Tom and Fia dead? Was I dead?

I saw an old man with a white beard and green eyes, who held a knife poised above my heart.

I flickered in and out of the Country of the Dead, and that could not have happened either, because no one could cross over from inside Galtryf. I was inside Galtryf, was I not? And there was a battle, after which Lord Solek fell on the green tiles outside Queen Caroline's door … or was that a different battle? I seemed to see the dead Lord Solek arise, his son Tarek behind him, and to hear them chorus at me, 'Where do they go, Roger?' while Leo played his lute as accompaniment.

Then, all at once, I was back, myself, Roger Kilbourne, with a jolting wagon firm beneath my back, my body so thin that even through the several thick blankets on which I lay, my spine seemed to touch the wagon bed. But I was back.

Sleep.

'I think his breathing is more even.'

'Aye, child. He will live.'

Sleep.

'How much longer, Jee?'

'Be two days more.'

'It's so by damn slow! And no one will let me ride a horse?'

'They care for the horses.'

Sleep.

'Why don't they kill him now? It makes no sense?'

'Hush, Rawnie. You'll wake Roger.'

'Nothing wakes him! He was more interesting when he was—'

'Hush! I mean it, young woman!'

Sleep.

Another awakening, and this time I knew I would live.

I lay on the bed of blankets, and above me arced a small canvas tent held above the wagon bed by bent and tied saplings. The wagon had stopped. Light rain pattered on the tent, and the fresh, sweet smell of rain-wet air drifted in the opening at one end of the wagon. Charlotte sat beside me on a low three-legged stool, reading a book. Where had she found a book? Where was I?

Not in Galtryf. Although it was difficult to sort the true experiences of my illness from what must have been either fever delirium or Jee's drugs, I was certain that I had flickered in and out of the Country of the Dead. Infant *hisafs* did, since they had not the will to control where pain sent them. I, too, had lost will and control, and that told me how close I must have been to death. Had I remained in Galtryf, the puzzling and complete barrier would have kept me from crossing over even involuntarily. I – we – had been travelling. Who? To where? And why?

Charlotte had not yet noticed my open eyes. She looked thin and worn. Was my father here, too? Rawnie? It seemed I had heard Rawnie during my illness, but it also seemed I had heard Tom Jenkins, and Fia, and my sister Katharine too, none of which was possible. I did not know how much time had passed.

Charlotte turned a page of her book and glimpsed my face. Her voice came soft as breeze: 'Roger?'

I tried to nod, could not, managed to croak, 'Yes.'

'Oh, thank the skies. We thought we had lost you!'

I tried to ask 'Maggie?' but was too weak to form the word. The next moment I was asleep.

When I woke, Maggie was there. The wagon moved again, slow as a funeral procession. Rain still pattered on the tent roof. Maggie smiled at me, tears in her grey eyes, and her fair curls fell over her forehead just as I remembered. 'Roger. I'm going to give you something to drink, and you must swallow it. No arguments.'

As if I were in any condition to argue! But now I vaguely remembered the taste of what she placed between my lips; I must have been forced to swallow it in my delirium. It was a medium-thin gruel, not unpleasant, but with the bitter undertaste of herbs. I guessed that the gruel, both nourishment and potion, was what had kept me alive after my wrenching return from the moor cur. Mother Chilton had been right. *Hisafs* had no business trying the arts of web women.

'Did he take it all?' said someone behind Maggie. Charlotte. And then Rawnie was there, too, pushing her freckled face between the two women, her red braids dripping rain upon my blankets.

'Yes, he took it all,' Maggie said, taking my hand in hers. 'Rawnie, stay back!'

'I'm sorry,' Charlotte said. 'Rawnie, you heard Maggie – stop dripping on Roger.'

'I can't help dripping,' Rawnie said, 'if I'm going to see him close enough to see him. Roger, I'm glad you're not dead. But you've been sick a long time, and so much has happened! Do you want me to tell you about it?'

'Y . . . yes.'

Maggie rolled her eyes. I saw her disapproval that Charlotte could not control her daughter. *My son*, Maggie's eyes said, *will never be allowed to behave like that*. I wanted to ask Maggie about our son, but I could not – no one must know about him. But she leaned close to me and, under guise of kissing my brow, murmured into my ear. 'He is safe.'

Rawnie crowed, 'He wants to hear *me* tell it!' I did. Rawnie would know more than Maggie or Charlotte, who both had probably spent most of this journey nursing me. Rawnie always knew more.

Charlotte gave up in defeat, moving off the three-legged stool. Rawnie plopped herself on it, ignoring Maggie, who kept hold of my hand. Her fingers felt warm and solid.

225

'Well,' Rawnie began importantly, 'there was a most wonderful battle at Galtryf. After you brought us there, Lord Robert's men all rushed around the castle, securing it, and I rushed right after them, helping.'

I remembered the guard restraining her in the doorway, but even if I could have spoken, I would not have. Let her tell the story her own way. Later I could sift truth from embroidery.

'It was easy for Lord Robert to win the battle, with all his soldiers. Some people were afraid that the bad *hisafs* might kill Mama and Papa and Maggie, but I thought they would keep them alive to bargain for their own lives with, and I was right. The only ones of our side who got killed were one soldier and Joan, and Joan was killed way before, after she let me out of Galtryf.'

Rawnie fell silent for a moment, her small face unchar- acteristically grave, and I wondered what she had heard of Joan's death. How had Joan died? Had that tormented woman, still grieving for Cecilia, been tortured for aiding Rawnie to escape? Even if I could, I would not have asked Rawnie. I could not bear to know.

Rawnie plunged ahead. 'Lord Jago was killed, I don't know how but I hope Lord Robert ran him through with a sword. Leo was killed, too, and I wanted his lute but I didn't end up getting it. Our army found Mama and Papa and Maggie and let them out of their cells. Papa was so happy to see me! Then we had to bring the old man with us. Papa said. Nobody will tell me why, or his name. I'll find out, though.'

Maggie tensed beside me.

What old man? And then I remembered the excitement and deference when someone had arrived at Galtryf, and later a figure standing above me in the pit, everyone again curtseying and bowing. A white beard, green eyes, a long white robe ... All at once I realized what I had been too fearful, and too busy, to realize in the pit: I knew him. He was the old man who had led the ceremony at Hygryll when I had nearly been murdered and devoured. He had held the knife above my heart as I lay bound on the flat rock, and only the arrival of Tom Jenkins and then my father's dogs had saved my life. 'At first,' Rawnie went on, 'Papa wanted Lord Robert to stay at Galtryf, but Lord Robert wouldn't, and they had a huge argument about it. I was hiding in a broken cabinet and I heard the whole thing. Lord Robert started like this!'

Rawnie jumped up, knocking over her stool, which fell onto me. Maggie snorted in annoyance and moved the stool. Rawnie, as Lord Robert, puffed out her chest, lowered her voice, and sent her eyebrows rushing together in a scowl. It was a performance that would have done Leo proud.

'"I will linger here no longer, Rawley. I was told by Her Grace's page" – and Roger, you should have seen the angry way he looked at Jee! – "that this place was the source of the witchcraft that lies upon the infants of The Queendom. The page convinced Her Grace of this, she ordered me here, and I am bound to obey Her Grace's orders. But the witchcraft has not lessened!"'

Rawnie gestured with her left hand as if slapping a bunch of papers in her right. 'And then Lord Robert said, "My couriers' reports! The witchcraft has not lessened! Children are still being tranced all over The Queendom. Taking this ruined outpost has done no good at all, and here I am at the ass end of the world instead of protecting the capital! The Young Chieftain prepares for war to recapture Her Grace, after that tawdry farce of a marriage ceremony with him, and I, commander of Her Grace's army, am here with— Fauugghh!" And then, Roger, Lord Robert got quiet and said, "We march tomorrow." And we did.'

Rawnie looked thoughtful for a moment. 'He's a good man, I think, but he's stupid.'

Maggie said sharply, 'You know nothing of the matter.'

Rawnie said, 'I'm talking to *Roger*, Maggie. He asked me to, remember? Anyway, Roger, Papa didn't like the way Lord Robert was talking to him, I could tell. Like Papa was a servant. But Papa didn't say anything. Then there was this big argument over who would leave Galtryf and who would stay. I didn't get to hear all of it because it was going on in different rooms and I can't be in more than one place at a time, can I? One problem was the old man, because Papa insisted he come with us and everybody is afraid that bad *hisafs* will rescue him. I don't know why they would bother, he doesn't look like much to me. I don't like those green eyes, and when he eats he gets crumbs in his beard. I saw it. Do you know who he is, Roger? Never mind, you can't tell me right now. It's just as bad as when you were a moor cur.'

'Rawnie!' Maggie's voice was like a whip. Charlotte, in the doorway of the wagon tent, made a soft, ineffectual sound.

Rawnie said, 'Nobody bad can hear me here! There's a whole army out there protecting us! Anyway, Roger, I'll find out about the old man. I can find out anything. Just yesterday I discovered Papa's command word of the day. That's the secret word that lets all the good *hisafs* know that an order really comes from Papa. There's a different one for every day and yesterday's was – no, I'm not going to tell you! It's a secret. I was hiding in an empty ale cask when I heard a courier give it to a guard *hisaf* when the courier brought Papa a report. I don't know where the courier came from, but not Galtryf. Papa gets just as many reports as ever Lord Robert did, and they're all secret. Nell has secrets, too. She gets hers from Mother Chilton.'

Mother Chilton? I had felt sleep coming over me again, either from bodily weakness or from drugs in Maggie's gruel. But Rawnie's words snapped me back to attention. What could Rawnie know of Mother Chilton? And who was Nell?

Maggie, watching me, said, 'Mother Chilton is not here, Roger.'

'No,' Rawnie said, with a resentful look at Maggie for the interruption, 'but she sends couriers. Or something. I'm not too sure about that part, but anyway she tells things to Nell. Interesting things, and sometimes Nell tells me.'

Maggie's gaze met mine, and in her eyes I saw the sudden wariness that was always provoked in her by mention of my crossing over, of Mother Chilton, of anything to do with ... I understood. Nell was one of the web women.

Maggie said, 'Nell joined us immediately after we left Galtryf. She is a healer, and she made the potions that saved your life.'

'Mother Chilton told her how,' Rawnie said, recapturing the stage by moving directly in front of Maggie in the narrow wagon. 'That's what Nell told me. But Nell knows all about plants even without reports from that old hag.'

I could see it all. Nell had been sent, probably in the guise of her soul-sharer, across Soulvine Moor to meet us as soon as we left Galtryf. Mother Chilton directed her through dreams. And those dreams would now be sent not through Stephanie, who was but seven years old and could not dream anything as complex as the recipes for potions. No, the dreams would be sent through the new conduit connecting all the web women and me, too: my son.

Nell would have also brought Maggie the news that

little Tom was safe. But not, I would bet my one good arm, of what our son actually was.

Rawnie burbled on. 'There's a great many things you can do with plants. Yew will poison a dog, did you know that? You should never let a puppy chew on a yew bow. Willow bark can ease a toothache. Selcane root helps you sleep. Holly—'

I managed to get out, 'Where is ... old ... man?'

'He's in the other wagon with a tent on it, and he sleeps all the time. Really all the time. Nell gave him a potion so he can't wake up ... Roger, are you listening? Don't fall asleep yet, I'm not done!'

But sleep pulled at me inexorably, a swift river current. Just before it pulled me under, I heard Rawnie's words speed up in an effort to finish her story before I should be unable to hear it.

'We've been travelling for over a week and Lord Robert curses because it's so slow because of the moor. Two days ago the old man's prison wagon got its wheels stuck in a bog and it took hours to get it out. Lord Robert hates this moor. A soldier fell into a bog hole and he sank up to his *neck* before they got him out – it was really exciting! However, in two more days we will be there.'

Where?

It was my last thought, and Rawnie's next words the last I heard before the river of sleep took me.

'What I don't know yet,' she said, 'is why Papa wants to go to this place called Hygryll.'

22

When I next awoke, it was to darkness, and this time a strange girl sat beside me on the three-legged stool, visible in the light of a single candle. The wagon was not moving. Maggie lay on blankets near the tent doorway, taking up most of the rest of the space. She, or someone else, must have decreed that I should never be unwatched. Maggie would have organized the watches. Even when the watch was not hers, she stayed nearby.

The girl knew the moment my eyes opened. In the flickering candlelight we studied each other, and my heart turned over. She looked like Cecilia. The same glossy chestnut hair, green eyes, small chin. But then I saw that this girl was older, firmer of mouth, steadier of purpose. She was what Cecilia might have become if Cecilia had been born with any talent for the soul arts and if Mother Chilton had trained her to use that talent.

'You are Nell,' I said. The words came easily. Sleep had drained my body of the potions in the gruel, and I was determined to take no more of them.

'I am Nell.'

I sat up. That, too, was easier than I had expected, although for a moment it left me light-headed. The feeling passed. 'Your drugs have saved my life and I thank you, but I—'

'It was not done for your sake,' she said.

'I didn't think it was,' I said dryly. 'You, Mother Chilton, Alysse, Fia – you web women are all so eager to make it clear that nothing was done for my sake.'

231

'What is at stake here is more important than any wayward boy.'

'I am not a boy. I am a man, and a father.'

'Yes,' she said, and even as I disliked her – why did all these web women feel such a need to berate me? – I was glad we had found some point of agreement. I did not want to anger Nell. She could provide me with information far beyond the knowledge of Rawnie, Maggie, or Charlotte. So I made myself smile.

'You have been teaching Rawnie about plants.'

'Yes. She has no talent for the soul arts, but she can at least learn enough practical lore to become a useful woman.'

Useful to whom? I did not say it aloud. Nell's antagonism towards me, which she either did not or could not trouble herself to hide, was disturbing. Yet I needed her.

'Rawnie says we are going to Hygryll.'

'Yes. That is why I am here talking to you.'

'To me?'

She didn't answer right away. Through the opening at the front of the tent I saw the moon rise, a thin crescent in a star-pricked sky. What time was it? The camp was not completely quiet; no camp of this size could be even in the deepest night. A horse stamped restlessly. A dog barked – was it really a dog, or one of the grey creatures from the Country of the Dead, carrying a *hisaf*? A soldier quite close to the outside of the wagon said something to someone, the words indistinguishable. Lord Robert would of course have night guards in and around the camp.

Nell shifted on her stool and candlelight danced on her hair, bringing out glints of cinnamon, gold, copper. Again I thought of Cecilia. I loved Maggie, I had finally committed my heart to her, I wished to spend the rest of my life with her. And yet I knew that Cecilia would haunt me for ever, with pain and regret.

Nell finally spoke. 'Rawnie will have told you that Lord Robert and your father carry a prisoner with this army.'

'Yes.'

Again that long pause, as if she weighed how much to tell me. 'The old man's name is unknown to us. Even now. Soulvine Moor is careful with names, as if they believed words carry power. They do not, but the old man does. More power than you can imagine. And that is your fault.'

'*Mine?*'

'At least in part. Were it not for all your meddling, Soulvine Moor would not have been able to gain so much power, so fast. Now much of that power is concentrated in this old man. There is a huge darkness of soul around him, like that around Galtryf. A huge concentration of power stolen from others' lives and deaths, including your sister's. But not only hers.

'Each time Soulvine Moor takes a circle of the Dead, their power is absorbed into the watchers at the centre of the circle. That is how the watchers gain strength. All the power that each dead soul has accumulated for years, decades, centuries – all stolen, and the Dead winked out of existence. Nothing can exist if robbed of its essence, which we call *vivia*.'

I had never heard the word before. I had only seen the theft of it.

'Accumulate enough *vivia* and, they are right, one can indeed live for ever – but at what cost!'

Now she had gone beyond my understanding. 'Cost? What cost does Soulvine Moor pay for living for ever?'

'They do not. We do, all the rest of us, both here and on the other side.'

I had seen that.

'But since all souls are connected in the great web of being, Soulviners must ultimately pay the cost, too.'

I had not seen that. I didn't know if I believed it.

'We call this old man "Harbinger", since we must call him something. But none of us understand this great darkness of soul, nor why your father insists he be taken to Hygryll. Lord Robert has unwittingly supplied Rawley the protection to do that safely. When we reach Hygryll your father will kill Harbinger. We—'

'That makes no sense,' I said. 'If my father wished to kill the old man, why not do so at Galtryf? Why take him on a long journey across Soulvine Moor, and so risk the chance of a rescue by the Brotherhood?'

'We don't know,' Nell said.

'There is no reason to take him to Hygryll. I have been there. It is nothing like Galtryf, it is merely a collection of huts burrowed into the ground, primitive and—'

I stopped. There was only one thing that made Hygryll different from any other small village. My mother, Rawley's first wife and Katharine's mother, had died there. And there, too, my sister had been born.

'We don't know why Rawley takes Harbinger to Hygryll,' Nell repeated impatiently. 'But here is the important point: the *hisafs* must *not* kill him. Do you hear me, Roger Kilbourne? So far we have strained the web of being but not torn it irreparably, and only because power has been kept in precarious balance. If Rawley kills Harbinger, a tremendous, monstrous amount of stolen power will be set loose with nowhere to go. The web will tear and . . .' She sobbed.

I stared. I had not thought Nell, who appeared so hard, capable of sobs.

In a moment she again had herself in control. 'Do you understand me, Roger? You must persuade Rawley not to kill Harbinger!'

'I do not have influence with my father. I have met him only once in my entire life.' And that meeting not a happy one. He had knocked me down. He had sent me on a dangerous journey with Tarek, the Young Chieftain. He had promised a rescue that never came.

'Nonetheless,' Nell said, 'you must do this! Harbinger must not die! The risk to the web is enormous! You must ensure that your father does not kill Harbinger!'

My father, who saw the war with Soulvine as a simple breach in fortifications, a gap in the barrier between the living and the Dead. He did not believe in the web of being. Did I? I didn't know what I believed.

'You don't understand,' I said to Nell. 'My father will not listen to me, of all people. How can I—'

'Hush!'

'I heard voices,' a man said. 'Are you alone, young Kilbourne?' One of Lord Robert's guards. I could see his head framed in the tent opening. Nell had vanished.

'Yes,' I said. 'I ... I cried out in a dream.'

The soldier's head disappeared from view. His tone had been as harsh as Nell's, and as fearful, although not from the same cause. Perhaps he remembered me from the battle at the palace three years ago; perhaps not.

Nell did not return. If she had become a mouse or a snake or a spider disappearing through a crack in the wagon bed, I never knew it. I was alone in ways the angry and fearful captain could not imagine. There was only Maggie, asleep a few yards away on the wagon bed. And although she could not help me with all that Nell had said, I stretched out my good hand until I could grab a fistful of her skirt. Maggie did not stir. Sleepless, I clutched the handful of cloth as if hanging on to a raft on a vast and violent and uncharted sea.

*

Before dawn the camp roused. Men shouted, horses neighed, dogs barked. Maggie woke and crept sleepily across the cramped wagon. 'Roger! You're dressed!'

'I feel much better.'

She kissed me carefully, as if I were very ill or very old, and I kissed her back as if she were neither. She felt so good in my arms! The kiss grew deeper yet, but Maggie, laughing breathlessly, freed herself. 'No, we can't, it's too soon for you, I'll get your breakfast!'

'No more selcane root in my food, Maggie.'

She stopped, turned, looked at me.

'I have slept enough. I wasn't ill, just weak, and the weakness has passed.' To prove this I got to my feet. Immediately I fell over.

'Roger!'

'Oh, don't fuss so! I'm fine.'

'If you were fine, you could stand up,' she said tartly, and already we were back to our old ways: her ordering and scolding, me resisting. I did not mind. She was Maggie; I was Roger; we were together. I got back to my feet, more slowly this time, and climbed down from the wagon into the first fresh air I had breathed in nearly a fortnight. Maggie followed me.

Soulvine Moor stretched the same towards all horizons: springy peat ground dotted with boulders, clumps of gorse and heather, shallow treacherous bog pools covered with sedges, and the occasional rocky tor. The morning was cool and fair. A pale pearly glow suffused the east, but the sliver of moon still rode high and the brightest of the summer stars were still visible.

Four broad-backed, deep-chested horses were being hitched to four wagons, two tented and two piled high with supplies. These four horses and two ponies were the only livestock; Sir Robert was marching his army home on foot. The soldiers had – thanks to me – arrived in

236

Galtryf with nothing but their armour and weapons, so everything else had been looted from the castle. It wasn't all that much. The men had slept, blanketless, on the bare ground, and they shared bowls and waterbags for their breakfast.

Jee appeared beside me in his soundless way. Over his tunic he wore a scarred leather breastplate that had been cut down to his size, the edges still raw. 'Ye be better, Roger?'

'I be better, yes.' I gazed at the eleven-year-old who had, through the child queen's attachment to him, brought an army to Galtryf to rescue Maggie. Jee had grown but little since I'd seen him last. Small, slight, his dark eyes as secretive as ever, he had changed the course of war. Under that borrowed armour beat the most loyal heart I'd ever known. Certainly more loyal than mine.

'Maggie,' I said, as she smoothed down Jee's unruly hair, 'I am hungry after all. Is there any breakfast to be had? Not gruel – something fit for a man.'

'I'll find you something,' she said, efficient as always, and bustled away.

'Jee, tell me why we are going to Hygryll. Nell didn't know – do you?'

'Nay,' he said in his slow way, in his unchanged country accent. 'But something happened at Galtryf. I saw it. Nell did not, nor many others.' He looked around. Two soldiers, perhaps camp guards, watched us and their expressions were not pleasant. Nor were the glances shot at me by soldiers loading the wagons. So it was starting again, the old suspicion and fear against Roger the Witch. That fear was dangerous to me. I hoped Lord Robert had his men in as good discipline as he seemed to.

I said, 'I'm going back into the wagon. Go away, and come back when you can do so unseen.'

I climbed aboard, relieved that although my muscles were weak from disuse, I felt no illness. Jee was already there. He had walked away, slipped back around the wagon, and climbed in over the wheel to slide between the tent ties. Nell herself, as rat or spider or whatever she became, could not have been more stealthy.

'What did you see in Galtryf, Jee? Tell me all.'

'It happed soon as we come. The soldiers ran from yer room. I saw ye were alive and with Maggie. Rawnie tried to leave. The guards seized her.'

I remembered Rawnie kicking and screaming in the stone chamber, and two men trying to subdue her without hurting her.

'They be busy with her and I got past them,' Jee said, 'to follow Lord Robert. Naught maun happen to him – Her Grace needs him. The soldiers went different places in the keep and I followed Lord Robert and his cadre. At the top of the keep a group guarded a room. *Hisafs*, some, and some Soulvine warriors. They fought hard but our soldiers killed them all. Lord Robert went into the chamber and I followed. The old man was there. My lord would not have killed such an elder, except that when he approached, the old man brought up a knife and wounded Lord Robert in the side. Not very bad. But the lieutenant rushed forward with his sword. And the sword went right through the old man without harm.'

My breath stopped in my lungs.

'I saw it. I did. It was as with the Blue army that ye brought back from the Country of the Dead. The old man cannot be killed. He maun already be dead. But the Blue army ... Roger, a fortnight lacks yet several days.'

I knew what Jee meant, and what Lord Robert must be thinking. But both of them were wrong. I knew what they did not, knowledge that froze my blood.

The Blue soldiers that I had brought back from the Country of the Dead could not be injured or killed here. Swords ran through them, fire did not consume them, they were exempt from death because they were already dead. But the Blues had vanished, one by one, after a fortnight in the land of the living, as had Cecilia and Fia. Their flesh had melted grotesquely, their bones had crumbled, their hearts and livers and lungs had rotted away in an instant. And their souls had vanished from existence on both sides of the grave. Death could not be cheated for long, and the length of that cheat was a fortnight.

But the old man had been in Galtryf longer than that. He had the invulnerability of the Dead, but he lived here, in the land of the living, and did not melt or crumble or rot.

'Harbinger' Nell had called him.

Soulvine Moor had succeeded. For at least this one person, the first person, they had succeeded. The old man could not be killed. He would live for ever.

Lord Robert did not realize this. He must have been badly shaken when the sword passed through Harbinger but he had seen that happen before, in the battle at the palace. He expected that in a fortnight, the old man would vanish. And meanwhile, what was there to fear? An old man, witched but feeble, no threat to robust soldiers as long as the old man was unarmed. So let the women deal with him.

Did Nell or my father know what Harbinger was? I didn't think so. Nell still believed that Rawley could kill the old man, and perhaps Rawley seemed to believe it, too.

To live for ever. Undying, unkillable. Safe. But why was Hygryll our destination? Nell wished me to find out, and so far I had not even laid eyes on my father since—

239

'Roger!' Maggie cried, climbing back into the wagon, 'Get down! An attack!'

Jee was quicker. He tackled me and I fell onto the nest of blankets just as a volley of arrows pierced the tent above.

23

None of us was hit. I grabbed Maggie and thrust her beneath me. I tried for Jee, too, but he was too quick. He crawled to the tent opening and raised his head above the wagon box to look out.

'There be many. Very many. They— Get out!' Another volley of arrows hit the tent, and these were tipped with fire.

Immediately the dry canvas caught fire. The wagon bed would be next. Maggie and I scrambled for the wagon box, on it, over it, down. Crouching behind the burning wagon, trying to shield Maggie – who was trying to shield me – I peered out at the moor, which in the rising light had become complete chaos. And yet not complete. The attackers knew what they were doing.

They were stationed behind and on top of a low, irregular tor that rose close by to the east. At that distance the archers had precision in their arrows and in the *guns* that now splintered the morning. But there must be a great many Soulviners out there because both arrows and *bullets* kept coming. The arrows were no longer afire, and only my wagon burned. So they knew where the drugged old man slept, and would not harm that wagon.

How had the Soulviners gotten so close without being seen by the guards? All at once, with a sickening lurch of the stomach, I knew. There were *hisafs* of the Brotherhood with them, and the *hisafs* had used my own stratagem. They had brought the Soulvine warriors here by carrying them through the Country of the Dead.

Lord Robert's army had been caught without armour or shelter. But they were trained and disciplined, and in less time than I would have believed possible they wore helmets and breastplates, carried shields, and formed a tight phalanx between the camp and the attackers. More soldiers ran to guard our rear. More *guns* fired – crack!

Crouching, I pulled Maggie towards the other tented wagon, a feat that took most of my strength. Jee followed. We had to clamber over the bodies of two soldiers killed in the first volley. I grabbed his shield and held it over Maggie's head. We dived under the wagon.

Jee cried, 'No!' but apparently not to me. The next minute he darted from under the wagon. Maggie clutched at him but got only air. His thin light figure ran over the ground to Lord Robert and shouted something in his face. Lord Robert batted him away, stopped, listened, and yelled orders I could not hear.

It was too late. His men had started forward towards the tor under cover of their closely aligned shields, like one giant tortoise. The rising sun flashed fire from the polished metal. Then the first few soldiers faltered, stumbled, and dropped their shields. The rest, responding to Lord Robert's shouts, retreated, still in formation. I had a clear view of the five who had stumbled.

In the gathering light the brighter green of the ground around the soldiers was becoming visible. It was a mire, a treacherous bog pool of mud and decayed plants covered by the sedges and mosses that nourished themselves at the top. The soldiers sank into the mud, and the more they struggled, the deeper they sank. Their fellows could not risk dropping their own shields to throw them ropes.

One man, at the far edge of the mire, managed to crawl out, only to be hit by a bullet. Three others died from bullets or arrows while they sank into the mire. The last soldier, trapped near the centre of the bog pool, sank rapidly. The mud reached his chest, then his neck. Maggie cried out in horror but there was no help for him. His mouth disappeared beneath the mire, cutting off his screams. Then the top of his helmet disappeared and he was gone.

Lord Robert continued his orders, but I knew his army was losing. The soldiers of the Purple had no way to reach the enemy behind and atop the tor. The army fired, and I did see a few Soulviners fall, who had no armour and who had injudiciously exposed themselves in order to shoot. The noise was tremendous; my ears rang with the sound of the *guns*.

Maggie screamed in my ear, further deafening me, 'That was a girl!' She meant one of the fallen Soulviners. I did not try, even if I could have made myself heard over the din, to explain that the warriors of Soulvine Moor included both men and women. Instead I gathered her into my one good arm and looked around for Jee, preparing to cross over with both of them into the Country of the Dead, away from the battle.

'No,' said a voice behind me, loud enough to penetrate the torrent of sound. 'Stay! They will have *hisafs* waiting for you there, Roger.'

I jerked my head to look over my shoulder. My father was crouching behind me under the wagon.

We stared at each other, backed by the nightmare around us. Maggie, who must have seen him many times since Galtryf, cried, 'Rawnie? Charlotte?'

'Inside this wagon. But—'

He didn't finish. He didn't have to, I knew what he did not say. *But we are losing.*

What would the Brotherhood, and Soulvine Moor, do to us if they recaptured us? The rescue was for the old man, but we would be rich prizes as well. Roger

243

Kilbourne, who had killed their centre of power, his mad half-sister. Rawley Kilbourne, a leader of the *hisafs* fighting the Brotherhood.

My father put his ear next to mine, so that even Maggie could not hear. I felt something hard and cold put into my good hand.

'If it comes to that, kill Maggie first, as cleanly as you can, and then yourself. Do it, Roger. They have vowed to torture her while you are forced to watch. I will do Charlotte and Rawnie.' And he was gone, crawling from beneath the wagon and vaulting onto the box above.

My mind reeled. Torture Maggie and Charlotte and Rawnie while we were forced to watch ... I had not imagined that much cruelty and revenge. The dagger felt twisting and poisonous in my hand, as if it were something alive. I thought, *I cannot do it.*

Nor could I bear the alternative. So I lay there, frozen, and watched the battle, concentrating everything in me on what was happening out there, to avoid what was happening within me.

I cannot do it.

I must.

I cannot.

Maggie said something and although I was aware of her voice buzzing in my ear, the words were meaningless. I may even have pushed her slightly away. Nor did I look for Jee. I concentrated on the battle as if I were fighting in it.

And so I saw when it happened.

More of Lord Robert's men had fallen. One, an arrow in his back, had tipped forward and lay half in, half out of the mire, which was slowly sucking him down. Some of the Soulviners, too, had fallen, but nowhere near enough. Hidden by the tor with its boulders, they had the advantage of position, despite their lack of armour.

Lord Robert turned to shout an order to the rearguard, and I saw the despair on his handsome face.

Then, all at once, the enemy *guns* ceased.

The enemy arrows did not fly.

And an image appeared in my mind, so hard and clear and shocking that I may have called out. Or not – I don't know. I do know that Maggie cried out as did, somewhere behind me, Jee.

The first Soulviner tumbled from behind the top of the tor.

Her body seemed to fall slowly, bouncing off rocks in a tumble that must have broken bones, except that she was already dead. Another warrior, a young man, followed her down. Two more slumped from behind a boulder. They were immediately fired upon by Lord Robert's men, but there was no need. They, too, were dead.

Even Lord Robert's disciplined soldiers fell utterly silent, looking at each other in wild fear.

The Soulvine warriors cried out and began to scramble away from their hiding places. Lord Robert's soldiers rushed to attack – then paused, utterly bewildered. One by one the enemy fell to the rocky ground, tumbling off the tor, thudding into the gorse, falling to the very edge of the mire. All cries ceased.

Silence stretched for an entire minute. Two, three. The image left my mind as abruptly as it had appeared. But I knew what was out there, and that in just a moment the first of them would appear. They waited for me. Or possibly for Jee.

Both of us raced up to the dumbfounded Lord Robert, me puffing with the exertion, Jee's face tense as lute strings. 'Ye maun not kill them!' Jee shouted, at the same time that I gave my one and only order to a Lord Commander of The Queendom: 'Hold your fire!'

'Upon who?' Lord Robert blurted, just as the first of

245

the web women staggered from behind the closest boulder, fell to her knees, and fainted.

'They were snakes,' I said, inadequately. Lord Robert looked at me as if I were crazed.

Again the vanished image burned in my mind, as clear as when it had come to me a moment ago. A small snake, grey as the rocks it slithered among, small enough to glide unnoticed to an ankle above a leather boot, to a wrist resting on a rock, to a neck backed up against a cliff face. To strike from a crack in the rock, from beneath a clump of gorse or bracken, from behind a pile of rubble slid off the tor. A small grey snake with a thin white line down its back, its little fangs filled with lethal and instantaneous poison. A dozen small snakes, that only yesterday had been guised as the women's own soul-sharers, patiently moving unseen beside Lord Robert's army, waiting for the necessary moment. And when it came, all the web women became snakes, slithered between and among the rocks and gorse, and struck. Again and again.

The soldiers panicked, but so good was Lord Robert's discipline that none fired upon the girls that now appeared, strewn around the moor like so many cut flowers. Most of them gasped for breath, pale as summer clouds, and I saw that one had already died.

Everything has a cost, Roger Kilbourne – when will you learn that?

'*Snakes?*' Lord Robert said. His men stood with raised weapons, *gun* or sword or knife or bow, looking wildly around for something else to shoot, their faces twisted with terror and uncomprehending anger. 'I *said* hold your fire!'

Two women climbed down from the tor, unaffected by their return to human form. One was Nell.

Lord Robert scowled at Nell, whom he knew only as Charlotte's serving woman. She strode up to him, fearless, and said, 'Well done, Lord Robert. Where is Rawley?'

He was there then, beside me, Rawnie racing to keep up with him. Nell said to my father, 'You are an idiot.'

He said coldly, 'We thank you for your assistance. Now you may go.'

Rawnie said loudly, 'But Papa, what *happened*?'

Nell said, 'Do not do this thing, Rawley. We will stop you, if we must.'

My father said, 'You cannot.'

Rawnie said, 'Stop *what*? Roger, what happened?'

Jee grabbed Rawnie and pulled her aside. She struggled but I heard him hiss, 'Stop! Have ye no sense? Come away!'

Lord Robert said, 'I will have an explanation, and I will have it immediately. Roger?'

Everyone looked at me, and in the eyes of my father and of the two women I read warning: *Say little. This is not Lord Robert's war.*

But it was. Children had been stolen from The Queendom, their lives extinguished to feed the immortality so ruthlessly sought by Soulvine Moor. It was Lord Robert who had rescued Rawley from Galtryf, and the men of his command who lay dead on the ground around us and in the foul mire. Lord Robert had a right to know what had occurred here. Curse this eternal secrecy among those who should be allies!

Or was I merely eager to defy my father?

I repeated, 'They were snakes, Lord Robert. All these girls and women. They are ... are women of the soul arts, which I think that Queen Caroline may have mentioned to you. They can guise themselves as animals, and these women you see became small poisonous snakes that all at once, upon a signal, struck at the Soulviners as you fought this morning.'

He gaped at me. I saw the word form on his lips: *Witches*. I saw the word die, perhaps too inadequate to be uttered aloud. I saw his mind seize on the one thing he could, as a soldier, understand.

He said, 'I neither heard nor saw any signal!'

It had been the image in my mind, that hard and clear image of a snake. And I knew it had come to all of them at the same moment, thus coordinating the attack, through the only means possible for such complex communication. The image had come to each of the web women, and to me, through the conduit: my infant son.

But I could not tell Lord Robert that. Not only had I strained his belief too far already, I would do nothing to alert anyone else to the existence of Maggie's and my child. All at once I became aware of her by my side, clutching my good arm.

I said, 'I am not privy to the methods of the women of the soul arts.'

Lord Robert said harshly, 'Nor are you in your full wits, Roger, a thing I have always suspected. You talk nonsense!' He glared at me, then turned to my father. 'What happened here?'

'I have no idea,' Rawley said.

'You, woman – where did you come from? You and these other maids?'

Nell gazed at him and said nothing.

There is a limit to what a man can accept. Lord Robert had been 'witched' from the banks of the River Thymar to Galtryf, far out on Soulvine Moor. He had been forced to accept me, the erstwhile queen's fool, in the body of a moor cur, and then had seen me returned to my own form, nearly dying in the effort. He knew about *hisafs* crossing from the land of the living to the Country of the Dead. He had seen reports of the tranced children, perhaps even seen some of the babes for himself. But he could go no further. The web women and their guising arts were new territory for him, and he could not make himself enter it. So do some animals stake out their hunting or mating grounds, and then never go beyond them. I saw the moment that Lord Robert rejected Nell, Rawley, me as completely as if we did not stand before him under the fast-rising summer sun.

He pointed southwest. 'My men and I are returning to The Queendom. You and your troupe of half-wit actors may do as you choose. We travel at your pace no longer. I have duties to my sovereign, Her Grace Queen Stephanie, and I will return to her to perform those duties.' And to his men, 'Bury the dead. We march for home within the hour.'

Lord Robert strode off, and his men, after exchanging stupefied looks, sprang to follow his orders. I could feel their relief, like a ripple of wind in tall grass.

My father said, 'They will find it difficult to bury the dead in peat.'

Nell faced him. 'You must not kill him, Rawley. You must not even think of it.'

My father snapped, 'I have thanked you for your assistance. You may go.' He turned his back and walked away.

Nell started after him. I caught her arm, afraid that she might turn back into a snake and slay him right then and there. 'Wait, Nell! Let me try first!'

She glared at me, but nodded.

I ran to catch up with my father. 'I would talk with you for a moment!'

'What is it, Roger?' He did not slow. I caught his sleeve and yanked him to a stop.

'Rawnie says we journey to Hygryll. Why?'

'That is not your concern.'

'I say that it is.'

He looked at me then, truly looked at me. His face, so like my own, took on an expression so intricate and layered that it was like the riddle boxes I had seen at court: box within box within box, all connected by delicate wooden levers without which the whole would come apart. On my father's face I saw – or thought I saw, for I too was part of the boxes and levers – a profound sorrow housed by guilt housed by a ruthless determination to accomplish his own ends by his own means. And all of it coloured by something in his eyes that did not look quite sane.

More shaken than I wished to show, I repeated, 'Why are we taking this old man to Hygryll?'

He did not answer, striding off alone in the direction of the tor. Behind me, I felt Nell's eyes watch him go.

24

Lord Robert left us two wagons, one containing Har-binger, but it did us little good since he left no horses. When he found it impossible to bury his dead soldiers in the springy peat the remainder of his army piled their dead, wrapped in blankets, into the other two wagons and had all four horses draw them. The ponies carried their supplies. We watched Lord Robert march his men away, towards The Queendom.

Jee went with them. 'I maun return to my lady,' he said to me.

'I know you must,' I said.

Maggie reached out a hand to grasp Jee, thought better of it, let her hand drop. She said, 'Thank you, Jee. I can never thank you enough.'

'When ye be home, send a courier to me,' Jee said, in the strangest mixture of his old loyalties and his new court life that I had heard yet. Maggie smiled, nodded, and kissed him.

Rawnie barrelled up. 'Jee, do you march with Lord Robert?'

'I do. Good day to ye.'

'Good riddance,' Rawnie sniffed, and flounced off. She had never liked Jee upstaging her, just as once she had disliked me for the same reason.

Maggie and I rested in the sun, on the south side of the tor. On the other side, in the shade and hidden by the rock, lay the web women who had become snakes. Two had died; I don't know what Nell and her companions

251

had done with their bodies. The others seemed to be recovering quickly. Maggie had organized food and water for them. Charlotte had taken Rawnie to hunt for grouse eggs not far off. I did not know where my father was.

Not that there were many places to go. The desolate moor stretched away in all directions, rising land to the south and undulating scrub everywhere else. The scrub was dotted with grey boulders, rocky tors, and the deeper green of bog pools and mires. Nothing moved under the morning sun except the retreating army.

Jee pointed south. 'Ye be no more than a day's walk to the border of The Queendom. If that be where Rawley wants to take ye.'

It wasn't, but I would burden Jee with no further knowledge. 'Thank you. Good-bye, Jee.'

'I maun go to my lady, or I would stay to aid ye.'

'I know you must. Keep well, Jee. We will meet again.'

He ran across the moor, expertly keeping to the hummocks and other higher ground, following Lord Robert's army. I watched until he, and they, were out of sight.

Maggie put her hand in mine. 'Nell still will not tell me where Tom is!'

'Better that you not know,' I said.

'How can you say that, Roger?' But the words lacked conviction. The attack by Soulvine warriors had badly shaken her. Maggie was meant for small, efficient, bustling worlds that she could control: a kitchen. An inn. A cook house. A farm. In these larger affairs her courage never failed her, but her assurance did. And she had just seen what the web women could do. They were better protection for our child than were his stranded parents or ruthless grandfather.

Which raised a question in my mind: Did Rawley even know Maggie and I had a son? I didn't think so. Nell certainly would not have told him.

As I sat on the moor trying to decide what we should do next, Nell ran full-tilt from the other side of the tor towards the tented wagon. When I saw her face, I knew immediately where my father was. 'Stay here!' I said to Maggie, who called after me but, for once, did not follow.

Nell leaped over the wagon box and hurled herself under the tent. I climbed after her as fast as I could. At the back of the wagon, my father held a knife at the throat of the sleeping old man. Perhaps the attack had made him reconsider, or Nell had. But he had decided not to wait for Hygryll. Before Nell could reach him, Rawley slashed the blade across Harbinger's wattled neck.

No blood. No cut. The knife might as well have been made of air.

Both Rawley and Nell stared. Rawley turned pale as the sun-bleached canvas above him. Nell shuddered and whispered, 'So they have succeeded.' And a moment later, 'See what you *hisafs* have done?'

My father rallied. '*We* have not done this, woman. Don't be so stupid.'

'It is you who are stupid, all of you men who think that killing can mend what killing has created. If your son had not brought the Dead back to the land of the living, the web of being would not be so strained. If you had not created those dogs, crossing into beings that have their own separate nature, the web of being would not be so strained. If you *hisafs* could not cross bodily now into the Country of the Dead – and that, too, is Roger's doing – the web of being would not be so strained.'

He turned to face her, the knife still in his hand, and at his look I shrank back. He said, 'There is no "web". That is a notion you women of the soul arts have constructed in your mind. We *hisafs* know better. We know there is a wall between the countries of the living and the Dead, a barrier, because we – and only we! – have crossed it.

Your knowledge is all conjecture, while ours comes from experience. That wall has been breached, and the only way to prevent further destruction of it is to kill the destroyers. Before all of them become like him!' Again my father pointed his knife at the sleeping Harbinger.

'And I can see how successful your effort to kill him was.' Nell's voice dripped sarcasm.

'It will be.'

'How?'

He didn't answer, but she must have known more of his thinking than I did because she said, 'You cannot do that. We will not let you.'

My father hurled the knife to the wagon bed, where it stuck in the wood, vibrating. 'You will not "let" me! How will you stop me? Become snakes again and poison me? And perhaps Roger as well? Why not Rawnie, too? She has no talent for soul arts, so perhaps she will grow up to champion the *hisaf* cause! Why not eliminate that threat now, you who claim to abhor killing but who just slew a small army of Soulviners?'

'It was necessary,' Nell said. The skin at the hollow of her throat beat hard and fast. She was controlling herself only by an enormous effort of will, and Rawley fought to do the same.

'So the killing you deem necessary does not affect your "web", but killing by *hisafs* will destroy it. Very logical.'

'I did not say that. Of course we have strained the web, you half-wit! But nothing compared to what you will do if you carry out this insane plan! Was it not enough that Roger here nearly tore the whole web by killing Katharine? Twice?'

'And yet your web seems to continue,' my father said. He had winced at the sound of my sister's name, and the wince seemed to further enrage him.

Nell's hands clenched into fists. 'You understand

nothing! Can you not suspend your own idea of a "wall" for long enough to see the larger truth?'

'Can you not suspend yours long enough to see the truth of actual experience?'

Their eyes locked and they glared at each other, both their hands curled into fists. Web, wall – was this then a battle of images? Or of men's gifts against the talents of women? And I – I did not know what I believed. Both seemed to be right, to me, and both filled me with dread.

I said to Rawley, 'What is it you are going to do in Hygryll that she objects to so much?'

Slowly both their heads turned towards me. Evidently they had forgotten I was there. Beneath them the old man slept on, his drugged breath turning musky in the close air. His flesh had gone even slacker, as people's do in sleep, and blue veins traced patterns across the wrinkles of his eyelids.

'Rawley,' I repeated, refusing to call him 'Father', 'how are you planning to kill someone who cannot be murdered?'

Perhaps Nell scented an ally. She said, 'Your father has a desperate idea, Roger. Desperate and dangerous and stupid. He knows now that he cannot kill Harbinger himself, neither in this realm nor that other. He has not the power. But he believes that others might. That those in Hygryll, the Soulviners most advanced in their obscene quest and so close to reaching immortality themselves, can still kill each other and perhaps Harbinger too. In other words: the only thing which can destroy power is more power. It is the sort of thinking that has brought us to this pass in the first place!'

My mind struggled to keep up, to sort this into sense. 'And . . . and is it true? Can others in Hygryll kill this old man?'

Nell was silent.

255

'You see,' my father said, 'she doesn't know. The truth is that no one knows until it is tried. But it is our best hope.'

Nell said despairingly, 'It may destroy us all. It—'

'Now you say "may"! A moment ago it was "will destroy us all"!'

Nell ignored him, speaking directly to me. 'We do not *know*. There is no precedent for any of this – how could there be? But consider, Roger. When you threw your sister into the vortex of watchers from Soulvine, we expected her power to be dispersed among the watchers. It was not – she entered one of the unnatural dogs. When she was killed by ... by that stray moor cur in the pit at Galtryf, we expected her vanished power to tear the web of being. Instead, it was dispersed among the Soulviners there, because they had learned to absorb it. They have also learned to drain babes of their *vivia*, using it to balance that taken from circles of the Dead. We did not expect that, either. But in each of these instances, the balance has been maintained, the flow of power between the land of the living and the Country of the Dead. What Rawley proposes will completely upset that balance. Where will the immense, dark power of soul around Harbinger go? It cannot go into any of us – power cannot be transferred among living men and women. Think, Roger, where will it *go*? And what will that do to the web of being?'

'This is all nonsense,' Rawley said. 'No more substantial than the light from marsh gas. We kill the enemy, they relapse into mindless tranquillity on the other side, and their "power" is gone. We are safe from them. It is my duty to protect The Queendom and the Unclaimed Lands, and I will do whatever is necessary to safeguard both.'

In my mind I heard Queen Caroline, three years ago, say the same thing: '*I will do whatever is necessary to rule my queendom well, for the greater good.'* Perhaps all in command had this same rigid determination, or they would not be in command. Certainly at this moment Nell's face and Rawley's resembled each other, both harsh masks of complete certainty.

Only I felt swamped by doubt.

I said to my father, 'But how will you persuade the Soulviners of Hygryll to kill Harbinger? He is their leader, and they are warriors. Won't they die themselves before murdering him?'

Silence. Then Nell said spitefully, 'Tell him, Rawley.'

My father gazed at me with no lessening of harshness. He said, 'People will do anything under torture, Roger.'

'You would torture people?'

Nell said, 'And if that does not work – and I think it will not – he and his *hisafs* will torture their children in front of them, until they trade Harbinger's life for their children's lives.'

I don't know what expression lay on my face. Whatever it was, it caused my father to burst out, 'Do not be so soft, Roger! The Brotherhood and Soulvine Moor have destroyed our children, have they not? You have witnessed it! This is war!'

Nell said, 'And you are but a warrior, Rawley. You are not the sword. Do not overreach yourself and so destroy us all!'

'I am trying to save us all! Even as you women, our supposed allies, thwart my efforts!'

I could stand it no longer. I stumbled from the wagon and sank to the ground beside one of the wheels. I think that if Nell or Rawley had come after me, I would have knifed either one. They did not follow me.

This, then, was the ruthlessness I had seen in my father's eyes, and the gloss of insanity upon that ruthlessness. Would my father really carry out his monstrous

plan? To torture children to manipulate their parents . . .
even the parents of Soulvine Moor. To do so in order to
force them to kill Harbinger, without even knowing for
certain if it was possible, or what the consequences might
be.

And what lengths would Nell and her web women,
who were equally determined, go to in order to stop
him?

If Nell killed my father, his men would complete the
plan anyway. Other *hisafs*, Rawnie said, had been
coming and going to 'Papa' ever since he left Galtryf,
spreading Rawley's orders throughout three countries
and two realms with the spoken 'command word of
the day'. No, killing Rawley would not stop his terrible
plan. Nell must know that. As must Mother Chilton,
far away in the capital and directing operations of her
own.

The web of being. I did not know if it was, as Rawley
said, just a notion. Mother Chilton had spoken of it, but
Mother Chilton, too, had been wrong on occasion.

A sound reached me then. Not Rawley and Nell, still
arguing within the wagon. Not Charlotte nor Maggie nor
Rawnie, picking bilberries out of earshot. Not the sudden
cry of a brace of grouse, startled out of the heather and
rising nearly straight up into the grey sky. No, what
I heard was dogs, baying to each other. Then I could see
them, dogs grey as the sky, barrelling across the moor.
Before I could even react, they were upon me. They
carried *hisafs*. Not the hisafs of the Brotherhood, for the
dogs did not attack. They leaped gracefully onto the box
of the wagon and then went inside, three of them. *Hisafs*
sent to protect Rawley against Soulvine Moor. Or against
the web women. Or both.

Rawnie, attracted by the arrival of the dogs, dropped
her bilberries and raced towards the wagon. I turned

away from her. Instead I stared at the wagon wheel beside me. It had slipped into a small patch of bog and was slowly sinking, deeper and deeper into the mire.

We dismantled the wagon, which could not be pried from the bog. There was no horse to pull it anyway. From the wood of the wagon sides and the cloth of the tent we made a kind of litter, and dumped the old man on it. Rawley and I carried this between us. It was not heavy, the old man being little more than bones and beard, and I had but one hand. Still, I managed with Charlotte and Maggie's help. Rawnie walked beside us, along with the three dogs. Nell and her web women had all disappeared.

Gone ahead, in their soul-sharing guises, to arrive at Hygryll first? Why?

Even Rawnie spoke little. That might have been due to orders from her father, the only one capable of controlling her. Or perhaps she had finally, in Rawley's presence, let go of her noisy bravado and become what would be natural: a frightened little girl.

Clouds had blown in from the west, threatening rain. We picked our way carefully across the low-lying areas, keeping to the higher ground and away from the greener patches of mire. These grew fewer. The ground rose steadily towards the Unclaimed Lands and the soil must have improved because now heather carpeted everything with tough-stemmed purple flowers that were pretty to look at but difficult to travel through. The occasional tree appeared, pine or stunted birch.

My father drove us onward until Maggie rebelled. 'Rawley, we must stop. Roger must rest!'

He glanced back at me. 'He looks stout enough still.'

'I am,' I said shortly, angry at Maggie for treating me like an invalid and determined to show no weakness in front of my father. And in truth I did feel stronger than expected, although my shoulder ached from carrying my half of the litter.

'Well, then, *I* am tired,' Maggie said, and sat down on a tussock covered with coarse grass. She looked meaningfully at Charlotte, who stood irresolute. Charlotte looked exhausted, probably as much with worry as with walking, but she would never defy Rawley. Had my mother been the same, so soft and pliant? From what I remembered of her, yes.

Rawley said, 'Oh, all right. Charlotte, can you give us something to eat?'

She had food in her pack. We laid the litter upon the ground and the five of us ate on the wide, empty moor, the dogs waiting hopefully for scraps. It was eerie to sit there, eating, as if on some macabre picnic. At our feet lay the old man who was – perhaps – immortal. My father contemplated the most monstrous crime I could imagine. Dogs that were not dogs watched us from green eyes. Grey clouds blew over the moor, but the real storm was within me.

When Maggie, Charlotte, and Rawnie all went behind a clump of gorse to relieve their bladders, I faced my father yet again.

'Why Hygryll?'

This time he answered me. His eyes hardened. I would not see any more complex, vulnerable expressions on that stern face. He said, 'We already hold the village. The inhabitants are already our prisoners.'

'So I guessed, or you would not be headed there with nothing to defend us but three dogs. I meant, why did Soulvine Moor choose that remote place for the first man to capture life everlasting?'

'They did not choose it. It chose them. And I think you already know why.'

260

'Because my sister was born there. Or rather, almost born there.'

'Yes,' my father said, and for a moment pain broke through on his rigid face. 'The bastard who abducted your mother took her there. She—' He broke off, shook his head, and looked away.

So it had been an abduction, my mother's second man, not a marriage. And my father had not known until it was too late. Where had I been? Perhaps already sent to my Aunt Jo. Abruptly I did not want to know more of my parents' history. Not now. Not ever. There is a limit to what the heart can bear.

Instead I said, 'Are you really going to do this thing, Rawley?'

If he registered that I called him by his name instead of 'Father' he gave no sign. 'Yes. And so are you.'

We stared at each other. Then Rawnie came crashing through the heather, the two women more sedately behind her. There was only time for him to say, 'If you are not with me on this, Roger, you are against me. There is no middle ground in this war.'

I did not answer.

Rawnie crashed up to her father. 'Are we nearly there, Papa? Mama says we are going to a place where there are wild ponies! Is that true?'

She stood hopefully before him, and not even Cecilia could have looked as artless and innocent. This, then, was where Rawnie had learned to play-act to get what she wanted. Despite himself, Rawley's face softened. He said, 'Perhaps. But now we must go, kitten.'

If this man had never left my mother, if he instead of Hartah had raised me, would I too have learned fawning and sweet, false deference as the only means to sway that stony will? Perhaps so. One thing both Rawnie and I had learned from our very different lives: how to survive the people who controlled us. I had survived Hartah, and Queen Caroline, Solek and Tarek. More: I had ended up, however blunderingly, defeating them all.

I did not see how I could defeat my father. The conviction was growing upon me that Rawley, whatever he once had been, was now so consumed with his goal that he had lost sight of its cost. But how could I, one-handed and seventeen years old, oppose him and his army?

And then, days later and just before we reached Hygryll, a plan was given to me. Not made by me, but given to me, and by the most unlikely person of all persons I had ever known.

Since, for one thing, he was dead.

'We must rest again,' Maggie said firmly. 'Charlotte can go no further.'

Rawley turned to his wife. 'Charlotte?'

'I can ... manage,' she said, although clearly she could not. She would have tried to walk across the open sea if Rawley had asked it, but she was not bred to this. So pale that the smudged skin under her eyes looked like ash, she swayed on her feet. Beside her Rawnie looked indestructible. Even Maggie, who had given birth less than a month ago, seemed sturdy as rock beside Charlotte.

Maggie said, 'Sit here, Charlotte. Rawnie, give her a drink from your waterbag. Rawley, surely another half hour can't matter to our arrival. Be reasonable!'

The last thing my father was, was reasonable. He was on fire with his monstrous mission. But after scanning the horizon in all directions, he nodded curtly. 'Half an hour, then.'

Maggie settled Charlotte on a blanket where she promptly fell asleep. Rawley took his daughter a short way off for a private talk, followed by all three dogs. I leaned against a large grassy tussock.

Maggie said gently, 'You are very troubled, Roger.'

'Yes.'

'Tell me what troubles you.'

I reached for her hand. But the words would not come. If my father carried out his plan, Maggie would witness it soon enough. If I told her now, I did not know what she would do. Scream at Rawley? Attempt to nag him? Neither would work. So I spoke not the first truth in my mind but the second one, also a reality. I said, 'I want to see our son.'

She believed me instantly, since for her this was the first truth. 'I know! I think of him constantly. But I've come to believe he is well cared for. And perhaps it will not be long before we are all three together.'

Maggie, hopeful and loving. Then, a moment later, Maggie managerial and practical. 'I have been thinking, Roger. When this is all over, we can find another cottage like the one at Applebridge and open another inn. It may take a year or so of work to save the money, unless Jee asks the queen to loan it to us. Do you think she would? I thought perhaps somewhere to the north, closer to Isabelle's queendom, since there—'

She talked on. I listened, but not well. It was the sound of her voice I wanted, not any specific course for the uncertain future. Above us, grey clouds moved in a slow wind. My head fell back against the tussock. My limbs felt heavy with the weariness I had been denying; it had not been that long ago that I lay dying. Maggie's voice faded, and I slept.

I dreamed.

Not a dream from Mother Chilton or Stephanie. Not a dream sent through my son, the conduit for dreams. Not one of the terrifying dreams I once received from Katharine, my mad, murdered half-sister. This was an ordinary dream, yet clear and bright, as some ordinary dreams are. And like some of those, it began as memory and then grew into something more.

I walked with Tom Jenkins, the only friend I had ever had, *through the Country of the Dead. Around us were the eerie stillness of the place, its drifting fog, the circles of the Dead in their mindless calm. Tom – courageous, feckless, life-loving Tom – had for the first time in his life confronted something that neither courage nor ale could conquer.*

'What's the good of being dead, Roger? If all you do is sit around for ever like some rock? For that matter, what's the good of being alive, if this is where you end up? You and me and George and everybody – just lumps sitting around in this awful place? Tell me that!'

'Tell you what?'

'What good is it? Death, or even life? Why bother?'

'Tom,' I said softly, 'have you never considered such thoughts before?'

'Of course not! Usual people don't think about such things! They think about hunting and farming and their dinners and bedding women and ... and usual things! But then this is where it all ends up! Here! I wish you hadn't brought me here!'

'But then Tarek would have killed you, and you'd have ended up here anyway.'

Tom groaned, the anguish of a man who truly never thought beyond the next dinner or the next girl and now was being forced to do so. I owed Tom my life; I must do better by him.

'Tom, this is not all there is. Not here, I mean.'

'There is what else? You have no answer! There ain't no more. This is the end – sitting around like lumps, everything inside us gone. I'd rather not have been born.'

'No.' I must give Tom some comfort, and it must be what he wanted. 'I don't think this is the end, Tom. Someone very wise once told me that the Dead are waiting.'

'Waiting for what?'

'I don't know. I wasn't told. But that there is more, eventually. First you will have a long and rich life, with all kinds of girls. And when you do die someday, and come here, it will only be temporary. Like a ... a ...'

'Like an inn on a journey?'

'Just so.'

'Some inn!' He snorted and looked around in disgust, which the next moment brightened into hope. 'You mean that after this, there's another place?'

I would not lie to him. 'I don't know.'

'But you think so?'

'I don't know.'

'But it's possible?'

'Tom, anything is possible.'

'Then in that next place, there might be all the good things? Food and hunting and girls?'

I chose the safe answer. 'I don't know.'

'But do you think—'

'I don't know!'

'Well, don't shout.' He brooded for a long moment. 'I think I better ask your mother.'

Memory, already altered by those last two words, ended, and into my dream *came my mother as I remembered her, dressed in a lavender gown with lavender ribbons in her hair. She walked between me and Tom, taking each of our hands in hers. Her fingers curled warmly around mine. Tom said, 'Roger is troubled.'*

My mother turned to me. Her voice, though sweet, was oddly cool and detached, like those of the old women I sometimes roused on the other side of the grave. 'You are looking in the wrong place, Roger dear,' she said. 'Do not look to Rawley, nor Hygryll, nor me, nor even Mother Chilton. Look to the sword.'

'Yes,' Tom said. 'By damn and piss-pots, yes!'

'Wake up!' Maggie said, and then it was her warm fingers around mine, not my mother's. Maggie's concerned face above mine. Behind her, Rawley demanded, 'Get up, Roger. We move on.'

He strode off. Maggie said, 'Can you stand?'

'Yes.'

'You called out something, I couldn't tell what. Were you dreaming?'

'Yes,' I repeated, getting to my feet and pulling her up with me. And it *had* been a dream, not any sort of visitation from my mother, nor from anyone else. By now, I knew the difference. Her presence had been created by my own mind, just as the memory of Tom Jenkins had been.

And now I knew what to do when we reached Hygryll.

25

Hygryll had not changed. It looked as it had on my first visit, when I'd been treated as an honoured *hisaf*, and on my second years later, when I had nearly been killed and devoured. The village still consisted of round stone huts, windowless and partially covered with earth, grouped around a central flat rock. The peat still felt as springy beneath my boots. The moor stretched away in undulations of gorse, heather, and low mosses. Boulders dotted the bleak landscape.

Rawley's men held Hygryll, but not only them; there were far too many men here to all be *hisafs*. And not all men. As we approached the village, accompanied by an outlying guard, Nell walked towards us. She was beautiful and implacable as ever, her green eyes hard as stone. Rawley turned angrily to the guard.

'What is she doing here?'

He was young, no older than I, and he stammered. 'Sh-sh-she is—'

'I know what she is.'

Nell said, 'We are your allies, remember, Rawley?'

He said, 'You will not stop me.'

Nell said nothing. Her eyes met mine. Under her probing gaze, I gave the tiniest of nods. Yes.

Yes, I will join you.

Yes, I will betray my father.

Yes.

Nell showed no reaction. Maggie's scolding voice leaped into the silence. 'For sweet skies' sake, Rawley,

Charlotte needs to rest. Roger, too. Where can I take them before it starts to rain?'

Not the least of my reasons for loving Maggie was her complete lack of fear of my father.

A woman came up to us. To my surprise, I recognized her. She was one of the women who had wailed and cried outside the mill with the dirty windows, the terrible morning when I had seen both the *hisafs* of the Brotherhood trance babes and the gasping *hisaf* who had just returned from inhabiting a grey dog. Suddenly I understood: These people who had taken Hygryll for my father were from The Queendom and the Unclaimed Lands. They had lost children to death trances, or were from villages that had. Rawley had recruited them in his fight against the Brotherhood. Lord Robert was doing nothing to avenge their children so they joined the outlaw who was, directed here by the couriers following Rawley's command word of the day. Not even fear of setting foot on Soulvine Moor had kept them from their hopes of revenge.

Had my own babe been tranced, I might have done the same thing.

The woman did not recognize me. Possibly she had never even seen me that morning. She took Charlotte's arm, half supporting her. 'Come with me, then. You, too, child.'

Rawnie, who always hated being called a child, scowled fiercely and opened her mouth. At a look from her father she closed it again and followed Charlotte. Maggie led me after them. I glanced sideways at Nell, whose tiny nod echoed my own.

The stone hut was as austere as I remembered, identical to although much smaller than the one where I had once eaten of what Hygryll offered. Then a fire had burned in a central brazier and pungent powders had been thrown on it, inducing trance. Now, in summer, the brazier stood empty. Stone benches ringed the walls, with baskets and bundles stowed beneath them.

The woman pulled out blankets, spread them on a bench, and helped Charlotte lie down. All the woman's movements were abrupt and jerky, as if she were under great tension. She did not speak. As soon as she had gone, Maggie rummaged in the other baskets, producing berries and the kind of flat, coarse bread that is baked on hot stones.

'Rawnie, are you hungry still? Eat this. Charlotte, can you eat a little? Roger?'

'I need to find the piss pit,' I said, inelegantly but accurately.

'How can you need to when you haven't even drunk any – oh, all right, we'll wait here. Charlotte? A few bites of bread?'

I left them, pushing aside the leather flap that served as a door. As I'd hoped, no one was about. Probably Rawley was making a report to his men, or receiving reports, in the large stone lodge I remembered all too well. Moving neither fast nor slow, I walked to the nearest large boulder, trying to look like a man in need of relieving himself.

Nell waited half hidden in a shallow crevice on the far side of the giant rock. I didn't know if she had gone there as snake or woman, but it didn't matter. Far out on the moor my father's guards prevented attack, and here we were unobserved.

The web women never bothered with niceties. Nell said, 'Did you persuade Rawley?'

'No.'

'He is *still* going to make Harbinger's own Soulviners kill him?' Her voice held outrage.

'Yes. But we are going to prevent it.'

She stared at me. 'We are?'

'Yes.' I wished I felt as confident as I sounded. 'But first – and quickly, Nell, I haven't much time – tell me what is "the sword".'

'You should not even have heard of the sword!'

'But I have. I think I have seen it.'

'That is not possible.' She shook her head, but her green eyes – Cecilia's eyes, Fia's eyes, the old man's eyes – had gone round and wondering. 'No, that is not possible.'

Somehow, web women were always telling me I was wrong. 'I saw it! We do not have much—'

'What is it you think you saw?'

'It happened when I brought the Blue army back from the Country of the Dead. Just as I crossed over with them the sky shrieked and ... and split open. Something roared out of that rent, something bright and terrible – I couldn't see it clearly. But it was real, and I – we – just escaped it. Was that the sword?'

'Perhaps. I ... I don't know.'

Nell, tongue-tied and indecisive! But I had no time for astonishment. 'What is the sword? What does it do?'

She looked at me, looked away, chewed her bottom lip. Finally she said, 'We have only conjecture. The sword ... It guards death itself. As such, it keeps the ultimate balance. None that I know have ever seen it. But there are reports, very old tales, from *hisafs* of bygone years. When one of the Dead has accumulated enough power, it ... it takes him.'

'Takes him? What does that mean?'

'We don't know!' she burst out, and I glanced around to see if we were overheard. A stupid action, since all I could see was the rock against which we crouched and the empty moor. Nell twisted her hands together so hard that the blood left them and they turned white.

270

'In the land of the living, one stroke of a sword can turn life into death. Just so, in the Country of the Dead – we think – the sword turns death into the next stage of life. All the tales report is that sometimes a circle of Dead, a very old circle from the ancient clothes worn, will vanish. There is the light and noise you have mentioned, the grey sky splits as if down a seam, and the Dead disappear. Perhaps it is a . . . a reward for the patience of the Dead, but we do not think so. It seems more a way to keep the web of being intact, to keep the balance of power. When a circle of the Dead has accumulated too much power, they must be taken away or the Country of the Dead will be profoundly disturbed. You know something of that, Roger Kilbourne – your meddling disturbed it enough once!'

And so I had. I remembered well the storms and the quaking of the ground I had caused in that place. My mind groped through Nell's words to find something solid to hold on to, something I could verify with my own experience.

'So you believe that when I brought the Blue army back to the land of the living, I upset the Country of the Dead so much that it called forth this sword? In order to right the balance?'

'When you next crossed over, wasn't the Country of the Dead restored to tranquillity?'

It had been, yes. And *I* had caused that, however unwittingly – but when hadn't I acted unwittingly?

This time. Here and now. For once I was going to affect the balance deliberately, aided by this information from Nell and by the dream prompted by the artless questions of Tom Jenkins.

Nell put her hands over her face. 'Oh, Roger Kilbourne, the risks you have taken of damaging the very web of being!'

271

'We all do,' I said, 'every moment of our lives.'

She dropped her hands and glared at me. But before she could retort, a child toddled around the corner of the boulder.

She was no more than two, dressed in a crudely woven gown of undyed wool, barefoot but with a bright ribbon in her hair. When she saw us she stopped, surprise in her green eyes. A small Soulviner, a child of Hygryll, one of those that my father would torture in front of her captive parents to force them to send the old man to the Country of the Dead.

Manipulating the balance in the web.

The child smiled at me.

A woman dashed around the boulder. 'There ye are, ye naughty girl!' It was the same woman of The Queendom who had led Charlotte to a stone hut. This woman had lost her own child to the Brotherhood, and now she had been set to watch this small Soulviner. Did she know what was intended for her charge? Surely she could not, and still minister to the little girl. Surely not!

She saw me, started, blushed. 'Oh, you're Rawley's son – I didn't know before. Beg pardon for intruding, sir. The little one escaped me. Come here!' She scooped the child up and went back towards the village.

No one crouched beside me. There was only a small grey snake coiled at the base of the rock.

'Nell, change back,' I said softly. 'I have a plan, and there is urgent work for you to do.'

What mattered most was time. But, then, when does it not? Time to live as fully as one can before death claims us. Or, in this case, to concoct a drug before death claims an enemy.

'I cannot do it,' Nell said. 'I have not the ingredients. No honey, no pounded flour, no—'

'Then do not make little cakes! Can't you put the drug into some other form? In water, even?'

'He would taste it.'

'In bilberries, then! There are some in the hut, I saw them.'

'Perhaps,' Nell said. Her eyes sought mine. I saw in them what I had never before seen in any web woman: doubt of herself. Often – very often! – they had doubted me, doubted queens, doubted *hisafs* – but never themselves. 'Oh, Roger, I don't think I have enough time! Not if Rawley intends to start the ... the torture right away—'

'I will see that he does not,' I said grimly. 'But you have the proper drugs with you?'

'Yes, I—'

'Then tell Maggie and Rawnie to come to me, and do your work in that hut.' Charlotte would neither interfere nor question; she was a little afraid of Nell. But what was I going to do with the other two? By the time they walked towards me outside the hut, I had decided.

'Listen to me,' I said conspiratorially to Rawnie. 'I have an idea for escape.'

She crowded close to me, even though there was no one else in sight. Her eyes shone. Maggie said, 'Escape? But we are not prisoners here!'

'No, not yet,' I said. 'But who knows what may happen? I think it wise to have means to flee, if we must. Now listen, Rawnie. I saw a herd of ponies on the moor just a moment ago. They are not wild because they wore bridles. They must have belonged to the people of Hygryll and somehow became loose without wandering far. Just a moment ago they went behind that closest tor. You are so good with horses – did you know, Maggie, that she stole a horse once and rode it back to The Queendom from Galtryf? Rawnie, we need those ponies, at least a few of them. If you could coax the lead pony to you and capture it—'

'I will!' Rawnie cried, at the same moment that Maggie said, 'Have you lost your *wits*?'

Rawnie said, 'I can do it, Maggie!'

'Roger, you would send a child out on the moor where there might be another attack, in order to chase ponies she most certainly cannot catch?'

'Yes, I can!' Rawnie said. Her freckles stood out dangerously. 'And I am not a child! I am eleven!'

'Maggie, there is no danger. You saw the tight ring of guards that Rawley has on the moor around Hygryll, and the dogs. Within that ring Rawnie will be just as safe as in the village. Perhaps safer. Hygryll itself will be the focus for any attack. And on the moor, she will see less.'

Maggie knew what I meant by that, even though Rawnie did not. Anyway, there was no stopping Rawnie now. She said, 'I saw some rope by that hut!' and dashed back into it. Maggie pushed her fair curls back from her forehead and gazed at me.

'Roger, I still don't think—'

'Keep watch on her, Maggie. I don't want her here for . . . for Rawley's plans.'

Maggie paled. 'Is he really going to do it? Now?'

'I don't know. But I want Rawnie out of earshot.'

Finally Maggie nodded. 'I can perhaps keep her on the other side of the tor. Oh, Roger, if it were our Tom—'

'Go,' I said, as Rawnie, carrying rope, raced back to us. Maggie had always been able to name hard truths. Sometimes I wish she could not. But she would keep Rawnie away from Hygryll while Nell worked. The indefatigable Rawnie would be a long time searching for ponies that I had invented.

After they had left for the nearby tor, I peered inside the gloom of the round hut. Charlotte lay asleep on the stone bench. Nell sat on the floor under a rushlight she had set burning in its holder on the curved wall. Around her were spread small packets of powder evidently extracted from her gown. She snapped, 'Close the flap, Roger, and stand guard so no one comes in!'

I closed the flap but did not stand guard. I must delay my father. Across the open centre of Hygryll lay the largest of the stone huts, where once I had been led to eat . . .

Do not think of that.

But as I passed the wide flat rock that sat in the middle of the circle of huts, memory was hard to keep at bay. The circles of the Dead with spinning vortexes in the middle. The circle of stone huts with the killing rock in the middle. Myself and Maggie and my son in the middle of this war I had blundered into.

Rawley emerged from the largest dwelling just as I reached it. His men, quiet and tense, followed. A few glanced towards the hut where the bereaved woman watched at least one innocent child. One *hisaf*, the youngest, was blinking back tears.

'Roger,' my father said, not gently. 'Go back to your hut and rest.'

'I am rested. And I must talk to you. Now.'

'You will not change my mind.'

'I do not intend to try. This is about something else. Charlotte.'

Alarm creased his face. 'She is not well? More than merely tired, I mean?'

'She is quietly asleep.' I did not want him blundering into the hut before Nell had finished.

'Then I will talk to you later.' He moved to walk around me. I stepped sideways to block him, and he reached out and shoved me aside. I think that was the moment I hated him the most. He had abandoned my mother and me, he had sent me into danger at least twice, and now he contemplated an act so terrible my mind shrank from picturing it. Yet it was that dismissive shove – *you are of no matter, get out of my way* – that enraged me most. So do our feelings lack proportion and balance.

Balance. That was, had always been, the key.

'Rawley,' I said, unable as ever to call him 'Father', 'I have information that will affect what you do now. Charlotte learned it in Galtryf, from Jago, and she told me. It is crucial knowledge!'

He paused. 'From Jago?'

'Yes. She didn't know if she should tell you, so she asked me just now, in the hut, before she fell asleep again.'

Irresolution appeared on Rawley's face. Behind him, two more men emerged from the hut. They were probably all *hisafs*, and the men on guard duty and holding Hygryll against attack were the ones recruited from The Queendom. Four, five, six *hisafs* – not very many, and one little more than a boy. Good! The rest of Rawley's forces must be scattered throughout The Queendom and the Unclaimed Lands, carrying out their part of the covert war. Whatever that part was.

Rawley spoke over his shoulder. 'I will come soon. Wait for me at the prison.'

The men nodded and started towards the farthest of the stone huts. That, then, was where Harbinger had been taken, along with whatever men and women of Hygryll had been left alive when Rawley took the village. Powerful men and women, made that way by the stolen power of the Dead. But their power was not yet complete, as Harbinger's was. And it had not kept them from being separated from their own children.

Rawley said to me, 'Now what did Charlotte learn from Jago?'

'Not here,' I said and started towards the large boulder where I had talked to Nell. My breath caught in my throat. Would he follow? He did.

Two minutes used up while we walked to the boulder. 'Well, Roger? Tell me!'

'It is difficult to say.' I tried to look like a man grappling with painful truths. Oh, that I had Leo's ability to act! 'Charlotte said ... she said ...'

'*What*?'

'I'm trying to remember the exact words.'

'I don't need the exact words – just tell me!'

'It was when Charlotte and Rawnie were in a ruined courtyard to walk a bit. Every day Charlotte was taken out of her cell for a while under the supervision of either Leo or one of the Soulvine women, although Rawnie had more the run of the keep because Leo—'

'Roger,' he said, and now his voice was low and dangerous.

'I'm trying to tell you! Jago was passing through and he said to her, "It isn't just dogs any more".'

Rawley's face changed. He looked at me hard. 'This was before you inhabited the moor cur?'

'Yes.'

'Had any of the Brotherhood – Leo, for instance – known that you contemplated such a thing?'

'How would I know what Leo knew?'

'But you hadn't told him?'

'No, of course not.' Did he think I was stupid? Apparently so.

'What else did Jago say to Charlotte?'

'I don't know. But you could ask her.'

'I will. Now. Why didn't you tell me this earlier? If Jago meant that the Brotherhood is training to do what you did ... but then why would he tell Charlotte, of all people?'

277

'I don't know,' I said, truthfully.

'This is indeed critical, Roger, but if – what is she *doing*?'

He meant Rawnie, who had appeared from behind a large boulder at full run, holding a rope. I shrugged. 'Playing some game, I suppose.'

'Well, it's safe enough this close to the village and maybe it's best that she not see—' He broke off, not meeting my eyes.

Had Nell had time to finish her preparation? And how was I going to get Rawley to eat it?

He said abruptly, 'I will talk to Charlotte,' and signalled his men to wait where they stood. Was that relief that I detected in his face? Perhaps even he was glad of an excuse to put off torturing the Soulviners. I said, desperate to retain him as long as possible, 'If the Brotherhood is indeed training to—'

'I wish to know exactly what Charlotte said. She may have misunderstood. Or you may have.'

'That is always a possibility,' I said, but he was already striding towards the stone hut where Charlotte lay. I followed. If Nell had not finished . . .

She had. Not little cakes, like those which once sent me into such a suggestible daze that I had bedded Fia. Not a potion, such as had once enabled me to watch Queen Caroline burn at the stake without understanding what I viewed. No, this time there was only an array of bilberries, the moor fruit glistening on a crude stone plate. Nell was gone. But the berries sent out an aroma stronger and sweeter than usual, and they glistened more redly, as if still fresh with dew under early sunshine.

Rawley ignored them. He bent over Charlotte, still asleep on the stone bench. She lay on her back, her hands flung palms up beside her head, in an attitude of complete vulnerability. In the flickering glow from Nell's rushlight on the wall, I saw my father's face soften. Her helplessness and dependence moved him. I thought how different Charlotte was from Maggie, and I was glad all over again that I had Maggie.

'Charlotte? Sweetheart?'

She opened her eyes and clutched at him. What had she been dreaming?

'It's all right, sweetheart. I'm here. I must ask you about something that Jago said to you, at Galtryf.'

'Jago? But he never—'

Over my father's shoulder, his back to me, I nodded vigorously. So it all came to this: The fate of my plan depended on a gentle woman's willingness to lie to her husband, and a ruthless man's hunger for berries. I pantomimed beseeching.

Charlotte, despite her timidity, was not stupid. And she knew what Rawley planned. Maggie, who always dealt the truth around like so many playing cards, had told her. Charlotte continued, with only the smallest of breaks in her voice, '—never talked to me much.'

Rawley probed. 'This was in the courtyard of the keep, when you were being led out to walk. Jago said something like "It isn't just dogs any more". Do you remember?'

I nodded vigorously.

'Yes, yes I do,' Charlotte said. Panic formed in her eyes.

'Tell me exactly what happened. Every word. It's very important.'

'Y-yes.'

I pantomimed eating the berries and pointed at my father.

'What did Jago say?'

'He said . . . he said . . . I'm trying to remember, Rawley. Oh, look! Berries! I'm very hungry, aren't you?'

'No. Try to remember, Charlotte.'

'Well, he said what you just said, about the ... about the dogs. Now let me think ....'

She had no idea what to say next, and she had not Maggie's wit to improvise, let alone her daughter's. Probably to stall, she reached for the berries. Before I could intervene, she had taken and begun to eat a great handful.

'Oh, these are so good! Please have some, Rawley!'

'Charlotte,' he said, and although his voice had not the flick of the whip he employed with me and his daughter, it held impatience. This flustered Charlotte even more. She quailed under his displeasure and looked helplessly at me. Tears formed in her eyes.

He saw them. 'Oh, all right, if it will please you—' He scooped up the rest of the berries and shoved them into his mouth.

When Fia had drugged me, and when Mother Chilton had, the potion had acted quickly. At least, I think so. Both times were a blur, although I remembered hallucinations. Rushlights and pine branches and Tom Jenkins had seemed to grow and shrink, grow and shrink. Flames had seemed to dance on Fia's white arms, turning them pink and gold and orange. Fia had asked me to promise her something and I had breathed 'Anything,' just as I had done anything Mother Chilton had asked of me when she had given me this drug.

But Rawley had eaten only half the dose.

Charlotte said, 'How strange you look! Your beard is a-fire ... no, you do not have a beard ...' She giggled.

In that bleak stone house, half-lit, the giggle was as shocking as a scream. Rawley rose and stared down at her. But he, too, was beginning to be affected. He shook his head, tried to focus his eyes. Whatever he was seeing, he did not speak of it. With a huge effort of will, he turned to me.

'You ... Roger ...' He paused, looking as if he wanted

to be sure of my name. Then, 'You . . . the berries . . . *Nell.*'

He fumbled at his belt for his knife. Even one-handed, I took it away from him easily. All his movements were slowed and clumsy.

'Nell?' Charlotte said. 'Do you think she is prettier than I am?'

This, too, I remembered. The drug dissolved inhibitions. Those taking it would say aloud whatever lay in their minds. I was counting on that.

'Rawley?' Charlotte said. 'Is Nell prettier than I?'

Rawley said nothing, glaring dazedly at me.

'Was Katharine? Did you love her more than you love me?'

Katharine. Not my mad sister, but my mother. The question must have lain a long time in Charlotte's mind, and never would she have spoken it aloud were it not for Nell's berries. Rawley did not answer. All his confused attention focused on me. I needed him to be as suggestible as she was. Everything rested upon that.

'Father,' I said, forcing myself to the word, 'sit down. There, on the bench.'

He did, stumbling towards it. Beside him, Charlotte struggled to sit up, and then leaned against him. They looked like two bewildered children – and it was that which hardened me. *Children*. What Rawley was prepared to do to children. I loomed over my father and said, 'Your men, Rawley. They are waiting for you outside.'

'My men,' he repeated, and nodded. 'Yes, my men.'

Charlotte, receiving no answer to her deepest fear, began to cry silently, tears coursing down her pale cheeks.

'Yes, your *men*,' I repeated, putting into my voice all the authority I could. 'They await your orders. What is the command word of the day, Rawley?'

'The command word . . .'

'Yes, the *command word*. For your men. What is it?'

281

'I—'

'*What?*'

He said nothing. It seemed to me that his face, turned up to mine in the rush-lit gloom, lost some of its confusion. He was fighting hard against the drug. He half rose, but fell again onto the bench.

I seized his shoulder with my one good hand. 'The command word! What is it!'

'There are no moor ponies out there!' a voice cried behind me. Rawnie tore into the hut and hit me hard on my shoulder. 'You lied, Roger! You lied!'

Rawley said, wonderingly, 'You *drugged* me.'

Charlotte put her hands over her face and wept.

And my great plan dissolved like mist on the dawn moor.

26

Rawnie stopped hitting me and stared. Her parents sat side by side on a bench, her mother crying and her father dazed. Fear crossed her face – these were the two people who kept her world together. But Rawnie was not her father's daughter for nothing. And Nell had been teaching her about plants. She looked at the stone bowl stained with unnaturally bright berry juice; she looked again at her usually indomitable father, red juice on his lips; she looked at me.

She said, 'You gave them something bad!'

'Rawnie, get out,' I said. To Rawley, trying to keep desperation from my voice, 'Tell me the command word of the day!'

'What did you give them?' Rawnie demanded. 'How did you know to make it? Where is Nell?'

'Here,' she said, appearing from a shadowed corner, where she had been ... whatever she had been. At the same moment Maggie, breathless and frowning, ran into the hut.

'Rawnie! You terrible girl, you can't just—' Maggie stopped, gazing around in bewilderment, trying to grasp the strange scene around her.

Rawley repeated, 'You ... drugged me.' The muscles of his face were still slack but his eyes were recovering focus, and they were harder and more immovable than the largest boulder on Soulvine Moor. He rose from the bench, stumbled, caught himself. And then he was on me, both hands around my throat.

Had he been completely himself, I would have gone permanently to the Country of the Dead. Or, had he been completely himself, he would not have attacked me at all. But he was half under the influence of the berries, and there was not enough strength in his hands to kill me. Maggie and Nell pulled him off me. Then Maggie hit him with the stone berry bowl, and he went down.

'Rawley!' Charlotte screamed.

'Papa!'

Maggie said, 'He was going to . . . I was just . . . he hurt Roger!'

But it was Nell who knelt beside Rawley, pried open his eyelids, felt his wrist and neck with her long fingers, listened to his chest. 'He will live,' she said, just as Rawley opened his eyes.

Maggie had recovered herself. 'Rawnie, give me that rope. I'm going to tie him. No, Rawnie, leave me alone. He attacked Roger!'

'Don't you dare tie Papa!'

'Rawnie,' Nell said, and there it was – the note of authority I had not been able to summon. 'Stop that. It is only until he recovers from the drug. You don't want him to hurt himself or anyone else, do you?'

'But why did you drug him? No, he said Roger did! Roger, I hate you again!' She kicked me in the shin, hard.

Charlotte, from her share of the drug, had slumped sideways on the bench into sleep – and that, too, I remembered. Perhaps Rawley would do the same. Certainly he now seemed quiescent, saying nothing as Maggie tied him with enough rope to hold a wild boar. Rawnie made up for both her parents' silence by flailing about in Nell's restraining arms and shouting at me.

'Why did you do that? Why? Papa is trying to save us, and he did save us, he brought us here where it's safe and – *why*? Are you that jealous of him because he's

284

powerful and good and he has two hands and you're a cripple? That's it, isn't it? You can't ever be what he is or have what he has and … and … you don't really want the command word of the day! I know you don't! It's all jealousy and … I'll prove that you don't have a good reason for tying up Papa and drugging him – no you don't, hateful Roger! I'll prove it! I'll give you the command word! I heard Papa give it to his captains this morning, when he didn't know I was listening! No, I won't give it to you, you're a terrible monster! I won't tell you anything, ever! So there!'

A sharp intake of breath from Nell. She let Rawnie go. 'You know the command word for Rawley's *hisafs*? Give it to me.'

'No!'

Maggie turned on me. 'What is happening here!'

Nell did not waste time arguing. She vanished, and a lethal grey snake slithered on the floor towards Rawnie.

She screamed and backed into a corner. I had just wit enough to say, 'She will do it, Rawnie, she will bite you and you saw what happened on the moor.'

Rawnie cried, 'The word today is "Hartah"!'

Hartah. My brutal step-uncle, who had raised me along with Aunt Jo. From what twisted motives of remorse or anger had Rawley chosen such a command word? For a moment I saw Hartah before me as he had been on that stormy pebbled beach, the night the wreckers had crashed the *Frances Ormund*. Rain streaming from his greasy hair, his face alight with unholy triumph, his knife bloody from sailors he had just killed. I pushed the image away, to be confronted by a sobbing Rawnie, broken down – finally – by fear and anger and Nell's betrayal.

So I was going to win by terrorizing children after all. Just like my father.

*

We had not much time. Eventually my father's men, waiting for him at the hut holding the imprisoned elders of Soulvine Moor, would tire of the delay and come to seek their leader. We must be ready. Five or six men here in Hygryll – but an army of *hisafs* throughout The Queendom and the Unclaimed Lands. I was going to make use of them all.

'Extinguish the rushlight,' I said to Nell. 'We need the men to be at a disadvantage. And when you strike, can you, can you . . .' I didn't know the words.

'They will not die,' Nell said. She had resumed her human form, and I was shocked to see it. Even though the snake was her soul-sharer, crossing in and out of it so often was taking a toll on her. Her face look ravaged, and her hands trembled. *'Everything has a cost, Roger Kilbourne.'*

Maggie, hands on hips, demanded, 'Tell me what is going on!'

I said to Nell, 'So your women – they can regulate the amount of venom? And where *are* they?'

'Yes. And you will not see them until it is necessary.'

'Roger!'

'Maggie,' I said desperately, 'I can't explain now. Please give me your trust on this. Tie and gag Rawnie so that she cannot make a sound. Please, sweetheart!'

Immediately Rawnie screamed and bolted for the door. Maggie caught her, pulled a cloth from a pocket in her gown – an apron or sleeve or something else, I know not what – and stuffed it in Rawnie's mouth. Between us we wound rope intended for the non-existent moor ponies around the girl's writhing body, pinning her arms and legs. Rawnie struggled, but I knew how strong Maggie was. I had always known. I depended upon it.

'Roger, you had better explain all this!'

'I will, Maggie. Soon.'

My father's eyes watched us with impotent, dazed hatred. His eyes were the last thing I saw before I extinguished the rushlight.

Then we waited. The wait seemed long, but probably was no more than ten minutes. Maggie, Nell, and I did not talk. Rawley, Charlotte, and Rawnie could not. I was aware of Nell's laboured breathing, but there was no remedy for that. My plan needed Nell.

Voices outside the stone hut.

Nell's hoarse breathing stopped.

The first of Rawley's men raised the door flap and entered, making a small wordless exclamation at the lack of light. Before his eyes could adjust enough to see, a small grey snake had slithered forward and struck at his hand. He barely had time to shout before he fell.

His shout brought the other four rushing in. And each fell, although this time I did not see the snakes. It was over in a moment. The door flap still rippled in place before each dark silhouette lay still on the hut floor, and three web women lay beside them.

Maggie fumbled with one rushlight, and then another. I stared at the floor, covered with bodies. Nell, gasping even more loudly, bent her head.

I said, 'You did not say – you didn't tell me—'

'You . . . asked if the . . . men would survive. Not . . . if we would.'

'But before . . . on the moor when they bit the Brotherhood . . .'

'Did you think,' she said with sudden fierceness, 'that they . . . could go on doing that indefinitely? I . . . could barely . . . two with enough strength left . . . They knew they would not survive. So your plan had better succeed, Roger Kilbourne!'

If it did so, it would be because of her. I did not say this. Sorrow flooded me for these three additional deaths

287

I had caused, but there was no time for sorrow. There was no time to think of Rawnie. Maggie would attend to her, to Charlotte, to Rawley. I could trust Maggie's competence.

'Roger!' Maggie said dangerously.

'Soon. There is more I must do. Please, Maggie.'

Wordlessly I helped Nell, even weaker than I had thought, to her feet, and we went outside to change the balance of the world.

It had begun to blow and spit rain. Not a storm, just the usual fitful moor weather, the clouds hanging grey and low. I helped Nell back to the shelter of the large boulder, on the side farthest from Hygryll. In some of these huts were more of my father's recruits, guarding Harbinger and the Soulvine children. I did not want us to be seen.

'*Where do they go?*' Stephanie and Mother Chilton had both asked me, in blurry dreams. I knew now what they had meant. And I knew the answer.

Nell collapsed into the crevice in the rock, breathing heavily, her green eyes huge in her weary face. I knew that she wanted to sleep, above all else, as I had wanted to sleep after crossing back from the moor cur, and also that she would not do so. Not yet.

I said, 'Are you ready?'

'Yes.' She tried to smile at me, failed. But I did not need Nell's smile. I needed her courage and her gift. This woman of the soul arts, whom I had not met until a fortnight ago, whom I did not even like, who looked so much like Cecilia – this woman was about to become closer to me than anyone living, even Maggie. Was *I* ready?

It didn't matter. It was time. I took her cold hand.

Nell closed her eyes. Rain blew past our crevice. In the grey light I could see the pale translucence of her eyelids,

288

veined with blue, and the intense movements of the eyeballs beneath. Nell was concentrating, perhaps harder than she ever had before in her life. She was performing an act of will that drew on all of whatever small strength she had left. She was trying to reach my infant son.

I could not. I had received my dreams from Mother Chilton and Stephanie through little Tom, the conduit. That's why they had been so blurry, sharpening as the days passed and the baby learned to see those around him. But never had I been able to initiate communication through Tom. I was not a web woman, and the soul arts were closed to me. That included the invisible shadowy web of dreams, which I could receive but not send.

Not so Nell. All at once her thin body twitched so violently that she scraped her shoulder against the rock. I gathered her into my arms and cradled her, as if she had been Cecilia, had been Maggie, had been my son himself.

'Reach Stephanie,' I said unnecessarily, for of course I had told her this already. 'We need the little queen!'

Nell wasted no precious energy on responding to me. I might as well not have spoken. But her body in my arms went completely still, the most ferocious stillness I had ever seen.

The message must go through Stephanie. When we were in the high western mountains with Tarek's army, the princess had had the power, untutored and lethal, to kill in dreams. She had to be standing close to her victim, and my mad half-sister had used that power to turn a six-year-old into an unwitting murderer. I was not using Stephanie to kill, even had that been possible. But only through the child's power, now shaped by Mother Chilton, could I also use my son to accomplish what must be done.

Nell's lips moved. She opened her eyes and said to me,

the single strangled word almost drowned by a sudden gust of windy rain, 'Roger . . .'

'Hold on, Nell! Tell Stephanie to go through my son. To send the message to all my father's *hisafs* at once. *All* of them. He can do that, my babe can . . .'

Could he? All at once this entire desperate plan seemed to me sheer folly. It depended on two children, one of them an infant. I did not even know if Mother Chilton happened to be with Stephanie at this moment, or if Stephanie would understand enough, or if my father's *hisafs* would obey this strange message, received in such a strange way . . .

'The command word!' I said urgently to Nell. 'You must make sure Stephanie gives them the command word of the day!'

A faint scowl on her pale lips, but she had no time for my fretting. I was the creator of this plan but, like an architect with the building of a palace, must depend on others to carry it out. *'Where do they go?'* All those children, whose power, whose *vivia*, had been stolen by the Brotherhood to balance the power stolen by Soulvine Moor from the Dead. It was such a precarious balance, that web of power. Destroy the bodies of the Dead, so that their power can flow to the men and women of Soulvine Moor in the land of the living. But then there is an imbalance in the Country of the Dead. So balance that by bringing over the *vivia* of the children. And put it where?

Into the darkness that was the other side of Galtryf. The darkness that prevented any soul arts from working in Galtryf. The darkness that I had seen on the other side, from a safe distance. I had also seen the glints of light in that darkness, the blurry flickering silver that was the life force of the stolen children, balancing the web.

Nell's lips formed my father's command word: *Hartah*.

The wind changed direction, blowing rain on her ravaged face. I shifted against the rock to shield her as best I could. What was she seeing? What was Stephanie doing?

And then I felt it, in my own mind. For I, too, was a *hisaf* that Stephanie could, through Tom, reach.

First the blurry colours, but less blurry than before. I glimpsed smooth polished wood – the side of a cradle? A woman bent over me, too close to see, all warmth and comforting smell. Cradle and woman vanished and I saw Stephanie. For a moment I *was* Stephanie. I felt my thin small body enclosed in an unfamiliar corset of bone, that was somehow not unfamiliar. I heard my skirts rustle around me. I held a hand, hard, and knew it was Jee's. Surprise and fear flooded me, and I felt my mouth make an O! Then all that was gone and I was Roger Kilbourne, receiving words as clear and crisp in my mind as if spoken into my ears by a lord commander himself. Impossible to tell that the vision, devised by Nell, came from a child queen through an infant who understood them as little as an aqueduct understands the water it carries.

'Rawley sends you this command through web women who have finally decided to work with us against the Brotherhood. The command word of the day is "Hartah". Here is what you must do, immediately.'

The brusqueness, the sound of authority, might have come from my father himself instead of being crafted by Nell with the last of her strength. Had I been one of Rawley's *hisafs*, I would have instantly obeyed.

The rain lessened. My mind emptied. I looked down, and I saw that Nell was dead.

I don't know how long I stayed there, in the damp and chill, holding her. It was Maggie who eventually found me. Maggie, usually so jealous of any other woman, who this time seemed to grasp the difference. She took Nell from me into her strong arms and then laid her upon the peat and moss. I realized the drizzle had ceased.

'Roger,' Maggie said with the gentleness that I saw only rarely, but always when it mattered, 'what have you done?'

'It is not done yet,' I said, before I knew I was going to say anything.

She knelt beside me and took my hand. 'What must I do to help you?'

'Nothing,' I said. But Maggie was not capable of doing nothing. She got me to my feet; I nearly tumbled over from sitting so long cramped in the crevice. She led me to another stone hut, blessedly empty of people. She spread a blanket from beneath a stone bench upon it, pushed me onto the bench, wrapped me in the blanket. I hadn't realized I was shivering.

'Now tell me,' she said. 'It can't be long now before Rawley's remaining men set him free.' But still I could not speak. The words would not come. I was too exhausted, too filled with doubt. What right had I to think that this insane plan would work? Just because once I had done ... had once seen ...

I could not stay here. I had to know: had Nell and I succeeded after all? Was there a chance? I was on fire to know what would happen – not here, but in that other realm, where it counted.

'Maggie ... please ... wait here. Please.'

I left her and crossed over.

Darkness—

Cold—

Dirt choking my mouth—

Worms in my eyes—

Earth imprisoning my fleshless arms and legs—

I stood in the Country of the Dead, among the low hillocks that, in the land of the living, was Hygryll. Fog drifted around me, for which I was grateful. I was taking a chance that *hisafs* of the Brotherhood were not waiting here to grab anyone crossing over. Although this was not as much of a chance as it would have been yesterday. If Nell and I were succeeding, the Brotherhood would have other concerns to occupy them.

Through the fog I glimpsed the boulder, as big on this side as on the other, where I had held Nell in my arms. From the boulder I set out southwest. I knew where I was going. I had been here before. Soon I came to the large circle of Dead, the one I had seen after Cecilia's death. The biggest of the circles, and the one with no spinning vortex in its centre. Instead, my mother had sat there, tranquil in the mindless calm of the Dead, with fresh blood inexplicably staining her lavender gown.

The circle was gone. So was she.

I almost cried out. Had Soulvine Moor taken her – destroyed her to suck the power from yet one more person? If so, I would never know. She would not exist anywhere, her chance at eternity gone to feed the monstrous desire of men like Harbinger to live for ever.

I could not bear it. But perhaps she had not been destroyed but only moved, perhaps even by my father . . .

And then I was running through the fog, searching, heedless of who might see me. My feet left no mark on the grey grass. I darted here and there, without plan, running – for how long? I didn't know. Time, like distance, is different on the other side of the grave, and impossible to gauge when light neither wanes nor waxes and no sun ever rises. Time here can stretch or shrink.

Eventually I came to a place where the fog had lessened and lightened: pale drifting wisps rather than dark shrouds. I could see better here.

If I crossed back over now, my father might already be

free. Rawley's men, tired of waiting for him in the prison hut, would go searching for him. They would find him and Charlotte and Rawnie bound in the hut where supposedly I lay asleep, but they would not find me. Not until I could see, without interference from Rawley, what Nell and I had accomplished. If we had accomplished anything.

So I walked north, or what would have been north in the land of the living, towards the border of the Unclaimed Lands. I walked a long time. This was the route I had once taken with Cecilia, and again with Tom Jenkins. It had not changed much.

But time had. More time must have passed on the other side, because shortly after I left the moor and reached the pine and birch woods of the Unclaimed Lands, I saw it happen.

Something materialized beside me. Four men, their arms laden. Immediately one of them shoved his bundle into the arms of another and seized me. 'I have one!'

'I am Roger Kilbourne!' I cried. 'Rawley's son!'

That stopped them. I did not know any of the four. The man who held me turned my face towards him and studied me. He said, 'Could be – there is a resemblance. But perhaps only by chance.'

I said, 'I know what you are doing. With the babes. Rawley sent a message through the web women to do it. With the command word "Hartah"!'

'Aye, he knows,' another said, and the man released me.

They carried sleeping infants. No, not sleeping: tranced. Three of the men carried two babes apiece, and the one who had grabbed me had carried one, now thrust unceremoniously atop another child, covering its face. It made no matter. These children could not be smothered, nor killed.

The men laid their burdens on the ground. As they bent, I saw the distaste on the face of the youngest *hisaf*, barely past boyhood himself. The one who had grabbed me demanded, 'Were ye with Rawley when he sent this order two days ago?'

Two days ago. Time had indeed shrunk here. What answer would be safest? I said, 'I was in Hygryll, yes, but I was not with him at that moment.'

'And what does he mean by it? It makes no sense!'

Now all four glared at me, ignoring the tranced infants lying at their feet. I shrugged. 'He did not tell me.'

'Do ye know nothing, then?'

I shrugged again. But I knew what my father, unlike the Brotherhood, had not known. The Brotherhood had understood the web of being. Rawley had been blinded, just as Nell said, by his own rigid idea of a breach in the fortifications between the living and the Dead. Jago, and Harbinger, and even vain and hapless Leo had understood the idea of balancing the powers of life and death. But I knew – better than most! – that solid bodies, not only the *vivia* of souls, could change the balance. I had learned that when I brought back from the Country of the Dead the bodies of Bat, of Cecilia, of the Blue army. My theft of bodies that belonged on the other side of the grave had so disturbed the Country of the Dead that it had nearly been destroyed.

And now my father's *hisafs*, unwittingly, were bringing over bodies that I hoped would disturb it again.

All over The Queendom, all over the Unclaimed Lands, every one of my father's *hisafs* were carrying tranced infants through the grave into the Country of the Dead. The men had stolen them in the night from cottages and manor houses and perhaps even from Glory itself, materializing as easily inside dwellings as once the Brotherhood had done to steal the children in the first place. So many infants, taken from their grieving parents. Taken, then returned in circles on the ground, as empty and mindless as the true Dead. Those little bodies balanced the soul power sent to the darkened Galtryf in the Country of the Dead, which in turn balanced the power taken from the Dead to go to the living men and women of Soulvine Moor. A delicate balance. A web of being.

Which I was now deliberately breaking apart.

All at once there came to my mind the image of the spider web in John Small's cottage, which had trapped a thrashing baby mouse all those months ago. The web straining under the mouse's efforts to free itself, until the wild Small children had seized the whole and swept away the web completely.

'I asked ye a question, young Rawley,' the *hisaf* growled.

'My name is Roger!'

'Whatever yer name be, I asked ye a question. What is your father doing?'

'I told you that I don't know.'

The man stepped closer. 'I don't believe ye. Ye were with him at Hygryll, and we were on our way there when this . . . this message invades our heads . . .'

Despite himself, the *hisaf* shuddered. I saw that he hated doing so, that he considered the shudder a sign of weakness. But I remembered the terrible dreams my mad sister had sent me, and I understood his shudder. The first time it happened, I had felt not only terrified and bewildered but also invaded, the wall of my mind breached by someone else.

The youngest *hisaf* pushed towards me, stepping on the hand of one of the tranced infants. I knew, however, that the child felt nothing. The boy cried, 'If he be lying, let us get the truth from him! Here, or there!' He raised his fist.

'Stop,' said the man who had grabbed me. 'We have our orders, Hal. Do naught to him.'

'But he—' The boy stopped.

Everything stopped.

In that land of silence, how can one discern an even deeper silence? But we all did, a sudden profound pause in the very air. My breath tangled in my throat. And then the ground heaved beneath us, throwing me off my feet. A sharp *crack!* filled the air, as of lightning right beside me, where there was no lightning. Someone screamed. The youngest *hisaf* vanished, fleeing back to the land of the living. A moment later the other three followed him.

I stayed. I wanted to see ... I must know ... I could not gather all seven infants to me, there was no time and I had but one hand. But I grabbed the closest two, clutching at some parts of their little bodies, I had no idea which. The ground gave another great heave, tossing us all into the air. Another great crack, and the sky above split and something roared from the great rent, something I could not really see but could feel in every shiver of my bone and every jangle of my teeth, something bright and terrible beyond belief—

The sword.

I never did really see it. Instead I crossed back over, the two infants squashed against me, and emerged beside a settlement of wooden huts. The other *hisafs* lay shaking on the ground, in a warm rain. Two of them shouted incoherently, and people burst from the huts and ran towards us through the rain.

I did not shout, did not get up, did not look to see who raced towards me. Instead I looked at the two children lying beside me, and the other five scattered over the sopping ground. All seven screamed in fear, wet and squirming and squalling and alive, alive, alive.

'Alice!'

'Dick!'

'Peter!'

I looked up at that, but it was not Peter One-Hand that was meant. One of the babes was named Peter, and his mother grabbed up the shrieking bundle and crushed it to her. She was a withered hag, used up by a hardscrabble life in this grindingly poor village, but not even Queen Caroline had been so beautiful in her joy.

People running, shouting, milling around, hugging the recovered children. A man seized me, a toothless and bearded man of such powerful build that his grip wrenched my shoulder. His country accent was so thick that I barely understood him.

'What did ye? What happened?'

How to explain? I could not. So I offered the simplest lie. After all, it had served me well before. 'The witches have untranced your children, and we brought them back to you.'

We were heroes. Old women rushed to fall on their knees and kiss our hands. My father's men liked this as little as I did. Too shaken to rejoice, they muttered something no one understood and tried to walk resolutely away along the narrow, faint track that led from the village. The leader thought to toss over his shoulder, 'More children to rescue!' and that released us.

When we were out of sight of the border settlement, the *hisafs* turned on me. 'What happened, young Kilbourne? And do not lie to us as you did to those villagers! What did Rawley do?'

What did Rawley do? Rawley, not me! A hot retort rose to my lips, but I must have learned some good sense in the last years, because I stifled it. This was my passage out. If I wanted to be able to slink back to obscurity with Maggie and our son, I must not take credit for the rescued children. Must not name little Tom. Must not explain

298

what had happened in the Country of the Dead.

What *had* happened in the Country of the Dead?

All at once, *I had to know*. That bright and terrible rending of the sky ... the sword ...

So I said to the *hisafs*, 'I don't know what my father did. He keeps his plans close to his chest, even to me.' That sounded like Rawley. 'I know only that he wished to have as many tranced children as possible cross over as soon as possible. I was on my way to a cottage with such a child when ... when *that* happened. More, I do not know.'

I watched them considering, weighing, finally accepting my story. The leader said, 'Then we will go to Hygryll and ask Rawley.' His face darkened. 'There is still the old man to dispose of.'

Was there? That, too, I needed to know. But not yet. I was on fire to cross over and see what had happened to the Country of the Dead. Would these men never leave!

The leader said, 'You can travel with us to Hygryll, young Kilbourne.' The youth glared at me, then lowered his eyes lest I see. He was easy to read. Jealous of me, Rawley Kilbourne's favoured heir. He knew nothing, the stupid oaf.

I said, 'My father told me to go to a particular cottage. I think I must, at least to see if what occurred here has happened to other babes as well.'

'Aye, that is sense,' the leader said. 'Anyway, Rawley can tell us more. Then travel easily, young Kilbourne.' He turned to stride back down the track and the others followed.

But I wanted to give Nell her due. Nell and all the other web women who had died for this redemption. So I called to the men's departing backs, 'I do know one thing more! My father is grateful for the cooperation of the women of the soul arts. He told me that whatever happens next, it would depend upon them!'

The youngest *hisaf* turned to glare at me once more.

When they had disappeared through the trees, I bit my tongue hard and crossed over.

Darkness—

Cold—

Dirt choking my mouth—

Worms in my eyes—

Earth imprisoning my fleshless arms and legs—

Tranquillity. Calm. Nothing of upheaval or fog. And nothing of that bright and terrible sword. The trees, still and dim, did not rustle above my head.

No path here, but I walked through the woods back to where the settlement had been in the land of the living. There were Dead here; probably families had lived in this little hollow a long time. The Dead sat quietly, singly or in one small circle. No fog around their heads, no vortexes stealing the power accumulated by their long-waiting souls.

'*We have only conjecture,*' Nell had said to me, with great reluctance to share even the conjectured lore of the web women. '*The sword . . . It guards death itself, a way to keep the web of being intact. To keep the balance of power, when the Country of the Dead is too profoundly disturbed.*'

So I had deliberately disturbed it as profoundly as I could. And the sword had righted it. Death had, however belatedly, guarded its own.

27

It was a day's journey back to Hygryll. I needed to rest often. Hunger gnawed at me, despite the roots and berries I found, and the occasional nut overlooked by squirrels. I did not pause to set snares, and anyway I had never been very good at it. By nightfall I had still not reached Hygryll. I spent a miserable night in the rain, huddled beside a great tor.

I reached Hygryll just as everyone else prepared to leave it. Only a few people remained in the stone village. Some laden ponies stood by the flat rock where once I had lain bound and moments from being murdered. Even now I could not suppress a shudder when I glimpsed it. But then Maggie was running towards me, and all shudders were over.

'Roger!'

She threw herself into my arms, and we both lost our balance and tumbled onto the wet peat. Not a heroic reunion. But that didn't matter. Nothing mattered except that she was with me, her sweet body in my arms and her straggling fair curls shoved into my mouth. I spat them out, pulled her upright, and murmured into her ear, 'Tom?'

'I don't know. There is no one to ask.'

No one to ask – of course not. Nell was dead. But why had not Mother Chilton or Stephanie tried to reassure me that Nell and I had succeeded, that Tom was all right?

Sudden fear swamped me, so strong that I went cold and then hot. I had never thought – what if the sending of so many simultaneous visions to so many *hisafs* had the same terrible effect on little Tom that it had had on Nell and the web girls? What if, in winning the war on Soulvine Moor, I had harmed my son? What if he were now—

My child, whom I had never even seen. If he lay dead by my own hand—

'What is it?' Maggie said. 'Why is your heart racing like that? Roger – is it *Tom*? What have you done?'

'It is nothing,' I said. 'I have no news of Tom. Truly, Maggie – I would tell you if I did. I know no more than you. Where are you going now? Those ponies are laden for a journey. Where is Rawley?'

'He left yesterday with all his men. The tranced children are all restored to life – but you already knew that, didn't you? I see it on your face.'

'And the old man?'

Maggie's eyes searched mine. 'Dead. He was found dead in the stone hut, without a mark on him. That was before the reports began to come to Rawley about the restored children. And *I* have been waiting! For you, for news of my baby, for someone to explain all of this to me!'

Any other woman, faced with so much uncertainty and fear, would have burst into tears. Maggie glared at me and clenched her fists. I took her again into my arms.

'You are right to wait—' As if she had any choice! 'I'm certain Mother Chilton will send a web woman about Tom. The war with Soulvine Moor is over. And we will go ...'

Where? I had nowhere to take Maggie, no home, no money. And I did not know where my son laid his downy head. For me, the war was not over.

'Roger!' It was Rawnie, barrelling out of a round stone hut towards the ponies. 'You're back! Where did you go?

Did you hear the news? I forgive you for tying me up. Papa explained why it was necessary. I would forgive Nell, too, except she's dead.'

That sobered her. To my surprise, the soberness lasted for more than a moment. Something dark rested in Rawnie's eyes that had never been there before. Not fear, for she was still incapable of more than momentary fear. But her eyes held sadness. She had seen and experienced too much for a little girl.

'Roger,' Rawnie said, 'Do you think Nell is happy in the Country of the Dead?'

No one wished to stay in Hygryll. For what was left of the day we journeyed north. In the evening we camped on the moor, perhaps two dozen of us: Rawnie, a very pale Charlotte, Maggie and I, plus a small band of men from The Queendom. I did not see the woman who had lost her child and then cared for the Soulviner children my father had been prepared to torture. I asked Maggie about her.

'When the first report came that the tranced children had been restored, she left with the first group of Rawley's men to go to her own baby,' Maggie said, her tone implying that I should have already guessed this. 'Most of the parents did.'

'And the children of Soulvine Moor that Rawley held at Hygryll?'

'Some women of the moor arrived just before you did. Ragged old women, no one that we could possibly see as a threat. They begged for the children and of course I gave them.'

Maggie gave them. I could easily picture it: Rawley and his men gone, Charlotte bewildered and uncertain of what Rawley would want, Maggie assuming charge. She would have been glad to give the children back, thinking all the while of her own babe but not giving way to tears or losing hope. Not my Maggie. She hoped for the best now; I could feel it in the grasp of her hand. And if the worst came, she would face that, too.

We sat around an immense peat fire, blazing on Soulvine Moor as if to announce to the sky that the war was over and we had won. Nonetheless, grey dogs patrolled the edges of the camp, along with men in rotating shifts. I did not expect an attack. The Brotherhood might chase Rawley for revenge, but they must also know he was not here. And without him to imprison, they had no use for Charlotte or Rawnie.

And me? I didn't know if they knew where I was. But the Brotherhood would now be in disarray, their war lost, their prize of immortality wrenched from their grasp. All this they would impute to Rawley, not me. If they could muster their fleeing group enough to attack, it would probably focus on my father, not me.

I had eaten for the first time in nearly two days. That and sleeplessness sapped my energy, but there was something I must do first. Having convinced myself that I was at no risk, I determined to take a risk. Just as I had to see whether the sword had righted the Country of the Dead, this was something I must do. Something I must know.

Maggie, however, would not let me go. She had waited too long. 'Come away from the fire, Roger.'

'It isn't time to—'

'Yes, it is! Come!'

There was no flouting that tone. I took her hand and we stumbled to an outcropping of rock. Maggie pulled me down and we sat with our backs to the cold stone. I put my arms around her.

'No, Roger, no kissing. Not now. Tell me!'

'Tell you what?'

'Everything. Everything you ... have left out since we met.'

It was the catch in her voice, the little sob on the word 'you' that undid me. That and the desire to finally trust, to be known, to love. I had been a long time coming to that. So I gave what she asked: everything. I told her about my mother, Aunt Jo, Hartah. About the wreck of the *Frances Ormund*, Mistress Conyers, Cecilia. Everything about Cecilia. And then about Mother Chilton, Queen Caroline, Tom Jenkins, Tarek son of Solek, Princess Stephanie, Lady Margaret. Everything I had learned from Alysse and the mouse-woman and Nell. And finally, all I had done to right the balance between the living and Dead, this realm and that other, Galtryf and the sword. Only one thing did I hold back: the part played by our son, and what he was. I talked until my throat was raw, and the blazing campfire visible across the heather had died to a ruddy glow in the darkness.

Did Maggie believe me? Perhaps, with her native scepticism, not all of it. But she listened without a single word. When I finally finished, she kissed me softly and said nothing.

'Maggie—'

'No, not now. No more talk now. We must sleep.'

We returned to the fire. Everyone else except the guards slept. When Maggie, too, gave way to exhaustion, I left her and made my way back to the outcropping of rock. To the guard I signalled a need for privacy behind a clump of gorse, and he nodded.

Alone in the shadows I bit my tongue and crossed over.

Night in the land of the living, an endless grey and tranquil day in the Country of the Dead. I began walking. All was as it should be in that quiet place, and the few Dead that I passed were as they should be, waiting for whatever it was that came next for them. If the sword had a part to play in that, I knew I would never witness it until, one far distant day, my own time came.

The walk back to Hygryll, unburdened by packs or ponies or Rawnie, did not take long. The round stone huts had all vanished, but the large flat rock was there. Upon it sat Harbinger.

I approached him warily, but why should that be? He was now just another of the Dead, this old man who had aspired to live for ever by destroying the souls of others. None of the Brotherhood, if that band still was in existence, surrounded him now. He was of no use to them. He sat calmly, his green eyes open and unseeing, and I passed him by as if he were just another boulder or tree.

What had I expected when I reached the circle of Dead that had surrounded my mother? What I feared was that she was still gone, another of Soulvine Moor's victims. She was not. The huge circle of fifty Dead, however, had vanished, and my mother sat beside one other Dead on the tranquil moor. Without the fog, even from a distance I could see the lavender of her gown. No – not another Dead. The figure rose. My heart clutched – an assassin from the Brotherhood?

It was my father.

'Roger,' he said tonelessly.

'What are you doing here?' I heard the harshness of my tone, and did not regret it.

'Are you surprised that I would come?'

'Very surprised.'

Anger broke from him, his usual defence. 'You understand nothing.'

'I understand that you abandoned her. And me.'

'I explained to you once, but I will do so again since you are acting like a sulky boy and boys need repetition: I left you both for your own safety. I did not know that

306

would make her less safe, nor that you would be taken by your Aunt Jo before I could find you.'

It must have been Rawley who'd removed my mother before, when I could not find her. He must have carried her to some place of safety. The realization didn't lessen my anger (and why had I not thought to do the same thing?). We faced each other on the desolate moor like two fighting dogs, two moor curs. He was stronger than I, with two good hands. If this came to blows—

It did not. My father broke. He put his hand in front of his face, but not before I saw the tears he immediately tried to blink back. He said quietly, 'I loved her, you great fool. I always will.'

And even though I saw that it was the truth, a lifetime of anger cannot be released that quickly. I wanted to hurt him, still. So I said, 'Really? And does Charlotte know that?'

The tears vanished. Rawley glared at me, but he had himself in control. 'There are so many things about love that you do not yet understand, Roger. I hope that someday you will.'

'Yes, with luck I may yet turn out like *you*.'

A faint smile, which reduced me to a child. Fresh fury rose in me. But his next words disarmed it entirely – as perhaps he intended.

'I have told everyone that it was I that brought an end to the war with Soulvine, that the victory was mine. I did so because there may be some of the Brotherhood, or of Soulvine Moor, who are not yet ready to give up. Now they will seek revenge on me, not you, and you and Maggie can live safely with my grandchild.'

I gasped, 'How . . . how did you know . . . .'

'It doesn't matter how I know. No one else does. Be well, Roger.' And he vanished, crossing back over.

My anger at him was replaced with a hollowness at my

heart. All these meetings in bitterness and anger, and I still did not know what Rawley Kilbourne truly was. Ruthless warrior, burning with vengeance. Tender husband to two women. Abandoner, betrayer, rescuer, protector.

Kneeling, I touched my mother's face. She looked just as I remembered from childhood. I could almost feel her arms around me, hear her voice singing to me. That could not come again. But she looked peaceful and calm, and there was no longer fresh blood on her gown. Whatever she waited for, she waited in peace. I kissed her tranquil cheek. 'Good-bye, Mother. Be well.'

I crossed back over, knowing I had seen both my parents for the last time.

When I returned to camp, it was past dawn. Maggie still slept, but the others ate breakfast or watered ponies, and someone was singing.

It was Rawnie. I had never heard her sing before. The voice from that scrawny, freckled throat was surprisingly full and sweet. Someone played upon a lute, and to its accompaniment Rawnie sang Leo's plaintive tune:

> Although you to the hills do flee,
> My love you can't escape.
> Your heart, my sweet, belongs to me
> Though you may change its shape.
>
> Never, never will I cease
> To follow where you go,
> And ever, ever will I be
> The hound upon your doe.
>
> Do what you will and what you can,
> Employ the arts you know —

Ever, ever will I be
The hound upon your doe.

The words struck me differently than they had when Leo had sung them. I squatted beside Maggie and put my good hand on her shoulder. She woke and smiled at me. I smiled back, not wanting to escape, nor to cease following her, nor to seek anything except her loyal heart and my infant son. And never let either of them go again.

28

There was still the gnawing fear for Stephanie. No vision had come from her since the sword had righted balance in the Country of the Dead. Was she ill from such great effort in the soul arts? She was but seven years old. Nell had been a woman grown, and her exertions had cost her life. Nor did Mother Chilton dream to me.

I had lost an entire night's sleep and during the next day's travel I stumbled along, half awake. Fortunately we halted early, just over the border between Soulvine Moor and the Unclaimed Lands. I fell asleep immediately, and I dreamed. It was, however, a dream so faint that when I woke, I could not be sure if I had only imagined it from the desperation of my desire – a dream of a dream:

A wavering swirl of grey, without place or colour. A figure, which I took to be a woman only by the high-pitched voice, although even about that I could not be sure. A single word: 'Wait.' I woke.

Wait! What was I doing except waiting – and how often had I been doing it before? Wait for Lord Robert, wait to recover from inhabiting the moor cur, wait to get to Hygryll, wait to see my son, wait for the sword to right the Country of the Dead! My life consisted of waiting, broken only by bursts of desperate, terrified action.

I waited. I did so with relief: the dream had undoubtedly come through little Tom, which meant he was alive. But my relief was mixed with yet more fear: Was it so faint because Tom, like the web women whose visions he passed on, was exhausted and ill from his efforts? They were not even really 'efforts'; he was like an aqueduct through which water passed with no exertion on its part – or so I hoped. But even so, an aqueduct can give way under a torrential flood.

Maggie knew none of this. And yet she never forgot anything, a trait I had cursed before and now had cause to be uneasy about again.

'Roger,' she said as we began the day's travel north, 'you look very tired. Are you worried about Tom?'

'Why would I be worried about Tom?'

She said slowly, 'You asked me something once. You asked if I had seen him "vanishing and reappearing". You would only ask that if you thought he was ... was like you. But he never vanished. He is not a *hisaf*, is he?'

'No.' I was glad to be able to answer her honestly, and I hoped she would ask no further. But then she would not have been Maggie.

'He cannot cross over to ... you know?'

'No. He cannot.'

'Can he do what Mother Chilton can? And those other women? Oh, Roger ... is he a witch?'

I heard the dread in her voice. 'No,' I said, again honestly, 'he is not as the web women are.'

'So *where is he*?'

'They'll tell us soon.'

'But how can you know that? Have you received word?'

'Only to wait. But I'm sure Mother Chilton will send word soon.' I was not sure.

By late afternoon even Rawnie was tired. Someone put her on one of the pack ponies, where she appeared to fall asleep. But not so, because from the greater height atop the pony she was the first to see the horsemen.

'Soldiers! Soldiers in the valley, coming on horses!'

The men looked at each other and drew their weapons:

knives, swords, a few *guns*. I strained my ears to hear shots, simultaneously looking around for a place to hide Maggie. That proved unnecessary. The horsemen wore the purple of Lord Robert's army and even before his horse had fully halted, the captain was swinging down from the saddle. 'Roger Kilbourne?'

'I am Roger Kilbourne.'

'You are summoned to the palace at Glory.'

We gazed at each other: I ragged, weary, scrawny, uncombed, without a bath in far too long. He, well-fed and clean-shaven, wore a new purple tunic and high boots. His breastplate and helmet shone in the sun. But his face held wariness and even fear. This captain was here under unwelcome orders, and he did not like dealing with whatever preternatural thing he considered me to be.

I said, 'Who summons me?'

'Lord Regent and High Commander Robert Hopewell, acting for Her Grace Queen Stephanie.'

'And why does Lord Robert wish to bring me to Glory?'

'I carry out Lord Robert's orders,' he said stiffly. I would get no more information from him, even if he possessed it. 'His orders are to bring you to Glory with all possible haste. Mount now.'

They had brought an extra horse, a great high beast of deep brown. A soldier dismounted, led the horse to me, and cupped his hands for my foot.

I backed away. 'I cannot ride.'

'You cannot *ride*?' the captain said, as if I had just announced that I did not know how to breathe.

'No, I cannot ride!' I repeated, at the same moment that Maggie said, 'If Roger goes, I go with him.'

The captain gazed down at her with profound distaste. 'Who are you?'

I said, 'She is my wife.'

312

A small, pleased sound from Maggie.

The captain said, 'I have no orders concerning your wife. Mount, Roger Kilbourne. You must be able to ride a little!'

'No,' I said. I had ridden donkeys, slow ambling beasts, and once I had ridden pillion behind a royal courier. But to sit alone on this huge horse ... and if Maggie rode behind me, I would only tumble her off, too, when I fell. As I surely would.

The captain sighed. He said to the soldier still cupping his hands, 'Throw him up behind Starkington.'

Another soldier, presumably Starkington, looked startled and unhappy. I said, 'And my wife? I will not go without her.'

Faced with the choice of wrestling with and binding one who had been summoned by the queen or of not carrying out his orders, the captain snarled, 'She may ride behind Everett.'

Two horses were walked up to the hand-cupper, who threw first me and then Maggie up behind soldiers. My horse shied and I gripped Starkington tightly around the waist. Maggie insisted on bringing her pack, which was fastened to the saddle. Rawnie leaped off her pony and tore over to us.

'I want to come, too!'

The captain did not deign even to notice her. He wheeled his mount and signalled to the others to follow. We moved off.

'I want to go too!' Rawnie screamed, the last thing I heard before the horses moved off. 'Roger, I hate you again!'

Two days later we reached Glory.

Again, just as it had three years earlier, the sight of the capital city filled me with trepidation. It rose on its river

313

island as a high wall of stone, above which soared the one palace tower. I had stood in or on that tower with Queen Caroline, or with Mother Chilton, or with nothing for company but my own pain and fear. Then the tower had flown Caroline's green banner; now Stephanie's purple flag furled and unfurled in the wind.

Our horses rode over the wide east bridge, hooves clattering on stone. Through the narrow, noisy ring of the city to the palace gates. They opened and we stood, as I had before so long ago, in a courtyard quiet, clean, and deserted.

Maggie dismounted first. 'We do not see the queen until we have bathed!'

The captain began, 'My orders are—'

'Forget your orders! Do you think the queen wishes to see us travel-soiled and stinking? I—'

'She does not wish you to appear before her at all, Mistress Kilbourne. She sent only for your husband.'

'—know my way to the servants' baths, and so does Roger,' Maggie finished, exactly as if the captain had not spoken. 'Both of us will need clean clothing.'

Everett, the soldier behind whom Maggie had ridden pillion, dismounted and seized her arm. He looked as if he would be glad to stop her, or imprison her, or just be shed of her. But the captain made a weary gesture, Everett released her, and Maggie started towards the women's baths. She said to me, 'We will meet back here shortly, Roger.'

Everett could not resist a jibe at me. 'Does she make all your decisions for you, Kilbourne?'

I smiled. 'Only when I deal with rabble.' For I could afford to be cocky with him: We had reached the palace, and I had the protection of the queen, whose queendom I had saved. Stephanie knew that, even if this oaf did not.

I bathed, shaved, and combed my too long hair. A page

314

brought me a crisp purple tunic, leggings, and boots of such a high polish that I could see myself in them. The feel of clean garments against clean flesh was almost startling – it had been so long! As I waited for Maggie, back in the soldiers' courtyard, servants came and went. None gave me a second look. Even if they remembered Roger the Queen's Fool, I no longer resembled him. Which was fitting, because I was not him.

Women take longer than men to bathe and dress. Finally Maggie appeared, her fair hair in clean springy curls, her trim figure clothed as country girls dress, in a borrowed white smock, tight-laced black stomacher, and a wool skirt hiked up over a striped petticoat. She looked pretty and young and not at all like a woman who had survived captivity at Galtryf. A passing soldier threw her an admiring glance.

But before I could tell her how beautiful she was, Jee burst through an inner gate and ran towards me across the cobblestones, and it was clear from his face that something was very wrong.

'Roger! Ye maun come!'

'I'm coming. What is it, Jee? Is the princess . . . I mean, the queen—'

'She will live. But ye maun come!'

Maggie rushed up to hug Jee. A brief hug, only – he grabbed her hand and hurried us both along. Jee had never spoken much, and he did not talk now. Nor, more surprisingly, did Maggie. Even as she ran, her shoulders squared for battle.

Jee led us past the throne room, its great carved doors closed. We raced on, servants flattening themselves against the walls as we passed, but scowling, too – Jee they knew, but who were these two upstarts with him? Then we came to rooms I knew all too well, the royal apartments. Jee waved his hand and the guards sprang aside. He was more than a page, then. He was what he had made himself: eleven-year-old protector, playmate, friend to the queen. What did Lord Robert make of that?

The presence chamber, as deserted as the throne room. Next the outer chamber, where a flock of ladies in waiting, all gowned in purple, sat sombrely sewing on benches or stools. These were not the chattering butterflies of Queen Caroline's reign but rather older women, motherly and sober, except for two little girls playing cat's cradle in a window embrasure. Then the privy chamber, where two men sat drinking wine at a great oaken table. One was Lord Robert, the other the court physician who had attended the nursery when Stephanie and her brothers still occupied it.

Lord Robert rose to gaze at me without warmth. 'So you have come, Roger.'

'I was sent for, my lord,' I said – stupidly, since of course he knew that. It was his soldiers who had brought me.

'Her Grace wishes to see you,' Lord Robert said. Something moved in his eyes, and for a moment I almost pitied him. It couldn't be easy to rule as regent for a seven-year-old queen who listened first to an eleven-year-old page and then to an old woman whom Lord Robert, being no fool, must suspect of 'witchcraft'. And now here I was back at court, the boy who had first brought that witch-craft to his child sovereign, and who had done something – no telling what! – to restore the tranced children of The Queendom. No, his position could not have been easy.

'Go in then,' he said to me harshly. 'But you, mistress, will stay here!'

Maggie opened her mouth, but then she closed it again. She had been a kitchen maid in this palace. It was one thing to defy soldiers – her brother had been one, after all, and she had no awe of the army – but quite another

316

to defy the Lord Protector and High Commander of the realm. Maggie cast down her eyes, dropped a grudging half-curtsey, and sat herself on the stool that Lord Robert indicated.

Jee led me to the queen's bedchamber, which I had never seen.

It was a curious room: half trappings for a reigning monarch, half nursery. Rich tapestries on the walls, polished oak chests, tables covered with embroidered cloths. On a dais stood a huge bed with carved headboard and purple silk hangings. The bed was empty. In one corner were two trundle beds separated by a low table covered with dolls and wooden toys. A woman dressed as a nursemaid sat on a low stool, and a stout lady in waiting, purple brocade straining across her bosom, leaned over one of the beds.

'Just eat a little, Your Grace,' the stout lady said.

'I don't want it!' The querulous voice of a sick child.

'My lady,' Jee said, and the voice changed.

'Jee! Have they— Oh, Roger!'

The stout lady in waiting moved, and I could see both beds. In one lay Queen Stephanie, her thin little face alight with pleasure despite the dark smudges under her eyes. She wore a white nightdress of some fine material and a matching cap on her lank brown hair. A withered crone I did not recognize slept in the other bed. And then I did recognize her. It was Mother Chilton.

Stephanie struggled to sit up. She could do so only with the aid of her lady, and I saw how weak and ill she really was. I dropped to one knee and bowed my head. 'Your Grace.'

'Oh, get up, Roger!' Stephanie said. To the purple lady, 'Please leave us, Lady Elizabeth.'

Lady Elizabeth frowned. 'Your Grace, Lord Robert said—'

'I said to leave us,' Stephanie repeated, and this time there was no mistaking the tone of authority. She was, after all, her mother's daughter, and her formidable grandmother's heir. But she was still also a child. She glanced at the nurse, who was not sent away. I raised my head to study the nurse. She returned my gaze steadily, her pale grey eyes telling me all I needed to know. This was one of the web women.

Lady Elizabeth left, her back rigid. Stephanie grinned at me. 'She is Lord Robert's sister and I am stuck with her. But she is not unkind. Roger . . . you came.'

'I will always come when you send for me, Your Grace.'

'Sit. We can talk with Philippa still here. She is one of us. Only . . . I don't want to.'

I took the stool beside her bed. Jee remained standing at its foot. I said, 'You don't want to talk while Philippa is here?'

'No! Not that—' A fit of coughing took her. Philippa rose, pulled a vial from a fold of her gown, and held it to Stephanie's lips. The little girl drank it eagerly. I remembered the drugs Mother Chilton and Fia had given me, and the one Nell had given Rawley, and a qualm took me. How much did this Philippa control Stephanie?

But the potion merely quieted her cough. Stephanie leaned back on her pillow and closed her eyes.

'Your Grace,' I said, 'you are very ill.'

'I am spent. And I do not want to do it any more.'

'Do what, Your Grace? You do not have to do anything you do not wish to.'

'I did have to. *You* made me! You and—' a fearful glance at the other bed '—Mother Chilton. And even you, Jee – you know you did! You, too, Philippa!'

Jee looked wretched. All at once I could see the scene here four days ago. As Nell and I sat huddled in the rain at Hygryll, Jee and Mother Chilton and her lieutenant

Philippa had all urged and directed and prodded Stephanie. It was necessary to do this for The Queendom, didn't she want to help those poor tranced babies, she could do this if she tried ... And Stephanie, a child and always a bit sickly, had exerted all the strength of her delicate body and half-developed soul arts, straining both to the breaking point. The greater part Nell had played had killed her. Stephanie had endured pain and illness, and now she wanted nothing further to do with the soul arts.

And Mother Chilton? I glanced at the other bed to be sure she still breathed. She, too, had paid the price. *'Everything has a cost, Roger Kilbourne – when will you learn that?'*

I had learned it well. But Queen Stephanie was seven years old.

I said gently, 'Is that why you summoned me here, because you don't want to do it any more?'

'Yes! Tell them, Roger – everyone listens to you!'

I gaped at my monarch. But from what little she had seen of my tale, it was true. I had directed Jee and Tom Jenkins, had outwitted Tarek to carry Stephanie away from his camp, had – in her view – defeated the *hisafs* who followed us. It was a child's view, and as a child monarch Stephanie had summoned the one person she thought could order the world as she wished. I thought of Maggie, endlessly ordering me, and I almost smiled.

'You should have said so to me, child,' another voice said. Mother Chilton's eyes opened.

Instantly Stephanie bowed her head. 'I'm sorry, madam.'

Madam. So did royal children address their governesses and nurses. But 'governess' hardly described Mother Chilton's relationship to the little queen. No word adequately described it.

Stephanie burst out again, 'But I don't want to!'

'Then you shall not,' Mother Chilton said.

'Really? But I thought . . . I thought . . .'

'No one need ask you to use your talent again. Whether you may eventually ask it of yourself is another matter.'

But this was too complicated for Stephanie, who smiled happily on her pillow. Mother Chilton turned her gaze on me, and once more I was shocked at the filminess in the sunken eyes, at the slackness of the incredibly ancient face. When I had first seen her, three and a half years ago, she had looked perhaps thirty. But her voice was still strong. What potion kept it thus, and had she been awake and feigning sleep from the moment I entered?

'Roger Kilbourne. You want to know of your son. He is well. The conduit does not suffer the same damage as the sender of visions.'

Relief flooded me, so strong I could taste it on my tongue, sweet and strong as new wine.

'Philippa will send someone with you to go to him. Where is Maggie?'

'In the privy chamber.' Once Mother Chilton would have already known that.

'Here? Have you told her what your child is?'

'No.'

'Good. Do not do so.'

I saw my chance. 'I will not. But Mother Chilton, I would join with Queen Stephanie in asking that my son be used no further by the women of the soul arts. The war with Soulvine Moor is over. We have won – *you* have won. Do not use my son again.'

Mother Chilton said, 'There is no need.'

'That is not what I asked. I want you to never—'

'There is no need,' she repeated and closed her eyes.

'Mother Chilton! I said—'

'Stop,' Philippa said, the first word she had spoken. 'She will say no more.'

'But she—'

'Enough.'

I glared at Philippa, then at Mother Chilton. What was I doing, shouting orders at a sick old lady? And this sick old lady would no more heed my orders than listen to a rock. She never had.

Jee stepped into the angry silence. 'My lady, ye have a reward for Roger.'

Stephanie, who had looked frightened during my heated exchange with Mother Chilton, smiled again. 'I almost forgot! Jee, help me.'

'Yes, my lady.'

He moved to her bedside, helped her sit up and swing her bare little feet over the side. Philippa did not protest. Seeing the respectful tenderness with which he assisted Stephanie, I saw that she was indeed and always would be his 'lady'. When they were no longer children, what would happen? That would depend on her strength of will, on his ability to survive court intrigue. I could not foresee their future. I could not even foresee my own.

Jee left Stephanie sitting uncertainly on the edge of the bed. From the chamber wall he took a sword with a great jewelled hilt. She could lift it only with his help. Stephanie said, 'Kneel, Roger ... good ... I dub thee Sir Roger Kilbourne!'

It was ludicrous. Jee must have known that the ceremony, carried out in secret by a little girl, carried no real meaning. Certainly Philippa knew. But Stephanie beamed at me, and I bowed my head and thought how Maggie would laugh and shake her head when I told her. At the same time, I was disappointed. When Stephanie had said 'reward' I had hoped for something more tangible.

Jee, bred to a hard life where money to eat mattered more than hypothetical titles, grinned at me. After he helped Stephanie lie down again, he said to her, 'My lady, the other thing?'

'What other ... ? Oh, yes. Fetch it, Jee!'

He took a key from his pocket, and this more than anything else convinced me of his influence with her. Was an eleven-year-old capable of winning a power struggle with Lord Robert Hopewell, should it ever come to that? I hoped it would not. Jee stuck his key into one of the ornately carved chests, pulled out a heavy cloth bag, and handed it to me.

'Open it, Roger!' Stephanie said gleefully.

Coins. Gold pieces, silvers, pennies. Stephanie had ruled for less than six months, and for much of that time The Queendom had been in turmoil. There had not yet been time to press new coins. These all bore the pure, lovely profile of her mother, Queen Caroline.

I stammered, 'Thank ... thank you ... I don't know what to say, Your Grace ...'

'I love you, Roger,' the queen said. 'But I think I'm tired now.'

She looked it. Philippa stood. 'I will see Roger out.'

Stephanie did not answer. She had Jee. I knelt, said, 'Good-bye, Your Grace,' and then went to bend over the other bed. 'Good-bye, Mother Chilton.'

She did not answer, either, but her eyes moved under their lids delicate and thin as the wing of a dragonfly.

As Philippa reached to open the chamber door, I said softly, 'Is she dying?'

'Her time is coming,' Philippa said. 'It will not be long now. Do not look so stricken, Roger Kilbourne, and do not grieve for her. Mother Chilton does not grieve. She is ready.'

For what? To sit tranquil and mindless in the Country

of the Dead – and then what after that? But I did not ask. Even if Philippa knew, she would not tell me.

She said, 'Take Maggie and go to the Sign of the Three-Winged Dove near the West Gate of the city. Wait there. Someone will come to take you to your son.' Philippa turned back to her charges.

'Good-bye, Sir Roger!' the little queen called from her bed, and giggled.

I returned to Maggie in the privy chamber. The stout woman in purple, Lady Elizabeth, swept past me with her chins in the air and her lip curled. Maggie lounged ostentatiously in a carved chair, drinking wine from a golden goblet, which was probably what had infuriated Lady Elizabeth. Maggie grimaced at her retreating back. I decided not to tell her that, in Stephanie's eyes anyway, she was now Lady Maggie. She might begin to order the palace guards about.

The money which Stephanie had given me lay heavy in my pocket. If the little queen was now free of her cares, so was I. Or rather, so would I be when I had my son.

EPILOGUE

'Roger! Roger!'

Maggie comes from the kitchen, holding a dirty cloth. Delectable smells follow her into the taproom, where I sit enjoying a solitary ale before the late-afternoon custom begins to arrive. Late autumn rain swirls against the window. Very soon winter will be upon us.

'What is it now, Maggie?' I say, looking at her in sheer pleasure. Maggie is good to look at. That was always true, but six months of good food and pretty gowns have made her even better. Her fair curls are bound with a purple ribbon, and her face flushes from the heat of the kitchen.

'Look at this filthy cloth! And that girl was going to wipe tankards with it! I am going to dismiss her, Roger.'

'You should *not*,' says another voice, coming in the door with Tom in her arms. 'Margery would not use that cloth on tankards, only on the floor.'

'She would!'

'Would not. Did ye ask the girl?'

'Da,' Tom says, and holds out his arms to me. Or maybe I just want the babbled syllable to be 'Da.'

'Give him to me, Joan,' I say, and Joan Campford dumps Tom on my lap, where he immediately reaches for the tankard of ale. I slide it across the table beyond his reach, and he puckers up his little face. I retrieve the tankard, which Tom promptly spills on himself and me.

I don't know how to be a father. Rawley, Hartah – these were the only 'fathers' I had known, and I would cut off my other arm before I would act as they had. Tom,

324

now a sodden happy lump on my lap, is infinitely precious to me. His fine, sparse hair, as fair as Maggie's and threatening to curl as soon as there is more of it, tickles my nose as I hug him. I breathe in his sweet baby smell, tighten my arm around his plump little belly. He spills more ale.

Meanwhile, the argument over Margery the scullery maid continues. 'I will dismiss her tomorrow,' Maggie says.

'That's for the master to say,' Joan retorts.

Maggie does not argue this point; she changes weapons. 'I will not run a dirty kitchen. Our custom depends on good food, good service, and cleanliness!'

'Half your custom stinks too much from months at sea to notice clean or not!'

'And you a laundress!' Maggie says.

'Not now. I now be a nurse,' Joan points out.

Both women are enjoying themselves. In a moment Margery, no put-upon timid underling but a stout seaport lass well able to defend herself, will dash out from the kitchen to join the fray, which will continue until the first patron arrives demanding ale. Then everyone will go back to work, the dirty rag forgotten. Margery will not be dismissed. Maggie ran through three scullery maids before she found one that could stand up to her and to Joan, and Maggie values Margery as much as she fights with her.

Which means she no longer fights with me. Our days, and our nights, are sweet and peaceful together. That was not true in the first weeks after a web woman found us at the Sign of the Three-Winged Dove. I knew immediately what the woman was, although Maggie did not, and I realized that Mother Chilton, and now Philippa, had these women of the soul arts everywhere in both city and palace. Lord Robert has no idea how much of his queendom is ruled by this shadow parliament.

The woman led us out of Glory and to a village several miles away, where Joan Campford lived with our small son as her own. On reflection, I realized that there was no one – or, at least, no one left living – whom I would have trusted as much. We spent a month in that cottage, and then journeyed east to the coast. Joan came with us, as little Tom's nurse. I had seen in that fortnight that much as she loved her son, Maggie would never be happy as a lady cottager waited upon by another woman. She needed to direct, to organize, to create. And I still feared being recognized that close to Glory.

So, thanks to Stephanie's money, we travelled comfortably to the far coast and bought two large cottages side by side. We live in one. The other Maggie has turned into the Red Boar, the best inn in this seaside city. Through the rainy window I can see the harbour, where ships come and go constantly with cargo from Benilles, from Gorwen, from a dozen other exotic ports. Running this prosperous inn is completely different from our poor alehouse in Applebridge. Here there is always news, interesting people, something happening. And there are no sheep.

The argument over the dirty cloth, so relished by all three parties, gives way as Maggie notices Tom. 'He's spilled ale on himself! Joan, why were you not watching him?'

'A little ale never hurt a babe,' Joan says. She lifts Tom off my lap. 'Let me take him, Roger.'

Tom clings to me for a moment, but then catches sight of window rain gleaming in the light from the bright fire on the hearth. He stretches his chubby fist towards the pane. 'Da!' Joan bears him off to be changed into fresh clothing, and I scrub at my ale-soaked tunic with the disputed cloth, which does not look all that dirty to me.

I am happy, although I know it is 'despite'. Despite the deaths of Tom Jenkins and Mother Chilton, of Lady Margaret, Alysse and Nell. Despite the loss of my hand. Despite the rumours of war, since Tarek son of Solek son of Taryn still claims to be the husband of Queen Stephanie. Perhaps that is what happiness always is – 'despite'. I do not know for certain.

'Roger,' Maggie says, 'can I bring you anything?'

I shake my head and smile at her. One thing I do know for certain: I will not cross over again. There is no need. Everything I want is here.

The door opens, and I rise to greet our first patron of the evening.